Doc

WOLVES OF IRON VALOR MC BOOK 7

DEX HAVEN

UNDER A TEXAS SKY PRESS

DEDICATION

EPIGRAPH

It's Hard to Say Goodbye

And I'll take with me the memories, to be my sunshine after the rain. It's so hard to say goodbye to yesterday. -Boyz II Men

ACKNOWLEDGEMENTS

Paula, thank you for your sharp eye for details that I missed and for making suggestions that helped make Doc read more clearly. I'm in your debt. Your clear thinking and quick wit helped keep me on track. I appreciate you so much and look forward to the next series.

Katie, thank you for late night chats and your creative ideas for characters's European names and possible histories. I love having you there to share my crazy ideas with and get immediate reactions. It's more helpful than you know. I'm looking forward to working on those Kozlov Vampire stories!

CONTENTS

TRIGGER WARNINGS

All of my books contain graphic intimacy, and likely some kind of physical violence—but always with a triumph-centered resolution. Guaranteed HEA. I don't believe in giving away the journey before it begins, but I believe in honoring your peace. If you know certain topics are hard for you, I encourage you to trust your instincts and read with care.

That being said, I thought it was important to note that there are scenes in Doc that include being held against your will (not sexually). And there are vampires in this story, so drinking blood to survive and during sex is involved. If these scenarios are triggering for you in any context, I do not recommend that you continue.

A complete list of warnings for all my books can be found on my website: www.dexhavenauthor.com

A quick note: Russian terms appear throughout this book. You don't need to memorize these—context will guide you—but this glossary is here if you'd like it.

Word	Meaning
durak	fool
glupaya devochka	silly girl
kotyonok	kitten
lyubimaya	darling
malen'kiy volk	little wolf
malysh kukla	little doll
malyutka	little one
moy volk	my wolf
moya lyubov'	my love
moya sestra	my sister
moye serdtse	my heart
sestrenka	sister
Sestrichka	little sister
solnechnyy svet	sunlight
solnyshko	sun
volk	volk

CHAPTER 1

LUCIA

You would think that nothing in Texas could ever feel cold, but as I stood in the guest room of Bronc and Juliet's log cabin, every knot in my shoulders burned with frost. The room reeked of hospitality—rustic Western trappings, antler lamps, a beautifully appointed quilt over the bed that was almost certainly sewn by a wolf who lived somewhere on this compound, and an actual stack of cowboy-themed books on the nightstand to amuse the out-of-town guests. I was *not* amused. Juliet, I imagined, had gotten a good giggle out of this. The *glupaya devochka,* I could see her laugh when she set them there.

The walls, hewn from local pine, glowed rich in the light of two wall sconces. They threw shadows that leaned and stretched across the room's single sitting area, where my father, the King of the Eastern Vampires, waited for me. He sat in a large, butter-soft leather wingback chair, looking every bit like the king that he was. He wore designer denim and a hand-tooled leather vest that should have looked ridiculous, but on him, looked stylish and fitting for the setting. His back was to a picture window that looked over the pastures that surrounded the Iron Valor compound, and I swear I heard a cow mooing in the distance.

My father is the greatest man I knew. He was the one against whom I measured all other men. And his love for me was unmatched as well; it was almost impossible for me to surprise or upset him. I knew I'd outdone myself this time, and there was no going back from the decision I'd made.

He watched me the entire time as I entered and walked toward him. He didn't bother to stand. His long legs were crossed, his hands steepled beneath his chin like a patient headmaster waiting for a wayward student to face the consequences of her wrongdoing. We hadn't spoken since I'd risked everything for Ryder "Doc" Lowrey of the Iron Valor wolf pack, since I'd given him my own blood to save his life. Vampires, not even the daughter of a king, have carte blanche to do this. To possibly turn a human much less a wolf, seemingly on a whim.

His hair, black as old lacquer, lay in a silken curtain over one shoulder, framing a face that was equal parts beautiful and predatory; with the look of a man no older than 45 but in reality had seen centuries pass. I hated how he could make me feel fourteen again, just by raising an eyebrow. He had been both father and mother to me since my mother died when I was five years old, and it always pained him to have to give any sort of discipline.

"You have not greeted me, Lucia," he said. His accent was faint, but it stained every syllable.

I ignored the rebuke and shut the door behind me with more force than necessary. I waited until the latch clicked. "Hello, Papa," I said. "Sorry, I forgot how much you like your entrances choreographed." I teased, but would never disrespect my father. He was everything to me.

He let my sarcasm pass, but did not fail to establish his position. "Sit. We need to discuss what you have done."

Every word landed like a blow to my body, but I did not want it to appear that I felt guilty. I did not. I would do what I did again a hundred times over. But one did not disobey my father, so I chose the edge of the loveseat across from him and slowly sat not bothering to hide my nerves. He could sense every twitch, anyway.

He stared at me for a full ten seconds before speaking, as if waiting for me to blurt out why I'd done what I did. When I didn't, he began, "I know the circumstances. I was there. But explain to me. Why did you force your blood on the wolf?"

I didn't flinch. "Because he was dying."

He moved his hands apart. The left hand landed on the armrest, fingers curled as if around the throat of some invisible prey. "You understand there was great risk to your actions? Did you not? So why would you put yourself and possibly my rule in danger, *solnyshko*?"

Sunshine. What he'd called me for as long as I could remember. An ironic term of endearment, as only the rare "born vampire" like myself could walk in the sunlight. I was resented already; perhaps he wanted to remind me.

"Because he was dying in front of me, Papa. I had to make a choice." When my father had laid Ryder Lowrey down on that rock, and I saw his blood—his life force—pooling beneath him, I had no choice but to act. The truth was, my world did not exist without him in it.

"Perhaps you should have let his life end." His words were flat, like it was a fact of nature.

"You carried him in your own arms, Papa! *You* could have left him in that canyon to die. But you didn't. Because you are not monster! And I couldn't just let him die because I am not a monster either!" My accent—picked up during months and years spent with my brothers in Romania—always spilled out stronger when I was upset.

My voice had gone quiet. "I couldn't just let him die in front of all of his family. I couldn't be so cruel when I had the ability to stop it."

"Vampire law forbids this thing, Lucia. The Council of Elders must be involved in the Turning."

"I didn't *turn* him. I just—*healed* him." Even as I said it, my pulse thudded in my neck, and I felt like a liar. "He's not a vampire, Papa. He's still a wolf."

He smiled and raised a perfect eyebrow as though he meant to say that he wasn't a fool. "Your blood is in him now. Do you understand what that means? What you have done?"

I stared at my knees, because looking at him hurt. "He's alive. That's what it means." And truly, that is all that mattered.

"You have made him part of us. Whether or not he turns, your blood will call to him for the rest of his life." He paused until I looked at him.

"You think you healed him. You did not. You cursed him."

I winced. Something in the way he said it—"Your blood will call to him"—made me burn. It wasn't an accusation, not exactly. It was recognition, a secret between us. I wondered if he knew the truth of it: that I'd always wanted Doc to look at me like I was more than Kazimir's daughter or just Juliet's best friend. I had somehow wanted to matter to him.

But I'd never admitted that, even to myself.

"It's not a curse," I said, more to the floor than to him. "He's strong. He'll handle it."

My father sighed, a sound like frost on old glass. "You are still so young, Lucia."

I flinched. He had used that tone with others when he was about to do something monstrous.

I stood slowly, like a chastened servant. My father had moved to the window, hands clasped behind his back, the Texas sun etching his profile in gold. "Do you know why I never forced you to Europe once you were a teen except for summers with your brothers?" he asked, his voice velvet-wrapped steel.

Because you respect my choices, I thought, but kept silent, waiting.

"Because you are my legacy," he said, turning. His gaze held me—not pinned, but cherished. "My only daughter. But you must think beyond impulse. Beyond... bleeding for wolves." There was no anger in his words, only the deep, familiar worry that lived in his eyes whenever my safety was at stake.

"I'm not a queen," I countered softly. "And Doc isn't a threat."

My father's chuckle was warm, almost proud. "He is nothing *but* a threat—to you. That *femoral artery*..." He trailed off, the memory of Doc's near-death, of my blood spilling into him right there outside of that cavern where we'd saved Brie from the Demon King Maltraz. "Your fierceness saved him. But exposing such power, Lucia..." He shook his head, the movement heavy with paternal fear. "My Council of Elders will see only transgression."

Exhaustion washed over me. "So this is my worry?"

He stepped closer. The scent of him—dry cedar and aged parchment—wrapped around me, a comforting anchor. "This secret must hold. My Council cannot know." Those ancient, unforgiving elders. "They must not know. At least not yet."

I met his eyes, the plea raw in my voice. "Then help me."

He studied me, a king weighing a daughter's heart against the weight of law. Then, a true smile broke through—rare, luminous, tinged with bittersweet memory. "You have your mother's spirit," he murmured. "All that fire... and not a drop of calculated cruelty."

"I'll take that," I whispered.

He adjusted his shirt cuffs, the motion precise, regal. "I *am* the law. What I sanction, stands." Relief threaded through his words; the decision made. "But caution, *moye serdtse*. There are those on the Council who'd demand your life for far less than saving a shifter."

My throat tightened. "You won't tell them?"

"Of course I will," he said, calm as stone. "When I control the narrative. Until then, live your life as normal." He moved to the door, pausing with his hand on the knob. "And I will inform your brothers. They deserve to know what you've done so they can shield you."

Warmth flooded me at the mention of them. Maksym, Taras, Nikolay, and Bohdan—my fierce, overprotective shadows. They'd move mountains for my happiness, not threaten it. Their only frustration would be that they hadn't been there to intervene in the first place.

My father kissed my forehead and then slipped out, leaving the door slightly open. I flexed my fingers, feeling the lingering warmth of his protection. The Council was a storm cloud, yes. But with Papa's unwavering love and my brothers' devotion at my back? I'd face it.

I could still hear his voice in my skull as I closed the guest room door behind me, careful not to let it slam. My father was gone—swept off in his own dust-devil of secrets and narrative control—but his words lingered in the old pine like the scent of a fire no amount of sage could clear out. I braced my palm against the smooth door and took two deep breaths. I wasn't sure if I felt relieved or abandoned.

The stairs creaked in protest as I walked down to the first floor. Bronc and Juliet's cabin always felt more like a lodge than a house; the ceilings impossibly high, beams thick as tombstones, everything oversized and rugged, designed for people built like Bronc. Lanterns hung in a row from the rafters, burning a pale amber that glowed against stone and wood. The fireplace was set with actual logs—none of that gas-log bullshit—and at the foot of the hearth, a stack of neatly folded baby blankets competed for space with several boxes of diapers, towels, and baby wipes. There was even a half-empty bottle of hand sanitizer, as if the wolves thought germs would dare challenge them here.

Juliet sat on the sofa, hands splayed wide on her swollen belly, her hair swept into a no-nonsense bun, and her eyes trained on the fire. I envied her composure. The glow on her face made her look serene, but the tension in her jaw said otherwise. Even the Luna wasn't immune to what was coming.

Bronc paced the hardwood in rugged, dust-covered boots. Each pass pounded against the aged hardwood floors. He had his phone in one hand, but he wasn't texting or calling—he was just gripping it, hard enough to crack the case if he weren't careful. He was always a bit unsure of me but never questioned my loyalty to Juliet or his pack. I'd been here for every battle since Juliet had become a part of Iron Valor. I'd met her in college, and she instantly became the best friend I ever had. That guaranteed my loyalty and devotion.

He clocked me the second I came into view, gaze pinning me as neatly as my father ever had. "Hello, Princess. Your father just left. Said he was heading back to Philly. I'm assuming there will be hell to pay when he gets there. It was a helluva thing you did back at the canyon."

I nodded, keeping my voice even. "Yeah, he'll have to do damage control for my impulsive life-saving decision."

He grunted, but the set of his mouth didn't change. "Did he tell you what happens if your blood screws up Doc's head?"

"Should I tell you that Doc would be six feet under without a thought in his head at all if I hadn't intervened?"

I crossed my arms and leaned against the stair rail, mirroring his conflicting emotions. "You can cease your worrying. Doc's not a vampire. He's not going to suddenly crave plasma or lose his mind to bloodlust. He's the same as he's always been. If something like that were going to happen, it would have happened immediately. I figured you'd just be happy your man was still on this side of the dirt."

"He's barely slept in three days," Bronc shot back. "He's not eating. He's snapping at people. Not like him at all."

I bristled, but Juliet raised a hand—quiet, but commanding. "Liam, enough."

He ignored her. "I trusted him to get us through this," he went on, voice rough. "Now I have to worry that the only doctor I trust is some kind of goddamn science experiment."

I forced a smile, but it tasted of rust. "He's *still* Doc, not a time bomb. He almost died out there, and yes, his body had a shock being emptied of his blood and restarted with new. But his heart beats, and his wolf lives. Isn't that what is important?"

"That's not the point," Bronc said, voice low. "The point is, you took a risk with my pack. With my mate."

Juliet finally intervened, resting her palm over Bronc's thick wrist and squeezing. Her fingernails were painted a luminous copper, elegant and sharp. "He's worried, Lucia. That's all."

I swallowed. "So am I, but the alternative was that he would die. He *did* die." I had to swallow the tears that threatened to fall.

The reality of it set in, and Bronc's eyes hit the floor. His chest rose with a resolute and worried sigh. "You're right, Lucia, I apologize. You did what nobody else could do. It's just my worry talking, and that's not fair. I'm thankful you were there. Once he gets used to whatever is happening to his body, I'm sure he'll get back to being himself."

Before I could reply, Juliet groaned softly and leaned forward, face blanching. The sound of her discomfort was so alien—so unlike the steel-clad Luna who ran this pack—that both Bronc and I moved at once.

She exhaled a shuddering breath. "My back," she whispered, then, louder: "Something's wrong."

Bronc dropped to his knees in front of her, hands careful on her thighs. "Where?"

She pointed just below her ribs. "It started an hour ago. Like a band, right here. Now it won't stop."

I sidestepped around Bronc and crouched beside Juliet, doing my best to project calm I barely possessed. "Pressure or stabbing?"

"Pressure. Then sharp."

"Any bleeding?" I asked, voice soft.

Juliet shook her head. "No. Not yet."

Bronc looked up at me, and the fight in him was gone, replaced by pure, naked fear. "Call Doc. He's in his office."

I was already reaching for my phone. "I'll get him."

I dialed, but it went to voicemail. The second time, he picked up, sounding like he hadn't slept in a week.

"Yeah?" The edge in Doc's voice could have sliced sheet metal.

"It's Juliet," I said, ignoring the way my stomach flipped at the sound of him. "She's got severe abdominal pain. I think she's in labor."

There was a pause. "Is Bronc with her?"

"He's here."

"Tell him to bring her in. I'll meet them at the hospital."

Bronc heard the conversation and gathered Juliet up like she were made of spun glass, and we moved out to his truck, placing her across the back seat. The softness of his movements was almost shocking.

Juliet's face was pinched, but she managed a smile. "I'm okay," she said to Bronc, and then, to me: "I'm glad you're here."

I didn't know what to say to that, so I just nodded as I sat with her head in my lap.

Bronc's hand trembled as he brushed hair from Juliet's forehead.

Doc met us at the emergency room doors with a wheelchair. He looked like Doc, just tired. I was glad he barely made eye contact with me because his focus was on Juliet. By the time they got her through the doors, Juliet let out a sharp cry and looked down at her lap at the puddle that was forming on the floor under her.

Doc gave her a beautiful, reassuring smile. "Looks like they got you here just-in-time Luna." He turned his eyes to Bronc who looked like he might pass out. "You remember what we practiced, Alpha?"

Bronc nodded.

"Good. Let's head back to a maternity room. I'll take care of you. Promise."

Juliet's expression melted, all her fight replaced by something raw and vulnerable. "Thank you, Ryder," she whispered.

The hospital was tiny; only three halls. He got her set up in a room that was equipped with everything he'd need to get her through her labor and delivery. He caught a nurse on his way in who stopped Bronc and me from entering the room. She handed us a set of blue scrubs to change into. We met outside her door before Doc opened it.

Bronc ran to her side, and Juliet called out for me. I hurried to her other side and squeezed her hand. She gripped back, strong as a vice.

"You look beautiful *malen'kiy volk*." I kissed her sweaty brow.

She looked at me, tears in her espresso eyes. "You better not have called me a cow in Russian!"

Everyone laughed, despite our worries.

"Little wolf, Luna. I called you a beautiful little wolf," I told her through the tears that had begun to drip off my chin. The baby heart monitor echoed with a cacophony of drumbeats through the room.

Doc stood at the foot of the bed, watching our exchange. His expression unreadable. Then, he suddenly snapped on latex gloves.

"We're doing this old-school," he said. "Just like we talked about." I didn't know how Bronc felt about his friend having his eyes all in his wife's business, but he remained calm and clinical.

"Let's get a measurement so we can see how close we are." His head popped up over the little sheet that had made a privacy tent. "You really *did* get here just in time. You're at six centimeters. It won't be too long."

Bronc took up position behind Juliet, propping her up and whispering into her ear. The words were too soft for me to catch, but the effect was obvious: her breathing slowed, her shoulders loosened. Even in pain, she was still Luna.

I stayed beside her, offering the useless comfort of a hand, but grateful to be needed at all.

Outside, the wind picked up, rattling the windows with a sound like distant applause. Inside, Doc took command, his voice calm and clear, and the room bent to his will.

CHAPTER 2

DOC

I'd been in countless delivery rooms, but none as loaded as this one. I'd set Juliet up in our newest birthing suite. The furnishings were comfortable, with nice lighting, stylish wallpaper, and dark wood accents. It had a big picture window overlooking a treed pasture and a field of wildflowers that were currently in bloom with bluebonnets and Indian paintbrushes; the kind of spring beauty that made even hardened doctors breathe easier. Bronc had appreciated the low lighting, as if that would keep the process more sacred, and I admit things felt oddly peaceful given all that had happened these past few days.

The machines beeped steadily, wires like tangled ivy looping from Juliet's belly to the fetal monitors. She lay on her side, already drenched in the hormonal fugue of late-stage labor, hair a wild halo on the pillow. Her hands, strong, and clenched at her sides when a contraction hit. She didn't complain. No one ever believed it, but pack Lunas always handled pain like she'd receive a big gold belt at the end of it all.

I checked her chart—six centimeters and holding, water already broken, contractions coming every three minutes. Right on schedule. Textbook, if you ignored the fact that her husband was also her Alpha and currently pacing holes into the tile by the headboard, and that a literal vampire princess kept drifting in and out of the room like a beautiful haunting.

I'd been dead a few days earlier. Or close enough that Lucia's blood had had to drag me back from the edge. My memories of that afternoon—crimson, bitter, cold, and then the odd velvet burn of healing—were already separating from the rest of my recollection, like a weird memory graft. I should have been weak, should have been out on my feet. For a while, I had been. But I'd woken up that morning feeling like I could run to Mexico. Or through a wall. The best explanation was magic, and magic was never a comfort for someone trained in battlefield medicine. Every time I washed my hands, the veins under my skin seemed bluer, almost pulsing with an extra charge. I had no idea how much of me was still mine.

But I was this pack's doctor, and so I would doctor; especially today; especially for Juliet. So I pushed every other thought aside.

Except Lucia. She floated into the delivery room with a basket of folded towels in her arms. She moved with her usual brisk, predatory grace, but I could sense the effort it took her not to look my way. Not after everything that night, not after what she'd done to save me, not after what she'd done had likely cost her.

I told myself to focus on the Luna. I *was* focused on the Luna.

"You're progressing," I said. "Steady is good. Pain management holding up?"

Juliet nodded, but her eyes flicked to Bronc, who had his arms crossed and his jaw set like he were prepping for a bar fight. "No way you're giving her too much, right?"

"No way," I replied. "Just enough. She's got a pain threshold I'd kill for, but I'm not letting her suffer for the photo op. You can trust me, Bronc."

"I do," he said, but he kept watching Lucia, like he was waiting for her to lunge at someone's throat.

Lucia placed the towels by the sink and hovered there, folding her hands. Her eyes, black as burnt coffee, flicked to mine just once. I swear to God my pulse went arrhythmic. The wolf in me wanted to climb right out of my skin and cross the room, bury my face in her neck, inhale every molecule of her, bite down until she screamed. It wasn't the usual shifter desire, either; this was new, raw, foreign.

I was aware of her, molecule by molecule, even when I turned my attention to the monitor and adjusted the strip.

"Doc, can I talk to you?" Lucia's accent, always a touch more dramatic when she was nervous, curved around the words.

"I'll be right back," I told Juliet, and stepped into the hallway. She followed, soft-soled boots silent on linoleum.

I meant to keep a safe distance, but she stepped in close, just inside my personal bubble, and the smell—something clean, then roses, mixed with the coppery memory of her blood in my mouth—hit me so hard I almost staggered.

"Are you all right?" She asked, voice low. "You look... better."

She was worried. I could see it in the set of her mouth, in the way her arms stayed rigidly at her sides. I almost reached for her hand on impulse, then stopped myself. Professional, I reminded myself. Professional.

"I'm fine," I said. "Better than fine, actually. It's almost disturbing." I made a joke out of it, but the truth was, every sense felt dialed up. I could hear Juliet's heartbeat through two doors.

"I am glad," she said. And then she did that thing where she looked at me, her eyes somehow sultry, and every logical part of me disconnected, and I had to lock my hands behind my back to keep from doing something incredibly stupid.

"I should check back in on Juliet," I said.

Lucia stepped aside. The door to the delivery room was three feet away. For those three feet, I was aware of her watching me—her gaze not heavy, but persistent, a hand at my neck. As I stepped through the threshold, I let my medical focus override the rest of me, at least for the time being.

Juliet was riding out her contractions beautifully. Some exhaustion was setting in as often does with labor, but Bronc was rubbing her back and massaging her scalp and doing all the things a good mate does. I checked the monitors and patted her shoulder. She squeezed my hand.

"I know this is your first," I told her, soft so Bronc wouldn't catch the edge in my voice, "but you're doing better than most of the first-time moms I've delivered. Just hang in there; you'll be to ten soon."

She nodded, a beautiful smile on her face.

I'd given her an epidural for her pain, and she was managing well. She was doing better than Bronc; that was for damn sure. Our Luna was made for this.

I made it another hour before I had to step out. It wasn't that I was tired—if anything, the unspent energy was making me edgy. I needed a moment to regroup, recalibrate, and pretend my only craving was for caffeine.

The hospital coffee bar had been retrofitted from a defunct vending alcove. We'd added a fancy coffee machine that dispensed flavored coffees and was a favorite of employees and visitors alike. I'd brewed myself a cup and pretended not to notice Lucia sitting on a stool by the window, flicking her phone screen in rapid, agitated strokes. Fuck if I didn't want to run my fingers through her long, silky black curls.

I should have taken my leave as soon as Nurse Amanda appeared. She'd had it in her head that we might hook up at some point. Never happened and never would.

"Hey, Doc." She leaned in, cleavage and all. "Didn't think you'd be here this evening."

"Luna's twins decided today was the day," I said, keeping it neutral.

She sidled up closer to me. "That's wonderful. It's always a happy time when pups are born." She looked over at Lucia with a curious glance.

"Sure is," I said, trying to wave her off diplomatically.

Amanda tried again, this time putting her hand on my arm. It was meant to be flirtatious, but the sensation was like static—unpleasant, wrong, more grating than alluring.

That's when the growl started.

It didn't come from me.

It came from Lucia. Not loud, not even audible to anyone without shifter hearing, but the vibration carried. It was a dark, warning sound—a subsonic thrum that rattled my bones and sent a message.

Amanda's hand jerked away. She laughed, nervous. "Rude, much?"

I looked at Lucia, who was now watching us openly, pupils dilated, jaw rigid. Her lips pulled back, just a fraction, and for a half-second I thought I saw the glint of fang.

Amanda started to say something more—another cutting remark about hospital drama, I'm sure—but I abruptly cut her off. "Hey, Amanda," I said with the authority that came with being the chief of staff and owner of the hospital. "The same rules apply for men as women when it comes to unsolicited touching. Okay? Why don't you take five. I'll cover if anything comes up in L&D?"

She was duly chastised and looked embarrassed and fearful enough to tell me she understood my point and quickly left for the nurses' station.

When she was gone, I exhaled. "You can't do that," I said quietly.

Lucia shrugged, but her cheeks were high with color. "I do not like her. Do you?"

"No."

"Good."

By the time I made it back to the birthing suite, the world had shifted. Juliet was curled on her side, eyes closed, breathing evenly. A good sign after her pain had spiked, earning her a small bump of epidural. She'd probably be dozing for another little bit if nothing changed. The pain, the panic, the whole storm of hormones had dropped to a low simmer. The epidural generally slowed the progression of dilation a tad.

Bronc sat on the upholstered sofa, hands steepled under his chin, staring at Juliet as if he could will her past the delivery. He didn't acknowledge me at first. The window showed a brilliant pink and blue Texas sunset. Perfect for the occasion.

I looked over the chart, reviewed the last three notations—her blood pressure was steady, fetal heart tones strong, no sign of distress. I adjusted the blanket over Juliet's legs and checked the monitor leads. All as it should be.

"You back for good?" Bronc said, not looking up.

I nodded. "I'll see her through."

He watched me for a long moment, then shifted on the couch. "You want to tell me what's going on with you?"

I shrugged. "Just a little medical miracle. I'm fine."

"That's what you keep saying." His tone was mild, but I heard the warning in it. "You died, Doc. For a minute, anyway. And now you're acting like nothing happened."

"Would you rather I act traumatized?"

He snorted. "No. But the changes—they're not subtle, you know. You're not eating, not sleeping. Saw you almost rip the door off the hinges earlier. And you look at her..." he jerked his chin at the door, meaning Lucia, "like you're about to eat her alive. I need to know if you're a risk to my mate, or anyone else."

I gripped the side rail and forced myself not to flinch. "I'm not a risk to Juliet. Or the babies."

"And Lucia?"

I hesitated. The wolf inside me howled, clawed at the base of my skull. I remembered the way Lucia's hair had shimmered under the fluorescent light, the way my body had reacted to her nearness, the heat in her skin when I'd brushed past her. It was everything I'd been trained to control—years of discipline, of pack brotherhood, undone in a handful of hours. I resented the accusation that I'd put myself anywhere that I'd be a danger to my pack.

"Alpha, I'd hope you'd respect me enough to know that I'd never put a member of my pack in any kind of danger. *Especially* my Luna and her pups. It's just *her*. She's... different," I admitted. "It's like I can't get enough of her, but I can't trust myself in terms of being with her, either. Not after what she did to me."

Bronc leaned forward, elbows on his knees. "So, what's your plan? You going to mate her?"

The word hung in the air, sulfurous and obscene.

"No," I said, sharper than I meant. "She's a vampire. That's not..."

Bronc didn't let me finish. "I didn't know Juliet was a wolf when I'd decided she was my mate. I'm a wolf. I didn't care. I knew she was mine. My *wolf* knew she was mine. The Goddess does weird fucking shit sometimes. Look at Papa and Aspen. He's a wolf; she's a witch/angel. Shit happens, Doc. If you need her—if your wolf needs her—maybe you should stop pretending otherwise."

"It's not that simple." My voice had dropped low and rough. "She's the daughter of the vampire king. She has a family, an empire. I'm just a..."

"Shut the fuck up, Doc," Bronc said, almost kindly. "You're the backbone of this pack. You're as much an alpha as any of the men on my council. If you wanted her, you could have her, and nobody would question it."

I looked at my hands; the blue veins vivid against pale skin. "I'm sending her back to Philadelphia. Once Juliet's safe, I'll make sure she gets on a plane."

Bronc's face softened, which for him was saying something. "You're going to break her heart."

"She's a tough one. She'll get over it."

He shook his head. "Will you?"

"I've been alone a long time and never intended on ever finding anyone. It's not a stretch for me to continue to be alone."

He just shook his head.

A silence stretched, heavy as a lead apron.

I got up to check Juliet again. "She's close," I said, changing the subject.

Bronc nodded; the conversation dropped.

I did a final sweep of Juliet's IV, then sat in the leather armchair and tried not to think about anything except the clinical facts of the situation.

But the silence wouldn't hold. My brain kept replaying every word Bronc had just said, and every second of the last forty-eight hours since Lucia—the growl, the heat, the ache in my chest that wasn't pain but hunger, something elemental. I'd convinced myself I could out-think the animal side of me, but now that I was only half-wolf, maybe I'd lost that edge.

I was still running those numbers when Lucia appeared in the doorway, arms crossed, back braced against the jamb. She wore a thin sweater over a black t-shirt, but nothing could mute the shine of her skin, the uncanny symmetry of her features. She looked straight at me, not blinking, and I realized with a sick twist that she'd heard everything.

I stood, then thought better of it. "Lucia," I said, barely above a whisper.

She gave a brittle smile. "Congratulations, Ryder. Your patient is doing well." Her accent, usually so soft, cut like broken glass.

Bronc looked at her, then at me, then back again. He stood, stretching his neck. "I'll go grab a coffee. Call me if she wakes up."

He left, the door hissing shut behind him.

Lucia didn't move. "So you are sending me away?"

I rubbed my eyes. "It's not about you."

She laughed, a sharp, cold sound. "No, of course not. It is never about me. Only about the precious pack, the Luna, the rules. Always rules." She uncrossed her arms, then shoved her hands deep into her pockets. "What if I do not want to go?"

"It's safer for you. And for us." The lie stung, but I made myself say it.

She closed the distance in two strides, stopping inches from my face. I could see the pulse in her throat, the twitch of her jaw. "You are a coward," she said, soft. "I saved your life. And now you pretend I do not exist."

I stared at the floor. "It's complicated, Lucia."

Her hand came up so fast I almost missed it, and she grabbed my chin, forcing me to look at her. Her eyes were endless, black and bitter, years of heartbreak crammed into a single glare.

"Da," she whispered. "Very complicated."

Then she let go, turned, and vanished into the hallway.

I sat back down, letting the silence press in. Juliet's monitor beeped, calm and steady. For a long time, I listened to it, trying to sync my breathing to its rhythm.

When Juliet finally woke, it was with a howl.

"Doc," she gasped, "it's time."

I snapped into action, the clinical part of me locking in, all muscle memory and algorithm. I checked her dilation—complete, ten centimeters, perfect. "You ready to push?"

She nodded, sweat already trickling down her temples. Bronc came barreling in, eyes wild, hair mussed, coffee forgotten.

"Let's do this, Luna," he whispered to Juliet, kissing her hand.

"On the next contraction," I said, voice even, "push with everything you've got."

The first twin crowned quickly, dark hair slick with amniotic fluid. Juliet was a champion—every push was coordinated, deliberate, like she'd done this a hundred times. The room got hot, thick with effort and fear and love. I caught the baby, wiped him down, checked his lungs.

A cry, sharp and beautiful.

"A boy," I said, holding him up. "Seven pounds, three ounces."

Bronc sobbed, the sound half-laugh, half-cry, then kissed Juliet's forehead.

"Second twin's right behind," I said. "You're almost there."

Juliet bared her teeth and bore down, the veins in her neck standing out like cables. I delivered the second baby—a girl, smaller but wailing like a banshee. Six pounds, ten ounces.

I handed the babies off to the postnatal nurse, then stitched Juliet up, cleaned the field. Bronc couldn't stop kissing her, over and over, murmuring little endearments that sounded like nonsense. I should have felt proud, or at least satisfied, but instead I was hollowed out, every joy cut with regret.

I washed my hands, made sure Juliet was stable, and then left the room. The hallway had filled with all my brothers and their mates overjoyed with the news of the pups' arrival. I passed them on my way to my office. The air felt empty, but I could smell the scent of roses, faint and fading.

I wanted to chase Lucia, to explain, to confess every ugly, hungry thought. But I didn't.

I walked to the window at the end of the corridor and watched as sunset turned into night and wondered if I could survive without her.

CHAPTER 3

LUCIA

His words looped in my head like a cursed melody—*It's not about you. Safer for everyone.* Over and over, until I wanted to claw my skull open. He never looked at me when he said it. Too busy playing the flawless doctor to notice how his clinical tone gutted me.

God, I wished he'd just said I disgusted him. Wished he'd screamed, hit me, shattered something—anything real. Anger, I could've understood. Respected, even. But that quiet cowardice? That, I couldn't forgive. I was glad my father had sent his plane back to Texas after he'd made it home. That way I'd not have to wait to return.

The weight settled deeper than exhaustion. Not the flight, not the heartbreak, not even the hunger. This was cement in my veins, my muscles dragging like anchors behind me. Every breath threatened to buckle me.

For the first time in my life, I wondered if maybe there was something wrong with me.

I shivered. I cannot remember ever having been ill. It is possible for a vampire to suffer ailments, but they don't *catch* them; they *happen* to them.

I closed my eyes and let myself slip, just for a minute, into the fantasy that Ryder Lowrey would call, would storm the jet at our private airstrip, would fight my father, my brothers, the entire damn kingdom if that's what it took. But the reality was worse: he would not even send a text. He would not want to know if I survived the trip, or if I was happy, or if I ever came back. He would convince himself he had done the right thing, and he would sleep soundly knowing he had kept everyone safe, including himself.

I hated him for that. At least I wanted to hate him.

Eventually, the fatigue overtook the rage, and I curled up on the wide leather couch, wrapped myself in a blanket, and let the soft whine of the engines lull me to sleep. My last thought before I drifted off was of my mother, the way she used to comb my hair and tell me that sadness was just another kind of hunger, that it could be starved if you had the right distraction.

I doubted she'd ever had a hunger like this.

When I woke, the jet was descending, and the view outside was black as the inside of a coffin. The lights of the estate's private runway cut through the void, a landing strip so smooth and bright it might have been painted onto the darkness by a vengeful god. I blinked, rubbed my eyes, and sat up slowly, the blanket pooling at my feet.

I checked my phone for messages. Nothing. No word from Juliet, or Bronc, or anyone from Texas. Not even a check-in from my brothers, who usually texted at least a meme or two when they knew I was in the air.

I needed to text Juliet tomorrow to tell her I loved her and to have her send pics of the twins.

I rolled my neck, patted my hair, and watched as the ground rushed up to meet us. The cold of the window glass bit into my skin, and for a moment, I could have sworn I saw Ryder Lowrey's reflection in the dark: sharp, angular, beautiful in the way that weapons were beautiful. But it was just me. Just Lucia Kozlov, the idiot who'd bled for a wolf and had nothing to show for it except an empty stomach and a heart that hurt.

The jet touched down with barely a bounce, tires screaming on the tarmac. I counted backwards from ten, breathing slowly, refusing to let the panic win. By the time the crew opened the main hatch, I was already at the door, chin high, ready for whatever waited on the other side.

The landing stairs yawned down from the jet's hatch, and I was halfway hoping Papa sent someone with a car when a figure appeared out of the darkness—a streak of a blue peacoat and faded denim, barreling toward me with the momentum of a freight train. My heart did a stupid, human skip before I even realized it was my brother charging me.

Bohdan Kozlov—Bohdi to anyone who'd ever gotten roped into his orbit—did not so much greet as ambush. One moment I was clinging to the rail, and the next his arms snaked around my waist, hoisting me off my feet with humiliating ease. I shrieked, a high, ugly sound I would've killed to keep inside. But even as I twisted to knee him in the ribs, he just spun me in a circle and whooped loud enough to scare every raccoon in the county.

"Bohdi, you bastard!" I yelped, pounding on his shoulder.

He set me down, grinning his lopsided million-dollar grin. "Surprise, *malyutka*. You look like shit."

"Fuck you," I muttered, but I was already hugging him back. He reeked of weed and Valentino cologne, but beneath it was the same warmth that had kept me entertained through countless summers in Budapest. "You're not supposed to be here."

He shrugged, hands already in his pockets. "Papa said you were coming in solo. Figured you'd appreciate the ride to the house."

"He wasn't wrong. Even though I could beat you with my superior speed." I shot back, then scowled. "I can't believe you snuck up on me. No one ever sneaks up on me."

He puffed out his chest with pride. "I am stealthy. Ninja of the night. Anyway, you wanna see the new ride?"

"Is it that orange McLaren?"

"Duh." He plucked my roller bag from the tarmac and tossed it into the trunk, then gestured grandly toward the car. "C'mon. Papa's waiting. And he's in a mood."

There was no refusing Bohdan when he got like this, so I followed him to the car. He dropped behind the wheel, shoved aside the Red Bull in the cupholder, and started the engine with a feral grin. I buckled in, bracing for the G-forces.

He peeled off the runway with a shriek of tires, sending pebbles rat-a-tatting against the fuselage. The roads through the Chestnut Hill estate wound like lazy snakes, and Bohdi took every curve as if he were being chased by a SWAT team. My head thudded against the headrest, and I gripped the dashboard just to keep my organs in place.

"Bohdi," I groaned, "if you crash, I swear to God I will maim you."

He cackled, shifting gears with a flourish. "That's the spirit!"

The mansion loomed ahead, ancient-looking even though it was barely a hundred twenty years old. My father had designed it to resemble some feudal Carpathian relic, moss-covered gray stone and imposing. Fifteen acres of woods surrounded it, the kind of privacy that kept out both neighbors and law enforcement. Even now, in the dead of night, the grounds were raked and trimmed, with not a leaf or cigarette butt out of place.

Bohdi killed the engine. "Papa's in the sitting room," he said, eyes darting toward the lit windows. "He's got council calls all night. He'll want to see you before you turn in."

I climbed out, feet heavy on the flagstones. Bohdi caught up and slung an arm around my shoulders, steering me toward the main doors. For all his bullshit, he knew I was teetering on the edge, and the weight of him kept me from crumpling.

Inside the house, the entry was grand with vaulted ceilings and polished floors, but I always got a sense of home when I walked through the doors. Bohdi led me into the main sitting room, where the fire was roaring in the massive hearth. Even so, I couldn't stop shivering.

"Sit," he commanded, shoving me gently onto the nearest sofa. "You need to eat."

"I need a shower," I countered, but the word "eat" turned my stomach with an ugly twist. "Please don't let Papa do the dramatic concern thing."

Bohdi laughed, then perched on the arm of the sofa. "No promises. You know how he is. You look like you haven't slept in a week. You sure you're okay?"

"I'm okay," I snapped. "I just don't have the energy for this."

He looked at me a little too long. "I don't know, Lucia. You're sweating."

"It's hot in here." The lie sounded pathetic even to me.

But before he could press further, the study door swung open and my father entered, every inch the immortal king in dark silk and midnight-blue velvet. His eyes—cold as Baltic ice—found me instantly.

He crossed the room in four silent strides and pulled me to my feet. The hug was quick but fierce, a reminder of the depth of his love for me. When he stepped back, he gripped my chin, tilting my face so he could see my eyes in the firelight.

"*Lyubimaya,*" he said, voice low. "You are not well."

"I am fine," I lied, ducking away. "Travel was shit, that's all."

He glanced at Bohdi, who shrugged. "She's been like this since I picked her up. I don't think she ate on the plane. If you ask me, she's a little lovesick."

My father made a noise somewhere between a sigh and a laugh. "Bring her blood. Have it warmed for her. She looks like she hasn't fed in days."

Bohdi saluted and vanished down the hall, calling for the kitchen staff as he went. I sank back onto the sofa, bones aching with fatigue. My father sat beside me.

"Did Juliet have her pups?" He asked, voice gentle.

I stared at the fire, letting the heat work its way under my skin. "She was just on the verge when I left."

His brow wrinkled in surprise.

"Ryder Lowrey thought it was better for everyone if I didn't stay." I looked at him, and for the first time ever, I couldn't hide the pain. "He sent me away."

"You could have stayed for your friend, Lucia. Fuck him."

That made me laugh. My father rarely used that kind of language with me. He was clearly irritated.

Then he sighed.

"Men are weak at times, Lucia. Even the good ones. Especially the good ones."

Bohdi came back in, glass in hand. I took it from him and sipped; the blood sitting sour in my stomach.

My father watched, eyes narrowed. "If you do not eat, you will die. This you know, da?"

I gave him my best smile. "Then I'll have to make it last."

Bohdi rolled his eyes. "She's being dramatic," he said, but I could hear the worry beneath the bravado.

"Let her be," Papa replied. "She has earned it."

The fire snapped, sending a spray of sparks up the chimney. I watched them, letting my mind drift to Texas, to the dark hospital corridors and the smell of Ryder's skin, the hunger that would not go away, the hunger for *his* blood.

When I finally spoke, my voice was barely a whisper. "May I go up? I need to wash off the travel."

Papa nodded, and Bohdi took my arm, helping me to my feet. We walked the length of the hall together, his grip just tight enough to remind me he was there.

At the foot of the stairs, he stopped and looked at me. "You're going to be okay, right?"

I mustered my best smirk. "Wouldn't you love to be the favorite for once?"

He shoved me, and I managed a real laugh. But as I climbed the stairs alone, the chill returned, gnawing at the edges of my bones, a reminder that the fire could only do so much.

At the top of the stairs, I looked back and saw my father watching from below, his face half-shadowed, eyes full of worry I'd never seen before.

I wondered as I moved down the hallway if this was what it felt like to be a ghost.

I entered my room and found it exactly as I'd left it a month ago—every surface polished, every blanket straight, the window cracked just enough to let in a sliver of Philly's night air. I cranked the thermostat and then sat on the edge of the bed.

I knew what I had to do, but it took a long minute for my body to catch up with my brain. The blood I'd swallowed was souring in my gut, churning, threatening to come up in a way that hadn't happened since I was a child. It was humiliating, but also kind of cosmic justice. I'd broken every rule of our kind, and now my body was staging a little revolution.

The door to my bathroom wasn't far away, but I staggered like I'd run a marathon. I barely made it to the toilet before I started heaving, violent and wet. The blood I'd consumed came up in a rush, splattering against the porcelain, turning the water a dull, muddy red. I retched until there was nothing left, then collapsed against the cold tile, shaking.

The aftertaste was of acid and regret. My mouth burned. My stomach felt empty, but not in a way that could be fixed. I wiped my face with a towel, then rinsed my mouth. I leaned on the edge of the vanity, staring at my reflection. The girl in the mirror didn't look like a vampire princess. I didn't know what I was becoming.

I bared my teeth and brought down my fangs. Still there. Still sharp.

"Maybe I need a spell," I whispered, voice hoarse. "Or a fucking miracle."

But magic didn't work that way, and neither did biology. I wasn't sure if what was happening to me was a side effect of giving Ryder my blood, or a curse, or just heartbreak taking a physical form. Maybe all three. I tried to remember if there was any precedent in the family lore, but this just wasn't done. I'd basically done the unthinkable, and I'd done it without thinking.

I wiped the tears off my cheeks—when had I started crying?—and stripped off my clothes, piling them in the laundry basket. The need for warmth was overpowering, so I turned the shower to scalding and stepped in, letting the water redden my skin.

Even then, I couldn't stop shaking.

It took a long time to feel clean. When I got out, I wrapped my hair in one towel and my body in another and went straight to the fireplace at the far end of the bedroom. I grabbed the matches from the mantel, lit the kindling, and coaxed the logs to life. The fire was real—oak and hickory, not a gas insert—and the smell of it brought back vague memories of my mother, of winters together when the world felt smaller and safer.

I finally dressed for bed and crawled beneath the massive comforter and slept a troubled sleep filled with bloody dreams of the hospital and Doc and me.

At 9:00 PM, after sleeping for nearly twelve hours, I heard it: the unmistakable sound of my brothers arguing outside my suite.

"I'm not going in," Bohdi said, his voice a nasal whine. "Last time I tried to wake her, she threw a lamp."

My oldest brother Maksym's voice was lower, patient. "That was years ago. She's not going to throw anything now. She probably just needs to talk."

"You saw her last night. How did she look?" Taras cut in, sounding almost identical to his twin brother, Maks, sharp as a razor.

Bohdi didn't hesitate. "She's not right. Her skin, her eyes—she's sick. Or she's hiding something. I say we go in and make her tell us."

"Great idea," Maksym snorted. "She'll totally open up when you start with the interrogating."

Their footsteps approached, and before I could burrow under the covers, the door burst open. All three of them spilled in: Bohdi in gym shorts and a neon tee, Maksym in black sweats and a Henley, Taras in crisp jeans and a white dress shirt, sleeves rolled to the elbow. They looked like the world's least effective SWAT team.

I glared at them from the bed, hair wild, skin probably translucent. "You're all insane," I said. "Go away."

"We're worried," Maksym said, moving to sit beside me on the edge of the bed. "You didn't come down for breakfast. Papa said you missed the call with the Philly council. Are you all right, *malysh kukla?*"

"Little doll?" I rolled my eyes. "You haven't called me that since you taught me to tie my shoelaces."

He smiled, the lines at the corners of his eyes deepening. "You were a small and sweet child. Now you're just small."

Bohdi howled. "That's quite a burn, Lucia!"

Taras ignored the banter. He planted himself at the foot of the bed and folded his arms, gaze boring into me. "Could you be sick, Lucia?"

"No. Seriously you can stop asking," I said. "I've just been going non-stop."

"That's bullshit," Taras snapped. "You've never been run so ragged. Not like this. What's really going on?"

"Nothing," I insisted, but my voice cracked.

Maksym put a hand on my ankle, squeezing gently. "You don't have to talk to us. But you can't hide it. We're not stupid."

I closed my eyes, fighting the urge to cry. "It's been a rough few days. That's all."

"You're not eating," Taras pressed. "You're not resting. Is it about the wolf?"

I opened my eyes, stunned. "What about the wolf?"

"We know you," Bohdi said. He plopped on the other side of the bed, sandwiching me between him and Maksym. "You only get like this when you're heartbroken, or when you're plotting something evil."

"This is not evil plotting," I said. "I promise."

"Then it's a heartbreak?" Taras demanded, voice softening just a little. "He hurt you?"

"No," I said, and meant it. "He just—decided it was best for me to go. It happens."

The three of them exchanged glances, a silent conversation I wasn't privy to. Maks squeezed my ankle again. "His loss," he said.

Taras scowled, but said nothing.

Bohdi nudged me with his shoulder. "If you want us to go kick his ass, we can do that."

I managed a weak smile. "It wouldn't help."

They sat with me for a minute, not talking. The comfort of it was almost enough to make me cry again, but I held it together.

"Get up, Lucia," Maksym finally said. "Fix your hair. Put on real clothes. If you don't, we're telling Papa."

I groaned. "Fine. Just leave."

They left in a single, clumsy herd, arguing all the way down the hall. When I was sure they were gone, I let the tears come, silent and hot.

After a while, I pulled the covers up to my chin, clasping my hands tight against my chest. Something unfamiliar pressed beneath my fingers, right over my heart. I glanced down, and in the dim light, I saw it: a small mark—a pale crescent, almost glowing.

I stared, utterly bewildered. What was this? What *was* this? Hesitantly, I pressed my palm flat over it and closed my eyes.

Suddenly, a rush of pure warmth flooded through me. It felt like sinking into warm honey, the first real warmth I'd felt in days. It lasted only a heartbeat, fading as quickly as it came, leaving behind just a faint echo of heat and that soft, persistent glow beneath my skin.

My heart hammered against my ribs as I traced the mark with a trembling finger. Awe washed over me. This wasn't normal. I *knew*, with a certainty that settled deep in my bones, that this mark was a tether. It connected me, irrevocably, to Ryder Lowrey. Somehow, saving his life had bound us.

I snatched my hand away. Did he feel it too? Or was I alone in this?

A sharp pang of sadness cut through the wonder. I couldn't even ask Doc. Not after he'd sent me away. He hadn't been cruel, but the rejection was clear: he didn't want me. Not really. Not enough to choose me. So what did this mark even matter? Telling my family... their worry, their questions, their inevitable attempts to "fix" it... it would only make everything worse. Let them believe it was just a broken heart. That, at least, was a pain they understood.

We were all hanging by a thread, and I wouldn't be the one to take a pair of scissors to it.

CHAPTER 4

Doc

The morning after a delivery was always a crapshoot—either I'd wake up feeling like I'd broken the tape at the Boston Marathon, or I'd feel like a cement truck had rolled over me in my sleep. Today was both, with a twist. I woke to the thud of my own heartbeat slamming my ribcage, hands trembling so hard it took two tries to silence the phone alarm.

The chill that rode my spine was concerning; it wasn't fever, wasn't the flush of a high-octane night. More like the hollow pulse you get after too many units of blood loss, the kind of hypovolemia that made medics sweat in the field.

You're a doctor, I told myself, and instantly resented how much it sounded like a plea.

Diagnosis: Adrenaline hangover, secondary to a wolf-sized dose of stress, grief, and sleep deprivation. Follow-up: general feeling of malaise, if I were being honest. This was the kind of thing you couldn't just fix with Gatorade and a breakfast burrito.

Swinging my legs out of bed, I planted my feet and waited for the goddamn floor to stop impersonating a ship deck. The piss-poor gray light at the window confirmed I'd slept, sure, but it felt about as restorative as a coma induced by a brick. I yanked on a faded Henley, raked fingers through my hair.

Lucia would've called me dramatic. Worse, she'd have nailed me with some crack about medical narcissism before reminding me other people had *real* problems. The thought hit like a sucker punch to the gut. *Forget her. Forget the loss.* That was the whole damn point of sending her back to Philly.

In the bathroom, I splashed icy water on my face, avoiding the horror show in the mirror. Bruised purple rings under bloodshot eyes stared back, anyway. Brushed my teeth like routine could magic this away. Spoiler: It didn't.

Downstairs, the kitchen's silence was broken only by the coffeemaker's grateful mutter—thank Christ I'd had the foresight to set it last night. Poured coffee. Watched the surface tremble like a seismograph picking up an earthquake centered squarely in my own nervous system. Took a scalding gulp. No nausea, no bitterness. Just the hollow, familiar disappointment of tasting absolutely nothing. Par for the course.

Time for morning inventory. Standard procedure on mornings when your biology throws a tantrum: *Temp: Subnormal. Check. Skin: Pallor, bordering on cadaverous. Check. Pupils: Slightly dilated. Check. Pulse: Still a tachycardic sonofabitch hammering against my ribs. Check. Hunger: Zip. Nada.* Not even a phantom rumble. Stomach? Empty ache replaced by a goddamn ghost pain right in the center of my chest. Like the phantom limb where something essential used to be. My wolf? Quiet. Not pacing, not whining, it was like he was pissed at me. I could scream my lungs out and get nothing but silence in return. Shock? Probably. Dying for two minutes before a vampire princess force-fed you her blood isn't exactly textbook recovery, asshole. More like his mistress had left him and he wanted to punish me.

I set the mug down hard. Yanked up my sleeve. Forearm veins stood out stark, dark blue-black tracery against too-pale skin. Pressed my thumb hard into my wrist. Watched the blanched spot fade sluggishly back to color. *Capillary Refill: 3 seconds.* Textbook says 2. Textbook, my ass.

"Not great," I muttered to the empty room. The pathetic echo of my own voice earned a harsh, humorless laugh. Yeah. Understatement of the fucking century.

I thought of Lucia again, and this time the absence landed hard. No echo, no anger, only the pang of longing. It was just the dull ache of something gone and never coming back. I pressed my palm to my chest and waited, half-expecting a burn or a sign. Then I felt it. Some weird pulse behind my sternum. I forced myself to ignore it.

I finished the coffee, dressed in scrubs, and headed out to the hospital, determined to muscle through whatever this was. I'd seen a thousand cases of post-op malaise, hormone dumps, existential spirals. I could white-knuckle it just as well as anyone.

But as I stepped into the dawn, cold air stinging my skin, I had the uneasy sense that I was walking into a future that didn't want me.

And for the first time since dying, I wasn't sure I could fix it.

The parking lot was empty except for a battered Honda and two bikes—Bronc's and mine—leaning against the curb like sentries. I ducked my head against the wind and made for the side entrance, badge flashing in the gray light. The smell of disinfectant and air conditioning hit me in the entry vestibule, and for a second I was anchored, comforted. Hospitals always had this effect: the illusion that things were under control, contained. Even when you were dying on the inside.

I walked the north corridor, blinking away the memory of last night's chaos. My footsteps echoed harder than usual, and when I reached the nurses' station, Amanda gave a tight little wave, eyes darting from my face to the clock and back again. There was a wary look on her face—probably from the way Lucia had nearly mauled her yesterday.

I nodded in her direction. "Morning."

She made a noncommittal sound, then went back to typing.

Juliet's suite was at the end of the hall, flowers already spilling into the hallway on rolling carts. I pushed the door open with my elbow, not bothering to knock. Inside, the lights were low, and Bronc was slumped on a visitor's cot, snoring with his mouth open. The twins' bassinet was next to Juliet's bed, each of them wrapped in a blanket. The boy, a wadded-up football of red skin and fists, his sister already making a game of sucking her own toes. Juliet lay on her side, back to the door, hair a tangle of golden blonde.

I paused, watching for a minute, waiting for her to shift toward me. Nothing. I stepped inside, moving as quietly as I could, which was less quiet than I wanted. My elbow clipped the IV pole, sending it shivering. I caught it, but the sound woke Juliet. She rolled over, blinking blearily.

"Morning, Luna," I said, softer than usual.

She smiled, but it was tired. "Hey, Doc. You bringing drugs?"

"Just myself," I said. "You need something?" She was sharp, even on no sleep.

Juliet's eyes narrowed, taking me in. "No, I'm good. You, however, look like you fell down a flight of stairs."

"That's the trend, apparently," I quipped, moving to the foot of the bed. "How's your pain, really?"

She shrugged. "They've got me on the good stuff. Feels like someone sat on my spine, but it's not too bad. Wolf healing, you know?" She nodded toward the twins. "I was a little sad that Lucia wasn't here to see them born. You know anything about that?"

I hesitated, then nodded and walked to the bassinet and looked down. The babies were trying to decide if they wanted to coo or cry. I knew how they felt. But they were about the most beautiful things I'd ever seen.

I wasn't in the mood to discuss my private life even with my Luna. "She needed to go home." I reached down and touched the boy's foot, the skin so soft it barely resisted my finger.

Juliet watched me with concern. "Hmm. It's not like her to leave without saying goodbye. Guess I'll talk to her later today. You sure you're okay?"

"Just a long night. My circadian's all out of whack."

She looked skeptical, but let me check her vitals. Her pulse was strong; her incision already healing well. The twins were also healthy: lungs clear, no murmur, no sign of hypoxia or the strange spectrum of illnesses that sometimes affected shifter births. I checked their weights again, just to be sure. They'd each lost a few ounces, but that's to be expected. They were perfect.

She reached out and squeezed my hand, gently but with that iron-laced empathy only pack Lunas seemed to possess. "You did good, Doc. Even if you look like you could use another eight hours of sleep yourself."

"I'll be fine," I said, but it came out thin.

"Did you hear what we decided to name them?"

I actually hadn't heard. "Tell me."

The baby boy had started to wail. "That loudmouth is named after his daddy. But we'll call him LJ, for Liam Junior."

Bronc jolted awake on the portable cot, snorted, and reached for the little red bundle. "Juliet?" he grumbled.

"I'm here," she called, smiling at the sound of her mate's confusion.

He grunted, then saw me as he pulled LJ to his chest and patted his back. "Morning, Doc."

"Anyway," Juliet continued, pointing to the pink bundle, "that sweet angel is Iris. She was named after my great-great grandmother. The only full shifter I'm aware of in my family."

"You want to hold her?" Juliet asked, nodding at Iris.

I started to say yes, but my hands betrayed me. "Maybe after rounds," I lied. "She's sleeping. Don't want to wake her."

Juliet's mouth twisted in a frown, but she didn't press. "Suit yourself. But you're missing out."

I looked away. "Shadbolt's coming in at noon," I said, shifting the subject. "He'll check on you, but if anything changes, call me."

Juliet made a face. "Shadbolt's not you."

"He's solid," I said. "I mean, he's not as charming as me, but shifter doctors who know their stuff are hard to come by. We're lucky to have him. And I wouldn't have hired him if he weren't a damn good doctor."

Bronc laughed. "Nobody's as charming as you, Doc."

I grinned. "Well, of course not. But I didn't hire Shadbolt as backup. I hired him because sometimes even the best of us might not be able to carry out our duties."

Juliet's smile dropped. "You aren't allowed to talk like that. You just lost charm points."

That earned her a genuine smile from me.

"I'm just saying."

The rest of the check-in passed without drama. I made a note to order more iron-rich formula from the pharmacy—Iris had a mild anemia, not unusual for twins—and promised Juliet I'd visit again after lunch. She'd supplement nursing with formula. She insisted on hugging me before I left, and I let her, though I was painfully aware of how little warmth I had to offer.

Outside the suite, I leaned against the wall, exhaling. My hands still trembled, and I pressed the heel of one palm to my temple, forcing myself to get a grip.

Down the hall, I caught sight of Shadbolt's reflection in the glass. He wore a white coat; always so damn formal. I huffed a small laugh to myself at how his hair was gelled into a neat helmet. He looked like the world's most boring fucking superhero.

He stopped beside me. "Ryder. You look..." he hesitated, searching for a word. "Tired."

"Yeah." He didn't know the half of it.

He shifted, eyes darting to the door behind me. "Is this a good time to discuss scheduling? I noticed you moved three appointments to next week."

I shrugged. "Needed to focus on the twins."

"I can take more calls if you need," he said, and for a second I saw something like real concern in his eyes.

"I'll let you know," I replied, already stepping past him toward the side door.

The air outside had started to warm. I walked to the end of the parking lot, ignoring the urge to scream or put my fist through the trunk of a nearby tree. Instead, I just stood there, letting the warm air sink into my bones, hoping it would numb whatever was happening inside.

For the first time in my life, I didn't want to go back inside the hospital. Didn't want to see patients, didn't want to see anyone. The certainty I'd always carried—my one superpower—was gone. I was improvising, and I was failing.

I looked down at my hands, not as steady as they usually were, and wondered how much longer I could keep faking it.

Not long, I suspected.

It was dusk when I made my way into the meeting room, trying to seem as normal as possible. There was a feeling in the air that told me that something was up. There was no pretending that I hadn't been through an awful trauma. I wasn't the first person in this group who'd faced death and recovered. But I *was* the first who'd been snatched from death's grip by sucking blood from a beautiful vampire princess. My brothers tried to play it off like everything was normal. It wasn't. And the effort of holding myself together was getting harder by the hour.

Bronc called the meeting to order by tapping his knuckles on the table. Papa, Wrecker, Arsenal, and Gunner all were looking no worse for wear, and they were all side-eyeing me like they wanted to be sure I wouldn't disappear. Or maybe they wanted to be sure I wouldn't suddenly grow fangs.

He kept it brief, the way he always did: status updates, new business, a rundown of the week's calendar. But tonight, he didn't dismiss the group after the formalities. Instead, he raised his voice.

"We've got a problem," he said. "We can't ignore the elephant in the room."

He didn't name me. He didn't have to. The guys looked at me all at once. It was like being in an MRI tube, every weakness on display. Gunner looked guilty, like it was his fault I'd managed to rip my artery open on a jagged rock—like it wasn't just bad fucking luck. I knew how the kid's mind worked. Arsenal was just sizing me up with his intense stare that never missed a goddamn thing. And Wrecker wore his usual smirk that made me want to wipe it off with my fist.

Papa cleared his throat. "We all lean on each other. We've survived worse." And he should know. He's one of the men who had all but died a few months ago. He looked at me, and his expression wasn't judgment—just worry, deep and open. He saw through the walls I'd built, and for a second I almost faltered.

"It's been a long couple of days," I said quietly. "I haven't slept much. I'll fix it."

Nobody looked satisfied with that, but nobody pushed. It was their way—don't press, don't pry. But the air was charged now, humming with concern.

Bronc spoke up, looking me straight in the eye. "We know that you tend to keep your business to yourself, Doc. We respect that. But not this time. We're gonna be checking on you. That's an order. When someone comes to your door; you *will* answer it. I can see you're seething over that. I don't give a single fuck. You are not allowed to handle this on your own. Tell me you understand this directive, Ryder."

I gritted my teeth so hard that if I'd had normal strength, they'd have broken. "Understood, Alpha."

A fist pounded the old wooden table. "Good. This meeting is dismissed."

Papa stayed behind, waiting for me to meet his eye.

He didn't ask if I was okay. He just put a hand on my shoulder and squeezed, a reminder that I wasn't alone, even if I wanted to be.

Aspen popped her head in the door. Her gaze met mine, soft but unwavering. "You know we're here if you need anything," she said, her voice the gentlest thing I'd heard all day.

I nodded, unable to muster words.

When they left, I stood alone in the meeting room, the echoes of their worry bouncing off the walls. I pressed my palm to my chest, feeling the empty thud of my heart.

Whatever this was, I couldn't fix it with denial. But I was damned sure going to try.

After ten minutes, I'd finally headed out. I almost made it out the back door when I was summoned to Bronc's office. Fuck.

I found him alone except for the bottle of Irish whiskey he kept for emergencies. He'd poured two fingers into a glass and was swirling it when I entered. He didn't look up.

"Close the door, would you?" he said.

I shut it and leaned against the wall.

He waited, then pushed the glass toward me. "Sit."

I sat, wrapping my fingers around the glass even though the smell made my stomach twist.

Bronc rubbed circles on his desk with his index finger. "I just talked to Kazimir."

He said it like a confession.

I didn't blink. "Why?"

"Because he's a father worried about his daughter."

"What did he say?"

Bronc exhaled, slow. "He said Lucia's not herself. She's sick, or something like it. She's not eating or feeding or whatever the hell they do. Can't get out of bed. Says she's complained of a bone-deep chill she can't shake. It's like someone cut out her insides. She's fading. He's scared, Ryder."

I stared at the wall, jaw locked. I thought of Kazimir, the vampire king, whose entire persona was built around glacial composure. Lucia was the light of his life. If he is frightened for her, then this is truly serious.

"He thinks it's got to do with what happened in the canyon. The blood. Said he's not seen anything like this in a hundred years or more."

The room got smaller. My heart pounded in my ears.

"He called it a tether," Bronc went on. "Some kind of bond. Said it runs both ways."

That landed. "Shit. What's happening to her is happening to me," I said, voice hollow.

"Yeah," Bronc said. "And if you don't do something about it, you're both dead."

The words hit like a freight train. I flashed through the symptoms, not just mine but hers—the sudden exhaustion, the chills, the loss of appetite, the emptiness. I was weaker than I'd let on. I was on the verge of collapse, and the prospect of Lucia suffering was a knife to my gut.

I thought of her, somewhere in Philadelphia, curled up in a room designed for royalty, dying by inches. I thought of how easy it had been to pretend her absence didn't matter, how the only thing that had kept me upright in the last thirty-six hours was her proximity during Juliet's labor. And now she was gone, and I was unraveling. How *I'd* done this. I'd sent her away because... why?

I looked at my hands, shaking harder than before. There was no hiding it now.

"How long?" I asked.

Bronc shrugged. "Kazimir says a week, two if you're lucky."

I let out a noise, half laugh, half groan.

"He should have told me sooner," I said, the anger flaring up.

"*You* should have told *me* how bad it was. I could have called him first," Bronc fired back, not unkindly.

We sat in silence, the only sound the ticking of the ancient clock on the wall.

"You know what you have to do," Bronc said. "You have to go to her."

I shook my head. "It's not that simple. I've got patients, I've got Juliet..."

"You've got a death sentence, unless you fix this. Plus, you hired Dr. Shadbolt months ago. He's capable of taking your caseload. We're wolves, Doc. We mostly heal ourselves, and I don't think any of the women in the pack are due to deliver anytime soon."

He poured more whiskey into his glass and downed it in one swallow. I knew he was right.

"You can't help anyone if you're dead, Ryder. You're the best we've got. Don't make me beg."

My pride wanted to fight. My wolf wanted to run.

I stared at the amber liquid in the glass and remembered the taste of Lucia's blood, the way it had burned and healed and bound me to her, whether I liked it or not. And I'll be goddamned if I didn't *like* it. That's what scared me most. I didn't *want* to become what I *knew* I'd become.

There was no dignity in this, no way to spin it as heroism. It was just hunger, pure and raw, and the only way to survive was to stop denying it.

I stood on unsteady legs.

"I'll go," I said. "But if I become a full-fledged vamp, I'm sucking you dry."

Bronc grinned, relief softening his face. "You'll have to get past Juliet, and not even vampire Doc would be strong enough to do that you fucker."

I left the whiskey on the table and walked out with a plan. I had a deadline. And I had a hollowed-out chest where my heart used to be.

Bronc didn't wait for my second thoughts. By the time I got back to my quarters, there was a text on my phone: *Jet leaves 3:00 pm. Papa & Aspen go with. Be ready.*

No questions. No negotiation. Just the Alpha taking care of business.

I should have been pissed, but all I felt was relief. Someone else was steering now, and maybe that was the only way this would work.

I threw a duffel together—two changes of clothes, my med kit, a flask of wolf-brewed whiskey in case I needed to cauterize anything on the way. I sat on the edge of the bed, staring at the bag, and tried to picture what would happen in Philadelphia. I'd never been to Lucia's world, never set foot in her father's kingdom. My only knowledge of it was her stories, half-joking, half-terrifying: midnight meetings in candlelit halls, brothers with fangs like ice picks, servants who could kill a man with a shoelace and smile about it.

I'd been to Kazimir's club a few times, but never to his home. His club was a place to play. It was controlled where everyone was willing and knew exactly what would happen before it happened. Now, I'd be walking into a completely unknown situation.

I'd done hostage extractions in Afghanistan. I'd pulled wounded out of collapsing buildings, and I'd never felt this kind of dread before.

Aspen called just after midnight. "We'll pick you up tomorrow afternoon," she said, voice calm. "Papa says bring your vitamins. We don't know what the vamps will serve for breakfast."

I smiled, in spite of everything. "Tell him thanks."

She hesitated. "You okay?"

"Not even close."

She didn't try to fix it. "See you tomorrow afternoon."

I put my phone away and tried to sleep, but the ache in my chest made it impossible. I lay in the dark, watching the ceiling fan trace slow circles, and let my mind think of Lucia, really think about her. About the night at the canyon. I thought of the way she ran through the caves, viciously killing the demons who'd taken Gunner's mate. How she fought beside us; not because she had to, but because she cared about us. I thought about her blood on my tongue, about the way she'd said my name like it meant something.

I looked back on the past months, how I'd noticed everything about her. Her beauty. The way she loved Juliet. How she fought with us for Menace and Savannah. She'd been there when we stood against the Green-briar pack and then when we'd rescued Brie. She was good. Period. And because of her species, I'd deliberately put distance between us. I'd been a fucking idiot. But it didn't matter now.

The emptiness inside wasn't just hunger—it was need, pure and perfect. This bond or tether or whatever it was, was a living thing, coiled around my ribcage, dragging me toward her.

I closed my eyes and, in the silence, reached for her across the distance.

I felt nothing at first. Then—faint, almost imaginary—a flicker of warmth, like the memory of a fire. It pulsed once, twice, then settled into a slow, steady thrum, as if two hearts were trying to synchronize from a thousand miles apart.

I held onto that, let it anchor me. I whispered her name into the dark, and for a second I thought I heard it echo back.

It was nearly noon before I could barely drag myself out of bed. I showered and dressed in a pair of slacks and a black dress shirt. I checked my reflection—still haunted, still hollow; but I managed to grab my bag and drag myself to the couch in the living room. The next thing I knew, someone was banging on my front door, yelling my name. It was Papa. He helped me to the truck for our ride to the Iron Valor airstrip.

Papa all but carried me to my seat and got me settled in. He covered me with a thick blanket, and I could see the worry etched on his face.

"Rest easy, brother. It won't be long until you're feeling right as rain." His giant hands tucked the blanket under my chin and around my arms to try to stop my shivering.

Papa, Aspen, and Oscar's voices carried through the cabin as I drifted in and out of sleep. I dreamed of Lucia and blood, and of a wolf who was no longer sure of what he was.

CHAPTER 5

LUCIA

You learn a lot about yourself in isolation. That's what I was telling myself anyway, lying in my bed and staring at the ceiling as the ancient grandfather clock in the hallway ticked off seconds like they didn't matter. When I was little, that clock used to soothe me. Now every tick was a nail hammered through my nerves.

I hadn't fed since that night in Texas. My father's kitchen staff—some combination of curious mortals and willing blood-servants—had left trays by the door. Most of it spoiled or congealed before I could force myself to even look at it. When I finally tried to drink, the blood went down sour and came right back up, painting the marble sink and toilet bowl with a grotesque swirl of crimson and black. It took me almost half an hour to clean it up, and the smell haunted the bathroom for hours.

Now, I lay flat on my back, arms folded over my chest like some waxwork in a museum, counting my own shallow breaths. On the nightstand, three feet away, sat a battered paperback of Anna Karenina that I'd read fifty times. I wanted it. Not for the story—fuck Tolstoy and his trains—but for the distraction, the old comfort of words. I flexed my fingers, felt the numbness tingling all the way to my elbows, and willed the book to come. Usually, telekinesis was as natural as blinking for me. But now, all I managed was a little tremble of the cover, a flutter, and then it flopped to the floor, face-down. I couldn't even muster the energy to curse. This was bad. Really bad.

I rolled to my side, pulling the comforter with me, and tried to make myself small. I couldn't tell if I was shaking from the cold, or from the panic. Both, probably. The blankets did nothing, but I piled them higher anyway, cocooning myself until the weight nearly suffocated me. I thought about calling for help, but I'd spent a lifetime refusing to play damsel. Besides, what would I even say? "Help, I'm dying of heartbreak; of wolf separation anxiety?" Fuck that.

My phone was somewhere on the bed, lost in the folds. I found it by feel, the glass warm from my skin. I checked for texts—Juliet had been telling me about her twins. We'd both obviously left Doc out of any conversation. I felt some relief at having heard the babies were healthy and beautiful. And beautiful they were. A boy and a girl; small and perfect. My chest hurt in a way that wasn't physical. I missed my friend.

I wasn't stupid. I knew some of what was happening to me. I'd broken something fundamental—had let my heart, my blood and my magic tangle in a way that no one in my family ever had. And now my body was punishing me for it, one cell at a time. The hunger in me wasn't for blood anymore. It was for something I couldn't name, something that had been ripped away before I could even understand what it meant.

A few hours later, I heard the thunder of boots in the hall, then the crash of a door against the wall. I was still in bed, still in the same position as when I'd finally fallen asleep, arms wound around my ribcage, head burrowed under the covers. The blast of air and noise jolted me in alarm.

"Wake up!" Maksym's voice, hoarse and ragged, was followed by the abrupt snap of my blackout curtains. He stormed across the room, big shoulders hunched, a thunderhead of black hair pulled back in a soldier's knot. He looked like a handsome linebacker on a mission to kill.

His twin, Taras trailed him by three steps, his silver hair parted in the middle and brushed back behind his ears. His white dress shirt, damask vest, and black slacks made him look like he were about to head to his office to count his coins. He paused just inside the doorway, hands tight behind his back, mouth set in a tight line that said he was not amused. Nik was in the mix, telling me this was serious.

Bohdi bounded in out of breath. His expression was worried, but the way he watched everyone told me he was already tallying up the casualties.

They closed ranks at the foot of my bed, all four glaring. For a second, I thought they'd planned it, rehearsed the choreography, but then Maksym started in without warning.

"Are you *trying* to die?" His accent thickened, a sure sign he was rattled. "Have you lost your mind, Lucia?"

"She's not going to die," Taras shot back. "It's impossible."

"Vampires fade, Taras," Maksym snapped, as if Taras were the idiot here. He turned to me, jaw trembling. "You gave him your blood. You fed a *wolf*, Lucia."

I rolled over, dragging the covers up to my chin. "I didn't just *feed* him. I saved his life. That's a little different."

"Different?" Maksym let out a sound between a laugh and a snarl. "How is it different when the fucking result is the same?"

"She's right," Taras said, but he didn't sound sure. "She *did* save his life. Father's Council is going to... *have* to see it that way."

Bodhan cleared his throat, flopping in an armchair. "The Council is already in a panic. The group chat was blowing up all night. Elders are calling for a full inquiry."

"That's not what matters," Maksym said. He was pacing now, back and forth, each step louder than the last. "What matters is our sister is lying here like a corpse, and nobody knows why." He pointed an accusing finger at me. "What did you *do*, Lucia?"

I tried to sit up, failed, then settled for propping myself against the headboard. I was still freezing, and the effort made me tremble.

"I did what was right," I said. "He was dying, and I—" My voice caught. I couldn't say the rest. I didn't want to tell them how desperate I'd been—how I couldn't imagine a world without Ryder Lowrey in it. How I felt the world lighting up as I poured my own blood into him.

Taras's face softened. He perched on the edge of the bed, careful not to touch me, as if I might shatter. "Is it the hunger?" he asked, voice gentle. "You need to eat, Luchka. We'll bring you whatever you want."

"It's not that," I said. "I can't keep it down. None of it."

Bodhan leaned forward, elbows on his knees. "It's a bond," he said. "You did more than heal him. You made a connection. That's why you're both falling apart."

"Don't be dramatic," Maksym barked. "Wolves and vamps can't bond. That's biology. That's history."

Nikolay cleared his throat, ignored him, and locked his gaze on me. "It doesn't matter if it's what we've always assumed about biology. What matters is you're weakening. Until it's fixed—" He stopped, shrugged. "You'll *both* keep getting weaker."

"So what?" Maksym rounded on him. "We're just supposed to let her die because of a mistake?"

"It's not a mistake," I said, and the words surprised even me.

Maksym stared, mouth open, as if I'd told him I was quitting the family.

"No one chooses this," he said finally, voice barely above a whisper.

"You don't know everything," I shot back. "None of you do."

He looked like he wanted to throw something, but he checked himself. They all did. Despite the anger, I could see the fear in their eyes, the way they glanced at each other when they thought I wasn't looking. Maksym's fists unclenched, and he knelt by the bed, just out of reach.

"We can fix it," he said, a plea in his voice. "Father is already working on it. He's making calls, pulling in favors."

Taras nodded, but his eyes darted to Nikolay, waiting for confirmation.

Nikolay looked at me, then at my hand, which still hovered over my heart. "Father will fix this."

I slumped back against the pillows, relief and dread tangling in my gut.

Maksym reached for my hand, then stopped himself. "Don't do this alone, Luchka," he said. "Let us help."

I wanted to let them carry me, like they had when I was a child and the world was different. But I couldn't. Not now.

"I'm trying to be strong," my voice felt far away.

"We're not letting you fight alone," Taras sighed. "Just say the word and we'll come back."

I watched them leave, their silhouettes framed in the door's yellow light. The room felt even colder now, the emptiness ringing in my ears. I pulled the covers tighter.

By nightfall, I'd managed to shower and dress carefully in a long, simple dress and ballet flats and make my way down the stairs. The house was in chaos, but carefully organized chaos. I recognized some of the faces, but most I didn't. My father had doubled his staff overnight. There were unfamiliar vampires everywhere, many of them with Slavic or Eastern European features, all on edge. I caught a glimpse of Maksym in the security office, barking orders into a phone. His face was drawn, sweat beading his forehead. I'd never seen him like this, not even in Budapest, not even when we were attacked as kids and had to barricade ourselves for three nights while Papa cleared the house.

At the solarium, I stopped, needing to sit. My legs had gone wobbly again, and the cold was creeping back, up from the soles of my feet this time, anchoring me in place. I eased into a low chair by the window and drew my knees up, hugging them tight. I couldn't stop shaking.

That was when I saw Taras, standing at the far end of the glass corridor. He was on the phone, voice clipped and urgent. I listened, barely daring to breathe.

"No, she's not feeding," he was saying. "We tried everything. It just makes her worse." A pause. "Father says the wolf can help. I don't know how. It's never been done before." Another pause. "Yes. Yes, I'll keep her safe."

He hung up, wiped a hand over his face, and saw me through the glass. He came in, closing the door behind him, and crouched in front of me.

"You shouldn't be out of bed," he said, voice almost gentle.

"I'm tired of my own company," I said. "Why all the guards?"

His gaze darted to the door, then back to me. "We're vulnerable right now," he said. "If word gets out about your condition, the Council might—"

"They'll think I've made Papa weak," I finished for him. "That I'm an abomination."

He shrugged, as if this was just how things went. "It's politics. Papa is making moves, but we have to look strong. He's the King of Kings. But *if* he can be hurt, it would be through you. He's just taking precautions."

I rested my chin on my knees. "You said the wolf was coming?"

He nodded, grim. "You're not the only one who's fading, Lucia. The wolf—Ryder—he's in just as bad shape. Maybe worse."

I closed my eyes, letting the truth of it settle. My stomach clenched at the thought of Ryder being unwell.

Taras hesitated. "Father has a plan," he said. "You just have to trust him."

"Do *you*?"

He thought for a long moment. "I trust *you*," he said finally. "If you say this isn't a mistake, then it isn't. And Father is the wisest man I know."

He helped me stand, his arm warm and steady. "Come on," he said. "Let's get you upstairs before the others see."

I nodded and let him walk me to the stairs. At the foot of the grand staircase, my knees buckled, and I clutched the rail, breath leaving me in a hiss. For a second, I saw black spots, then white, and then...

A sudden warmth bloomed in my chest, spreading outward like a sunburst. The mark over my heart pulsed, and for the first time in hours, I felt my blood quicken. It burned, not like fever but like the spark of life. My vision cleared. I stood taller, steadier.

A vase at the end of the hall began to tip, but I caught it midair with a flick of thought, the movement as easy as blinking. Taras stared at me, eyes wide.

"Are you...?"

I nodded, fingers trembling in a new way. "Something's changed," I said. "Something's coming."

The estate's front doors weren't meant for mortals. Each was twelve feet high, three inches thick, solid oak banded with iron and carved with a history older than the state of Pennsylvania. They didn't swing; they parted, like a curtain on a cathedral stage. Today, the drama was worthy of the entrance.

I stood on the third step, watching the wolf who came through the doors. He was a giant—Big Papa, the chaplain, dressed for battle in a tailored suit that somehow made his bulk more imposing. He stepped onto the marble like he owned the place, but his eyes swept the room, clocking every guard, every camera, every exit.

Even at a distance, I felt a jolt of respect. Most vampires came in afraid, always looking up, always outnumbered. Not him. He moved like he'd stormed plenty of castles before.

Oscar was right behind, a prairie dog in a Harris Tweed waistcoat, chin high, tail flicking with precise irritation. He took three steps into the foyer, craned his head toward me, and in a crisp British accent spoke, "My lady, you look quite unwell. I'm used to seeing you much more put together." He squinted at the art along the upper gallery. "I am most hopeful we've brought the thing that will restore your usual exquisite beauty. Between the two of us, you look like death."

I actually laughed. A bright, helpless noise, sharp as a snapped thread. It bounced off the stone and echoed, drawing every eye to the staircase, including my father's.

Our gazes locked. For a moment, neither of us blinked. I expected worry or maybe fear for me, but what I saw was... recognition. My father knew me better than anyone. He knew exactly what I was—what I was going through. I was a creature out of place, afraid to meet her destiny. He nodded once, so slight most would miss it.

Oscar rolled his eyes in my direction, as if to say, "Vampires, honestly," then bustled over toward the library. In his wake, the tension in the air went from suffocating to just moderately uncomfortable.

My father greeted Big Papa with a firm handshake, a signal to every guard that these wolves were to be trusted. He slowly moved back to join my brothers as the spectacle unfolded before them. Big Papa's demeanor was relaxed, and I got the sense he'd seen a thousand rooms like this and was aware that every conversation was a chess game, and every chess game ended with the possibility of a dead body.

I slowed. But the warmth in my chest was growing, not fading, and the idea of lurking in the shadows made me feel weak again. I pulled my sweater tighter and continued down the stairs, one slow step at a time.

When I was almost at the bottom, Big Papa's gaze met mine again. His eyes were kind, but not soft. He tracked every movement. As my feet touched the marble floor, he walked to me, making it clear he was no threat but no pushover either.

"Princess Lucia," he said, taking my hands and giving my title just enough weight to make it a joke between equals.

"Chaplain... Big Papa," I replied, feeling the corners of my mouth curl up.

His mouth twitched. "You holding up?"

I shrugged, which hurt more than I let on. "Better than I was."

He looked me over, but didn't comment on my appearance. "They're right behind me," he said. "The others."

I nodded, even though the thought made my pulse flutter.

I felt Aspen's magic before I saw her. She had a scent like wild lemon and something sweet and strange, utterly at odds with the cold elegance of the house. The air crackled, not with power, but with the promise of it. It wasn't a warning but a simple message: I am here.

She moved through the crowd with the kind of confidence I'd only ever seen in Juliet. She wore one of her signature swing dresses; this one pink with white daisies and a white collar. Her white go-go boots were classic Aspen. Her black hair framed her face in long waves, and her green eyes shone with concern. She didn't flinch at the guards; didn't shrink from the watchful stares of my brothers. She was clearly on a mission.

She locked eyes with me as soon as she entered. She cocked her head, studying me, and in that instant I knew she could see the change. Not just the hunger or the cold, but the deep, cellular alteration taking place under my skin.

She walked right to where I stood and stopped. She just stood there, silent and patient, letting the tension in the room bend around her. When I stepped towards her, she raised a hand, palm open and hovering inches from my arm. She didn't touch me, but I could feel the heat radiating from her skin.

"The bond is changing you both," she said, voice low but clear as a bell.

I opened my mouth to argue, but the words stuck. Aspen's eyes told me she wasn't judging, just observing—a scientist, not a priest. I nodded once, tight.

"Is it... bad?" I asked, barely above a whisper.

She shrugged. "It could be beautiful if y'all accept it." She smiled, small but real; her southern accent comforting. "Fighting it is what's killin' y'all."

I felt the urge to cry, or maybe just collapse. Instead, I laughed. Not a full laugh, but the kind you get at funerals, when the truth is too heavy to hold and so it leaks out sideways. Aspen's smile grew, just a little.

"Thank you," I said.

She nodded, her hands finally taking mine. "When he comes, you'll know what to do."

Oscar, who'd been eavesdropping from behind a potted ficus, piped up: "You see? Southern witches will always be more honest than the rest of us." He offered Aspen a dramatic bow, which she returned with a wink.

Big Papa had been watching all of this from the periphery, and now he stepped forward, his presence a buffer against the scrutiny of the room. He inclined his head to Aspen, then to me, and I realized he was bracing himself for whatever came next.

Around us, the room had settled into a kind of uneasy calm. The guards were still suspicious, the staff still edgy, but with Aspen and Big Papa flanking me, I felt insulated. Not strong, not yet. But no longer as weak.

I stood there, bookended by witch and wolf, waiting for the other half of my bond to come home. My father and brothers were an audience quietly letting things unfold before them.

I didn't have to wait long before I heard it—the deliberate footsteps of a man who knew he was walking into enemy territory. Ryder Lowrey stepped inside, and for a split second, everyone in the foyer stilled.

He was gaunt, sharp-jawed, skin pulled tight over high cheekbones like warmed-over death. His hair looked darker than I remembered, a sweep of storm over his brow. He wore black from collar to boots; slacks and a dress shirt showed the physique of a wolf but there was no hiding the exhaustion in his frame.

Our eyes locked across thirty feet of marble and silence.

I felt a warmth flood my body; my being. I heard nothing but the sound of his ragged breath and the shallow gasp that escaped my lips.

Ryder didn't move at first. He just stood there, knuckles white on the handle of a battered duffel. Every move he made was labored. Then he seemed to steady. His shoulders squared, color returned to his cheeks, and the line of tension that had cut through him simply vanished.

No one spoke. Not the guards, not my brothers, not even Big Papa. Aspen watched misty-eyed; so did Oscar with a prairie dog grin if there even was such a thing. Every vampire sensed something had shifted—something profound, irreversible.

But none of them mattered.

What flowed between Ryder and me wasn't hunger, or panic, or even lust. It was return. Completion. A circuit, closed at last. I felt it in every cell. The bond wasn't a leash; it was a homecoming. I'd spent days fearing it, fighting it, and now, in this cathedral of ice and history, I realized I wanted it more than I wanted to breathe.

He stopped and looked to my father. Kazimir nodded.

Ryder took one step forward. I mirrored him, the movement as natural as falling. I didn't care who was watching, if my brothers wanted to scold me, if it undid every rule my father had written in blood and stone. All that mattered was the heat, the pull, the possibility of being whole.

I couldn't help glancing at my father, who also gave me a nod of approval. Knowing he stood in my corner buoyed me above everything. I saw Maksym's face; a trace of relief crossed it along with a bout of confusion. For the first time in my life, I pitied him—he'd never felt anything this strong, this honest.

Another step. Another.

I was halfway across the foyer when the last of my fear dropped away. I was not dying. I was not less. I was more. I was alive. The tether was no longer draining me; it was feeding me; feeding us both. I felt it, and judging by the relief on Ryder's face, so did he.

We stopped, a foot apart.

He reached out, slow and careful, like I was a wounded animal. I caught his hand in mine, letting the current run through us. My fingers dug into his palm, and for the first time since I'd left Texas, I felt not just alive, but potent.

There were things to say, questions to ask, arguments to finish. But not yet. Not now.

He closed the distance, and suddenly his lips met mine, and the world made sense.

CHAPTER 6

DOC

My knees nearly buckled. The entrance hall's marble was cold against my boots, and the whole mansion seemed to tilt on its axis, like we were falling through a gravity well only she and I could feel. The crowd of vampires that included her father and who I assumed were her brothers, Big Papa, and even Oscar the prissy prairie dog—none of them mattered now. They'd faded into the background, and only the feel of Lucia's lips on mine registered.

For the first time in days, I felt awake. Not well—but lucid, like a man who'd suddenly been given life-sustaining breath. My fingers, numb and wooden seconds before, felt the softness of Lucia's skin as I caressed her perfect face. I wanted to devour her; but I kept my kisses light. It didn't matter. My cock still went rock hard. She consumed every part of me, and I wanted to inhale her.

Our bodies pressed closer together as my hands moved to her neck. The fit was perfect, like we were puzzle pieces molded to fit only to each other. Her skin was cooler than I remembered, but not cold—just below normal, like a fever in reverse. I could hear her pulse through her jugular, quick but oddly weak, as if her heart was running on borrowed time.

She pulled back slightly, eyes shining black, her lips moist from where mine had just been. "Ryder," she said, and there was a warning in it, as if she were worried I was about to fall over the edge.

She wasn't far off. Feeling strength suddenly come back into my body almost overwhelmed me. My own voice sounded distant, animal.

"The fuck is happening?"

I felt her breath in my ear. "We need to talk," she murmured, her accent thick.

Someone behind us cleared his throat, probably Big Papa. Or maybe one of the Kozlov brothers, their fingers already flexing as though they wanted to yank me away from their baby sister. Aspen's eyes were wide with alarm, but she didn't move. The entire foyer was holding its breath.

Lucia turned, still gripping my arm. "Excuse us."

Nobody tried to stop us. If anything, they looked relieved to see us go.

She hauled me up the stairs, moving carefully as we both still struggled for breath. The staircase seemed endless, but I barely registered it. All I could focus on was the pulse of her hand, the fire in my own veins, and the pressure building in my skull. By the time we hit the second-floor landing, my vision had started to tunnel. I let her lead me down a long corridor until we reached what I assumed was her wing of the estate.

She pulled me toward a heavy door and entered before me. The suite was a palace: gilded ceilings, an actual marble fireplace, velvet drapes. She turned to face me, really looking at me for the first time.

"You look like shit," she said, and there was no smile this time.

"Speak for yourself." I sounded irritated, but my voice was thin. "You've lost at least ten pounds since Texas."

"It happens when you're starving," she said, and closed the distance in a single step.

She grabbed my wrist, and the skin-on-skin contact was a flare of recognition that left me gasping. I watched, fascinated and horrified, as the veins beneath my skin darkened, surging blue-black, almost luminous. It was a pathology in motion. I felt the hunger lurch upward, eclipsing pain, eclipsing thought.

Lucia's hand slid to the hollow of my throat, fingers cold and careful, as if she was testing for a pulse. I shivered, not from fear, but from want. Her thumb pressed just above my carotid. "You need to eat," she said softly. "You need to feed."

"I'm not eating you," I rasped, "Not until..."

She shook her head, then forced my hand to her neck a small grin on her beautiful face. "No." She forced my hand to her neck, a small grin on her beautiful face. "I mean you need to *feed*. Now."

The moment I touched her skin, felt the pulse in her neck, a wave of heat crashed over me. The bond—whatever it was—had been waiting for this. I felt her heartbeat leap under my fingers, felt my own pulse sync to hers. Her scent was everywhere. I wanted to bathe in it.

She tilted her chin, exposing the pale length of her throat.

For a split second, my wolf howled, rising from the grave I'd shoved it into. It wanted to bite, to rip, to devour. But the hunger was not sexual, not at its core. This was deeper, more primitive, an ache that made my mouth water and my bones feel hollow.

I pulled away, staggering toward the nearest chair. "We can't do this," I said, but my hands shook so badly I nearly missed the seat.

Lucia stayed where she was, fingers still at her throat, eyes never leaving me. "We don't have a choice," she said. "This is the cost of saving your life."

Her voice was almost tender; I knew she was right. There was no choice. But it didn't mean I was happy about the long-term outcome. My choice had been ripped away from me in that canyon. And now it seemed my life was no longer my own. This hunger was beyond my control. Fuck. I craved her. Craved her blood. She'd turned me into a goddamn monster but one who only craved one woman.

I buried my face in my hands, breathing hard. "If I lose control..."

She laughed, bitter and bright. "Trust me, *volk,* you are still no match for me."

I looked up, meeting her gaze. "How did we get here?"

She came to me, knelt between my knees, and took my hands in hers. "Because it was the only way for you to live, Ryder." Her face was close, lips parted. "And now this is the only way we *both* get to. And I'm not ready to die."

She leaned forward, forehead resting against mine. "I took this risk for you—to save you. I guess you need to decide if you're willing to do what it takes for us to keep living."

My fingers curled into her hair, and I wanted to hold on forever, but contact alone wasn't enough. I could feel my strength going; my body shutting down. "Sit," I said, voice barely above a whisper. "Just—sit with me. Please."

She nodded, and we collapsed together onto the velvet sofa, limbs tangled, hearts beating in the same ragged, desperate rhythm. She searched my face with those endless eyes. "Ryder," she said, voice low and steady, "we do this once. Then we figure out how to break it, da?"

I nodded, though I already knew we were past the point of breaking anything. "Okay," I said. "But my way."

She smirked. "Wolves... always have to be in control."

"*This* wolf has to." My hands still trembled, but I steadied them against her hips.

"Fine," she said, lifting her chin. "Then do it."

I slid my hand into her hair, tilting her head back. The skin at her throat was flawless—no scars, no old bites, nothing but perfection. She closed her eyes, baring the length of her neck with absolute trust. That alone was almost enough to undo me.

I bent, lips grazing her pulse point catching the hint of roses, and something primitive, a note of smoke and dark honey that made my mouth water. My teeth—fucking fangs—descended, and scraped lightly, but not enough to break skin. I heard her breath catch, then slow, then catch again.

I couldn't wait another second. I bit down, and her blood surged into my mouth, hot and intoxicating. It was nothing like anything I'd ever known. It was pure, undiluted life that surged into my veins.

Lucia moaned, a sound I could only describe as ecstasy. I felt her fingers in my hair, nails digging deep, but she didn't pull me away. If anything, she arched closer, feeding me more, as if she wanted to be emptied. And goddamn if I didn't want to take every drop.

I forced myself to count the seconds, not letting the craving run away with me. My tongue caressed as my lips pulled, and I didn't want to stop. But I did. I let my jaw go slack, and the blood stopped, a single red line dripping down her neck. I dragged my tongue up the trail, not wanting to waste a single drop. She whimpered, eyes opening in a daze.

Instinct told me to lick the wound closed. Then I held her, waiting for the inevitable backlash; the frenzy. There was none. The desire to suck her dry was replaced with the wish to keep her safe; to only be careful with her. My strength returned in a rush of heat and clarity that wiped away the cold and the weakness in a single seismic pulse.

"Fuck," I whispered.

Lucia smiled, dazed and beautiful. "Is good?" She asked with a touch of vulnerability.

"It was... more." And that is what it was.

She just looked at me, glassy-eyed.

My need to take care of her overwhelmed me.

"Now, you." And I did something I'd never done for anyone. I made myself vulnerable. I bared my throat to her.

She straddled me, hair falling in a dark curtain over her shoulder. "I promise I'll be gentle." And she grinned. Even after having been on death's door, she was a smartass.

I turned my head, offering my neck, as much a challenge as a gift. "Careful. I'm worth a lot to the right people."

She laughed, and the sound vibrated through my chest. She bent, tongue flicking over my skin, finding the spot with surgical precision. The bite was gentle, a pinprick, and then her mouth was on me, drinking deep.

The sensation was nothing like what I'd expected. It was both violation and benediction—pain and pleasure, perfectly balanced. I let my head fall back, eyes closed, and felt every draw of her mouth run through my body. My hands found her hips, and I clung to her, steadying myself against the urge to roll her over and claim her completely. I faintly heard my wolf begin to stir, his voice in the back of my mind saying, *"Mate."* But that was ridiculous; impossible.

After several deep pulls, in what could have been seconds or minutes I didn't know. I just knew I didn't want her to stop. But she did. She released me and licked the bite closed. Her eyes held a promise when she looked at me. "You taste like eternity," she whispered, and the words landed somewhere deep, a place I hadn't known was empty until she filled it.

We lay back, chests heaving, the room spinning in slow, lazy circles. The bond between us was no longer a question, no longer a threat. It was a fact, a living thing that hummed in the air, as real as gravity.

She felt warmer than before—stronger—like the deficit between us had finally evened out. "Beautiful," I said, tracing her jaw with my thumb.

She made a face. "You sound sappy."

"Only with you."

She snuggled in closer, her head on my chest, her hand on my heart. "Don't let me go," she said.

I'd never heard Lucia Kozlov sound vulnerable before.

I held her to my side. "I don't think I could."

Fuck my life. For all the avoiding of this woman I'd done the past several months, how could I be irreparably tied to her now? Could we find a way to break this tether? Did I want to break it? All the while my wolf paced behind my ribs, growling at me as I contemplated this.

"No, mate."

"Shut the fuck up!"

Sleep finally took me, Lucia locked at my side, safe at last from the hunger. For the first time since the canyon, I felt whole.

We slept for nearly twelve hours. When I woke, the light outside the window was a blue so deep it could have been dawn or dusk. My mouth tasted of copper and roses, and my arms ached from the weight of her. Lucia was still wrapped around me, one leg slung over mine, her cheek pressed to my chest. If I didn't know better, I'd have thought she was dead. But the rise and fall of her chest, the heat of her skin, and the faint, satisfied smile on her lips told a different story.

I eased out from under her, careful not to wake her, and padded to the bathroom. My body was different—healed, energized; even the color in my face was back. No more shakes. No more tunnel vision. The world was sharp, saturated. I splashed water on my face and stared at my reflection, expecting to see something monstrous. But it was just me. Alive for the first time in days.

I found clean clothes in my bag and dressed, then went to the window to watch the dusk settle over the estate. The city's lights were visible on the distant horizon, a hard edge against the woods and rolling hills. There were guards moving in the gardens below, most of them pretending not to notice me. I knew better. Every move I made would be reported.

Lucia appeared at my side, silent as a wraith. She slipped her arms around my waist and leaned into my back her voice soft. "You look better."

"So do you," I told her. And it was true. The pallor was gone, replaced by a flush of health I'd never seen in her before. Her eyes were bright, skin luminous. I could almost believe we'd left the hunger behind.

"Are you hungry?" she asked, eyebrow arched.

I grinned. "Yeah. Like, hungry for actual food, not...you know..."

She laughed. "Yes, *moy volk*, I know. And yes, we eat actual food too. Born vampires enjoy good food. We don't have to eat as much as humans to sustain life. Blood does that for us. But, I'm guessing your wolf will need more. We'll just have to what...play it by ear?"

This is what my life had become. Endless playing it by ear.

The formal dining room had an old-world charm with dark-paneled walls and stone floors. The table stretched nearly twenty feet, set with delicate china and silver cutlery. There were only enough place settings for the family, and her father and brothers were already seated. At the head sat Kazimir, looking as he always did—perfectly composed. Her brothers surrounded him on both sides of the table. This should be a regular laugh riot.

We walked in together, almost touching, and the room fell silent. We presented a unified front—there was an "us" now, that hadn't been there before. I wasn't sure if that was good or bad.

Kazimir held his fancy stemware in both of his hands, elbows on the table. "Please," he said, "join us." His accent seemed heavier tonight, words like snow falling on marble. "Your friends flew back to Texas while you were resting. Mr. Rice said he would text you later."

That's when I looked around and noticed Big Papa and Aspen were not in the room.

Kazimir continued, "I don't know if you've been formally introduced to my sons." He gestured to the four handsome monsters seated on his left and right.

"I've not had the privilege." I was trying to play it cool. As cool as a wolf in a fucking den full of vampires could be.

They all rose and offered their hands to me. I'd love to say it was in friendship, but that would be a goddamn lie. They each seem to be trying to break my metacarpals with each handshake.

Then we sat. The conversation started slow, all meaningless pleasantries about weather, world politics, the latest Council drama. I let it wash over me, content to be beside Lucia and breathe in her scent.

It didn't last. Maksym, the oldest, couldn't resist. "So, Ryder Lowrey," he said, leaning forward, "tell us. How does it feel knowing that my sister bled for you?"

Lucia snorted. "Maksym, don't start."

He ignored her, gaze locked on me. "Did you enjoy it? It's why you're here, after all. Just survival, right?"

I took a sip of water, considering my answer. "Survival is paramount to both of us, as I'm sure you well know. And I am also certain you know I did not ask your sister to do this for me. I was all but dead, with death's voice calling and pulling me to the abyss. Your sister's voice happened to call more loudly than death's. And for that I am forever grateful."

The brothers tensed.

Kazimir watched it all with the calm of a man who'd seen a thousand family feuds. "Something has happened to you Ryder Lowrey," he said quietly, "and I do not yet know what."

The statement hung over the table. Nobody spoke for a long time.

Lucia cleared her throat. "Papa, the bond is now stabilized. We're not in danger."

Kazimir nodded and looked to her brothers who all still appeared as though they'd like to end me then and there. "Enough." He turned to me.

"You are changed, Doctor Lowrey. Not just by her blood, but by her. You have become... something new." He tilted his head. "Does it not frighten you?"

I shook my head. "Honestly, no. Look, I was a dead man. You know this, sir. I owe my life as much to you as I do to her. You could have left me in that canyon to bleed out. I don't take that lightly. I've never been a wolf who put much stock in destiny, but based on the shit I've seen the past few months; I don't discount anything now. What you and Lucia did for me was a gift. I intend to make the most of it." I meant it.

He smiled, a real one, small but genuine. "Good. There is no room for fear in this house. Only strength." He looked at Lucia. "And you? Are you satisfied?"

She nodded. "I am. I saved Ryder not on a whim. It felt... right."

"Then it is settled."

We ate in relative peace. The food was excellent, and Lucia even managed a glass of wine without gagging. I kept offering her glances, a silent reassurance that we were in this together. There were no more threats, no more tests, just the dirty looks her brothers tossed my way now and then.

After dessert, Kazimir stood, gathering the brothers with a look. "We have Council business," he said. "Ryder, Lucia, you are free to do as you please."

The excellent food settled like lead in my stomach. Kazimir's dismissal hung in the air. Fine. My own business couldn't wait any longer. I squeezed Lucia's thigh beneath the table, drawing strength from her warmth, then cleared my throat, the sound unnaturally loud in the cavernous room.

"Before you go," I said, locking eyes with Kazimir. All movement stopped. The brothers froze, their suspicion palpable. "I need to be clear. I appreciate the... hospitality. But I won't be staying. My place, my duty, is back in Texas with Iron Valor. My pack needs me."

Lucia's brothers looked murderous. "Father, you cannot allow this. It's his fault Lucia was just on the brink of death, and if he leaves, she'll be right back on death's door!"

The insults flew. "I knew wolves could not be trusted." "Selfish bastard."

Each barb landed, twisting the knife of guilt I already felt. They weren't entirely wrong about the danger. Staying apart *would* kill us both, slowly, agonizingly. But staying here? Trapped in their gilded cage? That was a death sentence for the man I was. Iron Valor needed me. *I* needed Texas. I'd already talked to Lucia about this. She wasn't staying behind. She'd be with me.

Lucia's hand shot out, gripping mine hard. She didn't flinch. She stood, her posture radiating defiance that silenced her brothers mid-tirade. Her voice, when it came, was low, cold steel cutting through the heat.

"Enough!" she commanded. Every eye snapped to her. "*My* choice." She turned her fierce gaze on me, then swept it over her stunned brothers. "He isn't *taking* me. I am leaving. *With him.* To Texas. That is *my* decision."

Kazimir stilled. He didn't shout. He didn't gesture wildly. He simply radiated an ancient, weary authority that instantly commanded the room. The brothers subsided into sullen muttering, their anger banked but still glowing in their eyes.

"Quiet," Kazimir said, his voice a rumble that vibrated in my bones. He looked at each of his sons, his gaze heavy with disappointment and understanding. Then he turned to Lucia, and a flicker of pride softened his stern features. Finally, his eyes settled on me, assessing, weighing.

He addressed the brothers. "Is this man dangerous? Perhaps, as dangerous as any wolf is wont to be. But he is not reckless. He is a healer—a doctor. He stood before us, knowing the cost, and spoke his truth. He fought for Lucia when he had no reason to trust us. He carries burdens heavier than you know." He paused, letting his words sink in. "He is a good man. A flawed man, like all of us. But trustworthy? With Lucia's life? Yes. I believe he is."

He shifted his focus back to Lucia, his expression softening further. "And Lucia... look at her. Truly look. She faced the darkness and emerged stronger than any of us dared hope. She has proven many times beyond any doubt that she is capable. That she can protect herself. That she can make her own choices." He leveled his gaze at his sons once more, his voice firm. "She chooses him. She chooses Texas. That is her right. Her *strength*. Respect it."

The silence that followed was thick, charged with reluctant acceptance simmering beneath residual anger. The brothers glared, but the fight had gone out of them, replaced by a grudging acknowledgment of their father's decree and their sister's unwavering will.

Lucia leaned into me then, resting her head on my shoulder. "You did good."

"I just told the truth," I replied, my throat tight.

"That's what scares them," she said softly. "They're not used to it."

Maksym walked up to me, sized me up eye to eye, and spoke through gritted teeth. "If you put her life in unnecessary danger; and she is harmed in any way; know this wolf... I will hunt you until you take your last breath on this earth."

"I wouldn't have it any other way."

I could swear I saw a look of respect in his eyes as he turned and left the room.

I huffed a shaky laugh, pulling her closer. "He's gotta be a big hit at parties."

She tilted her head up, meeting my eyes. "Not even a little," she whispered, a ghost of a smile touching her lips.

We stayed like that for a moment, the echoes of the confrontation fading, replaced by the distant tick of a clock.

"Now, the question is how the fuck are we getting back since Big Papa was my ride and he and Aspen already high-tailed it outa here?" I asked.

"Let me take care of that Ryder Lowrey," she said, her voice clear and strong. "Give me an hour, then let's go to Texas."

CHAPTER 7

LUCIA

The flight from Philadelphia to Dairyville was private, fast, and the single most claustrophobic three hours of my life. Maybe it was the enforced intimacy of the jet's cabin, all caramel leather and bone-white surfaces, the air smelling faintly of over-priced cologne and sterilized glass. More likely, it was the fact that for the first time in my existence; I was leaving my father's protection—and my brothers'—without the faintest assurance that anything waiting on the other end was going to be better. Or even survivable. I'd never lived outside the orbit of my family, let alone made a decision that bound myself to a surly ex-Army wolf medic who'd made it clear he didn't trust me—or himself—any further than he could throw me.

But I'd always been adaptable. I was a Kozlov, after all. We weren't survivors because of brute strength, like wolves, but because we could read a room, smell its weakness, and slip into the shadows before anyone even knew we'd moved. Now, I just needed to adapt to the gnawing certainty that I might spend the rest of my life glued to the side of Ryder Lowrey, the world's most reluctant hybrid.

Doc sat at the small table across from me, legs stretched into the aisle, arms folded over his chest like he was on the world's most inconvenient stakeout. He hadn't touched the bottled water or the array of snacks the jet staff had laid out for him. His gaze was fixed somewhere over my shoulder, jaw clenched so hard I could hear it pop every time we hit turbulence. Every few minutes, he'd shoot me a glance so quick it was like his eyes were trying to self-correct.

"You know, Ryder," I said, carefully tearing the foil off a protein bar and letting the wrapper crinkle, "if you keep scowling like that, you'll end up with a forehead like a Chinese Shar-Pei."

He blinked, then grunted. "You know, Lucia, if you keep calling me by my government name, you'll give me a complex."

"You like Doc better? Fine. But you do not have the bedside manner for it."

He almost smiled at that, the barest twitch at the corner of his mouth. "That's rich, coming from you."

I shrugged and set the bar down, not really hungry. "I'm very warm and cuddly. Ask anyone."

He snorted, eyes sliding shut for a second as if he were rewinding the last week and seeing just how much of a lie that was.

There was a lull. I picked at the cuff of my overshirt, watching his fingers as he tapped a silent rhythm on his biceps. I tried to ignore the ache at the center of my chest, the constant reminder that there was now a thread connecting us, pulsing every time his emotions changed.

"You really hate this, don't you?" I asked, softer than I'd meant.

He looked at me full-on, then. There was a strange kindness in it, buried under six layers of suspicion. "I don't hate *you*," he said. "I just... have no fucking idea what happens now."

"That is usually where adventure starts," I told him.

He grunted. "Last time I had an adventure, I bled out in a canyon and woke up with a new set of dietary requirements. Not really itching to repeat it."

I couldn't help it; I laughed. "You're very dramatic for someone with no imagination."

He shook his head, looking out the window. "Just being realistic. I know how to fix things. bodies, wounds, disasters. This? This I can't fix. There's no protocol."

"There is always protocol," I said. "You just have to make one up."

He grunted again. I liked the sound, the way it meant he'd decided against an actual retort.

We passed a few more minutes in silence. I could tell he was chewing over the last few days, and I wondered if he felt the same vertigo I did—like we'd both jumped from a plane and were waiting for the ground to decide whether to kill us or just break every bone.

I pulled my feet up onto the seat and hugged my knees to my chest, watching him over the fabric. "Have you spent much time with a vampire before?" I asked.

He snorted. "No. But you have."

"Only for my entire life." I let my accent thicken just to see if it would make him nervous. "We are not so different from wolves, you know. We just have better self-control and more hobbies."

He rolled his eyes, but the tension in his shoulders loosened a fraction. "You know this is going to be weird for everyone, right? I mean, the pack. They're not exactly progressive."

"You met my family, right?" I said. "But they are very good at pretending when they must."

He considered that. "Is it true you killed a man with a fountain pen?"

I arched an eyebrow. "Well... eventually. He did not die for several hours."

He laughed, and for a second, he looked like someone I'd want to know outside of a crisis. But then the warmth in his gaze flickered, and uncertainty crept back in.

The jet hit a rough patch. My stomach did a little flip. I felt it in him, too—the way his grip tightened on the armrest, the faint twinge of nausea that pulsed down the tether. I didn't comment, but it made me feel... something. Less alone, I guess. Or maybe just amused that, for all his hyper-competence, turbulence could still shake him.

"So," he said finally, "what's the plan when we land?"

I shrugged. "Juliet is meeting us. And you know Juliet. She'll want to be sure we didn't kill each other. Maybe make sure I didn't eat you." I laughed.

"Would you?"

I leaned forward, chin on my knees, and grinned. "Maybe a few nibbles."

He rolled his eyes, but I saw the color rise in his cheeks. That made my day.

"You miss them already, don't you?" he said, voice low.

I didn't pretend not to know who he meant. "Of course. My brothers were very upset with me. They have never watched me leave like that before. I mean, I always went to visit them at their homes for months at a time, and they'd see me off. But they knew I'd always return. Now, that's not a promise."

He nodded, like that made sense. "I get it. My pack... it's the only place that ever felt like home."

"Now you have two packs," I said. "Isn't that what this is? A merger. Like in business."

He looked away, jaw working. "Something like that."

I let the silence grow. I wanted to tell him that I was terrified, that I didn't know how to live in a place where no one remembered the sound of my mother's laugh, or the way to break up a fistfight without leaving a body behind. But I'd never been good at confession. Instead, I watched him, memorizing the way the lines around his eyes deepened when he thought hard about something, or how he chewed the inside of his cheek when he wanted to say something he'd later regret.

Finally, he asked, "What do we call this thing? Between us."

I considered him. "We call it what it is. A mess. But one where you're still alive."

He huffed a soft laugh, then leaned back, head against the headrest. "I've survived worse."

"Sorry. I can't say that I have." I found myself fighting back tears.

There was a sound from the cockpit, a polite ding. Doc looked up, alert again.

"Ten minutes to landing," came the captain's voice, cheerful and utterly oblivious.

I was relieved it was almost time to put some distance between us. "Saved by the bell."

I untangled my limbs and stretched. The cabin was quiet but charged, as if we'd both said more than we should have and now needed to pretend none of it had happened. We landed without incident.

Doc stood, flexed his hands, and reached for his duffel. I got up too, smoothing my wide-legged pants and checking my hair in the window's faint reflection.

When he looked at me again, his expression was complicated—equal parts relief, dread, and something softer.

"We're gonna be okay, right?" he asked, almost to himself.

I smiled, full and genuine. "We're going to be legend, Doc."

He shook his head, but this time, he didn't try to hide the smile.

It was early afternoon, and the airstrip's single runway stretched into nothingness. Out beyond the fence, I could see the silhouettes of cattle grazing in the pastures. I'd forgotten how empty Texas could be, how the horizon looked like it could swallow you whole if you blinked too slow. The whole scene felt staged for a Western, except the cowboys were wolves and at least two of the outlaws were technically monsters.

The moment the ground crew opened the door, I smelled her: Juliet, standing at the foot of the stairs, hair loose in the wind, eyes tracking every move. Bronc was beside her, looming, arms folded over his chest like he was two seconds from throwing a punch just to keep in practice. Doc grunted behind me, duffel in hand, already in motion before I could even think about stalling.

As soon as we hit the tarmac, Bronc beelined for Doc. He didn't run, but his stride was pure predatory intent, closing the distance with the confidence of a man who'd decided the world would step aside or else. He reached him, gripping his shoulder, words low and private. Doc nodded, not smiling, not exactly comfortable, but steadied by the contact.

Juliet cut me off before I could follow. She wrapped me in a hug so fierce I thought she might dislocate something. "You look way better than I expected," she said, her voice muffled against my shoulder. "All this is because of him?"

I hugged her back, hard. "Is good to see you, too, *malen'kiy volk.*"

She broke away, holding me at arm's length, her espresso eyes doing a full scan. "You good? You're not still having symptoms, right?"

"I'm good. I swear it." I squeezed her arm.

Her gaze darted past me to Doc and Bronc. Bronc was saying something with his head bent close to Doc's, but his eyes kept flicking to us, as if he was expecting Juliet to start a fight at any second. I almost laughed. She probably would if she thought it would make me feel better.

Juliet turned, her tone suddenly Luna-serious. "You two topped off? Or do you need to do your little bitey thing before I can get her away from you?"

Bronc actually flinched at that, like he'd caught her swearing in church. Doc just shrugged. "We're good," he said, but he didn't sound convinced.

She looked back at me. "Is he right?"

Juliet glared at him, then gave me a look that said, in all caps, MEN, I SWEAR TO GOD.

"He's right. We're good for a while."

She looped her arm through mine and towed me toward the big King Ranch pickup. "Come on. You can see him later, when you've had some sleep and he's gotten his shit together. I'm not sharing you with anyone tonight."

I let myself be steered, but as we got further from Doc, I felt a weird pull, like a tight band inside my ribs was trying to drag me back. I tried to ignore it, but it got sharper with every step.

"You okay?" Juliet asked, her grip tightening.

"Yeah. Just... the bond is annoying. I think it likes to be close."

She scowled at the jet, where Doc and Bronc were deep in a murmur, then shrugged. "He'll survive a few hours without you. Right now, you need a friend more than a boyfriend. Or whatever the hell he is."

"Would you call him boyfriend?" I snorted, climbing into the cab. "That is so... high school. We are more like hostages, both of us."

She slammed the door and started the truck, peeling out with zero regard for the speed. "Honestly? I think he's more lost than you are. He acts all tough, but you scare the shit out of him."

"He does not scare easily," I said. "He survived the Kozlov dinner table."

Juliet smiled, and it was like a sunrise breaking through storm clouds. "Yeah, but that's because you were there."

I stared out the window, watching the jet fade behind us. The ache in my chest eased a little, replaced by the warm, golden comfort of being in Juliet's orbit again.

"So where are your pups?" I asked, changing the subject as smoothly as I could. "Or did they already run away from home?"

Her face did the thing I'd seen a million times—absolute joy tinged with a tiny bit of terror. "Pearl and Maddie are watching them at the cabin. I wanted to meet you myself. It's kind of a big deal, you being here."

She didn't have to say it. I could see the truth in every line of her posture, the way her shoulders had squared up, the certainty in her hands on the wheel. Motherhood had made her more beautiful, if that was even possible. There was something wild and fierce and perfectly balanced about her now, as if the universe had finally put her exactly where she belonged.

I rolled down the window a crack, letting the wind slap my face. "You're happy."

She glanced over, smile gone soft and easy. "I am. But I'm happier you're here."

The words punched me harder than I expected. I'd been so focused on what I'd left behind that I hadn't let myself want anything from this place. Now, with Juliet at my side, I realized I could maybe want it, a little. Not because I'd lost everything else, but because for the first time in my life, I could choose to stay.

We passed pack houses on our way deeper into the territory toward Bronc and Juliet's cabin. There were fields full of pretty blue flowers everywhere. A person could find peace here if they looked for it.

"If being close to Doc is important to this whole bond thing, you should be okay. He doesn't live too far from the cabin."

My heart did a little flip at the thought of him being near.

"That's actually good news. Distance can cause us to weaken, I think."

Juliet hustled me inside before I could second-guess myself. The house smelled of baking bread, coffee, and something floral—maybe from a bouquet on the kitchen island. The only noise was the faint hum of the refrigerator and, from the corner, the soft cooing of two tiny wolves disguised as human infants.

There were two bassinets. Not the plastic hospital kind, but actual woven Moses baskets lined with quilts and fringed with lace. One held a lump of blue blanket; the other a riot of pink. For the first two seconds, I was convinced they were dolls. Then the blue one yawned, a wide, unself-conscious O that made my heart spasm.

Pearl appeared from the hallway, apron tied around her waist, her hair in a tight silver bun. She saw me, wiped her hands, and beamed. "Darlin', it's good to have you back." She hugged me with the kind of warmth that only mother's have.

Maddie, Bronc's little sister, trailed after her, balancing a tray loaded with cookies and milk. "I'll bet you could use some sugar," she said, winking at me. She had a way of making everyone feel at home and had always treated me like I were one of the family.

Pearl gave Juliet a look, then me, then back to Juliet. "We'll give you girls a minute. Holler if you need us." The two of them headed out the door with a tact only southern women seem to have mastered.

Juliet steered me to the bassinets. "Want to hold them?" Her eyes were shining; she was every bit the proud mother I'd expect her to be.

I nodded. "Please." My voice came out smaller than I liked.

She picked up the pink bundle first, tucking the quilt around the tiny, perfect body before handing her over. "This is Iris. She's the quiet one." She grinned. "So far."

I cradled the baby in my arms, and for a second, all my mental static went silent. Iris stared up at me, dark espresso eyes unblinking, as if she were trying to solve the problem of my existence. Her hand shot up, grabbed my finger, and squeezed with shocking strength. I expected her to cry, but instead she gummed her fist, then my knuckle, and stared some more.

"She likes you," Juliet said, happiness and exhaustion chasing each other across her face.

"She's perfect," I whispered, and meant it.

Juliet watched me, a question brewing. I braced for it.

She asked anyway. "Why'd you go, Lucia? Really?"

I looked down at Iris, then back at Juliet. "He sent me away. Before the delivery." I shrugged, trying to look like I cared less than I did. "Said it was safer for everyone. Not just him. Me too."

Juliet's jaw clenched. "He's a damn idiot."

"He's a doctor," I said, and managed a real laugh. "They always think they know best."

She shook her head. "He's in love with you, you know."

I almost dropped the baby. "He is not. He tolerates me because he has no choice."

Juliet rolled her eyes. "You're both idiots. I thought I'd seen little signs well before now. The way he watched you. And what you did for him when he was dying in that canyon. Well, I think that sealed it or something. Because when you left, he... I've never seen him like that."

I blinked hard, trying to hold it together. "It was bad. In Philly, because of the distance between us, I thought maybe I would die. My brothers kept asking if I was sick. Or if I'd been hexed."

"Were you?" she asked, half-serious.

I considered that. "It was worse than a curse. It felt like someone dug me out and left me hollow. I could feel him all the time. Even when I tried not to."

Juliet looked at Iris, who was now fast asleep. "Sounds like a mate bond to me."

"I am not a wolf," I reminded her.

"Neither is Doc," she countered. "Not fully. Not anymore."

We sat in silence, the only sound Iris's tiny breaths. I didn't want to move, or talk, or break whatever spell held the room together.

After a while, Juliet took Iris and swapped her for the blue bundle. "LJ. He's a handful already. Eats like Gunner and peed on Bronc this morning."

I grinned. "Now, *that* sounds like Wrecker."

LJ was heavier, warmer. He wriggled, rooting for something to bite. When he found my hand, he chomped down with his gums, growling under his breath. I let him. It felt right, in a way; nothing had for days.

I looked at Juliet over LJ's fuzzy head. "I can't go far from him. The bond—it's like a rubber band. When I get too far, I start to come apart."

She nodded, accepting it with the ease of someone who'd had to get used to magic fast or die trying. "We'll figure it out. We've got the perfect place for you to stay until things between the two of you settle. There's an apartment above Pearl's garage. I lived there when I first came here. It's cute. You'll love it."

"You sure?" I said, not because I doubted her, but because I still couldn't believe any of this was real.

She smiled. "I'll get Bronc to have some guys make sure it's all cleaned and freshened up. Besides, I want you close."

I almost said thank you, but instead I just hugged LJ a little tighter.

Juliet's eyes gleamed. "You can decorate it any way you'd like. It's pretty rustic now; not your style at all. But it's got big windows, and it's quiet. And you can bring in your own furnishings and whatever you want to make it feel more like it's yours."

"I do not have a style," I said, "but I will make it mine."

We traded babies back and forth until both of them were out cold. Then we curled up on the couch with mugs of decaf and plates of cookies, talking about nothing and everything—the pack, the town, Oscar's latest bakery marketing. The conversation was easy, the kind that made you forget for a minute that the world was broken and you were a stitched-together monster with no real home.

At some point, Bronc came in, did a perimeter sweep, and caught sight of us on the couch. He gave Juliet a look—half-exasperated, half-smitten—then nodded at me. "You good?" he asked.

I nodded. "For now."

He hovered a moment longer, then disappeared, telling Juliet he had church. I liked him. He was honest. And he loved my friend; there was no doubt about it.

My luggage was delivered by a young wolf about an hour after I arrived, and Juliet showed me to my usual guest room. I showered off the day's travel and put on a matching sweater set and met Juliet back downstairs for a light dinner. I was glad she understood my need to head back up to my room to settle in for the night.

I thought of Doc, and the ache in my chest was a dull, familiar throb instead of a jagged tear. I wondered if he was awake, if he was staring at the ceiling and thinking of me.

I wanted to believe we could make it work, that the bond was more than just a freak accident or a cosmic joke. For the first time, I actually wanted to try.

If you'd told me six months ago that I'd be living in Texas, holding babies, and mooning over a wolf who only liked me because I'd saved his life, I'd have laughed you out of the room.

But for a vampire princess who was out of choices, I think I'd choose this every time.

CHAPTER 8

DOC

The air in Bronc's truck had the heaviness of a staged intervention, only with less group therapy and more unblinking judgment. I sat in the passenger seat, feet planted, hands in my lap, and pretended not to notice the way Bronc studied me from the driver's seat. It was the kind of appraisal you got from a commanding officer right before being ordered to run a half-marathon with a sucking chest wound. The guy didn't just see you—he measured, dissected, and reassembled every inch.

What surprised me most was the absence of the old, familiar exhaustion. My hands didn't tremble. No cold-sweat itch along my spine, no wobbly heartbeat. Whatever had been broken before—whatever Lucia's blood had fused, remade, or corrupted—had settled. My pulse beat steady and strong in my wrists. Even the heaviness in my chest was gone, replaced by a strange, almost too-intense clarity. I felt so awake; it bordered on manic.

We sat in silence; him watching me with that flat blue gaze that made you confess sins you hadn't even committed. "You look like you could bench press a Silverado. A hell of a change from three days ago."

"Yeah," I said, and tried not to sound like I was bragging. "I'm good. Really. None of the post-resuscitation bullshit. No malaise, no crash, no fever."

"You always use ten-dollar words when you're hiding something."

I smiled because he was right. "I'm not hiding shit. I feel fine. Better than fine."

He leaned forward, elbow on the steering wheel. "How's the hunger?"

That got a laugh out of me. "You're gonna have to be more specific."

He didn't smile. "For blood."

I took a second just to be sure. I'd gone over every symptom a dozen times since getting back from Philly, cataloged every urge and deviation. "Only for her," I said. "It's not like a vampire thing. I'm not eyeing Amanda the nurse or wondering if Oscar would taste like pork rinds. I just want Lucia."

He grunted, satisfied. "And the wolf?"

That one made me pause. "Stronger than ever. More present. Like before, I'd have to call him up to the surface. Now he's just there. Like a subroutine in the background. It's... efficient."

Bronc nodded, chewing on that for a second. "You think you can control it? If things go sideways?"

"I'd bet my life on it," I said. And for the first time since the canyon, I meant it.

He exhaled, then dropped his gaze to his hands. "Look, I need to know. You and Lucia... is this a permanent thing? You think you're fated?"

"Fuck, Bronc. I don't know," I said. "Ask me again in a week."

He laughed at that, and the tension in the cab eased, just a little. "Her family wanted you dead, huh?"

I winced, remembering the dinner. "The brothers did. Kazimir was... not so much. But Lucia went full steel curtain on them. Stood between me and the worst of it."

He grinned. "Those Kozlovs are a different breed. I never imagined."

"Me neither." I hesitated, then decided I owed him the unvarnished version. "The bond is real. It's not just psychological. I can feel her even now. It's fainter because of the distance, but it's there. It's not sexual—not *only* sexual, anyway. It's... sustenance. If I cut her off, I get sick. Same for her. It's symbiotic."

Bronc absorbed that without so much as a twitch. "So she's here to stay."

"That's the deal. Until we figure out how to break the tether."

He studied me again. "Do you want to break it?"

I opened my mouth to say yes, but the truth got stuck in my teeth. I shrugged, noncommittal. "I want us to survive. Beyond that, I have no clue."

Bronc sat back, satisfied for the moment, then glanced at the clock on the dash. "You're due at church at six. You gonna be able to handle it?"

"Yeah," I said. "I don't have the shakes, Bronc. I'm not going to eat anyone."

He snorted. "Wasn't worried about the pack. I was worried about you."

That almost got me. "Thanks for the concern. I'm tougher than I look."

He gave me a look that said: *Not fucking likely.*

He pulled up to my house, and as I grabbed the handle, he stopped me.

"You did good, Doc. You survived. That's all anyone expects."

I didn't have a response, so I just nodded and let myself out.

I locked the door behind me. For the next hour, I puttered. Washed dishes. Ran a load of laundry. The monotony was grounding, a reminder that, for all the magic and madness, I still had socks to fold and bills to pay. Hunger never flared. I didn't even want a sandwich, let alone a vein to drain. By four o'clock, I'd convinced myself it was all going to be fine.

I spent the rest of the afternoon cataloging every new sensation, every deviation from baseline. It wasn't just that my pulse was strong, or that my skin felt hot and alive. There was an edge to everything—a humming, predatory alertness that made the familiar layout of my living room look strange, sharper. I could hear the scuttle of field mice outside the siding, and every so often, my nose caught a whiff of something a half-mile away: smoke from a neighbor's grill, or the iron-tinge of blood on the air from a deer carcass out by the fence line.

I tried to read, but the words wouldn't stick. I tried to nap, but every time I closed my eyes, I saw Lucia: the color of her skin, the exact shape of her canines, the precise way she arched her neck when she presented it to my mouth and whispered "Take." It haunted me—worse, it excited me. If Bronc or any of the others ever asked what really happened at the Kozlov estate, I'd have to invent some sanitized version. I didn't want to admit how much I'd enjoyed the taste. Or how, for a second, I'd lost myself completely.

I remembered her on my lap, straddling me, digging her nails into my neck, her lips at my throat. The moment before she bit, I was terrified—not of dying, but of what I'd become if I lived. And yet when her mouth closed over my pulse, I'd come alive. Not just as a wolf, or as a man, but as both, twisted into something neither of us had the right to be.

A shudder went through me.

I stood and paced back and forth, retracing the same six feet of hardwood until the urge to do something else became overwhelming. I hit the fridge for a beer, drank half, then poured the rest out, disgusted. It tasted wrong—too flat, too dead. I wanted something raw.

I looked at my hands. No tremor. No signs of withdrawal. Whatever was happening, it was stable, at least for now.

But there was still the question, the one I'd been avoiding since Lucia brought me back: Could I still shift?

The idea scared me more than anything else. The wolf had always been my anchor, the one thing I could rely on to get me through whatever hell the day brought. If that was gone—if the magic had been burned out of me by vampiric blood—I wasn't sure I could face what was left. I'd be useless to the pack. Worse, I'd be useless to myself.

Only one way to know.

I stripped off my clothes. For a minute, I just breathed, letting my heart slow. I tried to reach for the wolf the way I always had, but instead of the gradual build-up of heat and muscle, it slammed into me, violent and perfect. Lightning hit every nerve, and for a split second I thought I'd pass out.

Then it happened. My body contorted, bones reshaped, skin stretched. Instead of the old pain—the fire and agony I remembered from a hundred childhood shifts—this was instantaneous, a click like a dislocated joint snapping back into place. I didn't have to fight for control. I just let go.

Then, I was on all fours, claws digging into the carpet. I padded to the bedroom mirror, still half in shock, and saw myself for the first time.

My wolf was still white, but bigger. I must have weighed two hundred pounds—thick in the shoulders, deep in the chest. But my eyes, Jesus, my eyes. Not brown anymore. They glowed a deep, unnatural red, like old blood in a vial. I opened my mouth, saw the teeth, and nearly stumbled backward.

I was beautiful. And I was terrifying.

I stared, barely breathing, waiting to see if I'd snap back to human or just get stuck this way.

After a minute, I tried to change back. The shift was instant. No pain, no lag. My body reassembled itself without complaint. When I opened my eyes, I was standing upright, a little shaky, heart pounding in my chest.

I looked down at my hands. Free of scars. Lucia's blood saw to that. But it was the muscle that was most different—more defined, more cut, almost as if I'd spent the last month pounding weights in the gym.

Lucia's blood didn't just save me. It made me... more.

I sat down hard on the edge of the bed, trying to process it all. The only thing that kept me from completely losing my shit was the fact that I could still feel her, somewhere out there, a faint pulse echoing behind my own heartbeat.

She was safe. She was close. And so was I.

I didn't know if I should be grateful, or scared out of my goddamn mind.

But I was alive.

And that was enough. For now.

The club's church felt like a war room. Tonight it was all faces, all eyes, every patch-wearing Iron Valor officer pressed in around the battered oak table. Every one of my brothers sat, waiting to see if this was going to be just another Wednesday night bitchfest or something heavier.

Bronc stood at the head, posture rigid, voice soft but cut-glass clear. He ran through the opening business—treasury, patrol assignments, a brewing territory beef with some scab pack from New Mexico—then set down the folder and looked at me.

"Next order," he said, "is Doc. As you can see, he's vertical. Full faculties, more than before, by the look of him."

Wrecker grunted, slight smirk on his face. Arsenal didn't move, just kept his eyes locked on Bronc, like he was waiting for permission to exhale.

Bronc went on. "There's been talk about what happened in the canyon, what happened after. Let me make it plain: Ryder Lowrey is the pack doctor. He's one of us. Whatever changed, it made him better, not less."

Murmurs of agreement went around the table.

"Lucia Kozlov is also here in Dairyville. She's under our protection."

This was what they'd been waiting for. Every muscle in the room went tight. Gunner shifted, jaw clenched. Big Papa's eyes went wide only for a second, then he settled in agreement. Of course, he did. This is a man mated to a witch.

Bronc didn't hesitate. "You hear anybody, anywhere within this pack, showing any disrespect to her, consider that disrespect to me. I don't care if she's a vampire, a half-vampire, or a fucking Martian. She saved Ryder's life, and that debt is ours to honor."

He let that hang. Then, softer, "If anyone has an issue, they can take it up with me. If they want a challenge, do it the old way. I'll be waiting."

Nobody moved.

I tried to keep my own face blank. Inside, though, a cold spike of dread drove itself through my ribs. If anyone challenged Bronc, there was a less than zero chance he'd end up dead. And with him, everything holding this club together.

I sat up straighter at that. "Don't," I said, louder than I meant to. Every eye swung to me.

Bronc arched an eyebrow. "You want to say something, Doc?"

I couldn't stop the words. "This is stupid. You can't put yourself at risk over—over this. It's not worth it."

His face went stone-cold. "You think I can't handle it? Or you think *she* isn't worth it?"

I winced. "That's not what I said. You know damn well what I mean."

He didn't blink. "What I know is you and Lucia have a bond. That's not going away. If we're going to move forward, everyone at this table and in this pack needs to accept it."

Arsenal's "Damn straight" confirmed his agreement.

"Ryder is pack. Lucia is pack-adjacent." He smiled, sharp as a knife. "You all know what that means. They don't have to like it, but they'll respect it. Or they'll answer to me."

Gunner finally broke his silence. "Lucia Kozlov fought beside us when Menace and Savannah had trouble. She showed up in the fight against Greenbriar. And she damn sure helped us get Brie back from the hands of Maltraz in that canyon before she saved Doc's life. Hell, I'll fight anybody who has something to say about her. "

Big Papa spoke up next, voice steady. "A bond means everything. You don't let that go. I don't care what she is."

I nodded.

Bronc was just about done. "Keep your ears open. This will be a problem for some who aren't privy to everything that happens within the pack. They just need to understand what's out of bounds."

Then he tapped the table with his knuckles. "Dismissed."

Everyone filtered out. I lingered, feeling the weight of what Bronc had just done settle into my bones. He'd painted a target on himself, and for what? So I wouldn't have to look over my shoulder every day for the rest of my life?

We walked out together. Bronc put a heavy hand on my shoulder.

"I mean it, Doc," he said. "No more hiding. No more doubts. If you're stronger now, use it. The club needs you."

I nodded, not trusting myself to speak.

"Go get some sleep," he said. "I know you're better than you have been, but you honestly look like you been rode hard and put up wet."

"Not far off," I muttered.

He grinned, then peeled off to his bike.

I rode home, every mile a reminder that I was alive. Alive, and not alone. Not anymore.

If that meant having to fight off half the world to keep it, then so be it.

The first thing I did when I got home was head for the bathroom and strip off my shirt. I needed the kind of hot shower that could peel a layer off, something to burn the day away and let me reset. The overhead light was harsh, but I caught myself in the mirror anyway, unable to resist a good self-exam after everything that had happened.

My body was... insane. There was no other word for it. Every muscle stood out in relief, the kind of cut you got from months of boot camp, not a single night of viral death and resurrection. The plethora of scars I'd received from several tours and missions was gone. Vanished. I flexed just to see what would happen. My biceps bulged, the abs caught the light, and for a second I almost didn't recognize myself.

The memory of Lucia hit me like a fucking freight train, and my cock was already hard as steel before I could even process it. Thick, flushed, and throbbing, it strained against the confines of my pants, demanding attention. I braced myself against the bathroom counter, my hand instinctively sliding down to grip myself through the fabric. Fuck, I was already leaking, the slick pre-cum soaking through my boxers, and my knees nearly buckled under the weight of the need coursing through me.

Her scent was still fucking everywhere, burned into my brain—roses and honey and something so inherently *her* it made my mouth water. The memory of her legs wrapped around my waist, her hips grinding against mine as she sank her teeth into my throat, tore through me like wildfire. I remembered the sound she made—a low, guttural moan that vibrated against her lips as she drank me in.

I knew she'd been wet for me, her panties slick against my lap, her nails clawing at my shoulders as she pulled me deeper, wanting to take more. She'd felt the hard line of my cock pressed against her thigh, the way my hips jerked involuntarily every time she arched into me.

But now, alone in the bathroom? All bets were fucking off.

I yanked my boxers down, my cock springing free. I wrapped my fist around it, the heat of my own skin sending a jolt of pleasure straight to my core. I stroked slowly at first, savoring the drag of my palm against the sensitive head, my hips rocking into the friction. My breath came in ragged gasps as I closed my eyes, letting the memory of her consume me.

I turned the shower on, the water scalding hot, and stepped in, the steam wrapping around me like her arms. My hand moved faster now, slick with soap, the pressure building until it bordered on pain. I imagined her mouth on my neck, her lips trailing lower, her tongue licking a slow, torturous path down my chest until she reached my dick. The thought of her sinking down onto her knees, her dark eyes locked on mine as she took me into her mouth, nearly fucking destroyed me.

Her voice echoed in my head, husky and demanding. "Fuck, Ryder," she'd whispered, her lips brushing against my ear. *"You taste like eternity."*

My pace quickened, my hips thrusting into my fist, the pleasure coiling tighter and tighter in my gut. My thighs trembled, the water beating down my back, hot enough to sting, but all I could focus on was the memory of her skin under my hands, her nails digging into my shoulders, the way she'd moaned, the sound fucking primal.

"Lucia," I growled, my voice rough and desperate as I stroked myself harder, faster, my thumb brushing over the sensitive slit at the tip. The pressure built to a fucking breaking point, and then it hit me like a goddamn explosion, my vision going white as I came harder than I had in months. Ropes of cum splattered against the tile, my body shuddering with the intensity of it, my breath coming in ragged gasps as I rode out the wave.

I slumped against the wall, my chest heaving, the water rinsing away the evidence of my depravity. But, fuck, it wasn't enough. The edge was gone, but the need for her was worse than ever—sharper, more focused.

Tomorrow, I'd see her again. And then I wouldn't hold back.

Then, I'd take *everything*.

Chapter 9

Lucia

If heaven existed, it probably smelled like Buttercream & Blessings at ten in the morning on a Sunday—yeast and sugar, brown butter frosting, the sharp echo of espresso so fine it floated in the sunlight like pollen.

The bakery was open just for us. The supernatural faction of Dairyville—who lived among humans blissfully unaware. Aspen had reserved the round table by the window, where the sunlight pooled like spilled cream. There sat the women of Iron Valor royalty: Harper in pale blue, hair in a soft braid, her laugh a ripple of silver; Brie, her sister, pretty as a porcelain doll, a scarf thrown over one shoulder and sunglasses perched on her head as if she might be swarmed by paparazzi at any moment; Parker, in a band tee and black jeans, the piercings in her ears catching the light and giving her the look of a very tiny, fabulous pink feathered raven; and at the head, as always, Juliet, her golden hair falling in waves and both arms cradling a tiny bundle of pink. Surprisingly, Parker was rocking LJ.

"Lucia!" Aspen called, waving me over. Her voice cut through the noise, and in an instant the whole table turned, Juliet's eyes shining with the smug pride of a woman who'd not only made a family, but was now showing it off.

I slid into the open seat and did a quick roll call of the faces. "Good morning, ladies," I said, pitching my voice with just enough accent to make Juliet laugh. She'd always said I sounded like Dr. Evil when I did that.

Harper practically glowed with joy. "You look incredible," she said, eyes bright. "How are you feeling?"

I shrugged. "Back from the dead, so to speak." This got a laugh out of Parker, who was already two bites deep into a croissant the size of a fist.

Brie's lips twisted, nervous. "You really do look great, Lucia. Gossip says that when you were in Philly, you were in a really bad way. Like, super weak..."

Juliet shot Brie a look that could've frozen a lake. "Brie, don't—"

But I waved it off. "Is true. It was bad. I never experienced anything like it before." I let my gaze drift, casual, but I saw the way Brie flinched, fingers curling tight around her mug.

Aspen slid a plate of cheese danishes across the table to me. "Eat, darlin'," she said, the vowels stretched out like taffy. "There's nothin' that a sweet treat can't cure."

Oscar strolled in wearing a little prairie dog sized tweed blazer and bow tie. "It's true miss. It's very important that you continue to keep up your strength. Wolves are hearty. You need to be hearty as well."

I nibbled at the edges; the texture and sugar were a comfort. "Thank you for the advice, Oscar. I'll keep that in mind." I couldn't help but laugh.

I snuck a quick glance at the wriggling bundle in Juliet's lap.

She caught me staring and looked smugger than a cat in a sunbeam. "You want to hold her?" She asked, showing the pink-wrapped burrito currently flapping her hands in the air.

The urge to touch the baby was overwhelming. "Of course I do." My enthusiasm seemed to surprise the women at the table.

"She already loves her Auntie Lucia," Juliet said, and passed the baby into my arms with the ease of someone who'd done it a thousand times already.

The bundle was warm and smelled like sunshine. The baby opened her eyes—dark as obsidian—and blinked at me. I'd never seen a creature so small look so thoroughly unimpressed.

I adjusted my hold, careful not to jostle, and watched as the little wolf studied me. Her gaze was piercing, ancient. "She's going to be a terror," I predicted.

"That's the plan," Juliet wasn't even joking.

The other twin, in blue, was fussy, and Brie took him from Parker without waiting for permission. I watched with admiration as this little circle of women took turns pouring their love into these lucky pups.

Parker finished her croissant, dusted off her hands, and then blurted, "So, Lucia, is it true you and Doc are, like, bonded now?" No preamble, no tact, just pure Parker.

The table fell silent.

I took a sip of coffee, gathering my thoughts. I'd practiced answers for this, but none of them seemed adequate.

Juliet broke the silence. "She saved his life. That came along with other things, I'd guess."

Brie looked down at the baby in her lap. "I'm sorry," she said, voice so small I almost missed it.

Everyone turned.

Brie stared at the table, refusing to meet my eyes. Guilt sat on her like a weight she'd decided she deserved. "I'm the reason he was there. If I hadn't been so—" Her throat worked; the words stuck. "If I'd been smarter, if I hadn't gotten everyone involved with Maltraz—" She stopped, knuckles white.

I set my mug down, leaned in, and laid my hand over Brie's. She startled, but didn't pull away.

"Brie," I said quietly, "you are not to blame. Maltraz is pure evil. He chose to do something terrible. *His* choice. Doc made the choice to help. So did I." I gave her hand a squeeze. "None of us are the center of the universe, no matter how much we want to be. Sometimes fate is a bitch, and sometimes it gives you exactly what you need."

Juliet made a small, satisfied noise, like she'd been waiting for someone to finally put the matter to bed.

Harper cleared her throat. "So... bonded?" She pressed, her voice sweet as syrup. "What does that mean?"

I glanced at Aspen, who looked eager to hear my answer. The witch had probably read every book on the subject since I'd landed in town.

"I don't know," I said honestly. "It's new. My father says it's rare. Doc says it's impossible. My brothers say it's doomed." I shrugged. "But here I am."

Harper rolled her eyes. "You could do worse."

Parker managed a weak smile. "Doc's a pretty big grump."

We all laughed at that, the tension dissolving. I felt lighter.

I noticed Juliet watching me, her expression somewhere between pride and curiosity.

She leaned forward, elbows on the table. "So... are you going to, you know, mate with him?"

This time it was Aspen's turn to choke on her drink. I laughed genuinely.

"I honestly don't know," I said. "He's still a wolf. He'll probably want to take me on a picnic or something. I don't do outdoors."

Harper grinned. "It's Texas, Lucia. You'll have to learn."

"I guess I might."

I leaned back, let myself enjoy the comfort of being surrounded by women who knew every ugly thing about me and chose to stay anyway. The air was thick with the scent of baby powder, coffee, and something deeper, truer—kinship, maybe, or sisterhood.

I was lost in thought when I felt a tingle up my spine. Then the bakery bell chimed, and the room changed. A hush fell across the tables as three men entered, commanding all available oxygen. Bronc, in crisp jeans and a dark shirt, looking every inch the man who could level a city block with his jaw alone; Big Papa, whose presence softened the edge of the room, hands in his pockets, beard trimmed to a point that made him look like a Norse warlord on vacation; and in their shadow, Doc.

He stood in the doorway for a heartbeat, then started over. The world shifted. My whole body felt it. He looked... different. Taller, maybe. Broader. His eyes were sharp, the color even more vivid in the light. And his arms—God, the arms. His biceps were about to rip the sleeves of his shirt, and his chest strained the Henley, like he'd been airbrushed for a magazine cover. My mouth went dry. The bond didn't just hum; it sang.

Every woman at the table took notice.

"Holy shit," Parker muttered under her breath. "Doc's been doing CrossFit?"

Harper elbowed her, but she wasn't wrong.

Doc approached, moving with a confidence I hadn't seen before. He offered a smile—small, apologetic, but real.

"Morning," he said. He looked at me, and everything else faded. The room, the voices, even my own unease.

Juliet grinned up at him. "Looking good, Doc."

He ducked his head. "Thanks."

I could feel my cheeks flush, and if he noticed, he didn't let on.

Brie cleared her throat. "You're, um, looking... healthy."

Doc eyed her, then me, then nodded, slow. "Getting there."

He stood a step behind my chair, as if he was waiting for permission to join us.

Aspen pointed to the empty chair behind me. "Sit, Doc. Plenty of coffee."

He hesitated, then slid in. The chair creaked under his weight. He smelled like soap and cool water and just a hint of blood, which made my pulse stutter.

I risked a glance at his hands. They'd always been beautiful—surgeon's hands, steady and precise. Now, the veins stood out, blue and thick, and his fingers looked strong enough to snap bone.

He caught me looking, and for a split second, I felt the urge to bare my throat. It was ridiculous, but the compulsion was there, just under the surface.

Doc leaned in, voice pitched low. "You okay?" he asked me, soft.

I nodded. "I am now."

His gaze softened. "Good."

Across the table, Bronc and Big Papa conferred with Aspen about some club business, their heads close together. It was the perfect cover for Doc to reach under the table and brush his fingers against my knee. The touch was electric—warm, grounding, and a little dangerous.

I held his gaze and let myself smile, just a little. I wanted him to see I was all right.

The table was loud with laughter now. Parker told a story about her latest tech disaster, and Aspen was already making plans for a baby shower redux.

For a moment, I forgot the past, the blood, the danger. I forgot my father's warnings, my brothers' fears. All I saw was a future—hazy, unfinished, but possible.

Doc squeezed my knee and, in the hush between stories, asked, "You want to get out of here?"

His voice was low, but everyone heard. Juliet shot me a look that was half-motherly, half-devil. Aspen's mouth twitched.

I didn't bother to answer with words. I stood, slow, and watched as Doc rose beside me, towering. The bakery was a blur of light and scent, and sound, but the bond between us was all that mattered.

We said our goodbyes, collected a box of cinnamon rolls (Aspen's treat, "for the road"), and stepped into the sunlight, leaving behind the safe comfort of the bakery for the unpredictable world outside.

If heaven existed, maybe it didn't smell like Buttercream & Blessings at ten in the morning. I think it smelled like him.

The ride to Doc's house took fifteen minutes, not counting the two and a half where we sat at a stop sign on an empty road and pretended neither of us wanted to crawl across the center console. He kept one hand on the wheel, the other loose in his lap, but I could see the twitch of his fingers and the set of his jaw. I pressed my knees together, staring out the passenger window, and counted every fence post along the highway just to keep from clawing the leather.

It wasn't just the bond, though that was ninety percent of it. It was the memory of the night before—God, the shame of it—and how I'd been alone in the dark, minding my business, when the sensation hit. Not just his hunger, not just the aching want of his body for mine, but the sharp, blinding spike of his orgasm. I'd been reading in bed, Anna Karenina again, because misery loves company, and out of nowhere there was this wave of heat, this electric buzz in my core. My back arched, and I nearly kicked the damn lamp off the nightstand.

And then I heard it, not a voice in my head but an echo on the line: "Lucia." Ragged, desperate, full of a need that I hadn't realized could be shared across distance. It pulsed between my legs, hot and slick, until I gasped out loud. The book hit the floor. I bit down on my wrist and rode it out, every pulse perfectly in sync with his. When it faded, I was left tangled in sweat-soaked sheets, the silence ringing with what I'd felt.

I had not looked at myself in the mirror since.

Now, as I sat in Doc's truck, every jostle and bump made my whole body tingle. I kept my hands folded on my lap, fingers digging into my skin, and forced myself to breathe steady. The engine rumbled down my spine.

I tried not to imagine what he was thinking, what he might do if I said yes, I want you; I want you now, please.

He didn't say a word the entire drive. His profile was cut glass in the sunlight—cheekbones defined, lips pressed so tight it was a miracle they didn't shatter. I snuck glances and caught him glancing back, both of us feigning indifference with the desperation of drowning people refusing to call for help.

By the time we reached his place, my nerves were shredded. I gripped the door handle with such force the plastic creaked. He killed the engine and looked at me finally, really looked, and for a second the world stopped. He said, "You coming in?" in a voice so deep I felt it between my teeth.

I nodded, because what else was there?

Doc's house was a single-story ranch set back on five acres, the kind of place you bought if you were running from something or someone and wanted nothing but sky and quiet. He held the door for me, and I entered into a living room that was all clean lines and practical comfort—big black leather sectional, a massive TV, bookshelves full of medical journals and military biographies. There were throw blankets everywhere, which I would have mocked if they hadn't looked so inviting. The air was cool, not like the bakery's spring heat, and it made my skin prickle with anticipation.

He watched me take it all in, then gestured to the couch. "Sit. I'll get you something to drink."

I sat, arms crossed over my stomach, trying to project calm when every cell in my body wanted to vibrate out of existence. He was gone less than a minute, then returned with a mug of tea and set it gently on the coffee table.

"No coffee?" I teased, voice trembling just a hair.

He shook his head. "You don't need more stimulation," he said, eyes on my hands.

I wanted to roll my eyes, but the line landed. Instead, I wrapped my hands around the mug, the heat grounding me, and waited for him to sit.

He didn't. He stood at the edge of the carpet, arms folded, and stared at the floor like it held the answer to every question he'd ever had.

"We need to talk," he said finally.

My lips curled up, because wasn't that always the way? "About the bond," I prompted.

"And everything else."

He moved to the armchair opposite me; the leather creaking under his weight. The sunlight from the window cut across his face, picking out the new lines, the sharper jaw, the hunger in his gaze.

"I thought it was supposed to get easier," he said. "The longer you have it. The more you get used to it."

"Is that what they told you in medical school?" I sipped my tea, letting the burn of it distract me from the way he watched my mouth.

He laughed, the sound dry. "No. In medical school, they tell you to cut the cord if you can't fix it. Find the root cause and excise it."

I tilted my head. "Are you planning to excise me, Doc?"

He shook his head, mouth twisting. "I don't want you gone. That's the problem." He ran a hand through his hair; the motion restless. "I want you so much it's... fuck. It's pathological."

My heart stuttered. I set the mug down, careful, and leaned forward, elbows on my knees. "So what do you want to do about it?"

He looked up, met my gaze, and I saw the depth of it. The honesty. "I want you to stay. I want us to figure this out. But I don't know how to do that without..." He trailed off, searching for the word.

"Losing yourself?" I offered.

"Yeah."

I thought about that for a moment. About who I was, who I'd been forced to be, and all the ways I'd armored myself against the world. I'd never been anyone's mate, never even considered it. Now, my whole identity was up for renegotiation.

"I don't want you to lose anything, Ryder," I said. "But you're not the only one with a say in this."

He blinked, thrown by the change in tone. "What do you mean?"

I leaned back, stretching out my legs. "I mean, maybe you don't get to call all the shots. Maybe I decide when to feed, or when to fuck, or when to pretend this isn't the most terrifying, exhilarating thing that's ever happened to me." My voice was steady; my hands didn't shake. "Maybe I make you work for it. Make you earn it."

His eyes darkened, wolf surfacing just below the skin. "You want me to prove myself to you."

I smiled, slow and dangerous. "I'm a princess, Doc. You want my loyalty, you fight for it."

He grinned, teeth bared, and for the first time since the canyon, he looked alive. "That's not how it works for wolves."

I shrugged. "Maybe you should adapt."

For a minute, neither of us spoke. The air was heavy with the promise of a thousand unsaid things.

He broke first. "If I wanted to drink from you right now, would you let me?"

I let the silence drag, savoring the tension. "No," I said. "I don't want you to right now."

His jaw flexed. "Why not?"

"Because you want it too much. It's no fun if I just give in."

He leaned forward, elbows on his knees, matching my posture. "What if I took it?"

I arched an eyebrow. "You're welcome to try."

The line was drawn, and neither of us was going to cross it. Not yet.

He exhaled, the tension in his shoulders easing just a fraction. "You're something else, Lucia Kozlov."

I felt warmth spread through me, pride and relief and something sweeter, softer than I'd ever known. "You're not so bad yourself, Ryder Lowrey."

We sat like that for a long time, two predators circling, waiting for the perfect moment to pounce. The urge to touch him was overwhelming, but I wanted him to beg for it.

Eventually, he stood, crossed the room in three long strides, and held out his hand. "Let's go outside. I want to show you something."

I took his hand, the jolt of contact sparking up my arm and straight into my chest.

"Lead the way, Doc."

He did. And I followed, already planning how I'd make him chase me all over again.

CHAPTER 10

DOC

By the time we reached the edge of my backyard, late afternoon had sunk its teeth into the horizon. The woods beyond the fence glowed blue-black, shadows stretching long over the pool and up the trunks of the pecan trees. The pool lights kicked on automatically, turning the water slick and electric. Lucia walked at my elbow, her arms folded tight over her chest, but her face was open and hungry for whatever came next.

I stopped at the pool's edge, shed my jacket, and toed off my boots. Lucia didn't look away; her gaze tracked every movement with a focus that would've flattered most men and probably would have terrified a few. But not her. I took my time with the buttons on my shirt, working them loose, one by one. With each click, I watched her eyes narrow, lashes lowering in a slow blink as she processed the width of my chest and the new lines sculpted during days of near-death transformation. I shrugged out of the shirt, letting it drop to the flagstones.

"Is this part of your show?" she said, voice low, half-laughing.

"Consider it an anatomy lesson," I replied, starting on my belt. "You seemed more than a little interested in the changes, and I won't lie; I like your eyes on me."

She tilted her head, lips parted, and let the silence say more than any smart-ass remark could. I peeled away my jeans and boxers, stood naked for her inspection, and waited. The evening air cooled the sweat on my skin, but there was a heat to her stare that nearly set me on fire. My body was hard, not just my cock but every muscle, standing ready for inspection or battle or the other thing wolves and vamps were made for.

Lucia let her arms drop, hands loose at her sides. "Not playing fair, doctor," she said, her accent thickening like cream at the bottom of a coffee cup.

"Never said I was," I said. Then, with zero warning, I shifted.

The pain of it had always been there—a full-body compound fracture, skin splitting to fur, spine snapping into a new geometry. But now, thanks to the blood she'd forced into my veins, the change was instant; a collapse of bone and sinew and memory. One moment I stood upright; the next, I exploded into a two-hundred-pound beast, white-furred and wall-to-wall muscle.

Lucia startled. She took a full step back, shoes scraping on stone. Her mouth fell open, and for a second, the ever-confident Lucia Kozlov looked genuinely afraid. Then her eyes widened, her pupils going full black, and she let out a long, shaky breath.

"You are... enormous," she said. "And your eyes are red. That is... not typical."

I padded forward, claws clicking on the stones, and nuzzled her wrist. She hesitated, then buried both hands in the ruff of my neck, fingers diving deep. I let her, twisting so her nails could dig all the way down to the skin. It was pure fucking bliss. Every nerve ending in my body lit up—her scent, her touch, the feel of her breath as she pressed closer. If I could have grinned, I would have.

She nuzzled her face against me and studied me. "Does it hurt, the change?"

I shook my head, then bumped her with my muzzle. She laughed; the sound was music and wonder and it lit me up from the inside.

"Can you understand me?" she whispered, as if it was a secret.

I nodded.

She leaned in, putting her cheek against my fur. I licked her face once, a big, slobbery drag of tongue up her jawline. She squealed—actually squealed—and tried to shove me away, but I was too strong. She wiped her cheek, muttering, "Gross, Ryder!" but there was no venom behind it.

The wolf part of me loved the play. The man part needed so much more.

Without warning, I broke away, leaped the fence, and landed running. The ground was soft and spongy beneath my paws; the air loaded with the smells of bark—wet earth, fresh-cut grass, the coppery tang of her essence. I ran flat out, not caring where I went, just needing to feel the world move under me. Behind me, I heard her curse in Russian, then the slap of her shoes as she took off after me.

She was fast—vampire fast—and she caught up before I'd made it past the tree line. I looked back and saw a flash of red soles, damn Louboutin sneakers. She ran like she'd been born for it, black curls streaming behind her, face split wide with a grin. I let her close the distance, then juked sideways, doubling back toward the creek. She tracked me, never losing ground, eyes shining in the low light. I pushed harder, pouring on speed, but she kept pace. At the edge of the creek, I spun and faced her, lowering my body in a playful challenge.

She slid to a stop, laughing so hard she could barely stand. "You think you can outrun me, *volk*?" she called, hands on her knees.

I gave her a low growl, then barked once—an invitation.

She straightened and stepped forward, slow and deliberate. "Is this what you wanted to show me?" she said. "That you are faster, stronger than before?"

I shook my head and padded to her, pressing my body against her legs. She wobbled, then steadied, bracing her hands on my shoulders.

"Or maybe you wanted to show me that you are still you," she whispered, voice gone soft. "A magnificent wolf who will always know who he is."

I sat back on my haunches and let her pet me. Her hands were gentle now, stroking behind my ears, down my neck. She sat next to me on the grass, ignoring the wet and the dirt, and leaned against my side. We watched the sky turn indigo together. There was peace in it, something I hadn't known for months.

Eventually, she leaned over, put her mouth to my ear, and said, "Are you coming back, or do you want me to start howling with you?"

I chuffed, nudged her arm, and trotted a few paces ahead. She followed, never letting the distance grow too wide. We made our way back through the trees, moving side by side, like we were meant to. Every time she looked at me, there was a lightness in her face I'd never seen before. It seemed that all the other times we'd been together, we'd always been preparing for battles, never having time for rest. This was different.

At the fence, I paused. Lucia looked at me, then up at the house. "Should I go in first?" she asked.

I shook my head and launched myself up and over the fence, landing on the other side without a sound. She laughed, then scaled it herself, landing lightly. "Show-off," she said, dusting her hands.

I circled her once, then sat, waiting.

She came to me, placed her hand between my ears, and leaned in. "Thank you, Ryder," she said. "For letting me see you."

I closed my eyes and let the wolf savor it. For once, there was no pressure—no pack, no patients, no impossible choices. Just the two of us, the open air, and the easy rhythm of running together.

It was a gift. I wanted her to know it.

I led her to the back porch and paused. I nodded my head to let her know she needed to give me a little space. Amazingly, she understood. The shift was easier than before—like shedding a coat, stepping from one skin to another. I transformed and stood before her naked and satisfied.

To her credit she didn't even flinch. "That was fun," she said, voice gentle.

I faced her. "Thanks for humoring me."

She grinned, a toothy smile in the fading light. "You might be a better wolf than you are a man, Ryder Lowrey."

I laughed, the sound echoing off the pool. "Maybe that's true."

She nudged my arm with her elbow. "But I like the man, too." She looked me up and down. "I like some parts of the man very, *very* much."

I looked down at her, really looked, and saw the woman who'd saved my life, the one who was willing to risk her own to keep me in the world. I cupped her face in my hand. "I like *you*, Lucia Kozlov. More than I want to admit."

She raised an eyebrow. "You do not have to admit it. Just show me."

We stood there, wrapped in the afterglow of dusk, and I realized I'd never been happier to be alive.

Not for the wolf. Not for the pack.

But for her.

I motioned for her to follow me inside. Lucia hesitated only a second, then fell in at my side, close enough that our bodies brushed together when I shifted pace. We crossed the patio; her sneakered steps silent, mine heavy and deliberate. I felt her watching me, cataloging each muscle and the way my body moved with a new, effortless power. She didn't comment, but her breathing was just a shade quicker than before.

At the sliding door, I paused. She caught up, eyes catching the porch light's glare. "You want me to go in first?" Her voice was soft, almost teasing.

I shook my head and stepped ahead of her, the tile cold beneath my feet. She followed, pausing in the kitchen. I made no effort to cover myself.

Her gaze dragged over me, slow and unblinking, taking in the width of my chest, the scars now erased, the way every muscle stood in high definition. Her eyes went dark. The humidity from the run still clung to her skin, and her curls stuck to the sides of her face, framing her features with a wild, animal beauty. For a long moment, neither of us spoke.

When I did, my voice was rough around the edges. "I want more than a taste, Lucia. More than to feed. I want all of you."

Her eyes flicked to my mouth, then down. She licked her lips, deliberate. "You want all of me?"

I stepped closer, letting her feel the heat radiating off my skin. "Yes," I said. "Every fucking part."

She tilted her head, appraising. "Is this the wolf, or the man?"

"Both," I said. "They're not separate anymore."

She took a step back until her hips bumped the edge of the kitchen counter. "And if I say no?"

I shrugged, but it was a lie. It would break me. "Then I keep wanting. But I won't push. I won't take unless you say it."

Her lips quirked. "You're a liar, Ryder. If I said no, you would suffer."

I grinned. "Probably. But I'd survive."

She pressed her palms flat against the counter, arms bracketing her body. "I want it too," she said. "But I want to wait."

I blinked, surprised. "Wait for what?"

She searched my face, as if hoping I'd solve the riddle for her. "I don't know what happens when a vampire mates with a wolf. I don't know if it works, or if it is a disaster. I don't even know the mechanics of it." She smiled, a little sad. "I don't know if we feed while we make love or what. Just in case, we'll wait. We'll feed, but not with you inside me. Not until we explore what this is between us exactly."

She made me ache for her. When she mentioned me being inside of her, I felt it down to my cock. I reached out and caught her hand in mine.

Her fingers were cool, the nails painted a dangerous red. "You want to see if we can last," I said. "If this thing doesn't tear us apart."

She nodded. "Yes. I want to see you every day for at least a week and not try to kill you. Or myself."

I laughed, loud and honest. "That's fair."

She studied our hands, how they fit together. "I will give you my body, Ryder. But I want to know that you want my mind, too. My heart, my loyalty."

"I do," I said, squeezing her hand. "I want every piece. Especially the ones that scare you."

She closed her eyes for a second, and when she opened them, she was all steel. "Do you know why I like you, Ryder Lowrey?"

I shook my head.

"It's not the body, though I do appreciate the body." She squeezed my bicep, eyes twinkling. "It's because you put others before yourself. Your pack, your friends, even people you don't like. You think you are cold, but you are the most loyal person I have ever met. You respect your Alpha, and you respect your Luna. You take care of things, even when no one asks you to." She tapped my chest, just above the heart. "You can be counted on to take care of the important things, and you understand what those things are. That makes you the sexiest man I've ever seen."

I swallowed hard, not sure how to reply. No one had ever told me that before. It felt like being seen and forgiven, all at once.

"Lucia—" I started, but she cut me off with a kiss.

It was not sweet. It was not slow. Her hands were in my hair, then down my back, nails raking hard enough to leave marks. I pulled her up and crushed her to me, letting the heat and want and everything else I'd been holding in come out all at once. She moaned into my mouth, biting my lower lip hard enough to draw blood. I didn't care. I wanted her, and I wanted her to know it.

Then she lifted her head and looked at me, eyes soft. "You are really naked," she said, and we both burst out laughing.

"I told you," I said. "Anatomy lesson."

She rolled her eyes. "If you are trying to seduce me, you are going to have to do better than this."

I nipped her ear, growling low. "Give me a night, Princess. I'll show you what I can do."

She shivered, and I felt the tremor all the way to my bones. "I believe you."

We made our way down the dark hall, her hand tucked in mine. I felt the pulse in her wrist, a fast, skittering rhythm that matched my own. The urgency between us was a living thing, prowling the air, making my skin hot and tight. I'd never wanted a woman more than I'd wanted her in this moment. I nudged open the bedroom door and led her in.

My room was all shadow and quiet; the only light a dim lamp by the bed. The sheets were still rumpled from that morning, and the air carried the ghost of my soap and her perfume. I sat at the edge of the mattress and drew her between my legs so she faced me, close enough I could see the silver flecks in her eyes.

She looked at me with a question in her eyes—was I sure? Was I ready? The words got lost somewhere behind my teeth. Instead, I cupped her face in my hands, buried my fingers in her hair, and kissed her like it were the only thing that would keep me alive another minute.

She melted against me, arms around my shoulders, legs tucked inside mine. The kiss went on and on, deepening, sharpening, until we were both breathing hard and she was tugging at my hair, urging me closer. I broke away for just long enough to get the words out: "I need you out of these fucking clothes, Lucia." I felt the animal rising inside me.

She smiled, wild and sure of herself. "I need out of them too."

She slid back, stood, and faced me. For a moment, she just stood there, watching me watch her, letting the tension coil up between us. Then she began to peel off her clothes, slow and deliberate. First, the light oversized shirt one button at a time, letting the fabric slip down her arms and puddle at her feet. Next, the black bralette, small and lacy, showing off the sharp line of her collarbone and the soft fullness of her breasts. Her pants followed, then the scrap of red underwear, revealing everything—pale skin, bare pussy, curving hips, thighs strong and thick.

I drank her in, every inch. Her skin glowed in the lamplight, dotted with goosebumps from the cool air. Her nipples were already hard, pink against her milky white skin. She was perfect, but not delicate—she looked like she could tear me apart or hold me together, depending on which she felt like.

She stalked toward me, naked and unashamed, then crawled onto the bed, pushing me back until my head hit the pillows. She straddled my waist, her knees pinning my hips, and set about exploring my new body. I felt the strength in her, and it made me want to own her. Her hands mapped every muscle, every line, like she were memorizing it for later. Her mouth followed, trailing kisses down my chest, nipping at the line of my jaw, dragging her tongue across my abs. Her ass pressed against my rock-hard dick hot and insistent. She slid down my body, looked at it, then at me, and grinned.

"You were not joking about muscular perfection."

"Neither were you," I managed, and leaned up and grabbed her by the waist, hauling her up to my mouth like she weighed nothing.

She gasped, surprised, but braced herself on the headboard as I buried my face between her legs and ate her like there was no tomorrow. She tasted sweet somehow, with the tang of blood and the inexplicable taste of roses and honey that belonged only to her. I licked and sucked, slow at first, then faster when I heard her start to whimper, when I felt the tremor in her thighs. Her hands went to my hair, nails digging in. She rocked against my mouth, rolling her hips in tight little circles that made my tongue reach for her more.

When she was close, her thighs clamped around my head, and she made a noise that was half-growl, half-scream. I eased off, kissing her inner thigh, letting her ride the edge a while longer. She glared down at me, eyes burning. "Do not tease me, Ryder."

"I'm not teasing," I growled. "I'm only savoring this goddamn perfection. You are going to fucking end me." I gave her one more slow, deep lick.

She came apart then, shuddering and loud, her whole body tightening around me. I sucked her clit and lightly bit down, causing her to ride out her pleasure as long as possible, her wetness running down my tongue. I held her through it, gripping her hips so hard I was sure I'd leave marks. When the wave passed, she slumped down, skin flushed and damp.

She didn't give me time to recover. Instead, she slid down my body, lined us up, and lowered herself onto me, slow and controlled. The sensation was overwhelming—wet heat, impossible tightness. I nearly lost it right then.

"Jesus, fuck Lucia," I groaned, voice raw.

She just smirked, rocking her hips, her hands flat on my chest. She set the pace, grinding down, drawing it out, taking everything she wanted. I let her. I wanted her to have it all.

She leaned forward, bracing herself with her hands on either side of my head. Her hair curtained my face, shutting out the rest of the world. Her breath was sweet and sharp at once. "Do you like this?" she whispered, voice thick.

"You feel fucking amazing."

She paused, then she smiled, slow and genuine, and kissed me hard. "Good."

She fucked me harder then, rolling her hips, clenching down, drawing me closer and closer to the edge. I bent my knees and put my feet on the bed for leverage as my hips rose to meet her in punishing thrusts. I felt her building again, the muscles inside her fluttering, and I reached up to pull her tight against me, burying my face in her neck.

"Let go," she murmured. "Come for me, Ryder."

And I did. I came hard, hips jerking up, holding her tight as my body emptied into hers. She came with me, digging her nails into my shoulders, crying out my name.

"Fuuck."

After, we lay tangled together, catching our breath, the sweat drying on our skin. Lucia rested her head on my chest, tracing circles over my heart. "That was... incredible?" she asked.

"It was that and more."

She grinned. "Good. Because I don't think I am done with you."

"Oh, my little vampire. We're just getting started." I pulled her close.

I'd never felt stamina like this. A wolf could get it up pretty fast after emptying himself but needed at least a small bit of recovery time. This was apparently no longer the case for me. This is one advantage of being a wolf-vampire hybrid I could definitely live with. I was ready to take Lucia again, and I intended to take her wolf-style.

Lucia's skin was flushed—pale porcelain tinged with the faintest pink—evidence of the mess we'd just made of each other. She'd ridden me like a goddamn stallion, her vamp speed driving me wild as she took control, her hips grinding against mine, her tight little cunt milking me dry. But I wasn't even close to done. My wolf-vampire hybrid blood was fucking restless, primal, demanding more.

"Doc," she whispered, her voice husky, her black eyes locking onto mine. She knew what I wanted. My body left no doubt.

I didn't say a goddamn word. I just grabbed her slender waist and flipped her onto her stomach like she weighed nothing. Her ass—that perfect, round, fucking sinful ass—was in the air, begging for me to take her, to claim her, to ruin her. Her thighs were still wet with the evidence of our first round, and the scent of her—sweet, dark, and fucking intoxicating—was driving me mad. My wolf wanted to bite her, to mark her as mine, but I clenched my jaw, fighting the urge. Not yet. Not fucking yet.

I positioned myself behind her, my cock sliding through her wetness, teasing her, making her whimper. Her hands gripped the sheets, her nails clawing into the fabric as I pressed the tip of my dick against her. She was still so wet, so ready for me, but I took my time, savoring the way her body trembled, the way her ass shifted as she tried to push back against me.

"Now, Ryder," she demanded, her voice breathless and desperate. "Fuck me."

I didn't need her to ask twice. I thrust into her hard, burying myself in one brutal stroke. Her gasp turned into a moan, her back arching as I filled her, stretching her, claiming her the one way I could. Her pussy was fucking heaven—hot, tight, and throbbing around my dick like it was made for me. I grabbed her hips, pulling her back onto me as I drove into her again and again, my rhythm wild and untamed. She was mine; I knew it without a doubt, and I wasn't letting go.

Her ass slapped against my thighs with every thrust, the sound echoing through the room, and her moans grew louder, more desperate. Her hands were tangled in the sheets, her body writhing beneath me as I fucked her like the animal I was. My balls slapped against her clit, and I could feel her trembling, feel her cunt clenching around me as she got closer to the edge.

"*Volk*," she cried wolf in Russian, her voice breaking as I pounded into her, hitting that sweet fucking spot inside her that made her scream. "I'm gonna—oh, fuck, I'm gonna—"

She came undone beneath me, her body shaking. She squeezed me like a vice as she screamed my name. Her orgasm was magnificent, and I could feel it, feel her pleasure, feel her need. It pushed me over the edge; my own release crashing through me like a tidal wave. I buried myself deep inside her, my cum spilling into her womb, claiming her in every way except the most important way. I would claim her as my mate. And soon.

I had no idea what the future held, but I knew I was never going to let her go.

CHAPTER 11

LUCIA

Texas light is meaner than I expected. I thought the sun would filter gently through cream linen curtains, but the morning here comes sharp—cutting the corners of the apartment, painting the hardwood floors in brutal rectangles. It makes me feel like I'm under surveillance, even when the rest of the world is still asleep and I am the only monster awake for miles.

The apartment sits behind Pearl's house, tucked above her two-car garage like a secret she's proud to keep. The walls are new, still smelling faintly of primer and designer paint, but the furniture is mine—sleek, Danish, bought online at three in the morning during the sleepless nights I've had since landing in Dairyville. There's a breakfast nook in the corner, the kind with a little round table and two cheerful chairs, already set for tea because I can't stand the look of empty tables. The cabinets are filled with new dishes, and the shelves groan with the weight of books I'd had shipped from Philly—maybe as ballast, maybe as proof that the person I'd been could still exist here, surrounded by nothing but scrubland and cows.

I watched the sunlight crawl up the duvet where I lay, alone for the first time in two nights. The sheets were wrinkled, rumpled in a way that belonged more to wolves than to vampires. My body ached in a pleasant, unfamiliar way. I ran my fingers across my neck to the area where Doc had chosen as his spot. Phantom fangs piercing my flesh caused goosebumps to cover my body. When I thought of Doc, it pulsed, slow and warm and just this side of pain.

I'd never slept next to anyone before. Never wanted to. But when he fell asleep, he wrapped me up like I were the only anchor left on earth. The night at his house after we'd made love the first time, when it was all teeth and limbs, I'd awoken and he was still holding me, chest to my back, his arm thrown carefully over my side. His hand was so big it nearly covered my ribs, and I remember the strange, animal comfort of it. I'd almost cried, but didn't—crying was for people who expected something to end.

The first night had been... well. I still felt it in my thighs, my jaw, the tender inside of my lips. I'd wanted him so badly it hurt. But even in the heat of it, I hadn't let myself feed. Not when he was buried inside of me. I'd pulled away before I could take. I was terrified of what it might do—to him, to me, to the bond. We couldn't take the chance before we had more information about what true mating would do *between* us. What it would do *to* us.

Doc never pushed. Even when I felt his body tense under my mouth, even when his hands shook as he held me, he never once tried to force it. The hunger in his eyes went red, sure, but the rest of him held back. It's almost more dangerous, that kind of restraint. It makes you want to crack just to see if he'll catch you.

I got out of bed, pulling a sweatshirt over my head. The air was cool and dry, and the Texas wind sneaked under the window, hissing against the screens. I padded to the kitchen and put water on the stove, just for the comfort of something boiling. The cabinets rattled, and I half-expected to see Oscar the prairie dog pop out, offering unsolicited advice about hydration or omelets. But it was just me and the ghost of Doc's scent, which clung to the back of my neck.

I don't know if it was the hybrid thing, or if maybe my senses were finally catching up to my instincts, but everything about him lingered. I could taste the salt on my lips, feel the imprint of his hands on my hips, hear his voice in my ear—*"You don't have to be careful with me."* I'd never been careful with anything in my life. Not really.

After the water boiled, I poured it over an Earl gray tea bag and watched the color bleed out in lazy spirals. I sat at the breakfast table, staring out through the sheer curtain at the empty patch of grass and driveway below. It was nothing like the city, where every window offered a story, a tragedy, or at least a reason to leave the house. Here, the world waited in silence, and if you stared long enough, you started to see things. Tiny lizards doing pushups on the stone, a hawk carving loops in the sky, the shadow of a coyote slinking along the fence line. I could hear the chickens at the edge of the property, and the distant hum of a delivery truck on the highway. If I closed my eyes, I could almost feel Doc in his house, a mile away, brushing his teeth with military efficiency, counting the seconds until his first patient. The tether between us was like a live wire, buzzing faintly under my skin.

I touched my neck again, rubbing my hand back and forth. I'd read about mate bonds in the old books, the way a bite could tie two creatures together forever. But this wasn't a mate bite. This was just the spot where my lover fed—where he got his life-sustaining blood on the daily. In the morning light, it felt like more. We were certainly tethered together. But was it a bond? Yet to be determined I guess.

The other night, after he'd fallen asleep, I'd curled up on the far edge of the bed and watched his back rise and fall. He'd said there used to be scars on his shoulder, white and raised, like the rivers on an old map. My blood coursing through his veins had seen to it that they'd vanished. Now I stared at beautiful, pristine tanned skin that begged for my tongue. But if I'd gone in for a tiny lick, we'd be up for another hour, and he'd need his rest.

I put those thoughts aside and decided to dress for the day. When I slipped into a black halter maxi dress, I caught sight of myself in the bedroom mirror. I looked like someone who belonged here—a little lost, a little too pale for the sun, but alive in a way I hadn't been for months.

I'd barely made it back into my living room when the knocks came—four sharp, even raps, the kind that announced not just a visitor, but a visitor with no patience for being kept outside. I opened the door and there stood Nikolay, my youngest brother, in a button-down the color of wet ash, a pair of navy chinos and brown loafers; looking every bit the scholar he was. In one hand he held a set of car keys; in the other a battered black leather briefcase big enough to smuggle a child. He looked me over, head to toe, then grinned.

"Special delivery," he said, and pushed past me into the apartment without waiting for an invitation.

"Was the Old World running out of vampires, or is this a personal call?" I asked, shutting the door with more force than necessary.

He was already halfway to the living room, trailing a faint whiff of expensive aftershave and jet lag. "You always did love to play house, *sestrenka*. I see you have decorated with every shade of red known to man."

"Red is a sign of passion," I said, following him. "Or so says the internet."

He set the briefcase on the coffee table and turned, all business. "Father wanted me to bring you something."

That made me stop. "Papa's in Texas?"

Nikolay smiled, small and tight. "Da. He is in a meeting with your new Alpha and your bonded."

My claws threatened to break through. "And I'm not invited to the table. Of course." I felt my fangs extend, a half-second flash of rage that I barely caught in time. "What am I, a child?"

He held up both hands in surrender. "You are not a child. But you are new to being on the inside of this pack. And Papa wished to extend the Alpha his due respect."

I glared at him, wishing I could set fire to the briefcase with a look.

He relented. "Listen, Luchka. Maltraz is moving. There is rumor he may have struck a deal with Otero."

My anger vanished, replaced by something colder. "The king of the west would not stoop so low. He has to know Papa would crush him."

"You'd be surprised what men do when they believe they can grab power," he said, gaze flicking to the window. "But that is not why I'm here." He clicked open the latches on the briefcase and lifted the lid, careful, as though whatever was inside could bite. "This is for you, from Papa."

He drew out three objects: a roll of ancient parchment, bound with a strip of pale ribbon; a thin book bound in cracked leather; and a small metal tin, heavy as a weapon. He set them on the table in a neat row, then stepped back like a waiter at a Michelin-starred restaurant.

"What is this?" I asked, circling the table.

Nikolay plucked at the scroll and unwound a foot of it. The parchment was the color of old teeth, crawling with tight Cyrillic script and elaborate black-ink illustrations. He pointed to a diagram of two figures entwined, half-wolf, half-something else. Above their heads hovered a set of sigils that made my stomach twist.

"Hybrid pairings," he said, voice low. "The real kind. Not the council's fairytales."

I stared. "This is... impossible."

He shook his head. "It's rare. But not impossible. And you are not the first. You and your doctor—" He hesitated. "Your... wolf."

"Ryder," I said, refusing to give him the satisfaction of a flush.

"Yes, Ryder." He grinned, sharklike. "Being the first in over a hundred years is significant. Father believes it is important that you understand what this means."

I sat, knees barely bending. The diagrams were crude, but you could see the intent—two beasts fused at the heart, radiating something that looked like flame. The script beneath was dense, but I caught enough to get the gist. "They burned them," I said.

"Yes," said Nikolay, quietly. "They were destroyed. Their power scared the council. Some believed it could be weaponized. Others feared it would destabilize the balance."

"So we are a threat." I touched the edge of the parchment. It felt brittle as old bone.

"You are a target," he corrected. "When people find out, they will come for you. For him."

I processed this, letting the information filter through the slow, icy creep of anger. "Why would father send this? Why not tell me to run, or..."

"Because father believes in survival. He thinks if you know what you are, you'll have a chance." He reached for the book next, thumbing it open to a bookmarked page. "The old stories say that when the bond is complete, new abilities can surface. Healing. Strength. Some even say telepathy, though that's likely bullshit."

I smirked. "Telepathy. Sure. Next you'll tell me I can fly."

He shrugged. "It would be useful."

There was a moment where neither of us spoke. I could feel my body responding to the news—my nails extending to points, my temperature dropping further. I hated he could see it, that he'd know I wasn't as in control as I wanted to be; that my monster was rising to the surface.

I tried to regain ground. "So. Why now? What's the urgency?"

He folded his arms, face going serious. "Maltraz is trying to cause an insurrection or something. It won't take much. If he can prove that hybrids exist, and that they have some kind of exponential power, he can cause enough fear to make people want to hurt you. That would mean war. Father would never stand against you. It's ridiculous to fear something you don't understand. Even if you are the most powerful being in our world—which we know that would be a tie between Father and Archon anyway—you are no danger to anyone. It's why Father is meeting with the wolves right now. They know Maltraz better than anyone. If you and Doc can stay ahead of him, you might be the key to stopping him."

"And if we never completed the bond?"

"You know the answer, Luchka. You die."

I looked down at the scrolls, the diagrams of doomed lovers, the echoes of violence in the cramped text. "And if I can't stop Maltraz from starting this war?"

He hesitated. "Then you'll need to run. But it won't come to that. I promise."

I almost believed him.

He started packing up the scrolls, careful as ever, but I put a hand on his wrist. "Leave them. I want to read everything."

He looked at me, then nodded. "Okay. Just...don't let anyone see you with them. Not even Juliet. Not yet."

I rolled my eyes. "I'm not stupid, Kolya."

"No. You are the opposite of stupid." He smiled, sad this time. "You are what we always wanted to be."

He stood, rolling his shoulders. "I need to go. I promised Papa I'd check in on the compound. He'll be by when he's done."

The door clicked shut, and I was alone with a pile of history and the uncomfortable uncertainty if my life was about to be measured in days, not years. I wondered if Doc could feel my discomfort as I worried that we were like every creature who'd tried this before us and were living on borrowed time.

I leaned over the scrolls, letting the scent of ink and old paper fill my lungs. The world outside was still and bright, a mockery of peace. Inside, I could feel the ancient words rearranging themselves around my heart.

Then I saw an illustration of a woman and a wolf, joined at the wrists by a bloody thread. The text beneath read: "By blood and bond, neither shall die while the other lives."

I touched the drawing, tracing the outline of the thread. Clearly this meant we were bound in life and death. If one of us fell, the other would follow—but as long as one of us lived, so did the other. I needed to get my thoughts together because Doc deserved to know all of this before we completed the bond.

As if on cue, there was a light tap at my door, and I knew my father was on the other side. The tingle up my spine told me my mate was with him. We needed to discuss the completion of our mate bond. This should be a delightful conversation to have with my mate and my parent.

CHAPTER 12

DOC

The only car in the lot was a black SUV, parked and shining like a threat. I'd never known a vampire to arrive discreetly, but something about the precision of it—dead center, exactly equidistant between the lines—set my teeth on edge. Lucia had once told me her father believed in the power of entrances. If that were true, then the man was waiting for me inside the Iron Valor clubhouse, and he wanted me to know before I'd even set foot in the building.

I thumbed the lock on my truck, eyes on the glass doors. My reflection looked... like me and not like me, still. The new muscle hadn't faded, and the shadows around my jaw were more defined than before. I'd thrown on the usual hospital gear—a button-down polo, Dockers—but skipped the glasses for the first time since second grade. I hadn't needed them since Philly. Vision 20/10, thanks to Lucia and her impossible blood.

I walked up the steps, boots echoing in the emptiness, and pushed through the double doors. Bronc was waiting in the lobby. He wore the expression of a man who'd just finished a bank takeover and was wondering if it was worth the effort. His eyes met mine, and the half-second scan told me everything: Not injured. No one dead. Whatever this was, it wasn't an emergency. Yet.

"Doc," he said, and the voice that could make grown men piss themselves in combat barely registered above a murmur. "He's waiting."

I raised an eyebrow at the singular. He jerked his chin toward the conference room.

There were no baked goods on the table, no laughter making its way into the hallway. Bronc entered first, and I stepped in after him. The air inside was five degrees colder and smelled faintly of bergamot and coffee gone bitter.

Kazimir Kozlov was seated at the head of the table, hands folded in front of him. Up close, he looked like the genetic template for every James Bond villain—tall, impossibly handsome, skin too pale to be real. His hair was pulled back into a smooth tail that somehow managed not to be pretentious. His suit—charcoal, tailored—didn't wrinkle even when he leaned forward.

What struck me, though, was how healthy he looked. The man was a thousand years old if he was a day, and yet there was a vitality to him, like he'd drunk a gallon of sunlight before arriving. He smiled, a flicker at the corners of his mouth, and a hint of fangs were visible, but barely. "Dr. Lowrey," he said, "it's nice to see you looking... hale."

I snorted. "That's one word for it."

He gestured to the seat across from him. Bronc slid in at the midpoint, arms crossed, his every muscle broadcasting that this was his turf, no matter who sat at the head. I took my seat, careful to keep my hands visible. Old habit. You didn't hide anything from men like this.

"Coffee?" Kazimir asked. He already had a cup—white bone china, logo from some Vienna café on the side.

"I'm good," I said. "Had about a liter this morning already."

"Suit yourself." He turned his attention to Bronc. "Shall we begin?"

Bronc nodded. "We can skip the small talk. You're here for Doc, and so am I."

Kazimir's eyes glittered with something like amusement. "Direct. I always appreciate that about you." He looked at me. "How are you managing the transition?"

"Still upright," I said. "No side effects except what you can see."

"Excellent. But that is not what brings us here." He paused, then: "Maltraz is on the move. My sources say he has been asking about you. About your bond with my daughter."

Bronc's jaw flexed. "And why would he be asking about that? What does he know?"

Kazimir tapped a finger on the table, each click perfectly timed, like a metronome. "Enough to think he can break the Council's balance. There is an old story among our kind—about hybrids. You are the first in over a century. He believes he can scare them with stories about your power. Convince them that you and Lucia need to be destroyed and that he's the one to do it." The look he gave me wasn't pity. "Of course, he has no firsthand knowledge of anything. We need to keep it that way until we can destroy him."

I tried not to react. Instead, I asked, "Why would he care about the Council? He's a demon who lost his seat. He has no power there."

Kazimir smiled, slow. "The Council is more than a parliament. It is a reservoir of magic, one that keeps beings like Maltraz from simply burning the world to ash. If he can destabilize the Council, he can unmake the boundaries. He lost his seat, yes. But he's delusional enough to believe he can win it back by defeating me. And if he can destroy Iron Valor, all the better for him."

Bronc shifted in his chair, the movement slow and deliberate. "So he needs leverage. And we're it."

"Correct," said Kazimir. "You and Lucia are close to being a bond-mate pair. It is unprecedented. It will not go unnoticed."

I rubbed my forehead. The headache was starting, that tight band across my temples. "So, what's the plan?"

Kazimir looked at Bronc, deferring. "That is for your Alpha to decide."

Bronc gave a small, annoyed huff. "We protect our own. Nothing changes."

"Everything changes," Kazimir corrected, still polite. "If you think Maltraz will come for Ryder, you are mistaken. He will come for Lucia. He will use her to make Ryder... comply."

I pictured it. The old torturer's trick: Go for the soft spot. I felt my jaw clench, and the beast under my skin stirred, itching to shift.

Kazimir must have seen it in my face. "You are not yourself," he said, studying me like a new acquisition. "Not entirely."

"Neither are you," I said.

He grinned. "True enough."

Bronc glanced between us, then said, "Doc, is there anything else I should know about your... situation?"

I hesitated. "Lucia's blood. It changed me. Clearly, you can see the changes my body has undergone. I can barely fit into my clothes. But that's not the only change. My wolf has also... changed. He is bigger. Stronger. Sometimes it feels like the two are merging. It's not just physical."

"Explain," said Bronc.

I ran a finger along the wood grain of the table, organizing my thoughts. "Shifting is easier. No pain. It's almost instantaneous. My senses are... heightened, even when I'm not in wolf form."

Bronc sat with that, chewing on the implications. "So, if you challenged me right now..."

"I wouldn't win," I said, and meant it. "But that's because I've submitted to you as my Alpha. If you weren't my Alpha and I had just met you in battle as a stranger... toss-up. Of course, I love and honor you and willingly submit myself to you."

Kazimir made a soft sound, like he were taking notes. "Your Alpha is not threatened by you, Ryder. That is a good sign."

Bronc shrugged. "I trust you. Always have."

I looked at him. "He has nothing to fear from me. I don't know what this bond will turn me into, though. That's a little troubling."

Bronc's voice was flat and absolute. "You'll be Iron Valor. That's enough."

The silence that followed was heavy. Kazimir broke it, smoothing a hand over his immaculate hair. "We will keep this quiet as long as we can. Once Maltraz is eliminated, we will deal with my elders and then we'll deal with the Council. No one will touch you or Lucia."

"Easier said than done," I muttered.

Bronc leaned forward, forearms on the table. "What's the time-line?"

"Maltraz is not patient," said Kazimir. "He will move within weeks."

"Then we get ready," Bronc said, standing. "Doc, you got what you need?"

I nodded, though it felt like a lie.

I watched him walk to his Harley, back straight, no hesitation. I wondered if he ever doubted himself, if the weight of command ever made him want to run. Maybe it did, but he carried it anyway.

Kazimir insisted on walking the last hundred yards to Lucia's apartment. I don't know if it was a vampire thing or just an old-world power move, but he set the pace, and I followed. The compound was quiet—too quiet, even for mid-afternoon. I picked up the faint scent of honeysuckle from somewhere out behind Pearl's main house; the pear tree blooms floated in the air and the iron-tinged aroma that only supernaturals could register: old blood and magic, baked into the soil. My stride was longer than it used to be. Kazimir's was smoother, but mine covered more ground.

He didn't speak as we crossed the gravel, not until we hit the stoop under Lucia's porch light. He paused as if testing the air. "She is nervous," he murmured, not quite to me, not quite to himself.

Kazimir lightly tapped on the door. Lucia opened it instantly, fingers white around the edge, like she'd been holding her breath for hours and didn't trust herself to exhale. Her hair was down, wild and shiny, and she wore a long black halter dress that looked both expensive and designed to keep every inch of her armor in place.

"Papa," she said, voice level, but her eyes gave her away. I felt the pulse of her heartbeat—steady, but amped. She was always cool under pressure, but this was different. There was a new kind of fear, not for herself, but for me.

Kazimir swept her into a hug, brushed a kiss on each cheek, then stepped inside, scanning the apartment with a predator's interest. He didn't bother to hide it. "You have made a home here," he observed, and there was no judgment in his tone, but also no warmth. Just fact.

"Doc, you look worried," Lucia said, in lieu of hello. She reached out and touched my face, thumb skimming my jawline. The motion was quick, but it landed. "Should *I* be?"

"Remains to be seen," I said. "Guess we'll find out."

She rolled her eyes and motioned us to the living room. I saw the moment her gaze flicked to the old leather book and pile of yellowed scrolls on her coffee table, and her mouth compressed into a tight line.

Kazimir took the best seat, a wide club chair that looked tiny under his frame. Lucia and I took the sofa. Her leg pressed against mine, solid and reassuring.

He looked at us. "Show me your hands."

I held mine out, palms up. Lucia did the same. He scanned for tremors, for the pallor of illness, or the telltale blue around the nails. Finding nothing, he nodded. "You are both strong. Good."

Lucia bristled. "Is this a medical check, or are you going to cut to the point?"

Kazimir regarded her with a fondness so dry it was almost a parody. "Always so impatient, Luchka. Fine." He gestured to the scrolls. "You have read these, yes?"

She nodded. "All day."

"Then you understand what is at stake."

She sucked in a breath, and I could feel it through the tether, a band tightening across my ribs. "I do."

I wasn't sure I did, but I nodded anyway.

Kazimir leaned forward, elbows on his knees. "There are three elements required for a hybrid bond to form and hold. The old texts call them telo, krov, volya. Body, blood, and will. Most fail because they neglect the last."

Lucia's voice was flat. "Will. Intent. Not just the need to survive, but the decision to live, together."

He smiled, showing teeth. "Exactly. When you bond, the magic does not recognize passive acceptance. It is not enough to simply let it happen. You must choose it. If either of you hesitates, the bond will destabilize. At best, it will fail, and you will be as you are now—tethered, but leaking power. At worst, it could kill you."

I felt Lucia's hand curl into a fist, nails biting into her thigh. "And if we succeed?" I asked.

"Then you become... something new," Kazimir said. "The texts are unclear. Some say you will be stronger than any wolf, any vampire. Some say you will be more vulnerable. No one knows."

"Why?" I pressed.

He looked at me, dead serious. "Because all the other pairs were destroyed. By their own kind, by enemies, or by themselves."

A silence settled in the room, thick as honey.

Finally, Lucia broke it. "So what does it take? How does this work?"

Kazimir tapped a finger on the table. "The three elements must be present. Intimacy of the body—the act itself. Blood—shared in both directions, in equal measure. And, most importantly, will. At the moment you both take from each other, you must choose to bond. To lock it. You both must want it. Not as an accident. Not as a fix. As a decision."

I felt a blush crawl up my neck. "So, uh, just to be clear—you're telling us to go to the bedroom and fuck with intent."

Lucia elbowed me, but Kazimir only shrugged. "Americans. So blunt." He sobered. "But yes. Do not take it lightly."

She looked at the table, where the ancient script ran in neat lines across the parchment. "What happens if we don't?"

"You will remain as you are. Hungry. Not whole. But alive as long as you stay close." His voice softened, almost a whisper. "But if Maltraz captures one of you—he can use it as a weapon—through pain, leverage, or ritual. He'll use it against you, against me, against Iron Valor."

"We understand." I took a deep breath. "I intend to take care of your daughter, sir."

Kazimir stood, the movement fluid and final. "I will leave you *both* to decide. You don't have time to wait. He's making plans to move against us even now."

Lucia rose. She stood between us, head high. "We understand."

Kazimir regarded her, then me. For a second, I thought I saw pride in his eyes. Maybe fear. "I would not have chosen this for you, *solnech-nyy svet*." He placed a gentle hand on her cheek. "But I trust you."

He swept out the door without a backward glance, leaving the room full of old magic and an undeniable urgency.

Lucia waited until he was gone, then sat down hard, elbows on her knees, face in her hands.

I reached for her, but she shook her head. "He's right, you know. If we don't do this, we're a liability."

"We're stronger together, my lioness," meaning every word; knowing the truth of them.

She laughed, but it was brittle. "What if I'm the one who can't choose?"

I looked at her, really looked, and for the first time saw the fear behind the steel. "You already have," I said. "You chose to save me. You chose to come here. You chose me."

She shook her head, curls bouncing. "It's different. That was survival. This is... forever."

The word hung in the air, too heavy to move.

I slid closer to her, closing the gap until our knees touched. I took her hands in mine and felt the shiver of energy pass between us. "I want you. Not because I have to—because I choose to. And not just because you saved my life. I see the tough facade you show the world, but I see who you *really* are. I see the loyal friend you are to Juliet. How you'd lay down your life for her."

I brushed her hair behind her ear. "I know you were the one who, some fucking way, got that video of Declan Calloway that proved he cheated to rig the fight against Menace when the Council tried to nullify his mate claim on Savannah. And I've been consistently blown away by the way you always show up for Iron Valor whenever there is a fight we have to face. You've been one of us for months now. I've been stupidly fighting my attraction to you because of my prejudices, and I'm sorry."

She searched my face, and I let her.

"I want you too, Ryder Lowrey." A tear made its way down her cheek.

We sat in the hush of the room, surrounded by centuries of warning and hope.

Outside, a storm was rolling in. I could smell it—electric, promising a new beginning.

Or an end.

But right now, all that mattered was the space between us. And the choice we were about to make.

Together.

The storm arrived exactly as predicted—Texas punctual, right down to the first sledgehammer of thunder. It rattled the windowpanes and made Lucia's little apartment feel even more like a bunker. I could smell the rain before I heard it. Metallic, sharp, carrying the fragrance of wet grass and the bite that came with genuine change. A hundred new receptors in my body were all firing at once. I was wired for this moment.

Lucia sat near the center of her large bed, wearing a soft black satin nightie. She let her head rest on her knees, arms curled around her shins. From the outside she looked untouched, but inside our shared current, I could sense her emotions: anticipation, fear, relief, a grief so ancient it had no words. Her breathing had a rhythm to it, slow at first, then gathering speed every time lightning flickered.

I stood in front of her wearing a pair of boxer briefs. "I'm not sure I'm built for this kind of history." My voice wavered slightly.

She didn't look up. "No one is."

I took a seat on the mattress next to her, back against the headboard. The old wolf in me wanted to cross the space and wrap her up, but the new thing—the hybrid—wanted to learn restraint. To wait until she was ready to move.

For a minute, the only sound was the rain.

"I can feel you thinking," she said finally.

"Side effect of the tether, I think." I said, grinning. "Sorry."

She glanced back at me, and her eyes were not quite human. The blackness in them seemed to shift, like ink swirling in water. "What are you afraid of, Ryder?"

I thought about lying, but what was the point now? "Losing you," I said. "Losing myself. Not being able to tell where one ends, and the other begins."

She spun toward me and nodded, unsurprised. "I've always had that problem. With everyone."

I watched her hands, the way she kept flexing and unflexing her fingers. "But you picked me," I said. "You didn't have to."

She trilled a small laugh. "You think I had a choice?" She let the words hang. Then, softer: "I could have let you die. Wait. No, I couldn't. Something in you called to me. I couldn't have let you die out there anymore than I could have let myself die. I *needed* you to live."

My chest twisted, sharp. "And now?"

She hesitated, then unfolded her legs, stretching them toward me until her toes touched my knee. "Now, the only thing left is to see what we become together."

I reached forward, took her foot in my hand, and squeezed, gentle. Her body temperature was cooler than a wolf's, but perfect to the touch. "We can wait," I said. "You don't have to—"

She cut me off. "I don't want to wait."

That's when I noticed her pulse, how it thrummed in her ankle, a quick staccato. The tether flared, heat and promise, but this time I didn't fight it. I let it wash through me, taking stock of every cell that now answered to her.

"Do you think we'll be able to hide it?" she asked, quiet.

I shook my head. "No. What would be the point?"

She pulled her foot back, crossed the space between us, and sat next to me, shoulder to shoulder. Our energy merged, not just touching but overlapping. I smelled roses and honey, but also the familiar comfort of my own pack—the way a house smells when you walk in after a tour and your dog knows you're home.

Lucia leaned her head against my arm. "My father will know the second it happens. He'll probably throw a party."

I huffed a laugh. "Is that what you want?"

She turned her head so her mouth was close to my ear. "What I want is to not be afraid. I want to be a whole person, not just the half of one that makes other people feel better." She drew back, met my eyes. "You make me feel like more."

I slid my hand over hers. She laced her fingers through mine, the squeeze mutual.

We didn't say anything for a while, just listened to the rain beat its fists on the world outside.

"I'm not letting you go," I said, the words coming out low and sure. My voice didn't sound like mine, but I meant it.

She squeezed tighter. "Good. Because it seems that's not an option anyway."

I smiled for real. "It's a good thing I don't want a way out."

Her laugh was soft, the fear replaced with something else—relief, maybe, or surrender. "You think the world's ready for us?"

"Not even a little."

She let her head fall against my shoulder again. "Then fuck the world."

The old scrolls on the coffee table listened to us, silent witnesses to a story that had been written and burned a thousand times. But none of them knew this version. None of them had recorded our story.

She crawled across my lap until she straddled me, and every nerve ending in my body lit as if connected to a new power source.

"Are we doing this, *volk*?"

"I've never been more fucking ready for anything in my life."

Chapter 13

Lucia

The air in my bedroom practically vibrated with expectation, the kind of charged static that comes before a midnight storm. Or, if you were a student of the ancient ways, the sort of magic that felt like a gentle hum against your skin. These past days, I never knew what to expect. Tonight was no different.

I sat astride Doc's lap, knees bracketing his hips, trying to keep my breathing even as the preternatural glow from the bedside lamps painted him in honeyed gold. In the reflection of his eyes, I saw myself: black curls a wild corona, cheeks flushed, pupils blown wide. The world had narrowed to the space between our mouths. His hands—so careful, so expert—gripped the small of my back, thumbs kneading circles through the silk of my camisole at my waist. His eyes, always clear and unflinching, were rimmed with something wilder tonight. Hunger, yes, but also a hard resolve. The sort of look a man wore before jumping from a great height.

"Princess," he said, voice just above a whisper, "you sure about this?"

"So now I am your princess?" My retort lacked any real force. My voice was too breathy and soft; my body too busy wanting. "And yes. I'm as sure as a woman can be before she throws herself off a metaphorical cliff."

The ghost of a smile tugged at the corner of his mouth. "I just like reminding you that you're royalty. You're actually my queen." Now he wore a full-on smile. "Or more like my fierce lioness who fought for my life."

I brushed a dark strand of hair from his handsome face. "Mmm. Best decision I ever made. Now, let's go over again what we're about to do."

He leaned in, the bristle of his jaw grazing my cheek, and murmured, "Your father made it sound easy."

I shivered, not just from his nearness but from the slow invasion of awareness spreading through my every cell. I'd always thought of myself as a woman in command of her own fate—a walking, talking, fuck you to destiny. But with Ryder Lowrey; with this, I wanted more than just the illusion of control. I craved the surrender. Which was what we'd both need to do.

"Humor me. Let's go over details," I said, tracing my fingers along the line of his collarbone. I could feel his pulse, strong and steady, beneath my touch.

He drew back just enough to look me in the eye, his expression so earnest it would have been comical if not for the severity of the moment. "Three elements," he intoned, as if reciting a sacred text. "Physical union, blood exchange, intent. That's what your father said."

I snorted, letting the tension break for a second. "So clinical. We should have PowerPoint presentation and an after-action review."

His lips quirked, and for a moment I saw the Ryder who could banter with the best of them. "I'm a doctor, sweetheart. I like clear protocols."

"Physical union, I get." I ground my hips against him for emphasis, earning a barely there hitch in his breath. "Blood exchange? We've perfected that part."

He went still at that, jaw working like he was considering a hundred possible retorts and rejecting them all. Finally, he settled on, "And intent?"

That's where my bravado ran dry. I swallowed, tried for another quip, failed, and then let the truth slide out between my teeth. "I want this. I want you. Not because I'm supposed to or because it's life or death, but because... you're mine, Ryder Lowrey."

A silence fell between us, the kind that's not really empty but crowded with everything unsaid. In the past, I might have wanted to run from it, filled the void with a joke or a distraction or another mission from my father. But tonight, I let it linger. I let him see me.

He reached up and ran his fingers through my hair, his touch reverent, almost worshipful. "That's all I needed to hear."

The air in the room thickened, as if the magic was holding its own breath. I was keenly aware of every sensation—the silky feel of his skin beneath my palms, the faint scent of cedar and clean cotton that clung to his skin, the way his gaze never once flickered away from mine. When our lips met, it wasn't a gentle exploration or a hesitant overture; it was a declaration, a promise, a demand.

I let him take the lead. His mouth claimed mine, all heat and possessive intent, and I let myself melt into the sweetness of it. My fangs grazed his lower lip, drawing a bead of blood, and the taste was intoxicating—better than any vintage, more potent than any drug. I licked it away, savoring the tang, and felt a thrill run through him at the contact.

He broke the kiss, panting. "Jesus, Lucia."

"Scared?"

He shook his head, the movement almost tender. "Not of you. Never of you."

I pressed my forehead to his. "Of the bond, then."

He didn't answer, but he didn't need to. We both knew what was at stake. When we did this, there was no going back—not for me, not for him, not for anyone in our world. The daughter of the Vampire King, mated to a hybrid vampire/wolf shifter. The very notion was enough to set half the supernatural community on fire after they learned what I'd done to save him and what we'd done to seal the bond.

I grinned, letting my inner monster peek through. "Let's make history, Doc."

He growled—a low, vibrating rumble that started in his chest and ended between my thighs. "Physical union," he recited, and in a single, fluid motion, he rolled us over so I was pinned beneath him, his weight pressing me into the mattress. "Blood exchange." His tongue darted out, licked the spot where he'd bled. "Intent." He nudged my legs apart, his gaze daring me to protest.

I didn't. Instead, I cupped the back of his neck and pulled him down, our mouths colliding again, this time with teeth and hunger and a desperation that bordered on madness. My hands roamed his body—tracing the hard planes of his back, digging into the muscle of his arms, memorizing every line and angle. I wanted to devour him, to consume him whole, to make him a part of me in every conceivable way.

His skin was flushed, fever-bright, and I drank in the sight of him. The planes of his muscled abdomen, the tattoos, the sheer physicality of him. A god of war in a wolf's skin, and tonight, he was mine.

"Lucia," he whispered, voice raw, "last chance. If you want to stop..."

"Finish that sentence and I'll bite you," I warned, letting my nails rake down his spine.

He laughed, the sound dark and thrilling. "Promise?"

I bared my teeth, flashing fangs. "Promise."

He kissed me again, slower this time, drawing out the anticipation until I was practically writhing beneath him. His hands skimmed over my ribs, the curve of my waist, the inside of my thighs. Every touch was deliberate, measured, as if he were trying to memorize the shape of me.

"You're trembling," he observed, a note of wonder in his voice.

"I am not scared," I promised.

"I know." He cupped my cheek, thumb tracing the line of my jaw. "Neither am I."

The words hung between us, simple and profound. The only truth that mattered was this: I wanted him. All of him. Forever.

I arched up, pressing our bodies together, and felt the moment tip from anticipation into inevitability. My heart hammered in my chest, a frantic drumbeat that matched the rhythm of his pulse.

"Ready?" he asked, eyes locked on mine.

"More than ever."

He lowered his mouth to my neck, lips brushing the spot where my pulse fluttered just beneath the skin. I waited for the bite, the rush of pain-pleasure, but instead he kissed me there, soft and lingering, as if to remind me that this wasn't just ritual. It was love.

And that, more than anything, undid me.

We were ready.

Let the ritual begin.

Ryder didn't waste time. His hands, strong and sure, caught my wrists and pinned them above my head, palms splayed on the duvet as though he was testing my pulse through the bedsheets. I liked to think I was impervious to such alpha displays, but apparently, my body had other opinions on the matter.

He hovered over me, his breath ghosting across my cheek. For a split second, I glimpsed his wolf lurking in his gaze. Hazel irises swallowed by rings of burning red, pupils blown wide. If I were anyone else, I might have flinched, but with him, the monster was just another shade of him I wanted to taste.

He kissed me again, slower this time. His lips mapped the line of my jaw, the hollow beneath my ear, the sensitive spot where my neck met my shoulder. With every brush of his mouth, he left behind a trail of heat that made my skin ache for more.

When he finally released my wrists, it wasn't because I'd wrested them free, but because he wanted to see what I'd do with the power back in my hands. Challenge accepted. I tangled my fingers in his hair, tugged his head down, and bit his lower lip hard enough to draw blood.

He growled, low and dark, but the sound vibrated all the way down my body to my core. "How wet are you, Lucia? How drenched are you for your mate?"

I licked the blood away, savoring the sweet metallic tang, and arched against him. "My body knows who it belongs to and is dying for his touch."

He nipped the shell of my ear and ran his nose down my neck, one hand slipping beneath the hem of my camisole. "Fuck, but you smell like heaven."

"Your breath on my skin, your touch..." My voice broke on a gasp as his fingers found my bare skin, tracing slow circles around my navel.

He grinned against my shoulder, the curve of his mouth sending a shiver through me. "I want to savor every inch of your perfect body."

"Ryder," I moaned as he pressed me further into the mattress.

His movements were purposeful—never rushed, never frantic. For all the animal ferocity simmering just beneath his skin, he wielded it with surgical precision. It was maddening. I wanted him wild, teeth and claws and all, but what I got instead was something hotter: absolute control. Every touch was calculated to make me want, to push me right to the edge and hold me there.

He peeled my camisole away, slow and deliberate, and paused to admire the view. Not in a leering, possessive way, but as if he was taking inventory of the bruises, scars, and tattoos that marked my body as uniquely mine. He traced the outline of a particularly nasty scar on my ribs—a remnant of an encounter with a witch who had cut me with an enchanted blade when I was still stupid and reckless enough to think I was invincible.

"I love this one," he said, and pressed a kiss to the puckered flesh. "Proof you survived."

"I took care of all of your marks and scars when my blood entered your body in that canyon. But I know you've suffered *moy volk*."

"That's true. But you help me forget."

His mouth pressed against my sternum, working his way down with a devotion that bordered on religious. His tongue circled each nipple of my breasts as though they were delicate flowers he didn't want to bruise. His fingertips lightly grazed them, causing them to pebble along with the surrounding skin. When he reached the waistband of my panties, I lifted my hips.

"If you don't touch me here, I'll die."

He answered by hooking his thumbs under the fabric and sliding them down, baring me inch by inch. My nerves sizzled, every millimeter of exposed skin prickling with anticipation. The lamp's glow made everything more vivid—my skin almost luminous, his body shadowed and massive above me.

For a moment, he just stared. Then, reverently, he lowered himself between my thighs, and I swear I forgot my own name.

His tongue was soft, unhurried, like he were savoring the act for himself as much as for me. He circled my clit, not touching where I needed him most. His powerful tongue entered me in teasing thrusts before he came back to my clit alternating pressure, and when I tried to close my legs around his head, he held me open, spreading me wide for his attention. The sound he made—half growl, half-moan—echoed inside my bones.

"Fuck, you taste like everything I never thought I'd have."

I was close to unraveling when he slowed, drew back, and wiped his mouth on the back of his hand. "Not yet," he said, voice thick.

The command in his tone set off something wild in me. I sat up, grabbed his face in both hands, and pulled him into a kiss so deep I swear I felt his soul. He let me take, let me devour, and when I scraped my fangs against his tongue, he shuddered.

"I could lose myself in you," he muttered against my mouth.

He flipped onto his back and let me straddle him again, his hands gripping my hips with bruising force. My hair fell in a dark curtain around our faces, making the world feel small and secret. I raked my nails down his chest, leaving red marks in my wake, and watched as the pleasure-pain lit up his face.

"You are a goddamn dream," he said. Not like a line, but an honest-to-god prayer.

I lined him up and sank down slow, savoring the way he stretched me, filled me. We both groaned, bodies locking into the most ancient rhythm of all. For a minute, there was no magic, no supernatural drama—just two people coming together, sweat and breath and frantic hearts.

But then it hit: the charge of magic flowed through my veins. My senses, already heightened, blew wide open. I felt every ridge and vein of him inside me, the flex of his abs beneath my palms, the heat of his breath on my neck as he pulled me down and bit my shoulder—not to break skin, not yet, just to mark me.

Our heartbeats, once frantic and uneven, began to sync. I could hear his blood thrumming, feel the way his need merged with mine until we were one desperate, pounding organism. Magic crackled between us, a hot, buzzing current that threatened to short-circuit my brain.

He shifted, rolling us so he was above me again, his movements as graceful as they were overpowering. He drove into me, each thrust measured but inexorable, as if he was carving our bond into the very fabric of reality. I clawed at his back, desperate to anchor myself as the sensation built.

"Lucia," he panted, his voice more wolf than man. "Let go. Give your body to me as I give mine to you."

I did. I let the tension snap, let my body convulse around him, let my fangs descend and my cry shatter the silence. At the same moment, he buried his face in my neck, groaning out my name as he came.

Almost instantly his fangs descended as mine did the same.

His eyes had the familiar red glowing ring around the edges. "Your blood is calling to me."

He was still hard inside of me even though he'd just come. His hips rocked slowly as his nose nuzzled my neck.

I wanted to give him all of myself. "Take my blood. It's yours."

He dipped his head, lips brushing the spot he'd mapped earlier, and then he bit. Not a tear, not a savage rending, but a perfect, measured puncture—just enough for the magic to flood in. There was no pain, just a shock of ice and fire that lanced down my spine, and bled straight to my core. He continued to rock in and out of me as he drank, and I was close, so close to coming again. I gasped, arching up into him, letting the sensation take me over.

As he drank, I felt it—the bond stretching between us, a new tether woven from blood and want and need. He was precise, scientific, almost gentle in his ferocity. And he didn't take more than he needed. He took just enough.

When he pulled back, the wound closed in seconds, and I could already feel the blood knitting itself back together, magic stitching the flesh seamlessly. He licked his lips, a smear of crimson at the corner of his mouth. His eyes glowed, brighter than before, his wolf fully present but utterly tamed.

He shifted us again, rolling to his back, still fully seated inside of me. He tilted his head, baring his neck—the most vulnerable gesture a wolf could make. It was an invitation, but also a dare.

I leaned in and kissed the spot before I bit, a silent thank you for everything he'd given me. My fangs sank in, and his entire body went rigid, before he started pistoning into me from below. His hips relentless. A moan tore from deep within his chest. His hands locked onto my hips, anchoring us together, and the taste of him flooded my mouth.

It was... indescribable. Not just the flavor of his blood, which was rich and complex, but the sensation of his essence flowing into me. My senses exploded in a riot of colors and sounds. His heartbeat drowned out everything else. I could feel him inside me, in every possible way.

I drank my fill, and the magic sparked when we both came once more. When I pulled back, the wounds healed instantly, leaving only a faint hint of color behind. I licked his neck clean, then pressed my forehead to his, both of us panting, both of us dazed.

"Ryder," I breathed, "this is... holy shit."

He went serious as he squeezed my hands. "I choose you Lucia Kozlov. I choose this life and all that comes with it. I'm yours for all time."

I swallowed hard, overcome with emotion as I held his gaze. "I choose you Ryder Lowrey. You are my mate for all time. No matter what comes our way, we'll face it together."

The bond between us was no longer a whisper, but a roar. I could feel him, really feel him, in the back of my mind: his thoughts, his emotions, the tidal wave of affection and awe that crashed over him every time he looked at me. It was intoxicating. I wondered if he could feel mine—my deep, electric love, tinged with the terror of losing him.

Then a blinding heat raced through my chest, searing and sweet, and I knew without looking that the mate mark—the sigil—had flared to life. It burned under my skin, and I gasped at the intensity of it. I clawed Doc's back, desperate to stay grounded, and he held me tight, riding out the storm with me.

Our powers, once separate, braided together in perfect symmetry. The leak I'd felt for those days—the constant, maddening trickle of magic spilling out of me—was gone, replaced by a stable, golden hum. I felt... balanced, for the first time in as long as I could remember.

Doc stroked my back, soothing, until the fire faded. "It's done," he murmured.

I looked down at my chest, and sure enough, the mark was there: a crescent of runes intertwined with a wolf's claw and a single, perfect blood drop. I touched it, awed, and felt the heat ripple out through my veins.

Then I noticed something else. The cold that had haunted me since the canyon, the icy hunger that even blankets and sunlight couldn't erase—it was gone. In its place was a steady, comforting warmth, as if I'd swallowed the sun itself.

I laughed, giddy and disbelieving. "I'm not cold."

He smiled, eyes soft. "Good. You never will be again."

I sprawled out next to him, tracing the mate mark that had also appeared on his chest. It was unmistakable—a twin to my own. I felt a savage pride at the sight. No one else had ever dared mark him like this. He was mine, and I was his, and to hell with the rules.

I kissed the mark, then curled against his side, content for the first time in forever.

He reached up, cupping my face in his hands. "You okay?"

I nodded, then frowned. "Are you?"

He grinned, exposing a bloodstained canine. "Better than ever. I feel... I don't know. Like I'm finally home."

It hit me then: what we'd done. The ritual wasn't just about physical union or magical theatrics—it was about choosing each other, again and again, no matter how scary or inconvenient or batshit crazy it was. It was about intent. And mine was crystal clear.

I must have dozed, because when I opened my eyes again, the bedroom was steeped in the dreamy blue of early morning. Doc was already awake, propped against the headboard, his arms tight around me like I was something precious and breakable. Which was hilarious, considering I could bench-press him if I wanted to.

He pressed a kiss to the crown of my head. "You're thinking too loud, lioness."

I poked him in the side, then traced my fingers over the mate mark that had formed above my breasts. It was beautiful in a weird, gothic way: dark lines and angles, a crescent of runes surrounding a crimson drop and claw. I turned my head and found the twin mark on his skin, right above his heart. It looked right there, like it had been waiting all along.

We sat in silence for a while, just breathing. I felt the bond thrumming quietly in the background, not loud or showy, just a gentle pressure that made me feel less alone. I knew that Papa had to have felt it when the bond snapped into place. My brothers likely lost their minds. Maybe they were already plotting new alliances, new wars, or whatever he deemed necessary to keep me safe. The thought made me smile.

Across the compound, Bronc and the rest of the Iron Valor officers would have felt it too, I realized—the shift in the power dynamic, the way the pack magic had realigned itself around us. Good. I liked knowing I'd left my mark in more ways than one.

Doc disentangled himself, slipping from the bed and returning a second later with a bottle of water and one of my silk robes. He helped me into it like I were made of porcelain, then tucked the blanket around my shoulders for good measure.

"You're fussing," I said, amused.

He shrugged, looking almost sheepish. "Instinct. You're my mate now. I get to fuss."

I took a long drink and studied him over the rim. He looked different this morning—lighter, somehow, like a weight he'd carried forever had finally lifted. The mate mark suited him. Made him look dangerous, in a way that sent a thrill through me.

I reached out and tugged him back onto the mattress, straddling him with a grin. "Still want me?"

He snorted. "Princess, I'm never letting you go."

It was good because the world outside would come crashing in soon enough, with its expectations and wars and centuries-old grudges. But right here, right now, we were together. Complete.

CHAPTER 14

DOC

My family's kitchen was always a bit of chaos. My mom always insisted on family breakfasts with my sister Christine and me, and my father always indulged her. And that reminded me I'd avoided my family for the past few weeks. They weren't even aware their son was no longer the same fucking species as them. Dammit. I ran my hand through my hair as I put coffee grounds into the coffeemaker. I was a shit son. But as I stood in Lucia's kitchen the morning after I'd bonded with my mate, I found it difficult to care much. I'd fall on that grenade soon enough. This morning I felt too good. Too whole. The kitchen glowed with beams of sunrise cutting across the hardwoods; the coffee pot hissed and burbled like a medieval alchemist's lab, and the woman whose blood remade me was in the next room.

My phone vibrated on the counter, dancing a tiny jig by the sugar canister. I ignored it at first, focusing on the simple ceremony of dark roast dripping into a clear carafe. My hands were steady as I pulled two expensive mugs from the cabinet. It felt natural to be preparing coffee for my mate. My mate. I'd never imagined having a mate. As the other guys fell one by one, finding mates in the most remarkable of circumstances, I felt there was no circumstance wild enough to grant the same for me. Boy, had I fucking missed that one by a country mile.

The phone pulsed again. I flicked my gaze to the screen. Seventeen unread messages, all from my brothers. I'd known they'd feel it when Lucia and I sealed the bond, but I didn't expect the full Iron Valor group chat to light up before eight a.m. on a Sunday.

First was Gunner. It was always Gunner. The man lived for morning wolf runs and for busting balls. I snorted so hard I almost dropped the bag of coffee on the counter at his three kissy-face emojis and a GIF of Brad Pitt biting someone's neck. I scrolled to the next one.

God, I missed the days when nobody in the club knew how to meme.

Of course Big Papa sent a photo of a vintage condom box, and below it, a scripture reference about the power of the blood. Fitting.

Wrecker chimed in:

It was more sibling-mean than usual. Wrecker always pushed hard when he was happy. I grinned and let the burn of their affection seep in. A GIF of sexy lips with blood dripping in the corner. *Please clean those up before we see you.* Then a winky face emoji.

Arsenal, ever the tactician, followed, adding a smiling vampire emoji. And a bullet-pointed agenda for church at noon. Typical.

But it was Bronc's text that hit the hardest. It sat by itself, like a benediction after the sacrilege:

I scrolled past the rest—a mix of crude jokes and supportive, if slightly unhinged, brotherhood. Then paused, reading the last line again.

Bronc: Your girl eats with us now.

It wasn't a demand. It was a welcome.

My phone buzzed once more. *Bronc: Kazimir is gonna join via video.* I wasn't surprised the king would want to see Lucia after our mating had been completed.

I knew he'd want to see the mate marks.

I rubbed my chest. The sigil was fresh, a perfect fusion of a wolf's claw and a drop of blood over a crescent of runes. I was proud to have her mark. Our mark.

My fingers still tingled from tracing the fresh mate mark—Lucia's warmth lingering like a phantom touch. The bond pulsed once—sharp, wrong—and then the world dissolved.

One heartbeat I was staring at the coffee drip; the next, I was *elsewher e.*Hazy darkness swallowed me. Cold steel bit into my wrists—suppression cuffs, the kind that drains magic to a whisper. I strained against them, but my hybrid strength guttered out like a snuffed candle. Panic clawed up my throat. *Trapped.*

Shadows shifted. Maltraz stood a few feet away, arms crossed, his expression unreadable. Silent. Watching. To his left, Otero's lean frame leaned against a damp stone wall, eyes glinting with detached curiosity. Neither spoke. Neither moved.

Lucia. Her absence hit me like a physical blow—a hollow ache beneath my ribs. The bond stretched thin, screaming into the void. I tried to call for her, but my voice died before it left my throat.

Then it shattered.

I blinked, and I was back in the kitchen, standing at the counter, trembling hands around a coffee mug. The vision lasted seconds. Fragmented. Surreal. Like a nightmare half-remembered at dawn.

Stress. It had to be stress—the bond settling, the hybrid changes rewiring my biology, the weight of everything since the canyon. I scrubbed a hand over my face, the ghost of those cuffs still chilling my skin. Otero's cold stare. Maltraz's silence. And Lucia... gone when I needed her most.

I didn't tell her. Didn't tell anyone. Why worry them over a hallucination? Maybe it was a side effect—my human half fraying under shifter magic, or my new instincts misfiring. But the dread lingered, coiled low in my gut.

Wait, I decided, pouring the coffee. *See if it happens again.*

I buried the fear deep. Some secrets are safer kept.

I grabbed her mug along with mine and headed to Lucia's room. The coffee smelled normal, but that was the only normal thing about the morning. Maybe that would change. Maybe it wouldn't. I wasn't afraid either way. But I did wonder if the next time I had to sew up a brother, the sight of the red stuff would make me hungry, or just homesick for the woman in the bedroom.

I padded down the hall, the worn oak planks cold against my bare feet. I didn't notice how my body moved, not until I did: the little increments of speed and power, the way my hearing spiked every time Lucia moved the duvet. I was more now. Not less.

I stopped by her door, coffee mugs in hand, and let the sunlight halo her silhouette. She sat up phone in hand, hair a black river over one shoulder. Her pulse thrummed through the bond with a color and texture I'd never had before. It was love, yes. But also trepidation, determination, a dash of her father's arrogance.

She looked up and smiled, and my chest tightened.

"Morning," I said.

She set her phone down. "Papa felt it when our bond snapped into place. And my brothers...you don't want to know." Her smile was radiant.

"My brothers as well," I said. "The group chat is unholy."

She stretched, feline, and rolled onto her back. The mate mark on her collarbone shone like a gemstone, raw and unpolished. "Let me guess. Wrecker has already demanded proof of my existence."

I sat down with the mugs. "You're an instant legend. He wants to know if I still eat food or just..." I let the implication dangle.

She arched a brow. "He is so... so Wrecker."

I couldn't disagree and laughed and just watched her soak in the moment. She reached for her own coffee, still sleepy, and sipped it black as midnight.

Through the bond, I felt a flicker of her pride, and a warmth I could only call belonging. That was what had always drawn me to the club, and to her: the need to belong, to anchor myself to something bigger than the next mission or the next wound to patch up.

She set the mug down and leaned in, her breath warm on my neck. "You are different, Ryder."

"You're different, Lucia."

And when she stood, hair wild, the mate mark faintly glowing, I knew church was about to get a whole lot more interesting.

"I have to go home and shower. Change clothes. You should come with me. We can…" I caught myself, but I wasn't going to play shy, not after last night. "We can talk about what happens next."

She pressed her cheek to my shoulder, so close I could feel the hum of her pulse. "You mean, where we live?"

I nodded. "I will not live apart from you. That's not how it works for us. I want you with me. Always. But if you hate my house, or you want to turn the basement into a wine dungeon, just say so."

She rolled her eyes. "Americans. All you think of is basements and extra-large fridges. I'd like tall ceilings. I want a music room with large windows and a baby grand piano I can play."

She'd surprised me.

"I didn't know you played."

She went serious. "There are many things you do not know about me Ryder Lowrey. I am not all sex and teeth and claws."

I wanted to hold her; to cradle her, so she felt how precious she was to me. But I didn't know if she'd want that. I simply gathered her in my arms. "You are many things, Lucia Kozlov. Sex and teeth and claws are the smallest parts. You are beauty and you are light. And clearly, many things I have yet to discover. I can't wait to learn them all. And you will have your music room."

"That was easy. Let me think of other things." She laughed.

"You've seen my place. I never had the inclination to decorate. It's always been mostly a place to lay my head when I wasn't on a mission, at the hospital, or at the club, or out patching up our enforcers when they picked fights with the wrong guys. Do with it what you want."

Lucia watched me, and for a second I worried she'd find my loneliness somehow pathetic. Instead, she just gave my hand a squeeze.

"I will pack a bag. Of course, I need my toothbrush for when I bite you." She showed her teeth through a wicked grin.

"Fair," I said. "I'll swing by in an hour. We'll ride together."

"Ryder," she said, serious now. "This is what you want?"

I didn't hesitate. "It's actually the only thing I've ever wanted. I just didn't know it was possible."

She looked at me for a long moment, all the fire and hunger and hope of her focused right into my face. Then she kissed me once, quick and decisive.

"Go shower," she said, shooing me with both hands. "And in the future; bring me flowers. I will not forgive you if you do not."

I walked out, feeling the bond between tighten and hum and then settle into a steady pulse. I felt more alive than I had in years.

I didn't know how the world would take the two of us, but I knew this much: come hell or high water, I wanted Lucia by my side.

Iron Valor's conference room wasn't built for subtlety. Since the pack house was blown up a few months ago, it was rebuilt on the basement level with state-of-the-art technology. This room could double as a bunker if need be. The conference table is long and can seat the officers and their mates when the occasion calls for it; which today it does. On the walls hang several large-screen monitors for video conferencing.

Wrecker and Parker have outfitted the entire building with the most state-of-the-art tech available on the market and several items they created specifically for us. There are drones that fly above the compound, sending real-time images to techs who monitor screens around the clock. It only took one time when Iron Valor almost lost the entire pack for Bronc to have put in place measures to ensure that never happens again.

Today, the table groaned under the weight of food: platters of steaks, mashed potatoes, grilled asparagus, and enough rolls to feed a small country. There were also three kinds of pie, none of which matched, and a pitcher of sweet tea sweating onto a trivet. Pearl was in her element, swanning around with a tray of deviled eggs and scolding anyone who dared eat them all before I arrived.

I stepped into the room and was hit with a double-shot of sensory overload: the savory, bloody smell of beef (which now made my pulse stutter in a way it never had before) and the bright flare of a dozen familiar faces. Every officer in the pack had brought his mate, so the room was already filled with the sounds of familiar voices. Bronc presided at the head of the table, with Juliet beside him and Maddie, Bronc's younger sister, visible through the open door of Juliet's office wrangled a pair of sleeping twins.

Lucia entered after me, and the whole room stuttered for a beat. Not because she was out of place (she never could be), but because everyone knew we'd completed the mate bond and the air around us crackled with something different. She scanned the crowd, took in every face, and then pulled the chair beside mine.

Pearl descended on her instantly, enfolding Lucia in a hug that would have cracked the ribs of a lesser woman. "My dear, you look positively radiant. You hungry? You eat first; let these mongrels wait."

Lucia looked as though she'd been handed the keys to a secret kingdom. "Thank you, Ms. Pearl. It is beautiful to see you again. Everything looks delicious."

Pearl beamed and patted her hand. "Sweetheart, you are more than welcome. And you can just call me Pearl; drop the Ms. Part. Or better yet, you can call me Mama Pearl if you like. I'll be your Mama just like I am to the rest my dear."

Lucia swallowed hard. An emotion I'd not seen on her before crossed her face. "Thank you, Mama Pearl. It's my honor to call you this."

Big Papa raised his glass. "To new family," he said, and the room echoed him in a clatter of crystal and coffee mugs.

When we'd finally worked our way through the main course and the better part of a pie, Bronc rapped the table with a fork for quiet. "Listen up," he said. "We've got business, and the king's on deck."

A massive monitor flared to life at the end of the room. Kazimir's face filled the screen, black hair slicked back, eyes the color of arctic ice. He looked at Lucia first, and when he smiled, it was a strange mix of predator and proud father.

"Little one," he said. "You look well."

Lucia nodded, all the princess in her now. "I am well, Papa. Very well."

Kazimir's gaze flicked to me. "Dr. Lowrey. You look quite hale. Your eyes tell me a change occurred."

I straightened in my seat. "Yes, sir. It's safe to say my wolf has mixed completely with vampire blood. But he is feeling strong." I gave a subtle glance around the room and saw the raised brows of my brothers.

He gave a low, rich laugh. "Then show us. The sigil."

I unbuttoned the top few buttons of my shirt and pulled it back to reveal the place over my heart toward the camera. The mate mark had already healed, the edges of the skin closing over the inky blend of runes, wolf's claw blood drop. There was a beat of silence, then Kazimir's smile went soft, the kind reserved for family.

"Good," he said. "Now, be very careful, son. The world will not understand what you are and what you mean to each other. Lucia, you have the same mark?"

"Yes, Papa." She pulled the V-neck of her top slightly down and over to reveal the smaller matching mark.

Bronc cleared his throat. "So, Kazimir, tell us. What have you heard of Maltraz's knowledge of this? Does he know that you and Iron Valor are allied through the mate bond? If so, we need to coordinate with Rafe, Menace, Griffin and Slade ASAP."

Kazimir inclined his head. "I have scouts and spies gathering intel. But you must also prepare for Otero to betray us. The Western King despises me, and he has long dreamed of a world where vampires and wolves are at war again."

Wrecker folded his arms. "Bring it. He has to know that we not only have Doc as a hybrid but Aspen cannot be discounted as an angel/witch hybrid also."

Big Papa cut him a look. "I'd prefer you not flippantly toss my mate into the fray without using the utmost restraint, brother."

Juliet, ever the note-taker, asked, "What do you need from us in the next twenty-four?"

Bronc's voice was stone. "Security lockdown. Nobody in or out without three-factor clearance. No solo runs. If the wolves run, run in groups of at least three. If Maltraz wants a war, we'll give him one—but only on our terms. Kazimir, we'd appreciate being informed of any information you learn."

The vampire gave a regal nod to the Alpha.

Arsenal laid a Glock on the table (Pearl tutted but didn't try to take it away). "I'll run a full perimeter sweep. Then, see about setting up protections for Lucia and Doc if things get hot."

Harper rested her hand on his. "We won't run," she said. "Not from this."

Aspen piped up. "Oscar and I will reinforce the wards tonight." The prairie dog's whiskers twitched in agreement.

Kazimir watched it all from his screen, strangely silent. When he spoke, it was almost gentle. "Your pack never ceases to amaze me, Iron Valor. Not just warriors, but something more. Take care of each other. Lucia, we will speak again soon. Your brothers want to see you."

"Yes, Papa." They each nodded, and the feed went to black.

The meeting closed with a round of handshakes, hugs, and one last tray of brownies. Lucia and I lingered, letting the others go first. The conference room felt different now, less like a war room and more like a home.

She leaned into me, her voice low. "This was a good day," she said. "Tomorrow will be harder."

The vision I had in her kitchen kept scratching at my memory. I hoped tomorrow would *not,* in fact be harder.

CHAPTER 15

LUCIA

My feet made a slapping sound as they moved across the pale, hand-scraped hardwood floors. Doc's house was all light and space and unnecessary grandeur, the way the Texans liked. As if every ceiling needed to be cathedral-high to keep God from knocking his head on the molding.

And yet, I loved it.

The living room alone was bigger than the apartment over the garage at Pearl's, or the one I crashed in when Papa's Bratva "business" required me to lie low for a while. This place had a formal living room just off the entry, which was now my music room, a den for "real living," and a "formal" dining room that I'm sure had never seen an actual meal. The modern kitchen had an island and barely used matte stainless steel appliances. The entire space was clean and uncomplicated, just like Doc used to be.

Everything about the place reflected his former life. The life he had before it tried to bleed out all over a Texas canyon. Before I realized that I couldn't live in a world without Ryder Lowrey and decided to change our destinies. Or maybe I fulfilled them.

I laughed to myself; I'd turned into a *chmo*.

In only a couple of weeks, I'd managed to change this drab functional-only house into what I'd hoped was a living home that represented both

Doc and me. I never expected to be the kind of woman who cared about a wall sconce, but here I was, fussing over a pair of pewter-and-glass beauties I'd ordered online from some specialty store. I determined to install them myself, balancing on a stepladder in a pair of Chanel cropped pants and a cream-colored blouse, cursing in three languages as I twisted copper wire and tried not to fry myself into a crisp.

I had the interior of the house painted in a color scheme: sapphire blues and moon-gray, like the sky right before it decided to storm. Normally I gravitated to crimson, black, and gold—every other space I'd occupied in my adult life looked like a murdered Fabergé egg—but this time I wanted something different. Something that felt less like war and more like peace. Doc deserved that, and he told me to make the house "livable."

He was at the hospital most of those days, head-down, all business. He'd never say it, but I could tell he hated the sound of boxes being opened, the shriek of packing tape as it came unstuck, the persistent thud-thud-thud of my hammer as I built up our home one anchor at a time. He never said "our home" out loud, but I'd caught him once or twice standing in the entryway, stethoscope still around his neck, just looking at what I'd done. No smile, but a different tightness at the edges of his mouth. The kind of pride only a soldier could have for territory won without a drop of blood.

The music room was my last masterpiece. The white baby grand arrived a week after I did. It had taken all of my connections—and a small bribe to a vampire with moving-company interests—to get it in less than six months. The men who delivered it looked at me like I was out of my mind, but I tipped them anyway and even made them coffee before shooing them off my new property. The tuner came in an hour later. I had the men at the Iron Valor front gate cursing me, I'm sure. Security was at an all-time high since a demon might have wanted to kill or kidnap me, or Doc or both of us. But I had to make this house a home. We'd been through so much. And this music room was non-negotiable.

The moment the piano tuner's footsteps faded beyond the door, I lifted the lid. My palms hovered above the keys—ivory and ebony, cold as winter marble under my fingertips. But as I pressed down, warmth bloomed. The piano *breathed*, alive with the ghosts of every Chopin nocturne and Liszt rhapsody that had ever lived in my bones. Silence draped the house like velvet; even Doc's coffee pot hissed its percussive rhythm from the kitchen, a distant heartbeat in the stillness.

I sat, the bench's leather sighing beneath me, and let Rachmaninoff claim me. His Prelude in G Minor surged through my hands—not as notes, but as liquid shadow and silver. My fingers became conduits: every chord a fracture in the dam holding back centuries of sorrow and fury. The music wasn't played; it *unspooled* from some deep-buried place where the vampire and the woman bled together.

I bent over the piano, fingers flying with lethal precision. Music wept from the instrument, and with it, every unspoken grief we'd survived. A feeling without a name: part reverence, part sorrow.

Only when the final chord hung vibrating in the air—a solitary, resonant cry—did I lift my head. The room swam back into focus: the Persian rug, the bookshelves, the scent of coffee. And there was Doc, one shoulder leaning against the doorframe, his eyes glistening. He didn't speak. He didn't need to. The look on his face—a fragile, wondrous ache—said everything. In that silence, the piano's echo lingered between us, a testament to the soul even monsters could harbor.

He had stood unseen in the doorway.

I turned on the bench to face him.

The look on his face was hot, unfamiliar, tender.

"You are the most beautifully intriguing creature I've ever known, mate."

His voice was barely above a growl.

I sat silently before him.

"The first thing I want from you is for you to close the drapes around this room without leaving your seat."

I wanted to show off for him. Happy to have my vampire at full strength, I raised one hand and with a flick of my wrist; I loosened the tie backs one at a time until all the curtains closed, covering the three windows in the room. The room dimmed to the pale chandelier light.

"Now stand. Remove every piece of clothing. Then sit back down."

I was happy to do as he demanded. I did not waste time on a seductive show. It was not needed for my mate. His eyes told me of his hunger. He'd been seduced when I'd played the instrument. He needed nothing more.

I stripped quickly. My breasts were heavy with desire; my pussy was already drenched in need of him. I sat not caring that I would leave a puddle on the leather bench. He slowly stalked toward me, fully clothed, and carefully closed the lid of the piano, covering the keys.

"Now, lean back, my beautiful creature, rest your arms on your instrument while I take my time with this gorgeous pussy that is so fucking wet for me already."

Then he was on his knees, low enough to reach me with his talented tongue. His hands spread me wide, and calmly he lapped at me from ass to clit then thrusting inside and out until my hips rocked against his face. He alternated between flattening his tongue and bringing it to a point; the sensations were driving me crazy.

"Ryder, please."

His eyes caught mine over my body as I tried to reach for his hair. He tsked. "No, no." He laughed and pulled back. "Look at my vicious mate, begging so prettily to come." He inserted two fingers and pumped in and out as he sucked on my clit.

My moans filled the room, but he still did not let me come.

"I will be that vicious mate, I swear!"

His face became serious for a moment.

"We haven't fed in over a day, my love. I'm hungry, not just for your beautiful body, but for your blood. Will you give me your blood? Will you feed your mate, your delicious, life-giving blood, my fearless, magnificent lioness?"

"Always *moy volk, moya lyubov'*."

With his right hand still on my pussy, his left pulled my thigh back, and he bit. Pain flared—sharp, precise—then melted instantly into heat. My body felt like a switch had been flipped as I felt his tongue massaging the vein as he drank. His thumb stroked my clit, and the orgasm hit with a ferocity that almost made me black out. My hips rocked, and his hands grasped them to steady me in place as he took a few more pulls then released and leaned back to seal the puncture. I leaped into his arms and wrapped myself around him as he stood and walked me to our room.

"Now, *moy volk*, your vicious mate will take what is hers."

If you'd asked me on any given Tuesday what hell smelled like, I would have said the faint smell of motor oil and leather. That's how Bronc's office always smelled. Not the scent of evil, but of a man who'd rather work on a motorcycle than think about his feelings. It suited him. So when I got the text—Conference in Alpha's office ASAP—I knew two things: one, this was about pack business, and two, I'd rather eat a bowl of live bees than spend a morning with Bronc in his bunker.

Doc saw me eyeing my phone over the kitchen counter, raised one eyebrow, and not bothering to pause his protein shake blending. "You got the memo?"

"Shadbolt on call at the hospital, so you're free to go?"

He poured two glasses and slid one to me. "If the Alpha calls a meeting, Shadbolt is automatically on call. Something is up. Menace is dialing in too."

Great. Now we were having a summit, with all the subtlety of the Cold War. I dressed for the occasion: black wide-leg pants, a white wrap top, chunky necklace and earrings. I paired it with stiletto boots because I was feeling aggressive.

We walked up together. Doc's hand warm and heavy on my back was a comfort, which was funny, given he could have snapped my spine with a single flex. He still hadn't gotten used to how much stronger he was now. Sometimes I caught him watching his own hands, surprised by how easily they crushed things that once resisted him: jars, handshakes, the shifters who insisted on arm-wrestling him at the pack house bar. I was fascinated by it, too, but I'd learned not to ask questions he couldn't answer.

Bronc's door was open, but I knocked anyway. He was already at his desk, arms crossed and face set in that "I know more than you think I do" expression that made every underling in the building piss themselves. The giant coyote pelt that hung behind his chair looked extra menacing in the daylight.

"Sit," he said, then nodded at the large screen on his desk. Menace's face was already up, the image crisp and unflinching. He looked cool as always. I was surprised he wasn't wearing his aviators as usual. I guess since the Council wasn't present, he had no reason to be annoying.

"Princess," Menace said, with that little head tilt that was ninety percent mockery and ten percent respect.

I smirked. "Your Majesty."

Doc grunted and dropped into the chair beside me, stretching his legs like he owned the place. He kind of did. Nobody was going to tell him otherwise, not now.

Bronc wasted no time. "Menace, tell them."

Menace leaned in, hands steepled, eyes sharp as broken glass. "Word from the Council. They've been sniffing around for weeks, but today it was official. Inquiry into Doc's, ah, new condition."

Doc's jaw went tight. "What business is it of theirs?"

Menace's lip twitched. "You're the first documented wolf-vampire hybrid that hasn't self-immolated in the first month. It's historic. The Council has an interest in anomalies. Especially the ones that change power dynamics."

"And that's what I am now?" Doc snapped. "A threat to the balance of power?"

"Don't be dramatic," Menace said, but he didn't deny it. "They want details. Capabilities. Evidence you're still in control."

Doc snorted, leaning forward on his elbows. "What do you want to know? I'm stronger. Faster. I heal faster. My wolf is bigger. I can bench Menace now, which makes him cry into his protein powder every night."

Menace's eyes narrowed, but Bronc grinned, just a flicker at the edge of his mouth.

I cleared my throat, trying to inject some reason. "Look. The Council doesn't do anything unless someone waves a red flag. They're not proactive. So who ratted us out? It had to be Otero if he's working with Maltraz."

Bronc's face got even harder. "We're trying to trace the origin. It was submitted anonymously. Could be Otero. Son of a bitch hates shifters; especially Iron Valor shifters. He still might have an axe to grind."

"The hate is mutual," I muttered, then remembered my father's voice: Assume everyone has an axe to grind. Especially if you're holding the whetstone.

Doc was still simmering. "So what's the play here? They want to study me? Put me in a glass box and poke me with sticks?"

Menace shrugged. "You'll likely be asked to appear before the Council. They'll want a demonstration. A Q&A. If you refuse, they'll send enforcers."

"Let them come," Doc said, a little too loud. "I'm not some fucking test subject."

Bronc held up a hand. "Enough. We need to be smart about this. Iron Valor has never lost face with the Council, and we're not starting now. Lucia, what's your read?"

I'd been waiting for this. "They're scared," I said, locking eyes with the screen. "Of you, Doc. Of us. The last time a hybrid existed, it took half his pack to put him down. If they think you're a liability, they'll act preemptively."

"Well fuck. I understand why it was hard to put the last one down. He was fighting for his goddamn life. That's probably why he appeared crazy, also. If you knew people wanted to kill you just because you were different, you'd fight tooth and nail too. But it's not the 1800s, or the 1900s for that matter. I thought the days of witch-hunts were over. Now they just look to put down anyone who might wield more power than them, but just enough more that they can stop it."

He was shaking with his anger

Doc looked at me, really looked, and I could see the stubbornness flaring in his chest. "Why should I have to prove anything? I didn't ask for this."

I reached for his hand, squeezing. "Because the world isn't fair, and the Council is even less so. We do what we have to, and then we go back to living."

Bronc cut in. "First step, we find out who submitted the tip. If it's internal, we handle it. If it's external, we prepare for a visit."

Menace nodded. "You'll need to keep a low profile, Doc. At least for a while. If you show off too much, it'll spread. Wolves talk. Vampires talk even more."

I couldn't help but laugh. "Menace, do you know your brother at all? You think he, of all people, will show off? He can't help his physical changes. He doesn't have to be ashamed. But this man is the least showy of all of you bastards. But you act like bringing attention is a bad thing. Information is leverage. Maybe we leak something ourselves, a narrative that puts us in a better light."

Bronc raised an eyebrow. "You volunteering for spin control?"

"At least we'd be in control of what's being reported," I said, like I truly believed it would make a difference. I didn't.

The meeting broke, but the tension didn't leave the room. Doc stalked out first, practically vibrating with rage. I followed, but paused at the door, letting Bronc's presence settle over me.

He didn't look up from his desk. "Keep him close, Lucia. If they come, they'll come for him first."

I nodded, then left, heels clicking a warning down the hallway.

Doc was waiting outside, face stormy. "This isn't going to end well, is it?"

"I'll talk to my father," I said, because if anyone could read the Council's true intent, it was him. "For now, we do nothing. We give them nothing. We act normal. That's how you win these games."

He looked unconvinced, but let me wrap an arm around him. I could feel the power in him, coiled and barely contained.

As we rode home, I tried to catalog all the ways my life had changed since moving here: I had a partner who might be the strongest man alive, a house that was finally a home, and a threat that could burn it all down if I misplayed a single move.

It was the happiest I'd ever been.

Which, of course, meant something terrible was bound to happen.

It was a night for plotting, or maybe for drinking, but mostly for calling my father.

I'd never been nervous to dial his number before. But I felt it now: a clench in my chest, an urge to pace that I couldn't shake. I tried to fight it, but the room was too big and my worries too loud.

I called him from the bedroom, pacing the white carpet in bare feet. My toes curled with every ring, like I were bracing for a hit. It was almost comforting when his voice answered, so dry and cold you could practically see the fog on his breath.

"Lucia," he said, voice thick as a Russian winter, "I was expecting you."

"Of course you were," I said, flopping onto the bed. "What else do you know?"

He clicked his tongue. "That you would not call unless your pack was in trouble."

Your pack. Those words filled me with a kind of warmth I'd not felt since my mother was alive.

"You know the Council is investigating Doc," I said, not bothering to lower my voice. He could hear through half the walls in the house, anyway.

"Da," he said. Just that, as if I'd told him the weather was mild.

I rolled onto my back, eyes on the ceiling, willing him to take it more seriously. "He's the first of his kind in a century. They think he might be dangerous."

"He is," my father said, not unkindly. "But that's not reason to kill him. It's a reason to keep him close. The Council will want him in their pocket."

"They'll never get him," I said, braver than I felt.

He was silent for a moment. "They will try, and they will fail. Do not antagonize them unless you must. If you do, do it with purpose." There was the Bratva king; never use a hammer when a scalpel would do.

"They want a demonstration," I said. "An audience. A show of loyalty."

"Give them a show," he said, almost smiling. "But make sure it is your show. Not theirs."

I laughed, sudden and sharp. "You make it sound easy."

"It is not easy," he said, "but it is simple." He paused, then with a voice like a prayer: "You are my daughter. If you cannot outsmart a roomful of politicians, then perhaps I have failed as a father. But be careful. I fear there is more at play here. I fear it's more than the Council that has an interest in Doc and you. Do not let your guard down for even a moment."

"Yes, Papa."

He grunted. "You will be fine. You have more allies than you think. Even the Council wants stability. No one wants war."

I let myself believe him. "So we play along?"

"We play the game," he agreed. "And if you lose, I will bring my own army."

He hung up, no goodbye. He never wasted them. I lay there, phone still pressed to my ear, the warmth of his confidence thrumming in my blood.

But it wasn't enough to quiet the hunger. The need. The craving for Doc had sharpened, not dulled, with every stress the day threw at me. Maybe it was the hybrid thing, or maybe just my brand of crazy, but as soon as I thought of him, I felt my teeth ache.

Tonight, I decided I would make it beautiful for him. For us. If tomorrow brought Council trials and threats, tonight would be a memory worth keeping.

I lit every candle I could find—Doc always teased me about being a fire hazard, but he liked the scent. Bergamot and violet, and smoke. I draped a thin blue robe over my shoulders, but only for effect. I wanted him to see how little I was hiding.

Then I climbed onto the bed, propped myself up on pillows, and let my mind slip open. If the mate bond was good for anything, it was this: the way it let you send thoughts and moods across space, a little psychic telegram just for two. I let the hunger build, let it bleed out to him. I pictured his face when he walked in—stressed certainly, but greedy for what I offered.

I didn't have to wait long. I heard his heavy steps in the hall. The closer he got, the more the hunger pulsed, as if our bodies were arguing over who needed the other more.

He pushed the door open and stopped, backlit by the hallway light, jaw set in that way that said: I am not in control of this situation and I don't know how to feel about it.

I smiled. "Hi."

He stood there, drinking me in. The way his pupils widened, how his hands twitched at his sides—he was holding back, as always.

"You look like trouble," he said.

I let the robe fall open. "You look like you could use some."

He crossed the room in three long strides, all that military grace wrapped up in animal need. He didn't touch me at first, just hovered, as if his shadow alone could press me into the mattress.

"I'm serious," I whispered, letting the hunger thread through my words. "I need you tonight."

And for once, he truly let the night take us where we needed to go.

CHAPTER 16

DOC

The hospital was quiet in a way that always made me uneasy. The rhythm of the place usually thrummed, even in the dead of night: shoes squeaking on polished tile, the faint sigh of pneumatic doors, nurses murmuring just beyond sight. But tonight, three hours after the last patient left, the only movement was the second hand sweeping my office clock, and the only voice belonged to my own muttering as I reviewed lab values and the next week's surgery schedule.

I flexed my hand out of habit, palm and fingers devoid of their faded scars. Old reflex. But nothing haunted me quite like the memory of bleeding out on the cold stone, Lucia's frantic voice in my ear, her blood filling the void where mine had once been as she broke every law in her world to bring me back. That night had redefined impossible, leaving me with a pulse that was too strong, a wolf that felt too alive. There were worse things, but not many.

Paperwork. There was always paperwork, no matter how immortal or supernatural the clientele. My desk was an engineered disaster: patient charts, notes from the new physician about the upcoming influx of shifter babies, surgical logs, and schedules I'd been putting off for a month. I flipped through them, initialing, signing, and flagging the ones I'd pawn off to the office manager tomorrow. The constant friction of busy work was a comfort, in its own way—a reminder that whatever I'd become, I was still needed.

I leaned back, letting the old, familiar tension settle in my shoulders. My wolf slumbered somewhere deep, content for now. The hybrid thing was real, sure, but for the first time in days I could almost believe we'd pulled it off—dodged the crosshairs of the Council, bought ourselves time, maybe even left our little drama as yesterday's news in the eyes of the supernatural overlords. Lucia had called this the lull, the moment when the world lets you breathe again just to see if you'll take the bait.

I glanced at the clock—11:13 PM. I told Lucia I'd be home before midnight, so I needed to get my ass in gear. I started to reach for the next file, and that's when I noticed it: the temperature in the room had dropped. Not a chill, but an absence. The hum of the air system fell away, the fluorescent lighting softened, every surface suddenly too far away from the next, like my office had quietly doubled in size when I wasn't looking.

Another vision. I should have felt the usual warning: migraine blooming at the base of my skull, tightening behind my eyes like a vice, the whole world tilting at a wrong angle. I'd had them more frequently, but had dismissed them as waking dreams, not as some newly acquired power. But this one arrived without violence. My heart rate didn't spike. There was no pain. Instead, the world just... stepped out from under me.

I tried to move and found my hands still, fingers frozen mid-signature on a sheet of carbonless forms. The edges of my desk blurred, then sharpened, then faded to transparency. The walls of my office began to recede, pulling back like the tide, taking doors and windows and all physical boundaries with them. The ceiling above vanished, exposing a limitless dome of black. My feet stayed anchored, but the floor transformed beneath them, the industrial carpet shifting to a glassy, pitch-dark obsidian that reflected nothing, not even the glow of my own skin.

Then the black glass beneath my feet rippled, and from the darkness ahead a shape coalesced—first an outline, then mass and detail. A long, ancient table extended itself into existence, dominating the empty space. The thing was monstrous: a slab of stone; wide, inlaid with bands of gold and bone, resting on legs that looked disturbingly like femurs, as if judgment itself needed bones to stand on.

Chairs appeared one by one. Each was occupied by a presence, more sensed than seen, faces obscured as if blurred by static or warped glass. The figures sat unmoving, hands folded or resting on the table, their attention focused solely on the empty chair at the far end.

Mine.

I recognized the feeling—like being a test subject on the wrong side of a one-way mirror. Not hostile, but not gentle either. I had the distinct impression that whatever filled the seats at this table was there to decide my fate.

This was a trial.

I reached for my wolf out of habit, looking for that familiar feral heartbeat that had always been my anchor. Nothing. No echo, no resistance, no hint of the beast that had paced the bars of my soul since childhood. I didn't feel suppressed. I felt... amputated. Then I noticed I was wearing the same cuffs I'd seen in other visions.

The implications were immediate and chilling. Power suppression wasn't an act of restraint. It was a simple, elegant severing of connection, so seamless you barely noticed it was gone until you reached for it and came up empty.

My mind spun, searching for a way to hack the system, a medical loophole or backdoor. But there was nothing to grab onto. The old rules didn't apply.

The sigil on the empty chair pulsed brighter, and with a faint shimmer, the chair itself reoriented to face the others. No one spoke. The presences remained still, their features blurred and anonymous. I had the strangest feeling that if I tried to look directly at any of them, my vision would slide right off, like a needle skipping over a record groove. The only point of clarity was my seat, and the knowledge that I had already been chosen.

I looked down at the sigil in front of me and traced the lines with my mind. Claw, blood, crescent. All the pieces that made up the mate bond between Lucia and me, arranged in a code that no one else could have written.

I understood then: the Council didn't need to kill me. They just needed to know my weakness; my vulnerability.

The session ended not with a bang, but a simple, collective exhale. The table faded, the chairs collapsed in on themselves, and the void returned, smoother and emptier than before.

I was left alone, standing on the black glass, my reflection missing, my wolf gone silent. The invitation—or was it a summons?—hung in the air, heavier than any threat.

I knew what came next. They would call me to the table in the real world.

And when they did, I would answer.

The void held me in suspension, a paradox of total isolation and inescapable scrutiny. I waited for the next shoe to drop, the next rule to rewrite itself in my bones. Instead, the world shifted subtly—less a violent tectonic shift, more the nudge of a new element into the equation.

At the edge of my vision, a shape took form. Human, or close to it. Tall, lithe, black curls bouncing with each impatient step. Even in a world made of shadow and silence, I'd know Lucia anywhere. She stood behind a transparent barrier—a wall of glass, or something even thinner; the air itself hardened and made impassable. Her mouth moved. She was speaking, maybe even shouting, but not a sound reached me.

I could only watch as her fists pounded the other side, eyes wild. Even here, in a vision, the disconnect was total. A thread yanked from a tapestry, not a clean cut but an unraveling.

I wanted to rage, to call up the wolf and let it howl against the void. But the beast inside me was still absent, or worse, anesthetized. The anger that should have ignited instead turned inward, a cold, spreading dread.

A flash of movement in my peripheral vision. Two figures, barely visible, lingered at the outermost edge of the darkness, like specters content to observe the experiment from a safe distance. One radiated cold calculation and the scent of old, spilled blood—King Varek Otero. The other was impossible to miss: obsidian skin, a smile full of razors and lies. Maltraz. Neither made a move toward the table, or to Lucia. Their postures said everything—this wasn't their trial. They were spectators, not executioners.

I pieced it together in a flash, the same way you recognize a trauma pattern before the paramedics even unload the stretcher. Maltraz had called the play, tipped Otero to our position, let the Council do the heavy lifting. It was elegant in its simplicity: let the bureaucracy of the supernatural world do what centuries of violence could not.

Lucia caught my gaze, and for a split second I thought she'd found a way to reach through. Her lips shaped a word—my name, or maybe just a curse at the unfairness of it all. She pressed her palm to the glass, a stubborn hope in the gesture.

I pressed my own to the same spot, but the sensation was numb. The only thing real in this place was the absence.

A sound broke the moment—something mundane and jarringly out of place. The double-tap knock of a fist on wood, a heart monitor's beep, maybe even my own phone buzzing in a pocket that didn't exist here. The illusion cracked, fractured lines racing outward from where my hand met the glass.

The vision collapsed like a house of cards, and I snapped back into my own body with a force that left me gasping.

I was in my office, right where I'd left it. The lights were too bright; my paperwork untouched, the air suddenly heavy with the coppery tang of adrenaline. My skin was clammy, shirt plastered to my back with sweat.

My wolf came back in a rush, slamming into my consciousness with the force of a runner returning to a race after being benched. It paced, restless and unsatisfied, as if it knew exactly how close it had come to true extinction.

I sucked in a breath, forced my hands to steady, and looked around. Nothing was out of place, but everything had changed. I was the same man I'd always been, but the ground rules of my existence had shifted beneath my feet.

The only question now was how soon the Council would knock on my door in the real world.

And what they'd demand when they did.

I was still reeling from the aftershocks of the vision when I noticed the envelope.

It rested on my desk, dead center, too new for this world—thick, bone-white paper, sealed with a crest I didn't recognize. The very act of noticing it made my skin crawl; I'd been alone for hours, and nobody on this side of reality had come through the door.

I reached for it with the same caution I reserved for unexploded ordnance or a sleeping viper. The paper was heavy, textured, the kind that left dust on your fingertips. I cracked the seal with a thumbnail and slid out a single folded page. The ink was midnight blue, each letter calligraphed by hand, perfectly spaced.

Ryder "Doc" Lowrey,

You are hereby summoned before the Supreme Council of Supernaturals,

Two nights hence, at the hour of 2200.

Location: The Hall of Supreme Supernaturals, Chicago, Illinois.

There were no threats, no accusations, not even a reference to what, exactly, I was being summoned for. Just a time, a promise, and the expectation of compliance.

So that was that.

The Council didn't need to explain themselves. The invitation was an order, and the only alternative was running—a laughable strategy, given who and what would be sent to collect me. I'd spent enough years dodging things that went bump in the night to know you can't outrun a summons like this. You face it, or you don't face anything ever again.

But the memory of Lucia, pounding on that invisible wall, wouldn't leave me. Nor would the knowledge that whatever happened next was about more than just me.

I ran through the options. Bronc would want to know. Kazimir definitely would. Lucia... She'd break the world to protect me if I gave her half an excuse. Part of me wanted to shield her from it, but that was a lie. She was already neck-deep in this, whether I warned her or not.

I laughed, sharp and humorless. I'd survived actual war zones with less information and more at stake.

I set the summons back on my desk, retrieved my phone, and dialed the number of the man I trusted most in this world.

"Bronc," I said when he picked up. My voice sounded normal, calm, but I could hear the wolf in it, pacing. "We need to meet. Tonight."

He didn't ask questions, not over the line. "Usual place?"

"Yeah. And bring Luna if you can."

"Copy that."

"Talk to you soon."

I stood and took one last look around my office. The air was heavy with the scent of ink and fear. But somewhere in that mix, there was also resolve.

Two nights. That was all the time I had to set things right.

I owed it to Lucia. I owed it to the pack. And if the Council wanted a new piece on their board, they'd better be ready for a wild card. Fuck, they better be ready for an entire deck because I was coming, and I sure as shit was not coming alone.

The wolf inside me grinned, baring teeth in the dark.

It was time to fight.

CHAPTER 17

LUCIA

At three in the morning, when even the restless spirits of this land have resigned themselves to silence; my eyes snapped open to a cold emptiness at my side. Doc's place on his side of the bed was frigid. He'd never come home. Only an illusion of his scent lingered, quickly devoured by the air. A pit in my gut formed and took on an icy flavor. I could pretend it was nothing; that I could count on Doc to roll in with some legitimate reason for being away. But Doc was as dependable as the sunrise. He didn't do all-nighters without a text, a call—*something*. Ryder Lowrey was Mr. Reliable.

Some mates claimed they could sense their beloved's warmth from across continents. I reached for Ryder through our bond and felt... nothing. Not even the ever-present pulse of his wolf, the wild twin flame to his stoic, human side. The void gnawed at my bones.

He promised he'd be home by midnight. The echo of his voice from earlier—a calm, *"Go to bed, Lucia. I'll be along soon. Just a few things to finish"*—was now a taunt. My phone said 3:17, the digital face glowing in the gloom.

I hit Doc's number, but it rang five times and dropped straight to voicemail. I didn't leave a message. The second time, same deal. He never didn't take my calls. Especially in the middle of the goddamn night. No, this was bad. He was either incapacitated—or worse. I couldn't finish the thought.

I kicked the sheets off, stumbled out of bed, and pulled on the first things I found: black yoga pants, a faded Neon Moon t-shirt that belonged to Doc but he never had the heart to ask for back, and my tennis shoes. I was almost in a full-blown panic.

I could have driven, but the thought of buckling myself into the low-slung McLaren and carefully obeying speed limits while Doc might be bleeding out on the linoleum somewhere was just... no. My vampire was having none of that. I was faster on foot. The world blurred as I sprinted through the dewy grass, across the sleeping pack compound and down the hill toward Lowrey Hospital.

I tried Doc again. Still no answer.

The hospital loomed out on the prairie, state-of-the-art and glinting like a spaceship parked in the middle of Iron Valor wolf country. I slammed through the front door—thank you, keycard privileges, an upside to being the monster mated to the resident wolf/vampire Dr. McDreamy—and made a beeline for his office. Every footfall echoed like a gunshot. Each time my tennis shoes struck the tile, it was an accusation: Why weren't you fast enough? Why didn't you just call him at midnight like you thought about doing? Why is the only man who ever loved you a workaholic with a Superman complex?

The halls were dead quiet except for red rubber soles on tile. The only light came from the greenish glow of emergency exit signs and the faint shimmer of cleaning bots running their graveyard shift. My own heart was so loud it was almost annoying, and I willed it to shut up, to let me listen for anything. Doc's hospital was a fortress; there were cameras, sensors, and more alarms than the Fort Knox gift shop. But tonight, it might as well have been the Overlook Hotel. The emptiness crawled up my back.

Halfway down the east wing, I felt it: an arctic blast, the kind of cold that doesn't belong in a building kept at a steady 72, the kind of cold that bites all the way down to your immortal bones. It radiated from Doc's office, a shimmering frost halo around the door frame. I skidded to a halt, hackles up, every cell in my body screaming that something unnatural waited on the other side.

And then, just as suddenly, it vanished. The temp inside the office snapped from glacial to stifling, like a blast furnace had just kicked on. I pressed my hand to the door, felt the warmth flooding out, and for a second wondered if maybe I was the one having a stroke.

Papers rustled inside.

I shoved the door open so hard it slammed against the wall and rebounded. Doc was there, bent over his desk, a phone wedged between shoulder and ear, the blue glow of the computer screen washing his features out and making him look even more like a ghost. Except he wasn't—he was sweating, his hands shaking, and when he looked up at me, there was a mix of terror and wild relief I had never seen on his face. Not even when he'd first seen me in my father's foyer when we were both on the verge of fading away to nothing without each other.

"Bronc, I'll see you soon," he said, voice raspy. He hung up without waiting for a response, and in two steps he was around the desk and crushing me into him. His heart was doing its best impression of a hummingbird, and the bond between us finally blazed back to life, all tangled up and sharp with adrenaline and terror and a relief so fierce I could taste it in my throat. His eyes—hazel, gold-flecked, usually as steady as leveled guns—went soft with such a calm it almost broke me.

I buried my hands in his shirt and whispered, "Ryder. You're here."

He didn't answer. Just tightened his arms until I could barely breathe, his heart thudding like a frantic fist against my ribs. I felt everything he felt—his terror, his relief, his guilt. The bond was wide open, as if the walls between us had been blown apart.

"I couldn't sense you," I said into his collarbone, barely more than a breath. "I thought..."

"Lucia," he said, voice hoarse. "I thought I'd lost you."

We stood there a long time, the only sounds our heartbeats and the hum of the monitor on his desk.

Finally, Doc eased back, just enough to look at me. His eyes were bloodshot, but not from lack of sleep. I recognized the look: survivor's shock, raw and unhealed.

"What happened?" I asked.

He glanced over my shoulder, as if expecting someone to materialize behind me. "I had some kind of vision."

I wanted to laugh, because that was not a Doc thing to say. But something in the way he said it—the absolute conviction—made my mouth dry.

He still hadn't let go.

"Did it harm you?" I tried to inspect him, pushing back his sleeves, checking his pulse, looking for wounds. It was ridiculous; he was a supernatural now, stronger than anything short of a tank.

"Not physically, no," he said.

I didn't want to know. But I asked, because that's who I was, and because I'd never forgive myself if I didn't.

"What did you see?"

He swallowed, and for the first time I realized he was shaking. "I saw you gone. Like you never existed. And my wolf—" He shuddered. "I couldn't shift. Couldn't feel him. Couldn't feel myself. It was like being erased from the universe."

I pressed my forehead to his and let my relief wash over the both of us.

"I'm not going anywhere," I said. "You know that, right?"

He nodded, but the terror lingered in his eyes. I could tell he wanted to believe me, but he'd seen something he couldn't un-see.

"Tell me everything," I said. "No skipping the bad parts."

He drew a long breath, braced himself, and started to talk.

He didn't start with words. He started by folding himself onto the floor, right there in his office, knees drawn up as if to ward off a punch from the inside. I sat beside him, my back against his desk, the chill of it grounding. He took my hand, squeezed it until my bones creaked, and only then did he speak.

"Okay, so this isn't the first. They start out like a nightmare," he said. "First few times, I figured it was PTSD, or maybe just the new wiring in my head after..." He trailed off, unwilling to say *after you made me what I am*, which would've been bullshit. I'd saved him, but it changed him, and we both knew it. I knew he wasn't mad about it. It just was what it was.

"You know what a flashback feels like?" he asked, looking at our hands, not my face. "Like you're being forced to relive something, but you can't change the outcome, no matter what you do."

I nodded. "Da. I see my mother's death. My father's suffering."

He gave me a sympathetic nod. "These are different, though. Each time, they get more vivid, more real. First, I'm in the hospital, late shift, but the place is empty. All the lights are off. I'm looking for you, but you're gone. I try to shift, to run, and I can't." He flexed his fingers, as if the memory itself was enough to freeze him. "The next time, I'm cuffed to a chair. Silver. It burns. My wolf is howling, but it's not coming from me. It's... outside. And then..."

He stopped, knuckles white.

"Then what?" I prompted. I needed to know. Needed to stare down whatever monster was coming for us.

"I'm in a huge sort of cavernous stone room. There's a table. A slab of some sort. I'm wearing these cuffs. They make it so I can't access my wolf, my strength, nothing. Then I see Maltraz," he whispered. "He's not doing anything, just watching from the corner, with this... smile. And you're there, but not you. Shadow-you, like you're made of smoke. I yell for you, and the shadow just laughs, and then it's like I'm dying, but in slow motion. I can feel my wolf burning out of me, like someone turned off the moon. And when I wake up, I can't sense you. Not even a trace."

He looked at me, desperate for logic, for comfort.

"First time, I thought it was just stress. Then it happened a couple more times. Every time, it's more real. Tonight, I was wide awake when it hit. It was like—like I was outside of time, or time was inside me. I was terrified you'd vanished. I just came to, right before you came in. I was out for hours. Hours! Like whatever it was had control of me all that time. Fuck."

"I felt it," I said. "I woke up, and you were just... gone. Like you'd never been there. It made me sick."

He nodded, swallowing hard.

"Do you think it's possible?" he asked, voice gone thin. "That I'm seeing the future?"

I considered it. The supernatural world was a stew of powers, each more insane than the last. But even for us, visions of the future were rare. Costly, too. Nobody got them for free.

"Anything is possible," I said. "But if you can see the future, maybe you can change it. No?"

He frowned, and I could sense his doubt, thick and heavy. "I don't know. I was never the psychic kid. I was the science guy, the fixer. Now I'm a science experiment."

I smiled, reached up and brushed the sweat from his temple. "You're still *moy volk*. Maybe just supercharged, obviously."

That made him smile a small smile. "Don't get me wrong, I like having abs of steel and perfect vision, but I could do without the death prophecies. Although if they can help thwart the inevitable future, I'll take it."

"I'm glad you finally told me." I swallowed hard. "I actually have something to admit, too."

He looked at me, all focus, as if he'd forgotten his own problems entirely.

"My telekinesis has gotten... stronger. Sometimes things move with barely a thought. And..." I hesitated, not because I was scared of Doc, but because I was scared of what it meant. "I think I can somehow manipulate shadows. Not just hide in darkness, but actually... become it."

He stared, not blinking. "What do you mean?"

I looked around his office, which suddenly felt like the last place in the world for a conversation like this. Stacks of files, the sting of disinfectant, the cold blue glow of a computer screen left on in sleep mode, a whiteboard filled with his precise handwriting—medicine, order, reason. Nothing about this place fit what was happening to us.

"One time, in our bedroom," I said, "I saw my hand fade into the dark, like smoke. Only for a second. But then I tried to test it, and the more I focused, the more I felt like I could just... slip away. Lose myself in the dark. I didn't want to try it for real. Not until I talked to my father. Because I wasn't sure I could come back."

He covered my hand with both of his, even gentler now. "Why didn't you tell me?"

"Because I thought you needed time to adjust. And because I was scared you'd be scared."

He shook his head, squeezing me. "There is nothing about you that scares me, Lucia. Not even this. And now that I think about it; in my vision just now, you turned to smoke. That has to mean something."

"Shit." My mind was racing. "You're right. I don't know what is happening, but it's big."

We sat in silence. Doc's pulse was still erratic, but he was coming back to himself. Every minute, I could feel the mate-bond getting stronger, the gap closing.

"Do we tell the others?" I asked. "Or do we keep this between us?"

He thought about it, really thought, as was his way. "If I'm right, and something's coming for us—or for you—we need backup. You're not going anywhere alone, ever again."

I snorted. "Agreed. I never thought I'd need or want more than Juliet, my brothers, and my father in my life. I'm glad I was wrong. Life is better with more, even if all hell is coming at us."

"We're more alike in that way than you know my lioness. I've learned the hard way that life *is* better with more."

His smile broke through the tension a little. "But I agree, the next time you try the shadow thing, I want to be there with your father. Just in case."

"Same for you," I said. "No more secret visions. You must tell me so we can try to figure them out together."

We agreed with a small kiss.

We stood, and he picked up an envelope from his desk. His name was written in fancy scroll, and I immediately knew what it was. I had a feeling there would be an identical one waiting for me at home.

"This was on my desk when I came back to myself. Sort of suspicious, if you ask me. The Council or someone on the Council is aware of my visions or is behind the plans they have for me."

"Fuckers. We should call my father," I said, and Doc nodded.

Neither of us moved. Our bodies pressed close, mate-bond humming, anchoring us against whatever storm was coming. If we had to face the darkness, at least we'd do it together.

We wound up in Bronc's office. Juliet met us there as well. I needed her there to help ground me. Bronc's face held a worry I'd not often seen.

"You want to tell me why you sounded like you were about to chew your own hand off when you called earlier?"

Doc hesitated, then nodded to me. I squeezed his hand. "He needs to know everything."

We settled onto the leather couch in Bronc's office; Doc's arm around me and my head against his shoulder, both of us clinging to the mate-bond like it was the only thing keeping us from spinning off into the stratosphere. Juliet sat on my other side, clinging to my free hand.

Doc recounted everything: the visions, the fear, the sense of being erased. He kept it brief, clinical, but didn't hold back. When he finished, Bronc was quiet for a long time.

"Lucia," Bronc said finally, "did you feel anything like this?"

"I couldn't sense him," I admitted. "Not at all. It was like he'd been… unmade."

Bronc grunted. "Sounds like a fucking death omen or something to me. But let's not panic. Doc, what do you want to do?"

Doc's answer was immediate. "Well, clearly this summons dictates that we have to go to Chicago." He tossed the envelope onto Bronc's desk. "Need to talk to Menace and Kazimir, definitely. Get ahead of it. Talk to the Council, maybe any witches who might stand with us. For sure, need Archon. He may know if this is a warning or a curse."

Bronc barked out a low laugh. "Didn't take you for a guy who wanted a second opinion from witches, Doc."

"Neither did I," Doc said. "But I'm not taking chances. Not with Lucia."

Bronc's sigh was a white flag. "Okay. I'll call the others. Full complement is heading to Chicago. Spouses too."

"We have to leave by tomorrow," Doc said.

Bronc made a sound of approval. "I'll have the jet ready by dawn. Stay safe. Both of you."

We all stood. Juliet grabbed me and pulled me into a fierce hug.

"You're mine now, Lucia. Nobody messes with one of mine."

"Haven't things changed in a year *moya sestra*? You're not the same scared girl running from a monster. You've become the one who chases the monsters."

Juliet's eyes were wet with unshed tears.

"I'd never have escaped without you, my sister. You changed my life, and I'll be goddamned if anyone gets in the way of your happiness. I'll do whatever it takes to keep you and your mate safe."

I just nodded. No more words were needed.

My envelope was waiting on our kitchen counter when we entered the house. The cameras showed no one entering and no one exiting. The counter had been clear, then suddenly this envelope was there. Fucking magic.

I called Papa.

The phone rang twice before it connected, and his voice, rich and ancient and heavy with the weight of centuries, filled my ear. "Luchka. What's happened?"

"It's urgent," I said, and told him everything, even the parts I hadn't told Doc—the wild hunger for darkness, the feeling that the shadows wanted me to join them, the memories that weren't mine, that seemed to bleed into me from ancestors long dead. "Is this normal? For our kind?"

He was quiet for so long I thought the connection had failed. "No," he said finally. "But then, nothing about you has ever been normal. You are mine, which means you are unique. Born vampires were always rare, and always hated. It is said, when a vampire is born, the world will either accept them or want to end them."

That was not reassuring.

"But there are laws now, Papa. The Council—"

He made a low sound, almost a purr. "The Council is men and women like myself, playing at being gods. I will not let them harm you. Not now, not ever."

I tried to breathe, but the air was thick with his promise.

"Tell your mate," he said, "that he is not alone. That what he saw in his vision may be a warning, or a test, but it is not fate. You are not born to be erased. You are born to survive."

My chest burned with hope and dread. "Thank you, Papa."

"Do not thank me yet," he said, tone softening. "Prepare for war, my daughter. The world changes for people like us, or it destroys us. Stay close to your mate. Trust each other. And trust in the Goddess. She knows what she is doing, even when you do not."

He hung up.

Doc looked at me, brow furrowed. "What did he say?"

"He said we prepare for war."

Doc just nodded, like he'd expected nothing less.

We didn't talk after that. We just sat, the two of us alone in that terrible silence, mate-bond singing like a live wire between us. No matter what darkness was coming, I knew we'd face it together.

That was all the future I needed.

CHAPTER 18

DOC

We stepped off the tarmac into the weaponized glare of an Illinois spring, eyes squinting behind mirrored aviators, the lot of us dressed like we'd either stepped out of a high-end tactical catalog or a magazine ad for sports nutrition supplements. Parked at the bottom of the stairs, three black SUVs waited in a military-grade line of succession, each as matte and implacable as a shark's eye. The drivers stood at attention outside each vehicle, waiting for us to deplane. They nodded at us with the vacant, bulletproof politeness of career bodyguards as they opened the doors.

"Don't say 'men in black,'" Wrecker muttered in my left ear, low enough only I'd hear. "If you do, I'll shove you in the backseat with Parker and let her talk about Rocket for the entire ride." That damn ugly dog of hers was everything to her outside of hacking into highly secured servers.

"They're not even men," Parker replied, smirking, "unless you mean literal Renfields with GQ subscriptions." She shouldered her overnight duffel and nudged past Wrecker, who was now scanning the perimeter for snipers, shifters, or anyone worth punching before noon.

If there was ever a moment I felt like a supporting character in my own life, it was then, watching my brothers file into the SUVs like a very pretty, very expendable hit squad.

I waited for Lucia, who stood at the top of the stairs. She was deliberately last, jaw set and silhouette sharp against the white-hot sky. Black hair: perfect, as always. Makeup: just enough to say she'd worn it. Except for her lips. Those luscious, goddamn plump lips painted as red as blood with a shine that glimmered in the sun's glow. She looked down at me, and my chest did a funny, involuntary tripwire thing that made me almost forget the two-hundred-mile-an-hour context of this whole Goddess forsaken trip.

"You stare, Doc," she said, switching to the heavy Russian accent she exaggerated when annoyed. "Stare harder and your eyes will dry out."

"Pretty sure they're already dry. This is the Windy City, not St. Petersburg," I said, offering her my hand, which she ignored in favor of a five-inch heel landing directly next to my boots. She gave a long-suffering sigh, then stalked past me, not breaking stride as she knocked my shoulder with her purse. The scent—her scent, roses and honey with a hint of iron—lingered. I'd spent the past two hours trying not to think about that scent, or the way it made my fangs ache and want to descend.

We rode in silence, if you didn't count the clench-jawed breathing, the muttered obscenities from Wrecker (every time they hit a speed bump), or the constant flutter of Lucia's fingers across the touchscreen of her phone. Parker spent the drive pretending to nap, but every time I checked the rearview, her pupils were wide as coin slots, and her pulse thrummed at her wrist, visible just above the cuff of her denim jacket.

Big Papa and Aspen and that damn little prairie dog of hers, Oscar wearing a black jacket, vest, and a tiny cravat, were in the truck behind with Bronc and Juliet in tow. I couldn't believe that Juliet left the twins with Pearl. That's how serious the next two days were. And how much she loved Lucia.

Arsenal and Harper and Gunner and Brie rounded out our little army, taking up the final SUV. The Council may not realize it, but we were just mean enough to take them all down if pushed.

After winding our way through Chicago traffic and making it to the suburb of Highland Park, the SUVs pulled through a gate big enough to admit a tank. Past that, the driveway was all pale flagstone and precisely trimmed hedges, every square inch manicured to say, "You could disappear here and Google would delete your search results by lunch." The main house—no, estate—loomed above the drive. Faded red brick, cream trim, large windows, broad wings like the arms of a very pretty, very dangerous mother. And standing at the foot of the staircase: the butler. Six-two, snow-white hair, suit crisp enough to cut glass, posture that would make a Marine weep for his own lack of discipline.

He waited while the SUVs circled a large fountain and parked. Not just waited—performed a small, still opera of patience, like a chess piece that had never once considered being moved out of position.

Parker leaned close. "He's not even pretending to breathe. Watch."

We all watched. Not a blink, not a twitch. If someone had wheeled out a glass coffin, the guy would have climbed right in without wrinkling his shirt.

The doors opened in sequence, and we spilled out under the porte cochere. Lucia went first, her stilettos clicking off flagstone as she pulled up to the butler and—God love her—stared him down like she was the owner and he was just part of the landscaping.

"Princess Lucia Kozlov and escort," she said, with that cold, crispy authority that made you want to salute, or maybe run a mile and a half in under six minutes.

He bowed perfectly at the waist. "Miss Kozlov, welcome home. Your father is indisposed in conference, but asked that you and your companions make yourselves comfortable."

Wrecker grinned at "companions," probably because he'd already decided that sounded like code for 'pack of heavily armed assholes with nowhere better to be.'

The butler turned his gaze on me, and my wolf almost recoiled. No heartbeat. No scent but the faint, arid tang of something centuries old. I'd seen vamps do the predator-stare before, but this was next-level—if I blinked first, I was sure he'd pounce.

Instead, he smiled. "Mister Lowrey, I trust your journey was pleasant?"

"Efficient," I said, measuring the handshake he offered. Skin: marble-cold. Grip: fractionally too hard, as if he enjoyed the way my bones flexed.

"Please, this way," he said, and turned on a dime, leading us up the steps and into the shade of the portico.

Inside, the air dropped twenty degrees and switched from azaleas to expensive cologne and freshly cut lilies. We moved as a unit through the foyer, our boots and heels echoing against marble. The butler narrated as we went. "Your quarters are in the West Wing, as requested. Should you require anything, the house staff is at your service. Brunch will be served at precisely eleven o'clock in the Blue Room. The pool, fitness suite, and armory are at your disposal."

"Armory?" Arsenal said, lighting up.

"Of course. His Excellency believes all guests should be afforded the means to protect themselves, should the need arise."

He led us down a hallway lined with oil portraits and glass display cases. Every ten feet, another vampire waited, motionless, like a museum docent who'd forgotten to die. The butler stopped at a set of double doors and held them open.

The suite was bigger than our whole damn pack house basement. There was a wet bar, a billiards table, and couches in a U-shape around a TV the size of a billboard. Windows overlooked a pool sparkling so blue it almost hurt. And there, on the wet bar, were two glasses of blood wine set out with the same impersonal precision as a hotel mint.

The butler set our luggage down himself. "If you require breakfast, please dial zero. Should you need medical attention, and your doctor is not available; Doctor Hall is on call."

I smirked. "Is he human or...?"

"She is... competent," he replied, with just enough bite to make Wrecker snort.

Parker walked over to the window and pulled back a blackout curtain. She looked back at me, then at Lucia. "Are we prisoners or guests?"

Lucia shrugged. "Both, I think." She touched my wrist, and I felt her magic buzz underneath her skin—low-level, not the kind that could melt a man in place, but enough to send my pulse up a couple notches. I caught her eye and smiled, a private joke: if we had to, we could burn this place to the ground in under five minutes.

The butler cleared his throat. "His Excellency will join you at brunch." With that, he vanished, the doors clicking closed with a hush that was either supernatural or just very good craftsmanship.

For a second, we all stood there, listening to nothing. I heard the flutter of Juliet's pulse, the shift of Bronc's weight, the faint hum of air conditioning.

Wrecker made a noise. "I give it three hours before someone tries to kill us. Anyone want to start a pool?"

Bronc shot him a look. "For Christ's sake, would you cut it the fuck out? This is Lucia's family home. Kazimir is our friend."

Wrecker had the sense to at least look contrite. "Sorry, Boss."

It was Juliet's turn to let us have it. "If you could try to be on your best behavior, please, boys? You're representing Iron Valor here. We already have a shoot first ask questions later reputation. I'm not suggesting we don't shoot if the situation calls for it, but let's try not to kill anyone yet, hmm?"

Bronc looked at his mate, and I swear I saw hearts in his eyes. She was perfect for him.

"Listen to your Luna." He smiled down at her and gave her a kiss.

I ran a quick scan on the crew—old habits die hard. Parker: shallow breaths, adrenaline dump. Wrecker: baseline, but amped, which meant he was either ready for a fight or about to crack an inappropriate joke. Lucia: cool on the outside, but her hand trembled for a microsecond before she snatched a blood wine and sipped. Big Papa: always cool under pressure was scanning the windows. Arsenal: loved a good fight, seemed to want to protect Harper at all costs.

But Gunner was loaded for bear. He wanted Maltraz more than anyone. That bastard had kidnapped his mate just weeks ago, and he wanted his pound of flesh.

My own heartbeat was steady, but higher than normal, even after a lifetime of emergencies. I chalked it up to the unfamiliar: the glitter of the glass, the perfection of the setting, the circumstances of us being here in the first place.

Lucia leaned close and whispered, "Try to relax. My father values hospitality above all else."

I grinned. "Princess, you think I want to offend your daddy?"

She grinned. "Not on purpose. But tact isn't necessarily your strongest suit."

That stung, just a little.

Gunner was already at the TV, trying to figure out which remote did what. "You think he'll be in a coffin when we meet him?" he called out.

I looked at him. "Please don't ask him if he sleeps in a coffin you fucking moron."

Bronc agreed. "What he said."

I caught Aspen's gaze. "What are you thinking?"

She shook her head a little. "I don't know, Doc. Something feels very serious about this whole thing. I don't mean Kazimir. I trust him with my life. I mean the circumstances of this meeting. The entire thing stinks to high holy heck. I'm glad my dad will be there. We may need to meet with him separately."

I was glad to hear that. She's intuitive. Papa sidled up next to her and put his massive hand on my shoulder.

"We've got your back, brother."

Having my brothers here meant everything to me.

The suite Kazimir assigned to us was obscene. It was all moody grays and cold marble, with a centerpiece king canopy bed shrouded in a midnight-blue comforter and pillows that shimmered like dusted silver under the chandelier's hung crystals. I wondered if Kazimir had chosen this color scheme for our room so it would remind us of our home. It was damn thoughtful if so.

Lucia stalked the room's perimeter with her usual measured contempt, running one manicured finger over the gold leaf on the bed's carved posts, the mirrored surface of the armoire, the hardware of the French doors that led to a marble balcony and a view of the pool below. She paused there, back to me, silhouetted by the thin gauze of daylight that found its way around the blackout drapes.

I dropped our hanging bags on the fainting couch at the end of the bed and started to unpack, because the ritual of folding and stacking was the only thing keeping my hands from doing what they wanted: to close the distance between me and her, to bury themselves in her hair, her skin, anything she'd let me touch.

If she noticed me watching, she didn't show it. Instead, she sighed—a small, deliberate exhale, like a performer hitting her mark on stage—and pulled her hair loose from its clip. It fell in a black silken curtain down her back. The tension in her spine was impossible to miss, a tightness that went bone-deep.

"Lucia," I said, keeping my tone as clinical as I could, "we have maybe an hour before brunch."

I stepped behind her, close enough to feel the static rising from her skin. I pressed my lips to her shoulder, just below the line of her sweater, and felt the shudder run through her. "We both need to feed. I need more, though. You look good enough to eat." I said with a grin.

"You are always so American." She laughed, but her voice was threaded with something raw and dark. "All optimism and sex jokes."

"I'm all about efficiency," I said, sliding my hands around her waist, "and right now, my diagnostic tells me you're at eighty percent capacity for stress. That's medically inadvisable. We should…"

She spun so fast I barely registered it, and buried her fingers in my hair. Her eyes were fully dark, wide and wet, and dangerous. The perfume of her skin called to me; to my wolf. It was a lure, and I was the prey she'd willingly trapped. She pressed her mouth to mine, hard, and I tasted the force of her power, copper and iron.

Her hands found the buttons of my shirt and dispatched them with surgical brutality, popping two clean off and sending them skittering across the carpet. Her nails scraped my chest, leaving lines that were hot and tingling and would have bled if I'd been human. I let her push me back onto the bed, following her down in a controlled fall.

She straddled me, knees planted on either side of my thighs, and stared down with that predatory, appraising look that was hunger disguised as a beautiful face. "You want me to take the edge off, yes?"

"I want you to take everything," I said. It sounded needy, maybe a little pathetic, but after a day without her teeth in my veins, without the dizzying rush of her magic was one day too many. There was no point in pretending otherwise.

She leaned in and bit my lower lip, not quite breaking the skin, then ran her tongue along the crease. The world compressed to the three points where our bodies touched: her thighs around my waist, her hands in my hair, her breath hot in my ear. My pulse thundered. My wolf surfaced and wanted to howl.

She pulled back, lips parted, cheeks flushed in a way that was impossible for most vampires, but she wasn't most vampires. "You still fear what you are?" she whispered.

"Not anymore," I said, and I meant it. The old terror—the one I'd carried since the night she'd saved me, changed me, made me more than a wolf and basically a vampire—had faded. What replaced it was raw, unfiltered craving.

She reached down and peeled the cashmere over her head in one motion. Underneath: a creamy lace bra, the kind designed to be looked at and then destroyed. She arched just slightly, a cat stretching for the sun. I reached up, traced the curve of her ribs with my thumb, felt the pulse of her magic under the surface.

She laughed, low and smoky. "You look at me like you are starving."

"I am."

She slid her hands under my shoulders and pressed her body flush against mine. I ran my tongue up her neck, found the spot just below her jaw where the vein pulsed, impossibly fast for a vampire. I kissed it, then bit, just enough to leave a mark. She shivered, ground her hips against me, the friction sending an electric jolt all the way to my toes.

"It was thoughtful of Papa to put us in this room. Do you know why?" she asked, voice muffled by my skin.

"To remind us of our home. So we remember we have somewhere worth fighting for. Somewhere good to go back to."

She stilled. "Yes. I think so. Because we are good together. Better together."

I held her gaze for a moment. "I never would have known it if I hadn't died that day. If you hadn't saved me."

Her kiss was passionate as she slid her hand between us, palmed me through my jeans, and I bucked up, unable to play it cool even if I tried. She undid my belt and zipper with a flick of her wrist, and before I could say a word, my jeans were gone and she was on me, mouth hot and greedy. I gripped the back of her head, not to guide her but to steady myself, and try not to lose it in the first thirty seconds.

Her hands were everywhere: on my thighs, my hips, my stomach. She raked her nails down my skin, and I felt the cuts heal as quickly as they formed. When I pulled her up to kiss her, I tasted blood—my own, mingled with her spit—and the combination made my vision swim.

I pushed her back, reversed our positions, pinned her wrists above her head. She wriggled, testing my grip, but when she saw I wasn't going to let go, she went still, eyes bright as polished onyx.

"You need to feed." She demanded, her voice was rough.

"I do." I wanted her blood. Needed it.

"Take *moya lyubov*."

I bit her hard at the juncture of her shoulder and neck. The blood was hot, alive with magic, and sweeter than anything I'd ever tasted. It filled my mouth, and I felt my body absorb it like a plant soaking up the sun. My mind blazed white, all thoughts replaced by sensation. It always affected me this way. I wondered if it always would. She filled every corner of my mind. Our bond pulsed hotter; her feelings, wants, needs, became my own.

When I pulled away, her eyes were wild. She twisted her hands free, flipped me with a strength reserved for vampires alone. She ran her tongue across my shoulder at the junction of my neck, and bit. The sensation sent me higher. I pistoned into her as she sucked my blood into her mouth. She released, then bit my chest, and the passion started to rise again. I wanted to crawl inside her body.

The orgasm, when it hit, was almost secondary to the rush of her power inside me, a storm of ice and fire that collapsed every barrier I'd ever built. I saw stars. I saw visions: Lucia standing over a throne of bones, me at her feet, my pack howling in the dark.

I came back to myself gasping, her face inches above mine, lips smeared red. She licked them clean and smiled, slow and satisfied.

"You good?" she said, voice a rasp.

"Perfect," I said, and meant it.

We lay tangled together for a long minute, the only sounds our breathing and the faint thump of distant music from somewhere in the house. The wolf in me was satisfied, having taken his mate and marked her in every way.

She curled onto my side, head on my chest. "You think we are monsters?"

I thought about it. "I am a new species, and you are my creator. Monsters destroy things."

She laughed, soft. "You are such a nerd, Ryder."

"Can't help it."

I lay on my back and stared at the ceiling's plaster medallion through the sheer fabric of the bed's canopy. My heartbeat slowed from gallop to trot, and with every beat, I felt the raw pulse of her magic burrow deeper into my veins. I'd never understood the appeal of postcoital silence—until Lucia.

She rolled away, flopped onto the pillows, and stared at the far wall with the thoughtful frown of someone mentally disassembling and reassembling a Glock nineteen. I reached across the comforter, found her wrist, and circled it with my hand. Her skin was warmer now—an impossibility for vampires, unless you'd just consumed half a pint of hybrid shifter and a pint of your own adrenaline.

I pulled her arm gently, and she let me lead. We padded to the en-suite bathroom, which was bigger than the average Dairyville single-wide. The shower was a glass-and-marble cathedral, showerheads sprouting from the walls like something from a dystopian spa. I grabbed a hair tie from her toiletry bag and carefully pulled her hair up in a messy bun. She groaned, an honest, grateful sound, and rested her chin on my shoulder as I twisted the dial. Hot water hammered down on us.

We washed each other in silence, my hands mapping every inch of her skin, cataloguing old scars and the new marks she'd left. She returned the favor, digging her nails into my scalp, tracing my jawline, scrubbing until the blood from our bites ran pink and then clear down the drain. There was nothing sexual in it, not now—just the careful choreography of two animals tending each other's wounds.

When we were clean, I wrapped her in a towel and dried the base of her hair. We dressed in parallel, moving around each other with the ease of people who'd spent entire lifetimes together, even if we'd barely managed two months. She selected a black satin wrap dress; minimal but perfect. I chose slacks and a button-down, rolled up the sleeves, and used her hair dryer to give my hair a quick dry.

She watched me in the mirror, eyes narrow and amused. I watched her, too—the way she adjusted her lipstick, the way she fastened a silver locket at her throat. I wanted to ask if it was a ward, a weapon, or just an accessory. I knew better than to ruin the peace with a question.

When she was ready, she stood beside me at the vanity and met my eyes in the reflection. She smirked, lips curving just enough to show her teeth. I grinned back, more wolf than man for a second.

No words needed.

I checked my phone: ten forty-eight. If Kazimir's butler said "precisely eleven," he meant it.

I held out my arm. She slipped hers through. Together, we left the suite, walking in step down the hall—our bond humming, our bodies sated, and the whole future balanced on the tip of a knife.

We were monsters. We were pack. And today, we were ready for whatever king or council wanted to throw at us.

CHAPTER 19

LUCIA

The blue room had a name—"Sapphire Banquet Salon"—but my father's penchant for pageantry meant it was always painted anew in each guest's mind. Today, the space shimmered a pre-dawn cobalt, somewhere between royalty and bruise. The wall of arched windows framed the blooming trees along the Schuylkill, and a thin gray light washed the table in icy silk. The table itself—a monstrous piece of custom-cut walnut with legs carved in the style of something predatory and extinct—looked as though it might run off on its own if given half a chance.

We arrived early. Old habit: my father never tolerated lateness, not for brunch, not for assassinations, not for the sort of mid-morning blood feud brunches that defined "family time." Doc trailed behind me, his hair tousled in a way that made him look more beach bum than apex predator, though the glint in his hazel eyes spoke to the opposite. He was perpetually off-kilter in these settings—an effect I privately cherished.

"Always first, *kotyonok*," my father said from his throne at the table's head. Not a literal throne, but close enough: high-backed, velvet, the armrests shaped like twin obsidian lions. The sight of him was almost comical in its extravagance. He wore a black three-piece with a damask vest and a purple satin shirt open at the throat, and his hair—long, blue-black, and glossy—cascaded over one shoulder like a scarf. He was beautiful the way tigers are beautiful. To look away was unwise.

Doc stopped a pace behind me, eyes dropping automatically to my father's cufflinks. Even the most battle-scarred wolf knew to tread gently before the king of all vampires. "Sir."

Kazimir's glacier-blue gaze flickered over Doc, then returned to me. "Sit, Lucia. And your... mate, as well."

He could have used the term "companion," and the fact that he had called Doc "mate" spoke volumes. There was an unspoken dare in the word, an expectation that the arrangement would not fail, or combust, and would, at the very least, produce something worth watching. My father trusted in us.

I stared at him for a moment, at the way his eyes seemed to swallow all the light and reflect none back. I wondered, as I always did, how a man who owned a sex club and a multinational criminal empire could look so utterly untouched. The centuries had not left even the ghost of a wrinkle. Not on his skin. Not on his heart, either, it sometimes seemed.

He caught my gaze and offered a small, private smile. "You look well, Lucia."

"Thank you, Papa," I said, in English. I'd abandoned Russian with him years ago; it always made me feel six and foolish.

The double doors opened again, and the rest of the guests poured in: Bronc and Juliet first, all brawn and pressed denim, and my best friend who gave my father the smile of a daughter. Then Wrecker and Parker excitedly eyed the food as though they were starving. Big Papa, Aspen, Arsenal and Harper followed, chatting as they came through the large double doors. They greeted the others with radiant smiles and hugs. Then, finally, Gunner and Brie rushed in, straightening their clothes. We all knew what they'd been up to. A few eyebrows raised as they quickly took their seats.

Every chair filled, and still the table seemed empty in the center. The platters were there—cured salmon sliced thin as a lover's sigh, little towers of crepes, croissants, caviar nested in mother-of-pearl spoons, and fruit so vibrant I suspected it had been flown in fresh. There were eggs too, sausages, and bacon for the carnivores, and a carafe of orange juice and a thermal container of coffee.

Doc eyed the food. I felt him reach out, through that strange new part of our bond, to test if I was hungry. I could sense the way he catalogued the room—me first, then my father, then the exits, then the knives—and something about it made me want to laugh and cry at the same time.

I'd fed already, and so had Doc. The bruise on my shoulder was already gone. Vampires heal fast, but nothing compared to what we were becoming. Every day we grew stronger, becoming more. My father watched us now with a scientist's curiosity, a king's detachment, and the oddest hint of something else: pride.

He poured himself a glass of whatever the carafe contained (the color of raw rubies; probably not V8) and held it out to me. "To new alliances, *kotyonok*. May they be less troublesome than the old ones."

I clinked my glass to his, and he drank deeply, lips stained for just a second before returning to their usual colorless perfection.

"Thank you for the invitation, Kazimir," Bronc said, with a small bow of the head. His familiarity was a testament to the friendship they'd cultivated over the years.

My father inclined his head, gracious as a pope. "It is my pleasure to host. These are... interesting times." He shot a look at Doc, who had started eating. "I'm glad to see you eating, Doctor. Your metabolism is impressive. I would not want you to faint at the Council meeting tomorrow."

Doc's ears turned red, which amused me more than it should have. He muttered thanks and reached for more of the salmon. His hands, I noticed, did not shake. A few weeks ago, that would not have been the case.

Aspen, with a dapper Oscar by her side, raised a glass. "So. Council meeting. Any last-minute tips, Lucia?"

Before I could answer, my father did. "The person you need to watch for is Otero. Do not let him get under your skin. He feeds on chaos and confusion, and he will try to make you doubt your own nature." He said it with such calm, such utter boredom, that I knew he'd already planned for every possible outcome.

"Council sessions can be boring, right?" Gunner asked, with a small grin. "Or do they bring in circus bears for entertainment?"

"In Philadelphia, we use lawyers instead of bears," my father replied. "More vicious. Less fur."

Bronc snorted. "I don't know; have you met our representation?"

Even Doc managed a smile at that.

The rest of brunch passed in a blur of conversation and clattering dishes and not a small amount of tension. My father asked questions, polite but never quite harmless, and I answered them as best I could. There were small jokes, little moments of levity, but underneath it all ran a vein of dread, as icy and unyielding as my father's stare.

When the meal was finished, my father stood, and the entire room fell silent. He surveyed us all for a long moment, then looked at Doc.

"Walk with me, Doctor Lowrey," he said. It was not a request.

Doc met my gaze. His eyes said, Should I go? My nod was almost imperceptible. Yes. My father was not to be denied.

He followed my father out, their footsteps echoing down the marble hallway.

For a moment, I let myself breathe.

Juliet leaned over, voice low. "How are you really doing?"

I thought of Doc, of the new hunger in him, of the way my father watched us both like a chess player with too many queens. I thought of the Council, and Otero, and all the wars that had been fought with handshakes instead of guns.

"I'm... ready," I lied.

Juliet squeezed my hand, but said nothing.

I watched the doorway, waiting for Doc to return. Wondering if I'd sent him into the lion's den or to his confirmation.

My father, ever the gracious host, vanished with Doc for exactly twenty-three minutes—long enough for his guests to wonder if they should pretend everything was normal, or if they should send out a search party. He returned with Doc in tow. They moved in tandem, not predator and prey, but two surgeons scrubbing in for the same unexpected autopsy.

Doc's jaw was set, the bone white beneath his tan, but his eyes were clear and wild. I felt a flicker of him in my mind, a pulse of electricity: annoyance, curiosity, and something with serrated edges.

My father took his seat at the head of the table, the rest of us drawn in a crooked circle around him. He steepled his fingers and regarded us as if waiting for a jury to deliver a verdict.

"So," he said, slicing through the silence, "tomorrow's Council session will be... unorthodox."

"Unorthodox how?" Bronc rumbled, stretching his arms over the back of a chair. It was a calculated display of casual aggression—Bronc hated feeling outnumbered, and this house was nothing if not full of vampires and ghosts.

Papa smiled, all teeth, no warmth. "They have never summoned a shifter-vampire hybrid before. They do not know what you are, Doctor, and nothing terrifies the Council more than novelty."

Doc ran a hand through his hair. "I don't see what right they have to question me. I didn't ask for any of this," His voice was calm, but the words vibrated with a suppressed howl. I could sense the muscle memory of old wounds: years of being the outlier, the oddity, the problem to be solved.

My father nodded. "Precisely. That is your best defense. The Council is accustomed to power plays, not honest confusion." He glanced at me. "But they will try to provoke you. To force a display of your... uniqueness."

Parker leaned in, voice low. "Who started this whole 'witch hunt'?"

Papa's fingers tapped a drumbeat on the table. "My best guess is Varek Otero. He has been plotting something like this for decades, perhaps centuries. He is very clever, but not as clever as he thinks."

Bronc, arms crossed, grunted. "What's his angle? Why does it matter if Doc is... what he is?"

My father's eyes glittered. "Because there has not been a hybrid of this nature since the Dark Years. The Council fears disruption. Otero sees opportunity. He hopes to create precedent: to cage the wolf, to bind the vampire. To make all our kind just a little less free."

I felt Doc's hand brush my knee under the table. He didn't squeeze, didn't demand comfort, just made contact. It grounded him, and it grounded me.

"Sounds like he wants a war," Bronc said.

He shrugged with an elegance that made it clear he'd shrugged off greater threats than this. "He wants a bigger crown. The war is just a means."

Doc's voice cut in: "Can you tell us what to expect, specifically? I don't want to walk in blind."

My father's lips twisted, pleased. "Yes. They will begin with the ceremonial, the posturing. They will invite testimony, most of it irrelevant. Then they will ask you to perform." He made the word sound obscene. "You will be asked to prove your loyalty to one world or the other."

"That's ridiculous," Doc snapped. "I belong to both."

"Exactly." His gaze landed on me, then lingered. "And now, so does Lucia. She belongs to you as your mate, so she belongs to the Iron Valor Pack. She is also my daughter. She is the Princess of the Kozlov Vampires. She is both. And you," he looked directly at Doc, "By being her mate and a wolf/vampire hybrid with Kozlov blood flowing through your veins, are a Prince of the Kozlov line and thus belong to both."

Doc swallowed hard at the realization that my father considered him part of our family's bloodline.

The proclamation sent a small shockwave through everyone at the table as they realized my father had just declared Ryder as a prince in the Kozlov line. Of course, Wrecker was the most vocal.

"I'll be goddamned. Iron Valor now has a king with Menace, two princesses with Aspen and Lucia, and now a prince with Doc listed among our officers and mates. Are we gonna build a castle and install a moat next, or what?"

Bronc gave him a look that would freeze the blood of most men.

"How 'bout I install my boot in your ass, Wrecker?"

He cleared his throat, knowing their Alpha was in no mood for his smart-assery. "Apologies, Sir."

I felt the flush creep up my throat, a heat that was more anger than embarrassment. "If that Council tries to…"

"They will not touch you, *kotyonok*," my father said, soft but unmovable. "Not while I breathe."

The words should have comforted me, but there was a finality to them I did not like.

My father flicked a crumb from his sleeve and turned to Doc. "They may ask for your blood and to shift. To show both your natures." His eyes narrowed. "Can you do so at will?"

Doc hesitated. I felt him think through his answer, weighing what to admit. "Of course I can shift. They'll be shocked at my wolf I'm afraid. I've only revealed him to Lucia."

All eyes turned to him.

"He's big. Like, really big, and his eyes. They glow red."

Gunner looked awed. "Fuck me."

"There is no crime in having a large animal. I'd hesitate to give them your blood. It's new. I don't want them trying to synthesize it." He seemed deep in thought.

Juliet tapped her nails against the table. "What's the play if things go sideways?"

My father's smile was slow and sharkish. "If they attack, we kill them. Simple enough."

Bronc laughed, a short bark. "Wouldn't that start a supernatural incident?"

He spread his hands. "No one alive has seen a true vampire king's power in several centuries. They have forgotten what it means. If they wish for demonstration, I am happy to oblige."

Bronc met his gaze, not blinking. "You truly hold back don't you?"

My father's expression went soft, almost wistful. "I rule on reputation. It's possible demonstrations have to be made periodically. I'd prefer this not to be the case. I enjoy my life and rule as it is. I have children. Empires are for those who wish to die alone."

He let that hang in the air.

Harper spoke for the first time, voice trembling but clear. "If Otero's such a weasel, why do you let him get away with this?"

My father leaned back, considering her. "History lesson?" he asked, not really a question. "Nearly a thousand years ago, the Old World vampires warred among themselves for dominance. In the end, there was a vicious trial designed by the Goddess. The sovereign bloodline would be proven by survival—by who would be left standing. I did not seek the throne, but I won it by existing when all others fell." He sipped from his goblet, unhurried. "All vampires, even those not of my making, are bound to me; subject to me and me alone. Some, like Otero, resent this."

"So you came to America to get away from ruling?" Arsenal asked, incredulous.

My father smiled, rueful. "I came to America for change. The land is vast. The people, optimistic. For a time, it was enough."

He cast his gaze down the table, to where Doc and I sat. "But peace is fragile. Every age produces its own monsters. Otero negotiated for his territory—he wanted the West, and I did not care to argue. He thinks this makes him my equal." The contempt in his voice was glacier-cold.

Bronc spoke, voice low and steady. "You think he's working with Maltraz?"

His eyes burned. "He is too smart to get his hands dirty. But he and Maltraz both want to hurt me. And make no mistake, they want to hurt Iron Valor as well. If they can do it with Council tricks, so much the better."

The air thickened. Everyone at the table felt it. Tomorrow, the old games would play out with new pieces. For all my father's calm, the risk was real: if Otero's plan worked, if Doc or I faltered, the future of the entire supernatural world might tip.

Chapter 20

Doc

My brain wouldn't quit, not even at 4:00 AM with the air conditioner humming like a distant hive and Lucia's leg thrown across my thigh, her heel hooked at the edge of my boxers in a way that meant "mine." Her hair fanned over my chest, wild as black ink in water, one small fist curled beneath her chin. I traced the line of her spine down to the hollow where the sheet dipped over her ass and tried to count my blessings. Or count my fucking pulse, which was now a fifty-fifty shot at being measured in beats or whatever new metric the undead used.

Recently, I'd been a wolf shifter. Combat medic, surgeon, Clark Kent to this crew of superhero freaks. Today? I was a fucking hybrid wolf/vampire prince. The newest, rarest kind of monster in the country. Lucia's blood sang through my veins—her power, her scent, her anger, her need. I was still me, still a wolf beneath the skin, but every cell knew its new master, and the master wore red lipstick and could snap your femur with a look.

If I'd had an ounce of sense, I'd have let her let me bleed out on that rock outside Palo Duro Canyon. Sometimes you see the crossroads and walk away, anyway. But even half-dead, I'd never been the type. She'd bitten her wrist open for me, let her lifeblood pour into my mouth like communion wine, and now here I was, pondering the mechanics of eternity with her naked and warm in my bed.

It was the "with her" that caught me, snared me with all the ugly precision of a surgical suture. What had I gotten myself into? More important, when had I stopped thinking about her as a dangerous flirtation and started counting on her as a necessity? It must've crept up on me, all those nights she'd crashed around the compound while we waited for the various fucking battles we always seemed to be fighting these days. The way she handled a blade or a handgun with equal joy. The way she wore her loneliness like a diamond necklace—dazzling, hard, unmissable.

My wolf, whatever he was now, adored her with a fever I'd never let surface before. My new side—call it the vampire, call it the man who got back up off that rock—craved her like she was the first breath after drowning. I was hungry for her blood, sure, but I'd also kill to see her laugh or get her started on Dostoyevsky and watch her hands animate the air.

She stirred, lips parting in a silent protest, and I felt the little tug on our bond—a pulse of concern, the echo of my own unrest. It shamed me a little. She deserved better than this mess. Maybe I should've died. Maybe she should've let me. But when I pictured a world without her, the urge to curl up and fade to dust was worse than any fear of the unknown.

"Stop that," she mumbled, her accent syrupy from sleep. "You are vibrating with the gloom again."

I kept my hand tracing little circles at the base of her spine. "I didn't know I was broadcasting."

"Please. Your feelings are like a fire alarm in a tiny Russian apartment." She yawned and propped her chin on my chest, squinting up with those bottomless onyx eyes. "Tell me what you are thinking, Ryder."

Her voice, sleep-rough, hit me in the gut. No matter how many times she called me by my first name—rare, precious—I never got used to the gravity she gave it. Ryder. Not "Doc," not "*volk*," not any of the usual epithets she flung at my brothers. For her, I made sense as a man first.

I tried to play it off with a shrug. "Just recalibrating. Bit of an identity crisis."

She wriggled closer, thigh pressed tight to mine, and slid a palm up my chest. "You are strongest man I know, Doc. You could have died. Instead, you are here. With me. Council can go fuck itself."

I tried to smirk, but my lips were uncooperative. "The Council wants to see what happens when you mix two apex predators. My guess is they fear a lot of dead lab techs and a janitorial nightmare."

That got a laugh, one of those low, husky notes that said I'd earned another day in her orbit. "You think you are a monster now?" she asked, nuzzling my jaw.

I caught her face between my hands, rough thumbs brushing the sleep from under her eyes. "No. I think I'm myself, just with upgrades. But—Lucia, I don't know what happens if we lose this thing today. I don't want to lose you."

Her expression sobered; all humor leached away. "You will not lose me. Unless you get dramatic and throw yourself in front of a bullet or something stupid like that. And even then..."

I grinned for real this time, letting her see it. "Not planning on it. You're a terrible nurse."

She rolled her eyes, all drama and dark lashes. "So ungrateful. Some people die; then they are not dead and they say thank you."

I bent and kissed her, slow and deep, letting my fangs press against the inside of her lip but not break the skin. She let out a little moan—just for me, no performance—and I felt her hunger spark through the bond, a live wire tripping every nerve in my body.

"I need you," I said, and it wasn't a line. "More than I should."

Her smile turned dangerous. "Show me."

She pushed me down, her weight pressing on me. Lucia was small but stronger than most, all legs and hips and muscle, and she moved with a predatory grace that always left me disarmed. She straddled me, palms flat on my chest, hair sweeping across my chest.

The wolf in me wanted to flip her, take control, but the new instincts were different—more patient, more attuned to pleasure than to dominance. He'd have his turn. My senses were overloaded: her scent, her heartbeat, the way her skin flushed when she was aroused. I reached for her hip, but she pinned my hand above my head and grinned.

"Not yet," she whispered. "You will let me, yes?"

I nodded, biting back a groan. She leaned down, tongue tracing my collarbone, then the vein in my neck. I felt the cool press of her fangs, the anticipatory sting, and then...

God, if I thought wolf endorphins were a rush, the hit of her teeth in my throat was pure chemical euphoria. I felt her drink, the slow pull and the pulse of her own pleasure feeding back into me. My hips arched off the bed. My hands—still pinned—scrabbled for purchase, but she held me firm. My control was slipping.

She drank deep enough to make my head spin, but not enough to leave me weak. She released, then sealed the wound with a flick of her tongue, and immediately kissed me, sharing back a taste of my own blood.

"You taste like power," she whispered, and I could hear the awe in it. "Like a storm and starlight."

I paused, wanting to say something but not sure what. "I want you more with every fucking passing day."

She nodded, voice thick. "I want you. All of you."

I took control of her body and switched her onto her back. Her eyes were glazed with lust and power, and I knew she'd relinquished the control to me, but my wolf wanted to claim it. I ran my nose up and down the length of her neck; her fragrance of roses filled my senses before I bit. Her gasp was the most beautiful thing I'd ever heard. Her blood was rich, filled with strength and her arousal. I wanted to own this moment; to own her.

Her blood was on my tongue, fucking electric, primal, and thick with the heady perfume of her essence. Lucia. My Lucia. My warrior, my queen, my fucking everything. I couldn't stop tasting her, couldn't stop feeling her pulse thrumming beneath my lips, her veins hot and inviting as I drank her down. Jesus Christ, she was intoxicating, her essence flooding my veins, lighting me up like a goddamn inferno. My cock was already rock-hard, throbbing with need, strained against the fabric of my boxers.

I ripped them off, the fabric tearing like paper beneath my strength. I didn't give a shit about gentleness—Lucia didn't need it. She was an ancient huntress, carved from marble and steel, her body trembling with raw power as she clawed at my chest, her nails leaving angry red welts that healed almost instantly. Her breasts were perfect, bouncing with every ragged breath, her nipples hard and begging for my tongue. I took one into my mouth, sucking hard, biting down just enough to make her gasp and arch into me.

"Doc," she moaned, her voice low and rough, like whiskey and sin. "Fuck me. Don't you dare hold back."

I didn't need the invitation. I ground my hips against hers, my cock sliding against her slick, wet pussy. Christ, she was soaked, her arousal pooling between her thighs. I nudged her legs apart with one knee, spreading her wide, exposing her to me like a fucking feast.

I didn't tease. I didn't play. I drove into her in one brutal thrust, burying myself to my balls, her tight, wet cunt clenching around me like a fucking vice. She cried out; her nails digging into my back, her hips bucking against mine as I started to move, hard and fast, fucking her raw.

"You feel that, Lucia?" I growled, my voice thick with lust and the power of her blood coursing through me. "You feel how goddamn much I need you? How much I want you?"

She didn't answer—she couldn't. Her head was thrown back, her mouth open in a silent scream as I pounded into her, my hips slamming against hers with enough force to shake the bed. Her gorgeous breasts swung with every thrust, and I leaned down to suck and bite at her neck, her pulse racing beneath my lips as I claimed her again and again.

"You're mine," I snarled, my dick pistoning in and out of her, her cunt gripping me so tight it was goddamn torture. "You're fucking mine, Lucia. Always."

Her legs wrapped around my waist, her heels digging into my ass as she pulled me deeper, her body meeting mine thrust for thrust. Her moans were music, rough and primal, filling the room as I pounded her like the godsforsaken beast I was.

"I can't be gentle," I growled, my hands gripping her hips hard enough to bruise, my cock slamming into her with brutal, unrelenting force. "Not with you. Not now."

She came then, her body shuddering beneath me, her pussy clenching around me like a fist. I kept going, pounding her through her orgasm, my thrusts relentless, my cock taking her raw and deep.

"That's it," I snarled, my own climax building, my balls tightening as I neared the edge. "Take me, Lucia. Take all of me."

I reached down and tortured her clit with my thumb, and she came again; her scream tearing through the air as I fucking lost it, my cock pulsing inside her as I came hard, filling her up, her name a prayer on my lips.

We lay tangled for a while, the sheets a lost cause. My hand drifted up to her hairline, and I tucked her in closer, breathing her in. She kissed the fading bite mark on my neck with a reverence that made me ache.

"You are not broken," she murmured, half-asleep already. "Just different. Like me."

I didn't trust myself to speak, so I just held her. Later today, the world would want explanations and apologies, and maybe blood. But for the next few hours, I was just Ryder Lowrey—medic, wolf, vampire, hers.

Eventually, the sun peeked through the blinds, gold cutting across her shoulder. I studied the woman who'd saved my life and, in the process, ruined any hope I had for normalcy. I wanted to tell her I loved her, but the word didn't feel big enough. Instead, I kissed the crown of her head and whispered, "We're gonna knock them dead."

She smiled into my chest. "Da. Let them try to stop us."

We drifted together, strong and sated, ready to meet our fate.

By noon, the weather in Chicago was trying its damnedest to kill us with humidity. Sunlight bounced off the building's chrome gargoyles and banded windows, blinding as a migraine. Our convoy of black SUVs rolled to a stop in the horseshoe drive, flanked by a pair of nondescript sedans that even an idiot would clock as tail cars for private security or worse. Bronc had us all riding in a row—himself, Juliet, me, and Lucia in one; Arsenal, Harper, Big Papa, Aspen, Gunner, and Brie in the other. No one said a word for the last mile. Everyone was bracing for whatever circus the Council had planned.

From the outside, the building looked like a pocket version of the Chrysler Building, all art déco steel lines and geometric arrogance. Ten stories, maybe, but each floor was tall enough to house a basketball court. The main entrance was flanked by two massive stone wolves with obsidian eyes, their snarls frozen mid-lunge, and I felt a jolt in my chest at the detail. You could tell the artist actually knew wolves: the shape of the jowls and the set of their ears. It wasn't meant as a welcome. It was a fuck-you to anyone who thought they belonged here.

Lucia slid out first, looking expensive as always. Hair up in some com-plicated twist, wearing a long black lace dress, like she were sewn into it. She shot me a look—equal parts "let's eat them alive" and "try not to scare them to death." I wore a tailored Armani suit to remind these fuckers that Iron Valor weren't a bunch of backwoods rubes. We could buy and sell most of these jokers.

Inside, the lobby went from 2020s to 1920s in a heartbeat. Black-and-white checkered floor, gold leaf on every exposed surface, ceiling murals that would give the Sistine Chapel a run for its money. Most impressive to me? The temperature. A perfect 68 degrees, dry as a hospital. Someone had invested in both the magical and HVAC versions of climate control.

Behind the reception desk was a woman with hair the color of a four-alarm fire and eyes that sparkled an unnatural yellow. She wore a white Chanel suit; her nametag a tiny gold plaque with nothing but "Veronique." If you told me she ran a cartel in her spare time, I'd have believed you. She offered a bow so smooth it had to have been choreographed.

"Welcome, majesties," she said, voice bright and cold at the same time. "We have been expecting you."

Lucia raised one eyebrow. "I see drama level is cranked up to ten."

Veronique smiled wider. "Only for dramatic guests." She cleared her throat. "The Council is ready. Eighth floor, please. King Kazimir arrived an hour ago," Veronique said, her gaze lingering just a second too long on Lucia. "He is waiting for you inside."

"Of course he is," Lucia said under her breath.

Big Papa and Aspen came up behind us, Gunner and Arsenal flanking the women. Even out of uniform, the ex-military vibe was impossible to mask; the whole group moved in practiced sync, clearing corners and checking lines of sight without even thinking about it. Brie, still healing from her own trauma, held Gunner's arm with a grip of iron, but she tried to play it off as flirty.

As we moved toward the bank of elevators, I felt the prickle of active wards. Not just the usual anti-teleport stuff, but heavy-duty magical suppressants, something designed to keep shifters from shifting and witches from witching. They were subtle, like a very fine mesh of static electricity over your skin. It didn't hurt, but I was hyper-aware of the artificial stillness it created. I didn't think it would do fuck-all to *my* wolf.

"Council doesn't play around," I muttered to Lucia.

She leaned in, lips brushing my ear. "If they didn't, it would be the last thing they ever did."

The elevator was old, but beautifully restored. The doors closed with a satisfying thunk, and for a brief second, we were alone—a pack in a box, eyes forward, every nerve on edge. Bronc cracked his knuckles. Juliet took a slow, calming breath. The woman was a paragon of restraint. I caught Arsenal scanning the panel for hidden cameras.

"You ready for this?" I asked Lucia, quiet.

She turned, lips quirked. "Ready is not the same as willing. But I am with you. That's all I need."

I'd never believed in soulmates or any of that fairy-tale shit. But the look in her eyes made me think maybe, just maybe, there was something to it.

I reached for Lucia's hand, squeezed once. She squeezed back, nails digging in just enough to hurt. Everyone assembled into formation, ready for whatever was waiting.

Time to see if we were still the top of the food chain.

I don't know what I expected from the Council of Supernaturals—maybe an intimidating boardroom, maybe a Roman senate, maybe a Mad Max death pit. What we got was a bastard child of all three.

The chamber took up the entire eighth floor, oval and cavernous with a thirty-foot ceiling painted with apocalyptic murals: the moon bleeding red, wolves feasting on angel wings, demons swallowing cities whole. The real show was the thrones: a U-shaped sweep of twelve seats raised above a sunken central pit. Each throne was overdesigned to reflect its owner's House—blood-red velvet with silver fangs for Otero. Kazimir's wasn't quite as ostentatious, but over-the-top, nonetheless. Purple velvet and gold leaf, complete with matching ottoman and everything but a scepter for the vampire King of Kings.

The four wolf kings had large thrones that matched their personalities. Menace stayed true to his MC roots. His chair was black leather, and I'll be damned if the Iron Valor patch wasn't sewn into a small corner of the chair back. The other wolf kings ranged from white bone and gold leaf to more subdued mahogany and suede, and so on.

Below, in front of the thrones, ran a U-shaped table with smaller, ornate chairs for the various House reps. Apparently, being an immortal king or coven head wasn't enough ego inflation. They needed assistants to convey messages for them as though they couldn't stoop to our level.

We took the first two rows in the gallery, front and center. Bronc nodded to Kazimir, who sat on the East Vampire King's throne more regal and predatory than any other creature in the place. His purple satin robe over his expensive tailored black suit was as I'd expect. His black hair hung loose over one shoulder. He looked bored and dangerous, which I had learned, was his default setting.

The most regal and ethereal of all the kings, of course, was Aspen's father, the Angel King Archon Seraphel. I saw her give him a wink and a tiny wave, which might have been the most surreal thing I'd see today.

The Chairwoman banged a gavel made from some ancient, petrified wood. The room fell instantly silent; the air charged and humming.

"We are now in session," she announced, her voice amplified by magic or really good acoustics. "The Council will hear the case of Ryder Lowrey and Princess Lucia Kozlov."

I felt every eye swing toward us. I sat up straighter, never breaking contact with Lucia. We'd agreed—if they tried to divide us, we'd make it impossible.

"Ryder Lowrey and Lucia Kozlov," the Chairwoman called. "Please approach."

The walk up the aisle was worse than facing a firing squad. The gazes on us were not just curious—they were hungry, jealous, worshipful, and full of old hate. I'd seen battlefields with less threat-per-square-inch. We took our seats and waited.

The Chairwoman looked at her notes, then back at us. "Dr. Lowrey, you are aware that your current state is... unprecedented?"

I shrugged. "So I'm told."

A titter rose from the gallery—just enough to piss off the old guard. A witch coven leader raised a brow, like she were making a note to have me incinerated later.

Lucia leaned in, elbows on the table, voice carrying to the whole room: "If the Council had handled its demon problem, we would not be here at all."

Adramal's eyes glimmered with laughter. "I find your tone disrespectful, girl."

"Good," Lucia shot back. "Your former boss breaking several laws caused this. Which begs the question. Were you aware beforehand that he was going to be involved in murder and kidnapping before you usurped his throne?"

A hum rose in the gallery, and the Chairwoman banged her gavel several times.

"Ms. Kozlov, you'll refrain from addressing the panel unless you are asked a question."

Lucia leaned forward, gave the woman an evil look, and in a monotone voice that would terrify most said, "That's Princess Lucia to *you*."

The Chairwoman was quick to correct her mistake upon realizing it. "Of course, Princess Lucia."

I felt pride and terror at the same time. She wasn't playing defense. She was drawing fire.

The Chairwoman continued. "We are not here to debate the *Council's* actions. We are here to ascertain whether Dr. Lowrey presents an existential threat to the balance of power or to the community."

Bronc's voice, calm and full of Alpha authority, rose from the gallery. "With all due respect, Chairwoman, Dr. Lowrey is a decorated veteran and the Iron Valor Pack's doctor. If this were about threat assessment, you'd be evaluating the bastard who tried to murder him and the rest of us in the first place."

Some of the wolves in the gallery murmured in agreement. King Rafe Mayfield, the Southern Wolf King's eyes flicked to Bronc, and nodded in agreement.

Clearly, they weren't interested in any type of actual justice, only protecting their power.

The questioning started again with a parade of loaded questions and micro-aggressions.

Shashta Tierney of the Gloamreach Coven asked, "Mr. Lowrey, what were your intentions when you accepted the princess's blood?"

I kept my tone neutral, clinical. "Intentions were to survive. Bleeding out is contraindicated for long-term health."

"Princess Lucia, why not allow nature to take its course?"

Lucia bared her fangs in a flash. "Because unlike this Council, I believe in saving lives."

A few vamps nodded, but another witch rep looked disgusted. The room was a powder keg; the tension rising with every answer.

Adramal leaned forward, his gaze full of dark delight. "Tell me, Dr. Lowrey, how do you feel now? Is there a shadow behind your eyes?"

He wanted to goad me into some public display of monstrousness. I'd been trained for this. I gave him nothing. "I'm exactly who I've always been. I just have new parameters."

"And if you were ordered to harm your own pack?" Adramal asked.

I met his stare, unblinking. "I'd die first."

He grinned, showing too many teeth. "Then perhaps you are not such a monster after all."

The Chairwoman returned to her script. "Dr. Lowrey, have you experienced a loss of control, predatory urges, or phantom commands?"

It was the kind of question that sounded scientific, but was really an accusation. I took a breath. "No more than any other shifter. My loyalty remains with my pack and my mate."

Lucia slid her hand into mine, right there above the table. She looked at the thrones like she were daring them to object.

King Slade Stewart of the Western Packs spoke up. "If I may—my sources tell me the only reason you are alive is that in the act of rescuing a shifter who'd been kidnapped by Maltraz, the former demon king, your femoral artery was severed? And the princess took life-saving measures. Is this correct?"

I nodded. "Yes, sir."

He turned to the other Councilors. "Seems to me, we should be thanking these two, not treating them as a threat."

Kazimir, ever the showman, shrugged with a lazy smile. "If we as a Council cannot control our *own* monsters, perhaps we should hire better security."

The demon rep, Mosh, finally spoke, his voice slick as oil. "With respect, King Kazimir, we are not the only House with dirty laundry. Let us not forget the last time a hybrid was permitted to exist."

Lucia's eyes flashed, but I cut in first. "If you have specific concerns, state them. Otherwise, we're wasting time."

The Chairwoman tried for dignity. "The concern is precedent. You are the first hybrid since the Covenants. History tells us such creatures bring only chaos."

I folded my arms. "Again, with due respect, history doesn't have my credentials."

Juliet called out from the gallery: "He built the hospital on our pack land, saved the lives of shifters and witches and vamps alike. If that's chaos, we could use more of it."

A ripple of amusement moved through the gallery.

It was Otero's turn to turn the screws. He cleared his throat and raised a long, elegant finger. His flawless face belied the absolute horror of the man who dwelt inside his skin. He leveled an amber-eyed stare at us.

"That's all very altruistic of the good doctor; doubtless there's no discounting what he's done in the past. But we cannot overlook the fact that *now* he is not only a wolf but a wolf/vampire abomination. Throughout history, these... *creatures* have been destroyed to prevent them from turning into mindless killing machines. This has been for the betterment of all of our society. We cannot simply take the word of the creature's murderous pack or the assurances of the father of the hybrid's sire that he can be trusted not to turn on this very Council and rip us all to shreds. He must be studied and tested. His limits must be pushed to ascertain if he can be trusted within the confines of supernatural society."

This mother fucker. My blood was boiling, and I could feel my wolf rise to the surface. Otero was about to get his demonstration of my power if I didn't get myself under control. I knew my eyes had started to glow red as my control started to slip, but Lucia's hand on my thigh brought my rage back under control as my breathing evened out.

Kazimir had had all he intended to hear from Otero. "That is quite enough from you, Varic. You seem to have neglected to realize that Ryder Lowrey has Kozlov blood flowing through his veins. This makes the doctor a prince of the Kozlov House. I would advise you to tread carefully going forward with any remarks about my daughter's mate."

Otero stopped short.

"Of course, Kazimir. I meant no disrespect. I meant only to raise the concerns many on this panel have mentioned to me. I think these concerns can be quickly dispelled if the good doctor will submit to answering direct questions regarding his new powers, demonstrating those powers, and perhaps submitting to testing of his blood in a controlled situation."

I knew they would not be satisfied until I gave them what they wanted.

"I'm willing to show you the manifestation of my new abilities and prove to you I pose no threat to my pack or society."

A stir rose in the gallery once again.

The Chairwoman banged her gavel to regain control. "Thank you, Dr. Lowrey. We will recess and will meet at 7:00 AM in the labs where you will be asked to go through a few procedures."

Lucia tensed next to me and squeezed my hand tighter. I nodded.

"We'll see you in the morning."

"This meeting is adjourned."

Chapter 21

Lucia

Chicago after dark was not so different from the underworld: neon glances off wet pavement, shadows thick as ink pooling in alleys, and above it all the sky smeared purple and gold like a bruise in healing. I pressed my forehead to the glass of the SUV and watched the city recede, each block less alive than the last, until even the lights seemed weary of themselves.

Doc's hand, warm and heavy, settled over mine on the leather seat between us. The driver up front was a wraith in a black cap, silent and discreet. I caught our reflections in the window, two pale ghosts flickering through the dashboard-lit night. Bronc and Juliet sat quietly in the seat behind us.

"You know they want to kill you?" I asked, voice raw.

Doc smiled, but it was a moonless thing. "Without question."

I rotated my wrist under his, so our fingers linked in a proper knot. "They're not going to test you. Not really. They'll make you run a gauntlet until you fail, so they can call it mercy when they put you down."

He turned, gaze direct. "Then I don't fail. Not for them."

A part of me wanted to believe in his resilience. The other part—a cold, ancient splinter at the base of my skull—saw how the council had weighed him, measured him, and found him threatening not because he was unstable but because he was unprecedented.

"They forget who my father is," I muttered. I traced a lazy circle on the glass, watching fog bloom and vanish with each breath. "He is sovereign by trial. By death and by magic. Goddess-blessed since before their ancestors crawled out of their mud huts. He kept balance for our kind. Now they act like a single hybrid tips the scales."

Doc squeezed my hand. "What are you really afraid of, my lioness?"

A thousand terrors, all equally plausible: that I would lose him, that I would lose myself, that my father would destroy a continent to avenge me, and I'd never forgive him for it. I picked the simplest one.

"That I will watch you become what they say you are. That they will make you into it, and when it's done, I will still love you."

He lifted our joined hands and pressed his mouth to my knuckles. I felt the ghost of fangs behind his teeth—he still had to concentrate to retract them fully, especially when his emotions ran hot. "I'm not so easy to break," he said. "If tomorrow is the day, I want you to remember what we are. Not what they tell you."

I nodded, the motion scraping something sharp in my chest.

The city changed as we headed north. The towers thinned, replaced by stately homes lit from within, the whole block watched over by cameras and silent guards. Father's estate glimmered at the end of a gated drive, every window ablaze.

The truck slowed. A pair of sentries in designer suits stepped from the shadows and scanned us with black obelisks that whined as they sampled our auras. Doc tensed beside me, every muscle poised for the wrong answer, but the devices only pulsed green and the gates swung open.

We passed through the arches and up the circular drive. I saw my father in silhouette at the portico, arms folded, a living statue waiting to be animated by crisis.

Doc's hand slipped from mine as the car stopped. He looked at me, not with hope, not with fear, but with the iron resolve that had gotten him through every battle—on the field, in the operating room, in the haunted hollows of his own mind.

"Ready?" he said.

"No," I admitted. "But I will be."

I wanted to tell him a thousand things: that I loved him, that I would burn this city to the bedrock for him, that I'd destroy anyone who tried to put him in a box, even if it meant losing myself in the process. Instead, I just got out, letting the night air sear the back of my throat. He followed, close enough I could feel the heat radiating from his body. Juliet and Bronc followed along with the others from the following SUV.

We crossed the marble stairs together, two figures already carved into legend—at least in my own head. The council had their games and their tests, but tomorrow was ours. Whatever came, we would face it. Together, or not at all.

My father's great room had been many things in my childhood: a ballroom, an armory, a crypt for unwanted guests. Tonight, it was a war room. The white marble floors gleamed under too many chandeliers, the air sharp and tingling from recent magical warding. Soft Persian rugs covered the floors. Every plush sofa and sectional had been dragged to form a loose oval, all aimed at the grand hearth. My brothers—Maksym, Taras, Nikolay, and Bodhan—stood like sentinels behind Father, their faces set in the "I will listen politely before I kill you" mask our family favored for negotiations.

It took me a moment to register the sea of denim, leather, and wolf-scented testosterone: Iron Valor's inner circle, with a scattering of their mates. Bronc and Big Papa lounged at opposite ends of a sectional, boots on the table and eyes on the door as if daring an assassin to try their luck. Juliet and Aspen, with Oscar, of course, sat close enough to be a united front, and even Arsenal had found a place, his glare slightly less icy than normal. Harper sat on the floor, leaning back against his leg, grounding him.

I felt small suddenly—a little girl in her father's palace, afraid of monsters under the bed. I banished the thought. I'd become a monster myself.

I ducked upstairs to change—civilian gear: black leggings, an Iron Valor hoodie, hair in a topknot. When I returned, Doc was already seated near the fireplace, hands resting easily on his thighs. My brothers eyed him with familiarity, none of the chill I expected from ancient vampires facing a living paradox.

Father spoke first. "We have run every channel, probed every informant, and monitored every known hostile within three continents. The council's plan is apparently as stated: testing. They will not move until the outcome is clear. However, we have identified two units of private security arriving from Nevada. We presume Otero is hedging his bets. He wants to force a specific outcome."

"Varek Otero does not hedge," Taras muttered, knuckles cracking. "He preens. He believes he's the smartest man in the room."

"Still," Father said, "it bears watching. More important, we must know exactly what we are preparing for. Doc, Lucia, I ask you to be frank. No games. What changes, new powers?"

Doc nodded. "I'll start."

He ticked off changes on his fingers, voice matter-of-fact: "Bigger. Stronger. Faster. Don't tire. Shift is instantaneous, any time, day or night, no lunar tie. No pain. No loss of control. I can suppress the urge to shift, but it's easier to let the wolf out when there's a threat."

Wrecker interrupted, sharp and approving. "That's an upgrade, brother."

Doc allowed himself a brief smile. "I heal even quicker than before. Minor injuries—seconds. Major ones, minutes. I don't need food, just blood, but regular meals help keep me stable."

Juliet wrinkled her nose. "Human blood, or...?"

"Lucia's blood," Doc said, unblinking. "Any other is incompatible. I've tried animal, bagged, synthetic. Hers is the only one that truly works."

I'd flopped down in front of Juliet. She squeezed my shoulder; her warm assurance felt like affirmation. "Side effects?" she prompted.

Doc hesitated. "Some. Night vision is overwhelming—like living in day-glow. Hyper-aware of movement, even from miles off. And I have dreams. Prophecies, maybe. I've seen myself captured, caged, powers suppressed. And it always ends the same: I'm always taken from Lucia. Sometimes I see her body. Sometimes just smoke. But always gone. Don't know if they are premonitions since they haven't come to pass. But they don't happen when I'm sleeping. They're almost waking dreams."

A hush sucked the breath from the room. My brothers exchanged glances, a silent debate on whether this was sorcery or madness. Arsenal looked as if he'd been punched in the chest.

I felt my father's gaze like a solar flare. "And you, daughter?"

I swallowed. "My telekinesis is stronger. I can move things at a greater distance as long as they're in my line of sight. My speed and strength have also increased. But I've manifested a new ability. Shadows. I can move in them, manipulate them, and travel through them somewhat. I haven't tried very much. It's just started."

Father's lips thinned. He paced the front of the hearth, hands clasped behind his back. "Otero is afraid of this union. So is the council. Their worst fear is a breeding pair—one that survives. If tomorrow goes poorly, they will use every resource to prevent it from spreading. They hate my power. Always have. They can never be content with the power they have; always wanting more. And the idea of the two of you creating something even more powerful is more than they can abide. The Council must not find out about all of these new abilities. Hide what you can. Tomorrow needs to go well."

Arsenal cracked his knuckles. "Then we make sure it does."

Bronc leaned in, blue eyes flinty. "What's the play?"

Father stopped, looking older than I had ever seen him. He addressed the pack. "Do your best to remain close to Ryder at all times. The Council may attempt to separate you, as they did with Menace and Savannah. Do not allow it if you can help it. If you sense hostile magic or a compulsion, alert my sons. They will intervene."

"Understood," Bronc said, and I felt the pack's collective tension as a physical thing.

Doc took a long, deliberate breath. "If I lose control—if I attack, or… kill—take me out. Don't hesitate."

I shook my head. "No one is killing you, Ryder. Not while I breathe."

Father approached, expression carved from diamond. "Sometimes love requires the cruelest clarity. I will not risk you daughter, or my kind, for sentiment." But then his hand landed on my shoulder, and I felt the pulse of pride behind his words. "Still, I prefer your mate alive. He belongs to me."

Gunner raised a flask, the universal sign for *"crisis averted."* "To new bloodlines," he toasted.

Arsenal's smile was rare as gold. "And to no more fucking surprises, please."

We all drank to that, even if none of us believed it was possible. Especially me.

Doc caught my eye across the table, and for a moment, it was just us. I saw no fear in him. Only resolve, and a love so stupid it would stand up to the whole world. I squeezed Juliet's hand and let the warmth fill me, just for the night. Because tomorrow, the gloves came off.

The whiskey burned a slow trail to my stomach, but the memory of Doc's nightmare gnawed more fiercely than any liquor. Even with the laughter, the little jokes, the comfort of my best friend's hand in mine, I could not stop replaying his words. Every time I closed my eyes, I saw myself as a silhouette—smoke, body, then nothing. Always gone.

I had not planned on putting on a show, but when my father asked for a demonstration, I was not going to refuse.

"Let's see what my daughter has become," he said, voice all silk and razors.

The pack and their mates sprawled on sectionals and ottomans, but they leaned forward as if scenting a storm. My brothers flanked Father, expressions wary. Only Doc looked completely at ease, as if he'd already made peace with whatever I unleashed.

I closed my eyes and reached for the thin seam of darkness that trailed along the baseboard. Even with the lamps blazing overhead, shadows curled in every corner—hungry, living things. I whispered to them, not with my mouth but with the intent behind my mind. Instantly, they thickened and pooled around my fingertips, then snaked up my wrists in ribbons of black velvet.

Juliet gasped, breathless. Even Maksym, who'd seen some shit in his day, muttered, "Holy hell."

I smiled. With a thought, I sent the tendrils whipping across the coffee table, wrapping around a glass without shattering it, then let the darkness slither back into my palm.

But that was child's play. I stepped onto the marble, fixed my eyes on the deepest shadow at the far end of the room—an architectural nook beside a six-foot tall vase—and reached. The world stuttered, light spun dizzy, and then I was in the nook, heartbeat unchanged.

The pack erupted in yips and wolf whistles. Brie squealed and clapped. Bronc muttered, "Christ, she's a nightcrawler."

I returned to my spot in a blink, only slightly winded. The magic was exhausting, but not in a way I could explain. It felt like skipping meals, or holding your breath just a bit too long.

Father's face was impassive, but I saw the flicker in his eyes—a mix of pride and concern. "That is not ordinary vampire magic," he said, voice low. "You have inherited the old power."

Nikolay, who usually had jokes for every occasion, just shook his head. "Last I checked, only one vampire could do that. And he's standing right there."

Father did not deny it. "My bloodline is sovereign for a reason. Shadow-walking was lost to all but a handful after the Exodus. Now, it has found a new home."

Bronc leaned forward, tactical brain already in high gear. "How far can you travel? Could you scout the Council's chambers? Get someone out if it went bad?"

"Not sure," I admitted. "I've only tried it a few rooms at a time. I think distance is tied to line of sight—or memory of the place. But if I see where I'm going, I can be there."

Maksym nodded, grinning. "That's a game-changer."

Arsenal, ever the skeptic, asked, "Can you carry someone else?"

I hesitated. "Maybe. Small things, for sure. A person? I haven't tested."

Doc finally spoke, voice gentle but full of steel. "If you need to get out, lioness, you leave me. Understand?"

"Fuck that," I said, loud enough to quiet the room. "I'll drag you through every shadow on earth if I have to."

A few of the wolves chuckled, but my brothers just looked at each other—telepathic debate in real time. Maksym said, "If it comes to violence, remember that councilors always have backup. Their mages will try to cut off teleportation, or lay traps."

Father nodded. "Be cautious. This is not a performance. This is survival. This magic is untried for you, daughter. It could get you both killed."

A servant in a starched jacket appeared, pushing a cart heavy with food. The air filled with scents—rare steak for the wolves, raw venison for the vampires, salads and cheeses for the mates. The spell of tension broke for a moment as everyone piled plates and found new seating.

Juliet nudged me on the way to the buffet. "You didn't tell me you could do that."

I shrugged. "It's new. Every time I use it, it feels less like a trick and more like breathing."

She looped her arm through mine. "I know you're scared. But I think you just scared the hell out of them."

Juliet balanced her plate on her knees, already on her second helping of steak and salad. I stabbed at my own food, mostly to keep my hands busy. Even with a room full of heavy hitters, the only person who could make me relax was sitting an arm's length away in her bare feet, humming softly as she devoured food like she hadn't seen a meal in years.

She caught me staring and raised an eyebrow. "You're doing that thing where you overthink and under-eat."

I nudged her with my elbow. "I can't believe you left the twins for this. Bronc said you could have stayed back."

She wiped her mouth, swallowed, and gave me a look so honest it almost hurt. "Lucia. We're sisters. Not by blood, but... whatever this is." She waved at the gathered wolves and vamps and their tangled destinies. "We don't bail on each other. Not for anything."

I squeezed her hand, heart a little lighter. "I owe you, roomie."

She laughed. "You already paid up. You helped get me to a man with an ass like a granite countertop. Anything else is gravy."

Across the room, Taras—the most taciturn of my brothers—was locked in deep conversation with Arsenal and Harper. The wolf's mate smiled gently, explaining something with her hands, and Taras actually nodded as if the words mattered. I could hardly believe it; in every other context, my brothers treated wolves as useful but terminally stupid. Here, they deferred to the Iron Valor crew as equals.

Bodhan and Big Papa sat near the bar cart, sharing rare whiskey and war stories in alternating turns. I watched the way Bodhan listened—shoulders relaxed, head tilted, not hunting for weakness but actually enjoying the company.

Wrecker had moved to the hearth with Parker, who was talking to Nikolay about the latest in data center setups and how to leverage tech to try to save jobs. The details were foreign to me, but the way he listened intently to her in agreement was not.

Father stayed out of the main circle, watching from the picture window like a king in exile. He was not sulking—he never sulked—but every so often he'd catch my eye, and we'd share a glance sharp as a diamond. He trusted the room, and it was clearly a new experience for him.

I finished my plate and set it aside, letting the food settle. The tension in the room had changed—it was not gone, but it felt more like electricity before a race than the dread before a funeral.

Doc moved to sit beside me, thigh pressing into mine. His plate was clean; he ate with soldier's efficiency, every meal a mission. He studied my face, then leaned in.

"Tomorrow will suck," he said, voice low. "But I'd rather walk in with you than stand alone."

I let the words settle over me. It was not poetry, but it was everything I needed.

"Should we, uh, sleep?" I asked, suddenly aware of how heavy my limbs felt. "Or just fake it until morning?"

Juliet grinned. "Sleep is for the living. We'll stand watch. You two go do mated people things."

Harper snickered. "I can draw you a diagram if needed."

Doc rolled his eyes, but he didn't argue. He tugged me gently to my feet. The muscles in his hand flexed; his grip was careful, but absolute. We moved past the brothers, past the pack, into the long hallway lined with photos of my mother, my younger self, and ancestors whose stories were mostly warnings.

At the end of the hall, the glass doors opened onto a wide stone patio. The garden bloomed with a variety of late-spring flowers. The air was cool, but Doc's arm around me was an unbreakable line of warmth.

He spoke first. "You scared?"

I shook my head, then nodded, then shrugged. "Not of the Council. Not really."

He waited, as always, for the truth.

"I'm scared of losing this," I said, gesturing at the distant laughter, the friends and family I never thought I'd have. "I'm scared of being the last one left."

He pulled me close, so our bodies touched from hip to shoulder. "Not happening. I'll burn the city down first."

I laughed, high and wild. "That's my line."

He bent to kiss me, and when our lips touched, it felt like a binding. Stronger than law. Stronger than fate. The world could end tomorrow, but tonight, we were infinite.

When we finally broke apart, I stared into his eyes—wolf and vampire, healer and weapon, mine—and felt the old fear smothered by a wild, surging hope.

"Let them come," I said, voice barely above a whisper.

He nodded. "Let them."

CHAPTER 22

DOC

I tried to convince myself that my heart wasn't racing as we navigated downtown Chicago in the blacked-out Suburban, but my body had other plans. Beneath the pressed shirt and tailored suit, sweat prickled under my arms, and my pulse hammered behind my right temple. You'd think with all my combat experience, supernatural genetics, and recent resurrection, I'd have a better grip on existential dread. But the fact was, I'd rather be dropped blind into a Kandahar kill box than willingly submit to whatever the Supreme Council had in mind for me.

Lucia sat silent beside me the entire ride, her posture rigid, jaw clenched, refusing to look anywhere but straight ahead. Her left hand found mine; her ice-cool fingers wrapped around my own with a grip strong enough to break a weaker man's bones. I didn't need our new bond to know she was panicking under all that porcelain: even in her best poker face, Lucia's emotional tells always came through in the way she held herself, breath locked down tight in her lungs like she could dead-lift the world if she needed to.

I catalogued the rest of our convoy: Aspen in the way-back row, shoulders hunched, typing furiously into her phone and then glancing out the tinted window at every red light, like she expected pursuit. In the passenger seat, Kazimir sat with the eerie calm of an apex predator, radiating Old

World composure from his Italian suit; the only sign of life a single index finger drumming silent Morse against his knee. Bronc drove with the same focus he brought to battlefield extractions: every lane shift telegraphed, every blind spot pre-cleared. Juliet sat next to Lucia on the bench seat and fidgeted with the hem of her blazer and worked her tongue against her canine, like she were rehearsing arguments in her head.

We looked like a rejected League of Nations... and I'd become, the supernatural community's favorite new bug to pin and dissect. Shifter? Yes. Wolf? Absolutely. Vampire? Sort of, after Lucia's impromptu blood transfusion in the middle of a Texas canyon. No, I had a few extra bells and whistles. Some folks on the Council wanted me cleared as "not a threat" and sent back to the minors; others, especially the old-guard vampires who hated Kazimir, saw me as the perfect excuse to kneecap him politically and maybe, if they could swing it, get rid of me permanently.

So the only thing left was to prove I could be trusted. Or, failing that, to die more gracefully than last time.

Aspen's phone vibrated again—rapid fire—and this time she answered. "Yes, I'm sure," she hissed in her best library voice. "He's right here, and he's not going to...no, Dad, stop. I know." She cupped the phone and whispered, "It's my father. He's making sure the Council's not going to, like... disappear you."

I offered her a smile in the rearview. "Tell him I appreciate his concern."

She did, her accent curling like honey over the word "Doc." Then she frowned, listening, and the faint blue glow from her phone framed her face in soft witch light. "He says he'll be in the building the whole time. Just in case."

Lucia snorted. "Wonderful. The world's most powerful helicopter parent." She squeezed my hand harder, and I felt the ghost of a laugh through our bond—more nerves than joy.

Oscar, the most verbose prairie dog on the planet, wearing a dapper bow tie and waistcoat leaned over the seatback. "Yes, Princess. But never discount having an angel on call when dealing with devils."

"Thank you, Oscar. You're correct." Lucia gave him a smile. Genuine this time.

We pulled into the horseshoe drive, past a line of Mercedes and limos, and Bronc cut the engine with a finality I could feel in my teeth. As we spilled out onto the sidewalk, security detail materialized out of nowhere: men and women in unmarked black, with the blank, polite faces of private military, radios clipped to their wrists. None of them looked directly at Kazimir, which told me everything I needed to know about who actually ran this show.

The receptionist, Veronique watched me walk in and—this is a hell of a thing—didn't break eye contact once, not even to blink. It wasn't seduction, not even curiosity; it was more like a cat watching a pit viper crawl across her windowsill. I nodded, and she nodded back, her lips curving just enough to make me wonder if she'd heard every thought in my head.

Kazimir drifted to her side and exchanged a few words in rapid-fire Russian. The receptionist scanned her screen, then handed him a white plastic visitor badge and announced, "Second floor. They're waiting."

She handed badges down the line, pausing a microsecond longer on Lucia's name tag. "Princess," she said, and her voice held a peculiar under-tone I couldn't read. Respect? Pity? Dread?

Lucia accepted it with a brittle "Thank you." Her eyes were already losing their human shape—growing wider, more that ancient, hungry black. I knew she was scanning for threats, cycling through options. Her father stood behind her like a monolith. The entire tableau felt staged; everyone hitting their marks.

We made our way to the elevator. Bronc kept a hand lightly at Juliet's elbow, as if she'd bolt, and Aspen hung back, Big Papa at her side. We hit

"2," and I felt my stomach do a slow roll as the car ascended with the kind of smoothness that told me it was more magic than machinery.

The doors opened onto a waiting room lined with steel and glass, all sharp angles and cold white light. The art deco glamor of the lobby was gone, replaced by an antiseptic, modernist minimalism that screamed "testing facility" in every language of trauma. Menace and Savannah were already waiting, flanked by two Council attendants. Menace looked tenser than I'd ever seen him. The man usually radiated total confidence, but today he was scanning the corners, every muscle in his body taut as a piano wire. Savannah sat with her legs crossed, green eyes burning holes through the conference table.

Menace saw me and got up, crossing the space in three long strides. He didn't say anything, just wrapped me in a bear hug that compressed my ribs enough to hurt. "Hey," he said, voice pitched low. "You ready for this?"

"Define 'ready'," I said. "I brought my own blood."

He didn't laugh. Instead, he stepped back and appraised me, gaze landing on Lucia's hand still gripping mine. For a half-second, I thought he'd say something about it, but instead he gave me a tiny nod and motioned us to the waiting chairs. "They'll call you in as a group, but you'll go first. Just answer every question. Don't be a smartass."

"That's asking a lot," I said. The old Army humor was automatic, but even I could hear how flat it sounded. Menace wasn't reassured.

Savannah got up and hugged Lucia, whispering something in her ear too soft for me to catch. Lucia's face didn't change, but I felt a flicker of gratitude across our bond—she'd needed that, even if she'd never admit it. Aspen made her way to me and looped her arm through mine, squeezing tight.

The rest of our party clustered awkwardly, trading half-hearted banter while the real show got underway behind the double doors across the lobby. More than once, I caught the Council attendants watching me: some with curiosity, most with a kind of sterile interest usually reserved for test subjects or time bombs. The sense of being pre-judged was suffocating, and I found myself clenching and unclenching my hands just to keep from pacing.

Finally, a Council runner—a petite witch with owl eyes and a clipboard—called my name and ushered me through. Lucia started to follow, but the attendant blocked her with a raised hand. "Only immediate test subjects and their designated secondaries."

"I am his mate," Lucia said, voice like a razor blade.

The attendant didn't flinch. "Then you'll be tested as a pair. But the initial workup is solo. The protocol is very strict." The way she said it made it clear there was no argument to be had.

I looked to Bronc, who nodded once. "Go," he mouthed, like he were sending me into a burning building.

We were escorted to the "workup" room after they took me to a separate chamber to change into appropriate testing attire. The room was blindingly white, with glass walls on two sides and a bank of monitors on the third. Chrome fixtures gleamed from every angle. It smelled faintly of bleach, ozone, and something else—maybe old blood? The entire place was a shrine to sterile control, but all I could see were the subtle architectural details that would make it a great kill room: no cover, no easy exits, everything visible at all times.

A bank of medical techs waited by the table, all wearing identical lab coats. Behind them, in a raised observation area, sat the Council of royals, many of whom I knew personally; others I had no desire to know.

One of the techs insisted on ushering Lucia to the other side of the glass to sit with Bronc to watch the preliminary tests. I saw Savannah and Juliet through the observation window, watching from behind a tinted wall. Even from here, I could see Menace's face was stony and Savannah was biting the inside of her cheek. The others were forced to remain in a closed-off waiting room.

Lucia looked ready to burst through the glass, but she kept herself coiled, predatory, waiting for any hint of foul play.

I scanned the Council, noting who was bored, who was hungry, and who was already calculating whether I'd be easier to kill before or after the tests. Most eyes skipped right over me—except for the Angel, who nodded with a kind of benediction. I wondered if that was Aspen's influence, or just some angelic sense of fair play. Menace and Kazimir kept a steady eye on everyone.

The lead tech cleared her throat and spoke in English, crisp and oddly gentle. "We'll begin with verification. This is for your safety as much as ours."

I shrugged, not trusting myself to say anything clever.

She began the workup: saliva, a buccal swab, each sample disappearing into the bowels of the lab as soon as it was taken. The glass made everything feel twice as exposed, and every movement felt like a deliberate display for the crowd. The tech's questions came in a steady monotone:

"Name?"

"Ryder Lowrey."

"Species?"

I looked at her. "You tell me."

She did not smile. "Have you experienced any unusual abilities since your transformation?"

"Define 'unusual.'"

She hesitated, then ticked her eyes to the panel of observers. "Enhanced strength or speed, rapid healing, new senses, compulsion, altered appetites?"

"Check, check, negative, negative, and... check." I risked a look at Lucia, who nodded faintly. I didn't say more, but the tech wrote something on her tablet and moved on.

A few more questions. A few more tests. Then, the announcement: "We'll proceed to the observation phase. Please wait." They backed away in unison, leaving me standing alone in the middle of the white room.

I waited. Time stretched, turning to static. My skin itched with the urge to move, to do something, but I just stood there and memorized every inch of the chamber: the seam lines, the air vent, the thickness of the glass.

They were studying me. But I was studying them, too.

After ten minutes, a door on the far side slid open, and the tech beckoned for Lucia and Bronc to enter. I watched her as she crossed the threshold—every muscle trembling with anger and fear, her eyes black as a shark's, but she kept her cool. Bronc looked at me, scanned the space, then said in a low voice, "You good?"

"Never better," I said.

The door hissed shut behind them with a sound that might as well have been the click of a gun's safety disengaging.

I stared at the observation window, at the Council, at the coterie of supernaturals who had come to watch me break or bend. And in that moment, I knew: I was no longer here to prove I was safe.

I was here to see if the world could survive whatever I'd become.

The white room made every flaw stand out: the half-moon of blood under my thumbnail, the coffee stain on Bronc's cuff, the way Lucia's cheeks pulsed with color when she was close to losing it. She tried to stand with the same bored, aristocratic posture her father perfected, but the tremor in her hand betrayed her. Even the light in here was wrong, too bright, washing every emotion raw.

The lead technician returned with a tray loaded with everything but a bone saw. "We'll begin with bloodwork," she said, glancing at Lucia, then at the ceiling where cameras followed every motion.

A secondary tech, male, tall, with a receding hairline and the build of someone who'd never taken a punch, presented two vials and two butterfly needles. He pointed first to me, then to Lucia. "May I?" he asked her.

"Do it quickly," she replied. Her Russian was so thick, the 'do it' sounded more like an order to assassinate.

He did. No hesitation, but his hands were steady. The needle went into the crook of her elbow, and for a moment, the color of her blood was a shock: deep, rich, black-red, thick as syrup. I watched the way it filled the tube, swirling with lazy force, and felt a jolt of something—hunger? nostalgia?—that made my jaw clench.

My turn: my blood was... normal. The bright arterial red looked entirely human-shifter as it filled the tube. But I *knew* it wasn't normal human-shifter blood. This was the reason we didn't want to provide blood samples. Testing would reveal the anomaly. What specific anomaly? I wasn't sure.

The lead tech carefully said, "Now the test."

She unscrewed both vials, pipetted a droplet from each onto a clear glass slide, and fitted the whole mess into a device that looked like a microscope made by NASA. On the monitor, the blood cells swam into view. At first, there was nothing odd: wolf shifter red, Lucia's vampire black. Then, as the sample fanned out, the edges of the two touched.

And merged.

Not a blending, not a fight for dominance, but a quiet, unhurried consumption. The two fluids made contact, and in seconds, the cellular borders vanished. The monitor flickered: one cell type, then two, then an impossible lattice of hybrid structures that any hematologist would have called a fever dream. The lead tech's mouth hung open, and the other tech made a strangled noise in his throat.

Bronc leaned forward, arms crossed. He didn't need the science to tell him what this meant, but he wanted to see the proof. "That supposed to happen?"

"No," the tech whispered, her voice cracking. "No, this is..." She gestured, helpless, at the screen. "This isn't hybridization. It's... fusion. New."

There was a flurry of movement behind the glass wall. Observers started talking at once—too low to pick up the words, but the tone was pure panic-tinged excitement. Councilors leaned over one another, taking photos, sending messages on encrypted phones. One of the vampires, with a mane of white hair and skin so pale it looked blue, pressed a hand to the glass as if he could feel the change vibrating through the room.

The lead tech wiped her hands on her coat, eyes flickering between the monitor and me. "We'll have to run further tests."

Lucia snorted, not bothering to hide her contempt. "Of course you will."

It wasn't until the next step that I realized they'd been planning to separate us: two attendants appeared, each with a polite, professional smile, and gestured to Lucia. "If you'll please accompany us," the first said. "The subject—Ryder—must be unaccompanied for the next sequence."

Lucia whirled. "No. I stay."

"It's required by..."

"Try to move her," I said, "and you'll be picking your teeth out of the drywall." I meant it as a joke, but nobody laughed. Especially not Bronc, who looked like he was two seconds from shifting just to make a point.

The lead tech raised a hand. "If you promise to remain behind the marked line, Princess Lucia may observe. But no physical contact." She pointed to a red tape boundary on the floor.

Lucia glared, then backed up, arms crossed, heels right on the stripe.

The shift test was next.

I was ordered to the center of the room, where a circle of geometric symbols had been etched into the tile—sigils to destabilize shifters, make the change as brutal as possible. In the old days, these were used for exorcisms and executions. I recognized them from an occult manual I'd found in a rare book store. It was barbaric then. It was barbaric now.

"First, full shift," the tech said, voice a little shaky.

I nodded and stripped off my shirt, tossing it to Bronc. He caught it without looking. My body had transformed into a perfect male specimen. I grinned as I pulled off my pants and boxers. I think I heard a gasp from the Council gallery.

I know I heard Lucia's voice. "That's right bitches. Look at what belongs to me."

I shook my head and got to the task at hand. Most wolves—hated shifting in sterile spaces, the process being loud and messy. The last time I'd done it on demand for a crowd was my first shift. Shifting becomes natural after a while, and the pain barely registers. But this circumstance and this space were designed for pain.

The test didn't work as they intended. I called my wolf, and he was just... there. No pain, no bones breaking, no fire in the veins. Just a lurch, a crackle of white-hot energy, and I was on all fours, claws sliding against the tile. My senses sharpened, air saturated with the smell of bleach, fear, and a hint of Lucia's perfume. Her eyes met mine—wide, black, wet with pride and possessiveness.

The tech's hands shook so badly she dropped her pen.

"Now, partial."

I pulled it back, halting at the halfway point: hands elongated, teeth extended, eyes burning red, but otherwise still me. I towered over the lead tech, and for a moment, she forgot to breathe.

"Shift back to human form," she managed.

I willed it away. Became myself again. Human. Heart racing, but not out of fear—out of something deeper, some urge to show them what I was capable of.

A councilor behind the glass whispered to another. Their voices didn't carry, but my hearing had improved in ways I couldn't quite explain. "This isn't a wolf that learned control," she said. "This is a wolf that never lost it."

That landed like a bomb in the room.

The rest of the tests blurred together: neurological responses, olfactory stimuli, even a light-up panel meant to mimic lunar cycles. They ran each one three times, then again. Every result was off the charts. When they shined a UV lamp in my face, I didn't even blink; when they pricked my finger to see if the wound would heal, it closed before the tech could dab the blood.

The whole time, Lucia never took her eyes off me, not even to blink. Every time the techs got too close, she flexed her hands, fingers curling into claws.

By the end of the hour, the mood had changed. The first tests had been curiosity—clinical, detached. Now, everyone was just waiting to see when I'd finally lose control.

I didn't.

They made me repeat the shifts twice more, just to be sure. The last time, the demon in the observation gallery bared his teeth in a grin and clapped, slow and deliberate. He looked like he were already planning how to take me apart, molecule by molecule.

When they finally called a break, the techs backed out of the room as if it were full of hydrogen sulfide. I caught Bronc's eye; he nodded, approval written in the iron lines of his jaw.

Lucia crossed to me the instant the observers stepped away. She didn't say anything, just pressed her forehead to mine and exhaled.

"We're not done," she said softly.

I knew she was right. I could feel the next test coming—bigger, meaner, built to crack me in two.

I just wondered if anyone in this building had planned for what happened if they couldn't.

CHAPTER 23

DOC

It took them less than five minutes to reset the white room for the next round. The techs returned, this time in twos and threes, glancing sidelong at me as they rearranged the monitors and swapped out the bloodwork slides for something that looked like a lie detector on anabolic steroids. The audience behind the glass had doubled: every seat filled, some councilors standing in the back.

Lucia caught my gaze, her pupils blown so wide her eyes looked black. "Don't let them break you," she whispered. She didn't need to say it out loud, but I think she needed to hear the sound of it in the air.

Bronc said nothing, just clapped my shoulder and put himself at her side, silent and immovable.

A voice from the observation booth cut through the hum of the techs: ancient, low, as steady as the tick of a grandfather clock. Lucia looked at her father. They recognized this man. She whispered to me once more.

"That is the Romanian King; almost as old as my father. He is powerful."

The white-haired vampire spoke. "Ryder Lowrey. You will now submit to the will of this Council."

The words thudded against my skull like a bag of concrete, thick with compulsion. My knees wanted to buckle. I'd been trained to withstand interrogation, mind control, and every flavor of magical duress you could throw at a shifter, but this was different—more elemental, like someone was pulling on my spinal cord from the other side of the room.

Lucia hissed, but I shook my head—don't intervene. I let the pressure flood in, felt it cascade down my spine. But I didn't give in. Instead, I did something nobody in this room expected: I smiled.

"That's the reason we're all here, no?" I asked, and instantly, the force doubled. My vision blurred at the edges; my hands trembled. But I stayed upright, still myself.

The vampire's gaze didn't waver. "Shift," he commanded, and the order vibrated through my bones like a tuning fork.

"I will shift." I could barely get the words out. "But on my terms." I stripped out of my clothes again, then...

I shifted. Fast, precise, no pain. Held the wolf for a full ten seconds, then snapped back to human. I heard gasps from the gallery, saw Bronc's lips twitch in a hint of pride.

"Kneel," came the next command. I felt my body lean forward, legs itching to fold.

"Why do you resist?" the voice asked, softer now, almost curious.

"I don't," I said. "I just choose."

I dropped to one knee, head bowed, every inch the obedient hound. Then I stood up again, slower this time, and met the vampire's gaze with my own.

That sent a ripple through the room—anger, awe, maybe even fear.

"Submit. Release your wolf."

The words hit like a hammer, but I'd already learned the trick: let the command in, then channel it sideways, into something useful. I felt the wolf rise, hunger sharpening my senses and my teeth, but I kept control. I could've torn the table out of its moorings. Instead, I stood there, hands open, heart rate steady.

The councilor frowned. "Fascinating," he said. "Again."

He made me do it five more times—shift, kneel, stand down. Each time, I obeyed on my terms, never fully losing myself. By the end, the compulsion felt more like a test than a weapon, a gauntlet thrown down by someone who wanted to see if I'd blink.

Behind the glass, a demon—different from the first, bulkier, with horns spiraling from his scalp—muttered, "He's not a puppet. He's a free agent." It sounded like a warning, not a compliment.

That's when the aggression test started.

The techs triggered a series of lights and scents in the room: adrenaline simulants, faint ozone, and a droning bass note calculated to set a wolf's teeth on edge. A shifter would normally have gone into full combat mode. I recognized the protocol—escalation of threat; see how the subject responds under pressure.

They cranked it up to eleven.

A new attendant, this one broad and scarred, entered with a padded suit and started circling me. He made no direct eye contact, but his stance screamed challenge. In a normal wolf, this would trigger a dominance contest. For a hybrid—or whatever the hell I'd become—it was supposed to be irresistible.

I felt the urge to snap, to lunge, but instead I waited. The attendant feinted left; I sidestepped. He tried to grab my arm; I twisted out, pivoted, and put him face-down on the tile in one move. I didn't hurt him. Just stopped the threat.

Bronc let out a low whistle. "Well, shit," he muttered. "They're not gonna like that."

Lucia was biting her fist so hard her knuckles turned white.

The next test was uglier.

Two techs entered with a canine cage—large, reinforced, designed to contain a shifted wolf; not *my* wolf. Inside was a raw steak, slick with blood, and a spatter of fresh animal scent. They opened the door, stepped back, and waited for the reaction.

I looked at the steak, then looked at the techs. "You want me to fetch?" I deadpanned.

Nobody laughed.

The lead tech—her hands still shaking—said, "Retrieve the meat, please."

I did, barehanded, and handed it back to her without even a flicker of predator instinct. She took it, eyes wide, and nodded to the observers.

The final aggression phase started with a simulated attack. They brought Lucia into the center of the room—unrestrained, but surrounded by three guards in tactical gear. One of the guards made a show of shoving her, not hard, but enough to make a point.

My wolf growled, deep and cold, but I did nothing. Not yet.

They did it again. Lucia stumbled, caught herself, and fixed me with a look that said don't do it.

The third time, the guard raised his hand like he was going to hit her.

I moved.

Not fast, not wild. Just efficient. I closed the distance, locked his wrist, and spun him around so gently he didn't realize he'd lost the advantage until I'd disarmed him. I set him down on the ground, unharmed, and stepped back.

Lucia smiled then, real and dangerous. "You see?" she said to the councilors. "He is more than what you fear."

For a long beat, nobody spoke. Then one of the witches, a severe woman with hair like iron filings, muttered, "He's calculating, not reacting."

Another councilor, a shifter with wolf-gray eyes, added, "That's what makes him dangerous."

The aggression tests ended. The room was silent but for the faint buzz of the lights.

I stood there, breathing slow, and met the eyes of every councilor in turn.

They didn't see a weapon.

They saw a threat they didn't know how to disarm.

They let me dress, then kept me standing for the next phase. The white room had a new smell now—coppery, sharp, the tang of nervous sweat and adrenaline. I knew what was coming the minute the medical techs rolled in a stainless steel cart stacked with field surgery supplies and a tray of glass syringes. The observers, crowded two-deep behind the glass, leaned forward with predatory interest.

Lucia was gone from the room, but not from my sight. They'd moved her back behind the glass. Her lips were moving, silent curses or prayers. Next to her, Bronc hovered like a bodyguard, blue eyes as cold as a January morning.

The lead tech—she of the nervous hands—read her script with the dead monotone of someone trying not to think about what she was doing. "Council has ordered a threshold analysis. You will comply for each step. Please indicate if you experience pain or abnormal sensation."

I shrugged. "Define 'abnormal.'"

She didn't answer, just took up a scalpel and made a quick, deep slice along my forearm. Blood welled up, bright and arterial, and for a second she hesitated, waiting for a scream or a snarl. There was none. The flesh knitted before her eyes, skin crawling closed like it were embarrassed to have ever been open.

The gallery buzzed—some councilors excited, some visibly disturbed.

The tech noted the result, then signaled her assistant. He rolled up a pneumatic bone-breaker—normally used to set fractures—and clamped it around my wrist. "Next phase," he said, and the machine snapped.

I felt the crack, sharp and wrong, but before the pain registered fully, the bone had already started realigning, knitting, the swelling going down even as they watched. I flexed my hand. "Try the other arm," I suggested, and some joker in the back snickered.

They did. This time, the bone broke all the way through, and it hurt like hell, but the mending was even faster. I could feel the heat, the flow of new cells rushing in, the way the nerves rewired instantly. The tech's hands shook as she noted the data.

There was a brief consultation in the gallery. The demon councilor rapped his knuckles on the glass and said, "Internal trauma next."

They loaded a syringe with some kind of coagulant, then injected it straight into my femoral artery. The pain was blinding, but my vision didn't tunnel; instead, my blood pressure shot up, forcing the clot out with such violence that it sprayed red across the tile. The wound sealed. My leg held. The tech blinked, eyes wet with horror.

Somewhere behind the glass, an elder vampire whispered, "Weapon."

I knew what they were seeing: not a hybrid, not a monster, but something closer to a prototype, a proof of concept that could survive anything. The more they tested, the more obvious it became.

"Proceed," said the Chairwoman.

The final round was endurance. They clamped sensors to my chest, my temples and forced me to run a series of sprints on a treadmill built into the floor. The speed was set for supernatural maximums—no human or even normal wolf could've kept up. I did. I ran until my feet burned and my heart hammered like a piston.

They starved me, denied me blood, threw every environmental stressor in the book at me: heat, cold, blinding light, even sonic attacks. My body adapted in real time, vitals barely fluctuating. But every time they let Lucia into my line of sight, every time I caught the glint of panic in her eyes, my heart rate spiked.

The councilors noticed. One of them, a small, fox-faced witch with a stylus, circled the data point and marked it in red. "Subject's physical state is only affected by mate's distress," she said, not bothering to hide the awe in her voice. "Suggests bond is primary regulatory anchor."

That sounded right, but I didn't say it.

By the time the tests ended, the tile was smeared with dried blood, but I stood as strong as when I'd walked in. The techs looked at me like I was a ticking bomb.

Lucia was crying openly now, her face twisted in an agony I recognized from war zones and emergency rooms—the kind that only comes when you can't save someone you love. I wanted to go to her, to break the glass, but I forced myself to stand still. I owed it to her to finish this on my feet.

The Council withdrew into a huddle, talking in tight, urgent circles. Some wanted me contained; some wanted to keep studying. A few, I could tell, were already plotting the next phase. Menace and Kazimir were animated. Archon remained calm.

I stood there, healing, sweating, wanting nothing more than to get Lucia out of this place and never come back.

But I knew it wasn't over.

Not for me.

Not for her.

Not now.

They made me sit for the bond tests. Probably thought I'd have an easier time holding myself together if I was already close to the floor. I could see Lucia through the glass again. They kept the sound muted, so all I got was her expression: tight, white, panic biting at the corners of her mouth.

The techs stuck a dozen sensors on my temples, chest, and fore-arms. The lead tech—her nerves more shot than ever—spoke over a headset to the observation gallery. "Ready for the first phase."

The doors opened. Two new guards flanked Lucia and led her out of sight, into a room I couldn't see. The moment the door closed, the emptiness hit me—not pain, not even hunger, but a hollowness that set my teeth on edge. I gripped the seat, knuckles white.

"Vitals unchanged," the tech recited, eyes on her monitor.

They moved Lucia farther: another room, then a corridor. Each time, a council runner announced the new distance. At twenty meters, I felt the bond stretch, thin as a nerve. My senses started to blur at the edges—like someone dialed back the color in the world.

At forty meters, the tech said, "Heart rate rising. Blood pressure increased." She looked at me, a question on her face, but I stared past her, willing the bond to hold.

They moved Lucia behind magical obscurement next—some kind of shroud or dampening field. That's when I felt it. Like a sudden drop in cabin pressure, my brain reeled, and a panic older than language clawed at my gut.

It wasn't rage.

It was terror.

I barely managed a breath. For a moment, I understood the compulsion behind the wildness—why monsters lashed out when caged. But my body didn't go for violence. It just froze, paralyzed, desperate for any hint of her presence.

The councilor with the fox face leaned into her mic and said, "She isn't his weakness. She's his anchor."

The tech nodded, writing it down. Her voice came out soft, almost respectful: "Would you like her brought back?"

I managed a nod.

The moment Lucia reentered the chamber, the world snapped back into color. The shaking stopped. My breath returned. She ran to the barrier, hands against the glass, and for a second, nothing else mattered.

"Fascinating," one witch said, and I could tell she meant it.

Next was blood dependency.

They started with the basics: a synthetic blood cocktail, some animal plasma, even a bag of stored vampire red labeled "O NEGATIVE—TEST ONLY." The tech offered each in turn. My stomach recoiled; my skin prickled with revulsion. I could not have forced it down if my life depended on it.

Then they brought out Lucia's blood—fresh, in a glass vial, the scent as familiar as air. The moment I tasted it, my whole body unclenched. The hunger, the emptiness, every fiber realigned. I felt better than I had all day.

The gallery fell silent.

"She can't be replaced," said the demon councilor.

The fox-faced witch marked it in red: "Bond is exclusive. No alternative source."

I saw then what this meant. If they ever wanted to control me—turn me, starve me, weaponize me—they couldn't. Not without her. We were two halves of a closed system, unbreakable except at the cost of both. I could only hope our power would continue to adapt to overcome what they'd learned.

Lucia was crying again, but this time it was relief. I pressed my palm to the glass, and she mirrored the gesture.

I knew that, whatever came next, the Council was scared.

Not just of me.

But of what we could become.

They were done with subtlety. The final act wasn't even pretending to be humane.

They filed in, every seat in the observation gallery filled—no longer a testing panel, but a tribunal. The lead tech rolled in a black velvet-lined box and opened it with reverence. Inside, gleaming under the fluorescent lights, was a set of shackles. Not ordinary cuffs, but bands of old, heavy metal etched with runes so sharp they seemed to cut the light itself.

I'd seen them before. In my dreams, the ones I'd seen time and again since the visions started. I remembered the cold press of the metal, the way the script pulsed with a heartbeat all its own. Seeing them here—real, waiting for me—turned my stomach inside out.

Adramal stepped forward. His voice was almost gentle. "For your safety, and ours, we will now test the runic restraints."

Kazimir stepped up.

Lucia, brought in and recoiled so hard her chair nearly toppled. "No. He is not..."

"It's protocol," the demon interrupted, bowing his head. "There will be no harm. It is simply a demonstration."

"See that it doesn't." Kazimir left no doubt that he would not stand for much more.

Bronc stepped between me and the tech. "He's proven his control. This is overkill."

Otero smiled. "One never knows. The future is a dangerous place."

I felt the bond with Lucia flicker, vibrating with her terror and my own. For the first time since this started, I considered fighting—really fighting, tearing my way out and to hell with the consequences. But I saw the warning in her eyes: Don't. Not yet.

So I let them clap the cuffs on.

The effect was immediate. Power dampened, senses fuzzed, my wolf retreating into a distant, colorless fog. It didn't hurt, but it felt like being dropped into a vat of ice water. Every instinct screamed at me to get them off.

The councilors watched, taking notes. One of them whispered, "Effective." Another, more quietly: "Necessary."

I was pretty sure I knew what they were planning. If the bond tests showed I couldn't be starved or turned, maybe I could be caged. The shackles were a warning, not just to me, but to Kazimir, to Lucia, to everyone who thought this council played fair.

They left the cuffs on just long enough to satisfy themselves, then unlocked them. The runes burned cold against my wrists. The tech carefully removed them.

The session ended with a formality: "Testing is complete," the fox-faced witch announced. "The Council will deliberate."

Nobody cheered. Nobody smiled.

Lucia ran to me the instant they let her, arms around my neck; her relief was so complete I thought she'd collapse. "I'm sorry," she whispered. "I should have..."

I shook my head. "It's not over. We keep playing their game."

She held on tighter.

When it was time to leave, the staff ushered us to the exit. But instead of letting Lucia walk with me, they split us up—her to the left, with Bronc and the rest; me to the right, alone. "You will be escorted to change out of testing attire," a functionary said, voice polite and empty.

Kazimir bristled. "My daughter walks with him."

"I'm afraid protocol demands otherwise," the functionary replied. "It will only be a moment. He is safe here."

Bronc saw it immediately. He reached for the functionary, but security closed in, just enough show of force to make it clear. I tried to catch Lucia's eyes as I was led away, but she was already being swept up by the crowd.

The corridor was narrow, lined with doors every few feet. I was led to one marked "PERSONNEL ONLY." The functionary gestured inside.

I stepped through.

The door closed behind me, sealing with a hiss. The frame was etched with runes—identical to the ones on the cuffs. I realized, too late, that I'd just walked into a cage of my own.

And for the first time since this nightmare started, I was genuinely afraid.

The cell looked like any hospital changing room: a bench, a metal locker, a stack of neatly folded scrubs. But the second the door sealed, I felt the static charge of magic snap shut around me. It wasn't just the runes—they'd built this whole place as a containment trap, layers upon layers of wards and null fields. Even the air tasted flat, like the pressure had changed and sucked the oxygen out.

I tested the handle—solid, unmoving. The walls felt like plaster but rang hollow, deadening every sound I made. My senses went fuzzy at the edges; the wolf retreated into a place I couldn't reach, not rage or sleep, just... muted. When I tried to push power out, all I got was a tingling in my teeth and a mild headache.

The worst part was the sudden quiet in my head. The bond to Lucia, always there like a heartbeat, went faint. Not gone, but far away, like I was underwater and she was calling from the shore. Panic fluttered in my chest, more animal than rational. I beat it back and started counting the ways out: the vent (too small, sealed with more runes), the hinges (not visible), the bench (bolted down).

I paced the room, looking for a weakness. Nothing. I ran through the tactical checklist—escape, improvise weapon, feign injury—but every angle was already covered. I'd never been truly caged before. Not in any way that mattered.

On the other side of the world, I felt Lucia reach for me. Not with words, but with emotion: a single pulse of cold, sharp worry, then a muted flare of rage. I tried to send something back, but the cell just bounced it around, dull and useless.

I didn't know how much time had passed. The lights never changed. Nobody came.

I started to think in circles—what did they want? To study me, lock me up, use me as leverage? Or just to prove that even monsters could be contained if you built the right box?

When the door finally opened, it wasn't a guard or a functionary. It was the Otero, walking in like he'd been expected for tea.

He regarded me for a moment, eyes sharp as scalpels. "You understand this isn't personal," he said.

I didn't answer.

"Containment is necessary," he continued, as if we were old friends. "You're not the only one who sees the danger."

Still, I said nothing. He waited, then shrugged.

"This is the part you and that fucking so-called King of Kings don't understand," he sneered. "It's not about your power, or our safety. It's about the person who actually has had the *real* power all along."

I knew in that moment that I would never see Lucia again unless they found wherever they were taking me next.

CHAPTER 24

LUCIA

I'd braced myself for the long, slow agony of waiting through the Council's assessment, but I never expected that the pain would arrive as a single, slicing absence—like waking up to find you've bled out overnight. The mate bond I'd just begun to trust thinned to a filament, a cobweb strand stretched by hurricane winds, and in the time it took me to inhale, the other half of my soul—Ryder—had gone silent. Not just weak, but wrong.

He was gone. The guards had taken him to change, a token gesture before he rejoined his party. But that was forty-two seconds ago by the wall clock. Even with my father's knack for melodrama, forty-two seconds should not stretch to infinity.

I launched myself down the steps, grabbing the hem of my dress so hard I heard threads snap, the words "He's gone, he's gone, he's gone," on repeat from my mouth.

The tech assigned to escort Ryder's guards back up the corridor was still in the foyer, face half-buried in a clipboard, oblivious to the squall building in the chamber. I reached for his arm, but before I could so much as make contact, a shadow rippled over me, and my father's hand shot out instead, grabbing the tech by the throat.

There was a crack—maybe the clipboard, maybe cartilage—and the technician's feet left the floor. Kazimir's eyes were feral black, the pupils blown so wide they'd nearly erased all the white. His fangs, always slightly longer than even the oldest vampires, had erupted fully, slicing his lip. Blood, black in this lighting, glistened on his chin.

"Where," my father demanded, voice rumbling in registers that scraped the marrow, "is he?"

The technician made a gurgling, high-pitched mewl. His left shoe tapped out a frantic Morse code on the woodwork. I barely registered Aspen tearing past, her shoes making no sound on the stone as she sprinted for the rear hallway, Big Papa hot on her heels.

The tech's face had started to turn purple. My father rattled him harder, squeezing out a squeal. "Speak!"

"I—I—left him with the guards, Your Majesty, they took him to the changing room…" The technician's eyes rolled, searching for help, but nobody was moving except for Bronc.

Menace barreled through the side doors, his hair disheveled and shirt half-tucked, as if he'd just run a dead sprint from the edge of the headquarters. His hazel eyes darted from me to the struggling technician to my father, calculation warring with primal fury in his features.

Somewhere beyond the main doors, a chorus of shouts erupted—at least two dozen voices, some high and keening, others guttural with threat. The Council witches had arrived, flanked by the other supernatural royalty. The Starweaver Fallon herself was at the front, crystal blue robes swirling like a comet's tail. She pointed a delicate, ringed finger at the chaos in the chamber.

"Council Chairwoman!" she bellowed. "This violates all protocols! All test subjects are meant to be kept safe from any harm—who allowed his removal?"

The Chairwoman, a sphinx of a woman in a severe black suit, looked seconds from cardiac arrest. Her eyes scanned the hall, hoping, perhaps, that someone would step in and save her from what was about to happen.

Rafe Mayfield, King of the Southwest Wolves, strode in next, his every step broadcasting what his words soon confirmed: "Bring me my subject, now!" He glowered at the chaos as if it were a personal affront, his onyx eyes boring into the technician with a predator's focus. His hair, longer than was strictly fashionable for a king, brushed his collar as he jerked his chin toward me.

"Princess Kozlov—do you know where your mate has gone?"

"Do I look like I know?" I snapped, voice pitched higher than I liked. "If I did, would I be standing here letting my father do this?"

The room was now a funnel of sound, all voices converging on the same horror. The witches were shouting about broken supernatural law; the shifters were shouting about honor, and the vampire representatives had gone eerily silent. I realized suddenly that my brothers, Maksym and Taras, were nowhere to be seen—no, there they were, gliding along the back wall, eyes glittering with something almost feverish. They were waiting for a command. Bohdi was suddenly by my side, and I knew Nikolay was somewhere near.

That's when Adramal appeared. If demons could feel concern, then it showed on his face. The Demon King's obsidian skin was even darker against his snow-white shirt, the horns curling low against his scalp as he surveyed the damage.

He addressed my father directly, his voice low and vibrating like an approaching train: "Sire, with respect—if you kill the technician, we may never know who took him. Allow me."

My father hesitated. For a heartbeat he looked at me, and I saw the horror there—a king who had watched too many of his kind die, too many mates sundered from their pairs. He released the technician, who collapsed in a heap, and in the same movement turned to face Adramal with all the dignity a nine-century-old immortal could muster.

I moved to follow Adramal, but a dizzy spell staggered me; it was as if my inner compass was fighting not just to find Ryder, but to keep me upright at all. The bond pulsed again—this time sharp, like a hot needle poking from inside my sternum—and I knew, absolutely, that this was not an ordinary abduction. Ryder was being unmade, molecule by molecule, from the other side of whatever wall they'd thrown between us.

The chamber had devolved into chaos. The Chairwoman banged her gavel, but the sound was lost beneath the roiling din. Her voice, when it came, was shaky but determined: "Order! We will restore order—now! Security: Seal every exit. Nobody leaves until we know where Doctor Lowrey has been taken."

Menace, who had been vibrating with kinetic energy this whole time, bellowed over the crowd: "If you want to avoid a bloodbath, Chairwoman, I suggest you start with the techs who handled the cuffs. You don't let a shifter just walk out—someone facilitated this."

"You accuse my staff?" The Chairwoman's voice was brittle.

"I accuse anyone in this room who had access to the suppression cuffs, and the transport logs!" Menace jabbed a finger toward the back of the room, where a huddle of vampire techs had clustered, terrified.

Juliet leaned into me, her breath warm on my cheek, and whispered, "If Ryder is gone, we will tear this place down stone by stone. Just say the word." For the first time I saw the streaks of black in her hair, the way her pupils were still stretching, wolf pushing and pushing. I wanted to thank her, but my throat had closed up.

The Chairwoman managed to reassemble herself from the wreckage of the council chamber, lips pressed so tight they'd gone bloodless. She pounded the gavel for attention, but it was the kind of noise a child makes when trying to scare off a bear: ceremonial, pointless, and almost heart-breaking. The hall was a tempest of bickering delegations and posturing lieutenants, all of them bracing for a wider war.

In the charged silence after the sixth gavel strike, the doors swung open with a languid sigh, as if the building itself had grown bored with our panic. Otero finally strolled in, not hurrying, not even pretending. The West Vampire King wore midnight-blue velvet; his silver hair a perfect mirror for the pale moon of his face. He looked like he'd just awoken from a long nap, or maybe a satisfying murder spree. I didn't even wait for him to reach the dais.

I moved faster than any human eye could track; the force of my leap sending bench splinters across the tiles. Otero didn't flinch. His eyebrows climbed delicately as I landed two meters in front of him, fangs fully bared.

"Where is he?" My voice was raw, torn up by the burning in my chest. "You took him, didn't you, you snake-eating bastard?"

He held out his hands, palms up, in a theater-gesture of innocence. "My dear, I assure you—this is as much a shock to me as to anyone. Highly irregular. Highly suspicious." His eyes flicked to the Chairwoman, then back to me with a little smile. "It seems someone has an agenda."

My hands curled into claws. Every nerve was fire and acid; the mate bond now so tenuous I could barely feel Doc at all. For the first time since the council began, real panic overtook my rage. A physical pain opened in my chest, a thudding, empty ache. I could not breathe. I could not think.

But I could hate.

My brothers arrived at my sides as if by summoning—Maksym to the right, Taras to the left. Both of them, beautiful and terrible, eyes alight with an ancient promise of violence. Together we made a wall, the sort of unbreakable line only Kozlovs could forge. Maksym pressed his wrist to my back, voice pitched for me alone: "*Sestrichka*, if you fall, we will burn this city."

"I'm not falling," I whispered, a lie too thin to stand on its own. But they believed it, or at least they would fight for it.

Otero kept smiling, shifting his gaze from me to the furious crowd. "It is tragic, of course," he said, voice carrying with supernatural resonance. "But perhaps the council should consider who truly benefits from this disruption. After all, the timing is most... convenient." He looked at my father when he said that, and the implication sizzled in the air like a brand.

Kazimir's jaw knotted. I felt the ripples of his fury, but he'd already decided not to waste a king's energy on a public screaming match. Instead, he fixed Otero with a dead man's stare. "If you had anything to do with this, you will not live to regret it."

"I am wounded, Sire. Deeply." Otero grinned, showing a hint of fang. "But I suggest we first establish the facts. Where, precisely, was Doctor Lowrey last seen?"

The Chairwoman, desperate for a narrative she could control, motioned for the Head of Security to step forward. He did, hands trembling, voice barely above a whimper. "He was seen entering the changing suite, escorted by two guards and a technician from your staff, King Otero."

A rustle ran through the council, the words "from your staff" blooming into accusation. Otero feigned offense, then waved a languid hand. "And yet, no sign of the guards. Most interesting. A professional, surgical abduction."

Rafe Mayfield, who'd been suppressing his inner wolf so hard it looked like his skin might split, finally snapped. "I want my subject produced—alive, unharmed, or you'll face consequences even your sire can't protect you from." He glared daggers at Otero, but his real concern was with Bronc, who still shook with the unreleased force of his near shift.

Menace, never one for passivity, prowled up the aisle and added his voice. "Someone's playing all of us for fools. I don't buy this magical vanishing act unless it's inside help." He jabbed a finger at Otero. "And you're the only king who wasn't in the chamber."

Otero smirked. "Perhaps I simply value punctuality less than you do, Mr. Hardin."

"Enough!" the Chairwoman barked, the word echoing off the marble like a gunshot. "We have protocols. We will follow them."

I could not bear it any longer. My mate was being erased while we debated etiquette and blame. I let my aura expand, shoving every other supernatural presence out of my way until I was practically glowing, a blue-white halo of anger and dread.

I stepped closer to Otero, so close I could have tasted his aftershave if I'd wanted to. "You will tell me where he is, or I will rip it from your skull one neuron at a time. Do you understand me?"

He laughed, a light tinkle of sound that filled the void and made me want to bite a hole in his throat. "How adorable," he said, "but if I had done this, darling, you'd be dead already."

I opened my mouth to respond, but the chamber doors blew open with a thunderous bang. The wind that swept in was warm, golden, and smelled faintly of cinnamon. Archon strode into the chaos, wings furled tight against his back, eyes burning gold like twin suns. On either side of him were Aspen and Big Papa, both looking battered but unbroken.

Every head in the room turned. Even Otero's mask slipped a fraction, the barest widening of his eyes. Archon didn't need to shout. His presence alone shut down all noise.

He made straight for the dais, his seven-foot frame making every step a benediction and a warning. He paused in front of the council and swept a look around the room. "This must end now," he said, voice carrying on some resonance that bypassed the ear and hit you straight in the heart.

The Chairwoman nodded, the first time she'd truly looked relieved since sunrise. "Lord Archon, if you have evidence—"

"I have more than evidence," he replied. "I have the truth." He turned to me, and when he spoke, the words vibrated in my skull. "Princess Lucia, I sensed the mate bond fracture. And I found the mark of its destroyer."

My knees went weak. "Is Ryder... dead?"

"No," Archon's certainty was a rock in the floodwaters. "But he is being torn apart, and soon, your bond will be gone for good. There was a demonic signature in the hallway—Maltraz, without question."

The room was a vacuum; every whisper sucked out. Everyone but Otero looked surprised.

"Maltraz?" the Chairwoman whispered, but she was looking at Adramal, who merely nodded once, the motion heavy with meaning.

Archon continued, voice gentle but implacable. "Your mate was taken by force, but not yet destroyed. Maltraz has plans for him, or you, or both. But he could not have done this without access. Without help from within."

He looked at Otero, then at the vampires clustered behind him.

Otero straightened, the picture of offense. "If you're implying—"

Archon cut him off with a single gesture. "I imply nothing. But the last to handle the subject was your technician, King Otero. And your guards have vanished."

Otero bared his teeth, a flicker of predator beneath the courtier. "Anyone can manufacture a demonic signature. This is clearly an attempt to besmirch the honor of my house. I demand a thorough investigation, not this witch-hunt."

Menace made a rude noise, but the Chairwoman seized the opportunity. "Then you will make your staff available for immediate questioning. And you, Princess, will—"

She paused, looking at me with real pity. "I am so sorry. We will do everything in our power."

I ignored her, locking eyes with Archon. "How much time do I have?"

He hesitated, and it was the first time I'd seen him hesitate in my life. "Hours, at most. Once the bond breaks, even I may not be able to reach him."

Otero's voice cut through the moment like a stiletto: "Assuming you can reach him now, of course. It sounds like he's likely long gone at this point."

A ripple of terror lanced through the assembly. For a half-second, true silence ruled the chamber. Then, in a supernatural blur too quick for any but the oldest monsters to track, my father was across the room and had Otero by the throat, pinning him against the stone wall. The impact shook loose a spray of ancient dust from the masonry, and the force of it rattled the windows in their casements.

My father's claws were fully extended, each one glistening with a pearly sheen that made them look more like surgical steel than keratin. He lifted Otero off his feet, one-handed, as if he weighed nothing. Blood welled up in dark beads where my father's claws pierced skin, running down the side of Otero's throat in thick, slow ribbons.

Otero scrabbled at my father's wrist, face shifting from smug to panicked to an animal's blank terror. His feet kicked, seeking purchase, but there was none.

"You think we all don't know you were involved?" My father's voice was colder than the grave; his face more monstrous than I'd ever seen. "You think you can touch my blood, my family? I have buried a thousand like you. You are nothing." He shook Otero so violently the king's head bounced off the stone, cracking it with a sickening sound.

Otero tried to gurgle out a response, but my father wasn't listening.

"If you are guilty," my father went on, his voice now pitched for every shadow and echo in the chamber, "I will make it so you never know rest, not in this life nor any to come. I will keep you in pain and darkness until you beg for death, and *when* you beg, I will deny you." He let the words hang there, an icy fog.

Otero's body slackened. My father dropped him like a sack of bones, letting him crumple to the floor. Blood fanned out across the marble, a Rorschach pattern of defeat. Otero coughed, clutching his neck, and glaring up at my father with a new, terrified respect.

Menace and Rafe both stepped back instinctively, the former with a grudging admiration, the latter with a wolf's calculation—was my father now the biggest threat in the room? Even Archon paused, the tiniest smile tugging at the corner of his mouth as if he approved of the demonstration.

The world spun. My knees buckled.

Maksym and Taras were there, their arms locking around my ribcage. I barely felt their hands; the bond was flickering now, each pulse weaker than the last. My vision fuzzed, the edges graying out, sounds coming at me from odd angles and at the wrong volume. My brothers exchanged a look over my head.

"We need to get her out," Taras said, voice guttural.

"Now," Maksym agreed.

They half-carried, half-dragged me toward the exit. The Council blurred past—faces gaping, some in awe, most in horror—but none of them mattered. The only thing that mattered was the thread in my chest, the vanishing, dying light of Ryder's existence.

Juliet and Bronc joined us at the steps, Juliet's eyes brimming gold, jaw set for war. "We'll find him," she vowed, and in that moment I believed she'd murder her way through a continent to make it true.

Menace barked orders at the security staff, organizing a full sweep with Savannah standing tall beside him, the warrior queen she'd become ready for battle. While Rafe conferred in angry whispers with the witch council. Aspen and Big Papa moved to flank our group, a makeshift honor guard for a princess who could barely stand. Wrecker, Arsenal, and Gunner were sentinels of strength at my back. Parker, Harper, and Brie ready to battle any who thought to come against us.

My last memory of the chamber was Otero slumped against the wall, holding his bloody neck, hatred and terror warring for space in his gaze. My father didn't even look at him as he followed us out, every inch of him the unbreakable, ancient monarch he'd always claimed to be. His hand brushed my shoulder, not gently, but with an unspoken promise: they would not take me, or my mate, without a war that would shatter our world.

I closed my eyes, and somewhere, impossibly far away, I thought I heard Ryder call my name.

When I finally surfaced from the black ocean of pain, it was to the scent of old wood, waxed marble, and something faintly metallic—blood, maybe, or just the memory of it. My eyes fought to focus, each blink a battle, and I realized I was in the great hall of my father's estate.

I tried to sit up, but my arms wouldn't cooperate. My skin felt three sizes too tight for my bones, and I was freezing, even in the heavy velvet of my dress. I wanted to say something—an order, a curse, anything—but the words stuck in my throat. I felt like I did when Doc and I had first been separated after his turning. But this was worse. Then he was nearing. Now he's slipping away.

Juliet must have seen me stir. She was at my side in a heartbeat, her hands cool and sure as she wrapped a blanket around my shoulders. "You're safe," she whispered, but the wobble in her voice made it a question.

I managed a smile, or something like it. "Never been safer."

"Liar," Juliet squeezed my arm so hard it almost hurt. "Doc is still alive, Lucia. You'd know if he wasn't. Right?"

The mate bond was now a distant echo, a whisper of pain and longing. I nodded, though I wasn't sure it was true.

A ripple ran through the room, and then the air thickened, as if someone had cranked the gravity to maximum. The front doors opened without a sound, and Archon entered. He wore white, always white, and it glowed in the lamplight like fresh snow. His hair was loose for once, falling in a shimmering waterfall down his back. He brought with him the hush of deep forests, the hush of the last breath before something holy—or unholy—arrives.

Every supernatural in the room stood, even my father.

Archon approached, and as he drew near, I felt some of the pressure in my chest ease, like a tourniquet finally loosened. He stopped at my side, looking down with eyes that held all the sadness of an endless world.

"You are suffering," he said, not as a question, but as a statement of universal law.

"I've had better days," I replied, because sarcasm was the only shield I had left. "Is he...?"

Archon shook his head, soft but definitive. "He is alive, but not well. His essence is being siphoned. If it continues, the mate bond will rupture."

Juliet growled, low and involuntary. "How do we stop it?"

"Find the source. Destroy it." Archon placed a hand on my shoulder, and the warmth that flooded me was so pure I nearly wept. "Maltraz has hurt his last. We will end him."

My father moved toward Archon, cloak trailing behind him like night itself. "If you need an army, you have it. If you need a kingdom, you have it. But you will bring my child's mate back, or I will turn this world to ash."

Archon inclined his head, as if accepting an appointment rather than a threat. "It will not come to that, Sire. But I will need your cooperation. And your daughter's."

I wanted to say I'd fight until my last breath, but that my last breath could come at any moment. But Archon's grip on my shoulder was an anchor. I nodded, and some tiny, vital part of me returned to the surface.

He turned to address the whole room, voice rising to fill every alcove and every heart. "Maltraz and his allies seek not only to break a mate bond, but to shatter the will of this kingdom. If they succeed, Kazimir will fall.

If he falls, the vampire world fractures. If that happens, every supernatural alliance unravels. The demon king wants chaos, not just power."

Menace spat onto the floor. "So we're fighting a war for the future, not just for Doc."

"Correct," Archon confirmed. "But it begins with him. If they break the hybrid, they can break any bond."

Bronc raised a hand, a commander's gesture. "What do you need from us?"

Archon scanned the room. "All of you together. Your strengths, your unity. And your belief that bonds, once forged, are not so easily severed. I will do what I can to keep Lucia alive. But for Ryder..." He turned to me, his gaze merciful. "He must hold on. If he gives up, even for a moment, he will be lost."

My lips went numb. "Can he hear me?"

Archon smiled, the first real smile I'd ever seen on him. "Always. He is yours, as you are his."

The mate mark over my heart was faint, the blue of it nearly gone, but it pulsed with a stubborn rhythm. I laid my hand over it and closed my eyes.

Hold on, Ryder, I pleaded. Just hold on. We are coming for you.

And this time, when I prayed, I believed it.

CHAPTER 25

DOC

I woke to the absence of sensation.

Not pain, not exactly. More like a subtraction of every crutch that anchored a man to the notion of time passing: no hunger, no thirst, no need to piss, nothing but a hollow float in a world engineered for neutral misery. I opened my eyes—or I thought I did, because vision didn't change. The light was omnipresent, colorless, a soft-edged fixture that backlit everything without so much as a gradient to cast a shadow. No walls, no doors. I could have been in an MRI tube or in a waiting room at the edge of a void. I tried to move my head, and something in my neck rebelled—heavy, slow, like my muscles had spent a week submerged in syrup.

I took inventory, as I had been trained to do. Awareness check. I was on my back, resting on something neither soft nor hard, neither warm nor cool. My wrists and ankles tingled with the specific burn of circulation gone askew, and I felt the numbing pressure of restraints. I flexed my left foot and heard the faintest chime of metal—a runic shackle, heavy enough to be felt but not enough to tear skin if you thrashed. I could taste the metal in my spit, acidic, copper-bright. I braced to shift. Nothing happened. The wolf inside me didn't so much as shudder; my new, hungry side felt like it had been vacuum-packed in Saran wrap and shoved in the fridge.

Someone had built this place with a deep, specific hatred for creatures like me. It wasn't a cell so much as a lab, a negative space where every possible escape was not merely blocked, but erased from the laws of physics. Even my brain chemistry felt foreign. I thought, then, about the first time I'd woken up restrained: the trauma ward in Kandahar, fourteen years ago, local anesthesia wearing off while a Navy corpsman cranked my arm back into place. That pain had been bright, quick, and personal. Of course, that medic did not know my wolf status, so when the pain eased quicker than humanly possible, I acted as though it hadn't. The pain here was the unending low drone of a hospital alarm that never stops, but never gets loud enough to warrant action.

My skin itched. My scalp burned. I tried to swallow and realized I couldn't remember the last time I'd needed to. Time itself was meaningless; it could have been minutes or months since I'd lost consciousness in that rune-covered cell. I ran down the list of bodily systems, one at a time. *Heart rate: slow, steady, not the panic spike of captivity. Blood oxygen: low, but not hypoxic. Pupils: Did they respond?* I couldn't test. I couldn't even raise my hands to my face to check, which told me something about the degree of immobilization. My healing factor was gone or suppressed, which meant this was no ordinary binding. Silver would have stung; iron would have made me nauseous. This was neither. This was something else—something more.

I tried to focus, to count breaths, but the air itself rebelled. It was thick, moist, and unscented. No hint of bleach, piss, rot, nothing to orient me in space or time. If I licked my lips, I'd have bet they tasted like the inside of an airlock—sanitized and dry and faintly reminiscent of static electricity. When I tried to inhale deeply, my lungs hit a wall; the pressure in the room was just north of comfortable, like the cabin of a plane right after takeoff.

It struck me that if this was torture; it was not designed for quick answers or sadistic satisfaction. This was a waiting game, an erosion, the kind of psychological warfare you reserved for beings that could not be broken by pain alone. It felt like a psychiatric specialist had designed hell: no violence, just slow decay and interminable monotony.

My hands started to throb. My body wanted to move, to cycle through its normal calibrations. I gave in to it and let the micro-movements roll through my fingers. I pictured the layout of the shackle on my right wrist, seeing the pattern of runes in my mind. It didn't track like anything Slavic or Norse, and the lines were too clean for cuneiform. I ran my mind through a pharmacopoeia of possible suppressants and drew a blank. Whatever was muting my regenerative system was baked into the hardware, not the air.

I shut my eyes and waited for the flicker of internal night. There was none. The room wasn't merely luminous—it existed outside the language of light and shadow. The absence of change was a kind of violence. The longer I stared at nothing, the more my thoughts tried to loop, running wild and starving for stimuli. I thought of Lucia—her laugh, sharp as a crowbar; her hands, always cold, always hungry. The memory flickered, then flattened. I could barely feel her in the bond. That should have terrified me, but it didn't. It just felt like losing a sense, and knowing you couldn't get it back.

I began cataloguing. If I were going to be a subject, I would make it my own damn research project.

1. No doors, windows, or seam lines—probable pocket dimension, or at least a bunker-level isolation room.

2. Sound was weird: my breath echoed back at me, but never the noise of a settling body, no rumble in the chest, no tinnitus. Like the air itself was flat.

3. No scents. Zero, zip. Not even my own. Not even a memory of it.

4. Bodily needs suppressed. Probably designed to keep me conscious and compliant as long as possible.

5. Shackles: high-tech and supernatural. Every time I tensed, the pressure adjusted, like they anticipated muscular changes and recalibrated. There was an algorithm at work, or maybe even a sentient control. But they also clearly had suppressed my powers.

6. Temperature: neutral. No sweat, no shivers, no vasodilation. Whoever built this chamber wanted me to lose track of everything but the slow, crawling need to move.

I flexed again, testing the slack. My joints responded, but there was zero give. I tried to cycle up the wolf, even just to taste the shift at the edges of my skin, and nothing happened. The hunger was a little different. It felt—weakened. If I tried to focus on it, it retreated, like looking into a microscope and finding the specimen on the slide disappear.

Maybe this was hell for hybrids like me. Maybe this was where monsters went when they outlived their usefulness.

I heard a noise, then. Not from outside, but from the inside of my own head: a slight static, an electric pop. I recognized the pattern as a neurological readjustment; the brain working overtime to create stimuli where there was none. Hallucinations would start soon if I didn't find a way to anchor myself. I started reciting med protocols from memory, step by step. Triage, first aid, field surgery, starting from the basics and moving upward, each one a stone in the river to keep my mind from washing away.

I remembered the day I almost lost my arm, back when I still bled like a regular wolf. How Bronc had held me together with nothing but duct tape and piss-poor jokes. I thought of how he got me to my hospital, the crisp sheets, the nurse who'd handed me a morphine clicker and said, *"Don't be a hero, Doc."* I remembered my own hands opening Parker's skull to relieve the pressure after she'd been blown to hell by a bomb meant to kill us all. I did it with practiced indifference, knowing she'd make it, then walking outside and throwing up anyway.

If my body were being denied its nature, my mind could still serve its function.

I began monitoring myself in real time, counting every second, every twitch. The monotony was a gift if you knew how to use it. I couldn't see my watch, couldn't even tell if I had one, but I started the clock anyway. I would measure every damn heartbeat, every breath, every time the shackles twitched.

Whoever came to get me would find me ready.

Or as ready as a man could be, chained up in hell's waiting room.

The first sign of a visitor was the shift in air pressure. Not the hiss of a pneumatic door, but a pulse that rolled over my skin and left the follicles standing at attention. I tried to prepare for pain, but what came was worse: recognition.

Maltraz entered with the slow, sure gait of someone who never had to rush. Behind him glided the tall, silver-haired vampire with skin so pale and smooth it looked airbrushed. They wore suits, though Maltraz's was a ruin of old blood and new tailoring; the other wore his like armor, every seam a challenge. The duo stopped an arm's length from the slab where I lay shackled, and for a moment neither spoke. The light in the chamber bent around them, refusing to touch their edges, as if the room resented the intrusion.

"Ryder Lowrey," Maltraz said, rolling my name around in his mouth like he were savoring the taste of each consonant. "We meet at last. Awake, alert, and as spirited as I had hoped." His voice felt like a toxin; I could almost trace its journey from my eardrums to the shudder in my spine.

I didn't answer. I stared at his buttons on his vest instead; shiny silver filigree, with tiny onyx stones inlaid. Hell's own prom king.

The other man—Otero, whom I hadn't seen since he'd trapped me in the cell under the noses of the Council; wasted no time. He produced a slender needle and a tube; the kind used for arterial blood draws. He didn't ask for my arm. He simply gripped my bicep in a way that suggested if bone snapped, it was my fault for being so fragile. The needle sank in with predatory grace. No antiseptic, no ritual. The pain was real, sharp, but measured. They wanted a clean draw.

Otero watched the blood spiral into the tube and made a thoughtful noise. "Fascinating. Still red, despite the null. I expected more purple." His accent was old-world, but his diction was precise—every word a little knife.

Maltraz folded his hands and leaned forward. "We're not here to torment you, Ryder. Not directly. This is a scientific survey. You should be proud: in all my eons, I have never found a specimen quite so... chimeric."

I spat on the floor—more reflex than protest, though I noted with detached interest that the saliva was pale, almost pink. "You want a sample? Take a swab and fuck off."

Maltraz smiled. "Oh, I will. But in stages. We have time." He flicked his eyes at Otero, who uncapped the second needle.

The next insertion was at my carotid, as if they wanted to see how quickly I could clot. They ran through ten tubes in silence. I tried to keep count, but the silence made time slippery. Each draw left me weaker, the world's edges going slightly soft. I watched the men work—efficient, detached, almost bored. Maltraz paced the perimeter, hands in pockets, while Otero monitored my pulse with one hand and the drip rate with the other.

When they finished, Maltraz leaned over me, his face close enough I could count every leathery pore. "You're wondering how you heal in here. The answer is: slowly. Your cells want to adapt, but the field recalibrates every millisecond. Fascinating, really. If we let you die, you'd come back, but less... each time. And we need you alive. Our interests aren't just... scientific. Your mate holds particular interest for us as well. She's the key, really; her father's weakness. Together, the two of you will topple a kingdom."

He straightened, flicking an imaginary speck from his lapel. "We will return. Rest well, Doctor."

They left, but not before Otero tucked a little sensor under my ribcage—just above the liver. I felt it click, then dissolve, as if it were made of sugar. Data, I realized. They were tracking everything.

I drifted. Time lost meaning again. The shackles felt heavier; my body sank deeper into the slab. At some point, the white light flickered, just once, and I caught a sliver of something familiar: the scent of roses and cold air. Lucia. My heart pounded against my ribs. It was gone as quickly as it arrived, replaced by a metallic tang and the sickly sweet smell of decay.

The next time Maltraz returned, he didn't bother with needles. He placed his palm on my sternum, fingers splayed wide. I felt a gentle tug—like a strong magnet under my skin. It didn't hurt, but I watched the veins in my arms rise and pulse in time with the rhythm of his touch. He closed his eyes as if listening to a distant song.

"You are holding onto something," he murmured. "A link. That's very dangerous, Ryder. Your mate cannot find you. Why resist the inevitable?"

I met his eyes, tried to muster contempt. My tongue was thick, slow. "You're not as clever as you think. You have to ask yourself—what if it goes both ways?"

He laughed. It was almost genuine. "Oh, but I hope it does. Our plans demand it."

They kept up the sampling, always at intervals I could not predict. Sometimes it was blood, sometimes a thin shaving of skin or a sliver of marrow. Sometimes, they simply talked, asking questions I refused to answer:

How long have you felt the bond?

Do you dream in color?

Did you ever fear your wolf?

What would you give to be normal?

After the third session, the hollowness set in. It was like standing on the edge of a cold pool, knowing you'd be thrown in, but not knowing when. I caught myself watching the light for signs of change, but it was always steady, a never-ending sunrise. My muscles felt as though they had atrophied; my mind ran loops of useless data. I thought about med school when I did my psych study. I remembered the kids who stared at nothing in the psych ward, how the only thing that seemed to help was the presence of another living thing. Even a goldfish.

When the psychological warfare started, I was almost grateful. Maltraz would enter the room alone, sit beside me, and speak softly, as if to a child:

"She's moving on, Ryder. She's alive, but her memory of you is fading. The bond thins every day."

"I can restore you. There's a way to erase the pain. You could be free."

"You are wasting energy for nothing."

The words didn't stick, but the images did. Sometimes I'd catch a flash in my peripheral vision—a face, a curl of black hair, the flick of a smile that belonged to Lucia. Once, I swore I heard her laugh, but it echoed wrong: too high, too brittle. They were trying to break me, not by force, but by erosion.

I focused on the only thing I had left: cataloguing the enemy.

Maltraz: Hands always clean, never a mark. Eyes that flickered red when the testing got interesting. Moved like a dancer, but the steps were always rehearsed. Voice modulated—never raised, never monotone. He liked to see how long I could hold his gaze before looking away.

Otero: The technician. All business, no affect. Once, I caught him humming under his breath—an old Russian hymn, maybe. He kept his tools immaculate, never repeated a question, and seemed annoyed when I wouldn't respond. If Maltraz was the showman, Otero was the scalpel.

Every hour—every session—I lost a little more. My body shriveled, my mind wandered. But the bond... the bond stayed. Even as the illusions flickered in and out, even as the light pressed in and the air grew stagnant, I knew she was out there. Fighting. Searching.

One time, Maltraz leaned close and whispered, "Let her go. If you release the bond, you'll be reborn. Otherwise, you both die." He smiled, as if sharing a secret. "There are worse things than death, Doctor."

I wanted to tell him to fuck off. But all I could do was stare at the blank ceiling, fighting to remember the sound of Lucia's voice. Every time I tried, the image went fuzzy, like a cassette tape stretched thin and ready to snap.

I wondered, not for the first time, if that was the point. Not to kill me, but to hollow me out so completely I'd volunteer for the end.

I gritted my teeth. I focused on the math—blood volume lost, cellular regeneration lag, the odds of surviving another day in the tank. I let the calculations fill the void.

I'd beaten worse odds before.

But this—this was a war of inches. I just had to make sure I never gave them the last one. I knew Lucia had to be weakening as well. I was certain that was part of their plan. I just hoped she'd find me before we were too far gone to save.

If Maltraz ever doubted I was a threat, he didn't show it. But the longer this game played out, the more I saw the tension in his jaw, the bored impatience in Otero's movements. The experiment had a timeline, and I was screwing up the results.

There was a rhythm to their visits, though not one I could measure in hours or minutes. The only clock was my own body—its slow decomposition, its refusal to let go of the smallest spark. Maltraz started coming less, but when he did, he stood longer at the edge of the slab, staring at me like a gambler watching the last card in the deck. Sometimes he said nothing. Sometimes he muttered in a language I didn't recognize, rolling the syllables over his tongue like a death sentence.

Otero came too, but his role was reduced to maintenance: check the shackles, log the readings, ensure the system held. But he was no longer collecting. They had everything they needed, or maybe they just got tired of the data always coming up the same.

I wasn't supposed to survive this long. That was the point.

It was in that stasis, that limbo, that I first noticed the change.

The bond didn't just ache—it throbbed, sharp and unpredictable. At first, it felt like a spasm, a cardiac arrhythmia firing off inside my soul. Then it was a spike of heat, burning through the fog of the null field, rattling the shackles. The runes on my wrists flickered—once, then again, brighter every time the bond surged.

Lucia.

I didn't hear her voice, but I felt the intent: a surge of desperate, reckless energy, like defibrillator paddles to the chest. It didn't heal me, didn't make me stronger. It just told me I wasn't alone, and it was enough.

The field fought back, cycling power, tightening the screws until my skin screamed with it. The lights stuttered, shadows skating across the floor for the first time since my capture. The air sizzled. Every cell in my body wanted to curl up and die, but I forced myself to hold onto that one last fragment of her.

Maltraz must have sensed it, too. He burst into the chamber in a blur of tailored rage, no Otero this time. He paced the length of the room, talking not to me but to the air, to whatever demonic god kept score in this place. He looked terrified. I wanted to laugh, but I was too busy trying not to bleed out through the holes in my soul.

He stopped at my side, looming, face gone all bones and predator's teeth.

"You can't win this," he spat. "You are not even a real wolf, or a real vampire. You are a mistake."

I grinned, or tried to. "Funny. That's what my high school guidance counselor said."

He slapped me hard. The impact rang but didn't hurt. "You want to be a martyr? You want her to die for you?"

He didn't understand. He never would. It wasn't about dying. It was about denying him the victory.

I kept my eyes open as the light went haywire, as the air temperature dropped to arctic then snapped back to boiling in the space of a single heartbeat. The walls pulsed, breathing with the force of the null field's machinery.

That's when I felt Lucia again. This time it was a thought—a wordless, panicked plea, but also a promise. She was coming. Not as a cavalry, but as a dagger, aimed right at the weak point.

The runes on my shackles sparked, throwing off little blue arcs. I flexed my wrists and felt, for the first time, the ghost of strength returning to my hands. The bonds still held, but the suppression field was no longer smooth—it rippled, stuttered, opened tiny fissures and closed them again.

Maltraz didn't see it. He was too busy yelling at the walls, his voice gone feral. The room began to warp, sound stretching and shrinking as if underwater. My hearing tunneled, then snapped back, every sense flipping between numb and hyper-acute.

Then I smelled her—roses and ice and blood, real and sharp and impossible to counterfeit. The bond snapped taut, nearly pulling my heart out of my chest.

And I knew: Lucia was here. Whether that meant in my mind because I was dying or in reality either way, I'd be with her soon.

The last thing I saw before darkness took over was the look on Maltraz's face—not anger, not even hate, but pure, undiluted panic. He'd built a box to kill a monster and instead woke something else entirely.

I let go of the slab, of the field, of the pain, and rode the bond into oblivion.

Next stop: wherever Lucia was.

CHAPTER 26

LUCIA

I woke to an emptiness so complete I nearly mistook it for death. There was nothing—no warm, solid weight pinning my thigh, no phantom brush of stubble at the back of my neck, not even the familiar scent of Doc's skin on the sheets. It was as if he'd been unmade from the fabric of the room, and all that lingered was the faintest echo of him in the way the pillow next to me curved, missing its shape.

My brothers held vigil at my side. "Don't sit up yet," Maksym said, not looking at me. "You're still—"

"I know," I rasped. My voice sounded like an old recording, played back too slowly. "Where *is* he?"

A silence stretched, fat and miserable.

"We'll find him," Nikolay answered, barely a whisper. "We will, Lucia, I swear to God, we..."

The rest of his words blurred in a sudden rush of static in my ears, as if my body's internal wiring had been stripped out and replaced with cheap speaker wire. It had been days since Doc had been taken. And each of those days I had become weaker. My magic stuttered within me, sparking weakly; the shadows that usually hovered at my fingertips pooled limply under the covers, sticky and inert.

I tried to sit up anyway, because the one thing I couldn't stomach was lying in bed like a victim. I managed an inch, then another, but it cost me. The room grayed at the edges, vision tunneling to nothingness.

I fell back, gasping. The ceiling bulged and pulsed, and for a moment I thought I saw something beyond it—a glimpse of Doc, maybe, or the place he'd been pulled to. But it was gone so fast I couldn't say if it was real or just a wishful hallucination.

That's when the temperature in the room changed.

Not in degrees—a thermometer wouldn't have noticed it—but the way the air moved, the charge of it, like standing in a cathedral just before the organ pipes howl. I felt it on my skin before I even saw the light: a pressure at the base of my skull, a pulsing on the inside of my eyelids.

Archon Seraphael entered with his usual disregard for doors, or for any kind of plausible deniability. One moment the space was as it had been; the next, a low burn of gold radiated in the center of the room, casting even the shadows into nervous, blue-tinged relief.

My father entered the room as though he'd sensed the angel king's arrival.

Archon nodded a small greeting to my father, and it was returned.

The Angel King wore a white shirt that should have looked out of place here—perfectly pressed, with buttons that shimmered like mother-of-pearl—but on him it just made the rest of us seem more tarnished. His hair, as always, was a ridiculous mane, white-gold, flowing past his shoulders and catching the wan light as if it belonged on a Renaissance fresco.

"May I approach?" he asked, and in that voice was the music of bells, of funerals, of battles just won, and the quiet afterward.

My father waved him to my bedside. Maksym grunted, the syllable shaped like a threat but landing like surrender at my father's raised eyebrow.

Archon knelt beside my bed. His presence crowded out everything else, but in a strange, welcome way—a kind of gravity that made all lesser concerns fall into order. He looked down at me, and I saw the golden flicker of his eyes, the depthless pools that held neither kindness nor cruelty but the simple fact of observation.

"You are diminished," he said, not unkindly.

"I'm aware," I replied, or tried to. It came out as a hiss of an exhale. "I need... he needs..."

He reached out—no slow, polite request, just the inevitability of his touch on my forehead. I expected a shock, something purifying, but the sensation was different: a spark, yes, but one that ran down my spine and into the root of my magic. It wasn't warm; it was all colors at once, a kind of cosmic static.

He withdrew his hand, then closed his eyes, as if accessing a radio station that only archangels could tune in to.

"The bond persists," he murmured. "But you are not anchored in this world. Your tether is through him, and the other end..." He opened his eyes, voice gone hard and analytical. "Maltraz is clever. The pocket he's made is outside the usual reach. Not even the Council could find it with all the witches of the Eastern Seaboard. But you..."

"I can find him," I said. The admission tasted like blood, but it was true. "If I could just..." My hands curled, then uncurled on the sheets, desperate for something to shape, to command.

Archon's smile was sad. "You are of a kind of darkness," he said, and it wasn't an insult. "I can light the way, but only if you walk it. Will you?"

I couldn't tell if the question was rhetorical or a test, but there was no universe in which I'd say no.

He didn't wait for an answer, anyway. Instead, he turned to Maksym and Nikolay. "Hold her," he instructed. Taras bristled a bit. My father nodded his consent.

Maksym crossed to my side and put both hands on my shoulders, gentle but immovable. Nikolay took my wrist. They were anchors, grounding me to this world, so I wouldn't slip out too soon.

Archon braced his palm against my sternum and spoke, but the words were not in any language I'd heard—nothing I could translate, but their weight was enormous, flattening all the air out of the room. My magic, dull and empty just a moment before, began to vibrate.

"You will focus," he told me, voice suddenly sharp. "Remember your mate. Picture only him. Let the bond lead you, and nothing else."

The ache in my chest became a compass. Every fiber of my being screamed toward Doc: not the man, not the wolf, but the exact meaning of his presence in my life, the steadiness, the light that he'd given me, the way he fit perfectly into every broken piece of me.

I let myself fall into that, using it as a hook to pull myself through the sludge of my own depleted magic.

It wasn't easy. The distance was not in miles but in metaphysics—a separation of soul, of time, of cosmic geography. It hurt. Every muscle in my body seized, and a cold sweat broke out across my skin. My hands clenched, and this time, black mist did gather, trembling and weak, at my fingers.

Archon's magic was a pressure at my back, like the light of a million suns filtered through lace. Together, the darkness and the light built—slow at first, then with gathering force.

I saw it: a line in the universe, a seam, a flaw in the perfect glass of reality. There was a tug, and then the world bent, and a sound like fabric tearing filled my ears. I screamed, not in pain, but in relief, because in that moment I could feel Doc on the other side. His mind, battered but alive, his hand stretching back along the line toward me.

"Open it," Archon said, the word like a blast of wind.

I did. I tore at the seam, my shadows threading it wide while his light seared the edges, cauterizing what would otherwise have bled us both dry.

The air split, and the room filled with the roar of unfiltered power, a torrent that made my nose bleed, made Maksym and Nikolay grunt with effort as they kept me anchored.

The opening shimmered, unstable and strange, but there it was—a window, a mirror, a path.

He was out there, and he needed me.

I slumped back, spent, but I did not let go. The line remained, humming with promise and threat.

My father showed the concern etched on his face. "Is she well?"

Archon leaned close. "Well enough," he said, and I could have sworn, just for a second, that I saw real pride in his face.

I expected some grand moment—the squad gathering in a blur of battle prep, maybe a rousing speech, or at least a silent group prayer. But that's not the Iron Valor way. The wolves gathered, not with fanfare but with the deliberate, silent efficiency of men who'd spent lifetimes going to war and coming back only a little less whole each time.

Bronc was first, striding in like he'd been called to handle a slow-burning fuse in the shop. His voice was soft but set the room's tempo: "Maksym, Nikolay, Taras, you're on outside perimeter. Bohdi, can you stay here and watch over our mates?" He never had to say the rest: If we don't come out, torch the compound. Don't let them take it. "Juliet, I need you to stay here. You are capable and strong, but our pups need their mother more than we need another warrior in battle."

She leaned up and kissed him and stepped back into the line of the other mates.

I sat on the side of my bed, and he knelt beside me, a mountain of calm, and put a hand over mine. "You ready to do this, Princess?"

I didn't trust myself to speak, so I just nodded. My hands shook so badly I could barely thread my own shadows together, but the look in Bronc's eyes made it feel like that was the only thing I'd ever need to do.

Menace appeared next, all coiled wire and unshed violence. Even in human skin, you could see the wolf pacing beneath—every muscle twitching for the chance to get bloody. He barely glanced at me, eyes instead locked on the tear in reality I'd opened. "You sure this thing'll hold?" he grunted, a challenge for Archon, but it was the kind of challenge that only came from desperate hope.

Archon, standing at the foot of the bed, regarded Menace with an odd serenity. "If your resolve matches hers, yes. If not, we'll all be unmade together. I gave you your life back for such an occasion, Highness."

Menace growled, but Bronc shot him a look, and he fell silent, radiating fury and impatience. He began pacing tight circles, as if winding a spring.

Wrecker and Arsenal came in together. Wrecker's eyes never left the tear, his mind working overtime, cataloging risk and possibility. He moved to the edge of the opening, leaned in close, and made a few sharp gestures at Arsenal—two fingers, then one, then a fist. Arsenal nodded and immediately set about checking the corners of the room for threats that only he could see.

Big Papa was next, and his entrance shifted the mood as if he'd opened a window and let in fresh air. He clapped Bronc on the shoulder, knelt by my other side, and looked me full in the face. "You got this, Lucia. You are the daughter of a king. And you got a whole damn cavalry right behind you." His palm, massive and scarred, landed on my shoulder. The simple warmth of it grounded me more than all the magic Archon could conjure.

Gunner took up position near the window, eyes flicking between the perimeter and the tear in the wall of the world. His hands moved with mechanical precision, loading and checking and rechecking the weapon slung across his chest, and packing more in the bags at his side; even though we all knew bullets wouldn't mean much in the place we were headed.

My father stood near, my ever-present bulwark against any danger that might try to assail me.

The portal itself was an insult to physics. It hung in the air like a wound, a vertical line of roiling black edged with luminous gold. Even looking at it made my teeth ache. Light seemed to leak out, but not in any direction I recognized; it just sort of diffused into the room, making the shadows deeper and the skin on the back of my neck crawl.

"Doc's on the other side?" Bronc asked, his voice so gentle I almost missed the tremor in it.

I closed my eyes, tried to breathe past the pain, and reached for the bond.

It was there—thin, desperate, singing with agony. He was still Doc, but he was changed, not just in body but in essence. If I reached further, I might shatter myself, but even the brush of my magic against his let me know two things: he was alive, and he needed me. The rest I'd figure out as I went.

"Yes," I said. "He's waiting."

Menace grunted again, this time with a note of approval. "Then let's go."

Wrecker stepped forward, eyes on the portal. "Recommend standard breach formation, Bronc. Lead with Menace, then me. Arsenal and Big Papa anchor. Lucia and the angel in the middle. Gunner brings up the rear. No telling what's on the other side, so we go loud, then quiet."

Gunner rolled his shoulders, adjusting to the weight of the weapon. "Ain't never seen a door like this. You sure it ain't a trap?"

Archon's smile was a slash of white. "Everything in that hellscape is a trap. But the only thing more dangerous than stepping through is not stepping through."

Big Papa helped me to my feet. The motion nearly buckled me, but he caught me before I fell and kept one big arm around my waist. I tried to focus on the support, not on how every joint in my body felt welded together with fear.

All their mates stood as we headed for the breach. Somewhere along the way, they had become my sisters, and I knew they'd be here when I brought my mate home.

Menace went through first, without hesitation, disappearing into the dark with a flex of his fists and a low, animal snarl. Bronc followed, then Wrecker and Arsenal. Bronc turned to me and Big Papa, gave a single nod, and said, "We end this." My father followed.

The portal was cold—colder than anything I'd ever felt. My magic flared in protest, shadows trying to claw back from the threshold, but Big Papa's grip and Archon's presence kept me upright. We stepped through, and for a moment there was only the sensation of falling, not down, but in every direction at once.

Then everything changed.

The landscape was impossible—a churn of obsidian and bone, the sky the color of old cement, the ground littered with strange sigils that pulsed with sickly red light. Everything smelled of rot and sulfur.

But through it all, the bond pulled at me, a cord made of equal parts need and memory. I staggered forward, barely holding on, but I knew—Doc was close.

Big Papa's hand on my back kept me from pitching over. "We got you," he said, and in his voice was the unbreakable promise of every pack, every brother, every battle line drawn in the dirt.

I drew myself upright. Even at my weakest, I was the daughter of Kazimir Kozlov. If Hell wanted to break me, it was going to have to try harder.

I looked to my father and saw his confidence in me. "Let's finish it," I said.

We moved into the dark.

The ceiling arched overhead, impossibly high, and from it hung shapes that could have been stalactites or maybe the teeth of something lying on its stomach, waiting to clamp shut. The air was viscous with rot and static, an unceasing whisper in the back of your mind that told you to lie down and just stop.

Menace didn't give the place the satisfaction. He grew in size, eyes gone gold and wild. He threw back his head and howled—a raw, rupturing sound that was equal parts challenge and promise. It shook the whole space, setting the runes in the walls to throbbing at double tempo.

All around us, as if summoned by the howl, were things that might once have been human, now corrupted into parodies of desire and fury.

Menace didn't hesitate—he went straight for the largest creature, claws raking the walls and feet pounding. The others followed suit: Gunner laid down a covering fire of silver rounds, Wrecker and Arsenal peeled off to the flanks, while my father and Big Papa kept me boxed in, as if I was a queen worth protecting and not just the weakest link in the chain.

I tried to run, but my legs turned to water. The effort of holding the portal open, of resisting this world's gravity, was sapping my reserves fast. My magic rebelled, threatening to burst out and leak away into the dead air.

Big Papa grabbed me under the arm, lifting most of my weight. "Lean on me, girl," he said, and his voice was a lighthouse in a sea of static. "You're not falling here."

Arsenal, already fifty feet ahead, ducked into a side corridor and reemerged with a face as pale as death. "Wrecker, abort left," he barked. "You do not want what's down that hall."

Wrecker didn't argue, just changed direction on a dime and made for the central pillar—a spire of obsidian tangled with writhing symbols and heavy chains. He dropped to a knee and started tracing patterns in the air, as if trying to hack the language of Hell itself.

Meanwhile, Menace collided with another monster in a cacophony of bone and magic. The two grappled, the impact sending shockwaves through the floor. And somewhere Maltraz's laugh sounded. It was a sound that hurt in ways laughter never should.

"You come to my domain with toys and hope?" Maltraz sneered.

Wrecker, oblivious, kept working the pillar. "Suppression field. It's dampening our magic—Lucia, can you see it?"

I couldn't see anything but the blur of my own failing sight, but I tried, reaching out with what little magic remained.

There it was, like a dirty blanket thrown over the fire inside me. I hissed, shoving back as best I could. My shadows, weak and ragged, clung to the pillar, searching for a seam.

Wrecker's fingers flashed, tracing a rune backwards. "Three more, then you're up," he said, calm even with a horde of hellspawn barreling down on us.

Gunner's rifle jammed, and he went full wolf, tearing into a beast that was mostly teeth and sorrow. Arsenal covered him, fending off a swarm of smaller minions. Bronc, meanwhile, stood between me and the chaos, his presence a brick wall of pure intent.

"Once the field is down, you go for Doc," he told me, not a suggestion.

"What about the rest of you?"

He smiled, and for a moment he looked younger than he was. "We'll handle the mess."

Maltraz appeared and ripped Menace's shoulder open, spraying the air with blood. But Menace just laughed, even as he bled, and clawed at Maltraz's throat. It was beautiful, in a hideous way.

The pillar began to strobe, its runes flickering faster. Wrecker swore. "Last one!"

I pulled on every memory of Doc—his patience, his warmth, his unwavering certainty. I let it fuel me, reaching for the bond. It was faint, but suddenly, as the last suppression rune went dead, it rushed back—like a dam breaking, power and pain and hope all at once.

I nearly screamed from the force of it.

"There!" I shouted, pointing to a wall behind a jagged wall. "He's through there."

Arsenal nodded, sprinting over and planting a charge. "Stand clear!"

The explosion was more silence than sound—a vacuum that sucked all the air from the room, then dumped it back in a rush. The wall crumbled, exposing a spiral stair that led down into pure blackness.

Big Papa scooped me up, bridal-style, and bolted for the opening.

Behind us, the world devolved into a blur of claws and curses. Bronc and Menace tangled with creatures too monstrous to describe, Gunner and Arsenal looking for where Maltraz had disappeared. Wrecker covered our descent, picking off anything that got too close.

Archon and my father were also on the hunt.

Down the stairs, the cold increased. My breath smoked in the air. Each step sent needles of pain into my skull, but I didn't dare close my eyes.

At the bottom: another door, this one locked with magic and misery.

I reached out and pressed my palm to the center. "Doc," I whispered, and the bond flared, as if his soul heard me.

The door screamed—literally, a sound of a thousand condemned souls—then gave way. Big Papa set me down gently, and I staggered through.

There he was.

Strapped to an altar of obsidian, skin gone pale, eyes open and haunted but alive. The sight of him made the world snap back into focus, colors returning, even if just a little.

I fell to my knees beside him, hands already working the restraints. "I'm here," I said, over and over, like a prayer. "I'm here."

He managed a smile, though it was mostly pain. "It can't be you."

I kissed his forehead, salty with sweat. "Look at me, *moy volk*."

He was weeping. I wasn't sure if he believed it was me or not.

Big Papa's voice cut through the static. "Brother. Your mate is here. Your brothers are here. We love you and we're getting you out of here. Look at your mate."

Then his eyes cleared for a moment.

"Lioness."

My tears wet his face.

Behind us, the fight above reached a crescendo. I could hear Menace howling, Maltraz screaming, and the rest of the wolves giving everything they had. It was a race now—not just against the demon, but against the unraveling of the world itself.

Big Papa braced the door, holding off a surge of shadow-creatures that poured down the stairs. I worked faster, freeing Doc's arms, his legs. He collapsed into me, barely conscious, but his fingers locked around mine with a desperation that nearly broke me.

"Can you walk?" I asked, wiping blood from his lip.

"If you hold me up."

"Always."

We ran blind, the only direction that mattered: away from the altar, up toward the howling vortex that used to be a corridor, through the ruin of a world that didn't want to let us go. Doc's weight on my shoulders was a buoy and an anchor all at once.

We staggered for the exit. Big Papa cleared the way, Doc leaning into me, every step a miracle.

Above, the chamber shook—cracks forming in the obsidian, runes sparking and dying. Maltraz's world was falling apart, and it wanted to take us with it.

But the bond, now blazing, pointed the way home. And nothing in this hell was going to keep us apart.

Big Papa blocked the stairs behind us, keeping a three-headed thing at bay with nothing but the bulk of his frame and the rumble of his voice. Wrecker and Arsenal worked in tandem, picking off the most dangerous targets and then moving on, never still, never letting the enemy get a fix on them.

I looked for my father, for Archon, and found them both standing apart from the carnage, ringed by a crowd of unmade ghosts. Otero—King of the West Vampires, now barely even a silhouette—stood at the center of the circle, defiant but melting by degrees.

It was then I realized that for all Maltraz's strength, for all his demon king bravado, this had never really been *his* show. He was the muscle. Otero was the mind, the planner, the one who'd known how to wound people in ways that never fully healed. Otero was also the only one in the room who looked at my father and flinched.

My father didn't bother with a speech. He stepped forward, faster than logic, and had his hand around Otero's throat in a heartbeat. Otero tried to shift, to slither or turn to mist, but my father's grip was metaphysical: it held the very idea of Otero, not just his body. With a flick of his wrist, he snuffed him out. There was no final gasp, no curse or threat, just a growl, then the space where Otero had been, folded in on itself, and he was gone.

My father didn't even look back at me. His eyes went to Archon.

The angel king was less beautiful than before, his wings out and torn at the edges, feathers singed black. But he looked almost happy—at peace in a way that made the whole room feel like a church after a funeral. Maltraz saw the look and howled, throwing Menace and Bronc off in a burst of energy.

Archon stepped forward, holding up one hand.

"Be silent," he said, and the world listened.

Maltraz went quiet, as if the word had stolen his voice.

"You have committed crimes against Creation," Archon intoned, and his voice echoed up and down the corridor. "You have made war on the living and the dead, and you have broken covenant with the light. You are owed no trial. You are owed nothing."

Maltraz tried to open his mouth, but no sound came out.

"Therefore, Maltraz, Demon of Hell, I unmake you," Archon said, and this time the words were not for ears, but for the bones of the world.

Maltraz convulsed. His body twisted, then unfolded, layer by layer, until there was nothing left but a ripple of shadow that ate itself as it collapsed. There was no blood. There was no scream. Maltraz just stopped being.

The dimension shuddered, then started to come apart for real. Runes peeled off the walls and became fireflies of raw data, burning holes in the floor as they fell. The ceiling caved in chunks, each one dissolving before it hit the ground. It was the end of a story no one had wanted to tell.

Big Papa shouldered through the collapsing debris, caught me and Doc both, and started hauling us toward the light leaking from the original tear. Bronc, Menace, Wrecker, and Arsenal fell in behind, battered and bloody but alive. Gunner covered our retreat, picking off the last of the minions with surgical contempt.

My father and Archon walked together, serene in the chaos, and when they reached the portal, they didn't even pause—just stepped through, shoulder to shoulder.

We followed.

The jump was less dramatic this time. No sense of being unmade; just a stumble, a rush of cold, and then sudden, blessed calm. We landed in the same room where we started, and when the last of us exited the portal shank to a pinprick, barely enough to bleed light. Then it was gone.

Doc collapsed to his knees. I went down with him, neither of us caring about the floor or the onlookers, or the state we were in. My brothers were there, Maksym and Nikolay, who both rushed forward and grabbed us up,

Taras too; hugging with the desperation of people who hadn't been sure they'd ever do it again. Bohdi stood in the doorway, relief etched on his face.

For a long, strange moment, nobody said a thing. The silence wasn't awkward; it was sacred.

Doc, head against my shoulder, finally spoke. "Not the prettiest rescue, but damn if it wasn't the most memorable."

I kissed him, a small kiss, weak as a kitten, and he laughed—a broken, raw sound that still had more life in it than the entire world we'd just left.

My father crouched beside us, his eyes impossibly gentle. "You're safe now," he said. It sounded less like a fact and more like a promise he intended to keep forever.

Archon leaned over us, his hand on my brow, and I felt something—something like a blessing or maybe just the assurance that what was broken could, in time, be repaired.

I checked the bond. It was there: not as a wild surge, but as a low, constant hum. Steady. The kind of love that survives even when you don't think you can.

I looked at Doc, at the little lines at the corners of his eyes, the healing cut across his jaw, the wild tumble of his hair.

"Next time," I whispered, "I'm rescuing you with a pizza and a bottle of tequila."

He smiled, the first true one since I'd found him. "How 'bout there not be a next time?"

Juliet tackled Bronc to the ground with kisses. Savannah did the same to Menace.

My father's ever-helpful butler handed robes to them since they'd shifted back and were now naked in a room full of people. They helped each other to the couch, both limping but smug. Wrecker ran a hand over his face, sitting with a worried Parker on his lap, taking inventory of all his injuries. Harper wrapped herself around Arsenal and peppered his face with kisses, and Brie acted like she would never let Gunner out of her sight again.

Big Papa pulled up a chair, set Doc and me in it, then stepped back to give us space. Aspen had tears running down her face as she clasped his hand as Oscar ran up his leg and perched on his shoulder.

Archon and my father watched over all of it, like gods who'd actually cared about what happened to mortals.

In the end, it wasn't the war or the victory that stuck with me, but the way Doc's hand found mine, fingers twining even though both of us were shaking.

The world had tried to come apart. But us? We held.

CHAPTER 27

DOC

Waking up after surviving demonic torture is about as surreal as you'd imagine. I'd been doing it daily for the past three days and I'd been doing it in the lap of luxury. I never imagined I'd be sleeping in what amounted to a castle. I also didn't imagine becoming half-vampire, but here I am; waking up in my mate's suite in the Kozlov estate: ceilings etched with gold leaf and ornate crown molding, velvet blackout drapes that could probably smother a pack of wolves, and a king bed larger than my first apartment, sheathed in sheets softer than most women's skin.

I lay flat on my back for a solid minute, just breathing. The room was so perfectly climate-controlled I couldn't tell if it was day or night; only the faintest line of city light eked around the edges of the drapes. My mind ran a quick diagnostic, out of habit more than need. No fever, no disorientation. My lungs filled and emptied without effort. The relentless throbbing in my thigh—the agony that had screamed through my arteries as Maltraz filleted me like a Sunday roast—was gone.

I flexed my toes and let my hands drift down, checking for the places he and Otero had used me as some kind of twisted science experiment. I felt for the areas they'd stripped skin for sampling, slits cut into flesh to insert who knows what under the skin, and the pockmarks of endless bloodletting. But there was nothing. Not a scar, not a raised ridge, nothing. Even my tattoos—seemed sharper, more vibrant than before.

And then there was the other thing.

My mate mark, hummed like a live wire against my skin. The beautiful crescent of runes that circled the claw and blood drop pulsed in time with my heartbeat, warm and insistent. I drew my hand to it, and when I pressed my palm against the spot, something like a static charge zipped up to my brain. I exhaled slowly, like if I went too fast I'd short-circuit the whole system.

I was alive. Or something close to it.

The memory came then—Lucia's face above me, her eyes glassy and furious, the taste of her wrist on my tongue as she jammed it into my mouth. There'd been shouting, voices surrounding me as natural light finally hit my eyes. The copper tang of her blood, thick and ancient, blotted out everything else. I remembered clutching at her arm, not wanting to let go, the pulse of her life fusing with mine.

Now, even the faintest trace of her scent—roses and honey—lingered in the sheets. It anchored me to the here and now, keeping the nightmares at bay. I grinned like a fucking idiot, feeling every inch alive, and letting myself be grateful for once.

A door opened. Steam billowed into the room, and Lucia emerged from the bathroom, wrapped in a towel the color of midnight. Her hair was damp and tangled, fat ringlets clinging to her throat and shoulders. She looked at me, one eyebrow arched in either challenge or concern. Or maybe she just liked what she saw. I sure as hell did.

"Is miracle," she declared, her accent slicing through the syllables. "Three days ago, you looked like bad roadkill. Today, you look like you want to run a marathon."

I smirked. "I've run enough marathons for two lifetimes. Where's my coffee?"

She marched over, every stride a flex of authority. Lucia wore nothing but that towel, which seemed to exist solely to make me imagine the rest. "Coffee later. First, you tell me how you feel."

"Like I got run over by a cement truck, then resurrected by a beautiful Russian scientist." I hesitated. "You have a way of doing that, don't you?"

Her lips quirked, but there was a worry line between her eyebrows. "No one will ever take you from me. I will always find you."

"I'm glad, Lucia. I'm yours." My words surprised us both. "You're stuck with me now."

She stepped to the edge of the bed, careful not to break eye contact. The towel slipped higher on her thigh, revealing skin so pale it looked blue in the weird light. "You mean this, Ryder?"

"How can you ask that, lioness?" I propped myself on an elbow. "Can I ask *you* something?"

She snorted. "Anything."

I ran my thumb along my collarbone, where her mate mark burned like a beacon. "Are you ready to have me for the rest of your life?"

She was quiet for a long moment. "I would never want anyone but you." She reached out, tracing a finger down the line of my jaw. "Are you strong enough to take me now? Because I've waited as long as I care to wait."

I sat up, letting the comforter drop to my lap. My body had miraculously come back almost to its pre-torture form. My muscles mapped out in shadow and light. I felt... predatory. Hungry. The towel was no defense for her; I reached out and snagged it, tugging gently until it fell away.

She didn't flinch. Instead, she let her chin tilt up in that regal way she had, as if daring me to take what I wanted. Her breasts were perfect—full and pale, the nipples dusky and tight from her want for me. I wanted to devour her, body and soul.

"Come here," I said, my voice going rough.

She slid onto the bed, straddling my lap, the heat of her radiating through me like a fever. Our mouths collided, and for a second I lost all sense of who was leading. She kissed like she fought—no mercy, no quarter, just an all-consuming need to win. But I'd been reborn, and something primal in me snapped the leash.

I flipped her, pinning Lucia to the mattress. She gasped, but there was laughter in it, wild and delighted. I nuzzled into her neck, breathing in the scent of her. "You want to know how I survived?" I murmured.

"Yes," she breathed.

"You." My lips found the pulse point in her throat. "I felt you, even when I was gone. You never stopped calling to me."

She arched her back, hands threading through my hair. "Of course. You are my mate. Was always going to find you, even in hell."

"You're extraordinary," I said, meaning every syllable. "I don't know what the Goddess was thinking when she made you, but I'm grateful she did."

Lucia's fingers dug into my shoulders. "Talk less. Fuck more."

That was a royal order I could obey.

Her scent filled my nostrils, and I was fucking drunk on it. She lay beneath me; her pale skin glowing like moonlight, her onyx eyes burning with a hunger that mirrored my own. The vampire princess. My savior. My obsession.

Her breasts pressed into my chest, and I felt the hardness of her nipples. I groaned, my lips crashing onto hers in a desperate kiss. Her tongue met mine, cold and wet, and I fucking devoured her, sucking on her like she was the last drop of water in a desert.

Her claws raked down my back, leaving trails of fire in their wake that I knew disappeared almost in an instant. I realized then and there I wanted her to fucking own me. She moaned into my mouth, her hips grinding against mine, and I could feel the wetness soaking me.

"Fuck me like you mean it."

Her pussy was bare, slick and glistening, and I couldn't resist burying my face between her thighs. My tongue dragged through her folds, lapping up her essence like it was honey. She tasted sharp and sweet, and I drowned in her.

Her hands fisted my hair, pulling me closer as she bucked against my mouth. "Yes, yes, yes!" she hissed, her hips jerking uncontrollably. I sucked her clit into my mouth, flicking it with my tongue until she screamed, her body trembling with pleasure.

But I wasn't done. My fingers replaced my tongue, thrusting into her tight, wet heat. She was so fucking tight, squeezing my fingers like a vise. I added a third, stretching her, thrusting them into her until she was shaking and begging for more.

"I need you inside me," she whimpered, her voice breaking. "Now."

I didn't need to be told twice. I sat back and stroked my cock a few times before lining it up with her dripping entrance. I plunged into her with one hard thrust, burying myself. She gasped, her nails digging into my shoulders, her fangs bared as she threw her head back.

"Fuck yes," she moaned. "Harder!"

I obliged, slamming into her again and again, her walls clenching around me taking all I had to give her. Her legs tightened around my waist, her hips meeting mine with every thrust. The sound of our bodies slapping together filled the room, mingling with her cries of pleasure.

"You are a part of me," I growled, my lips brushing against her ear. "The best fucking part of me."

She moaned, a dark, throaty sound that sent a shiver down my spine. "And you belong to me," she replied, her fangs grazing my neck. "Body and soul. I'm never letting you go."

I reached between us and rubbed her clit until her body bucked against mine. Then I leaned over her and licked her neck and sank my fangs in deep. She came with a deep wail as her sweet blood filled my mouth. I released her clit and continued to pound into her incredible pussy as I drank her down. Her orgasm was long and uncontrolled until I released my bite and sealed the wound.

She immediately leaned up and struck my neck with a bite of her own, and my thrusts became erratic. I came with a roar, my release filling her as she clamped down on me, as another climax tore through her. She moaned my name, her body trembling uncontrollably as she clung to me.

I lost myself then. There was no world outside this room, no past or future, just the wet heat of her and the white-hot sensation of being made whole. Our bond flared, twin fires burning as one. I could feel her, not just under me but in me—her heart pounding, her mind sparking with pleasure and need. It was almost too much.

She released her bite, and we collapsed onto the bed a tangle of limbs and contented sighs.

Brunch in the House of Kozlov was less a meal and more a production. When we walked into the grand dining hall—a room big enough to park a fleet of trucks, with crystal chandeliers that probably cost more than my house—every head turned to us.

No one spoke at first. The Kozlovs looked at me like I'd just stepped out of a fucking crypt. Maybe technically, I had.

Lucia slipped her arm through mine, a small gesture that said more than words. She wore a royal-blue dress that hugged her in all the right places, her hair pulled back with a silver comb. Even here, she radiated command. For once, I didn't mind being the arm candy.

We made our way to the far end of the table, where Kazimir sat in a carved chair that made him look like the vampire equivalent of a handsome King Charles. At his right hand was Maksym, whom I just noticed was a dead ringer for his father, but with less of the ancient menace and more of a bored rock star. Taras, the younger twin, lounged next to him, rolling a coin across his knuckles and giving off the vibe of someone just waiting for a fight to break out so he could enjoy the carnage. Nickolay, the "professor who could kill you with his pinky," was next, and Bohdan, the clear playboy of this Bratva vampire royalty sipped a Red Bull I could only guess was spiked with blood.

Kazimir stood as we approached, his expression somewhere between "proud patriarch" and "Grand Inquisitor." "Lucia, my daughter," he boomed. "And Ryder, my new son."

I braced for the worst—maybe a stare-down, maybe a test of strength. Instead, Kazimir smiled, arms open wide. "So good to see you up and around. Please, sit. Eat. You look like you could use ten pounds."

The other four men grinned in varying degrees of menace and amusement. Lucia took her seat without ceremony. I hesitated, just long enough for Kazimir to gesture to the empty chair at her side. I dropped into it, still half-convinced I'd set off some hidden alarm.

The table was covered in a spread that would make a Roman emperor blush: slabs of roast beef, smoked salmon, caviar by the bowlful, pastries so delicate I thought they'd break if I breathed wrong. A pitcher of something red—almost certainly not tomato juice—glistened in the center.

Nickolay filled my plate without asking, like I was a new recruit at a football team dinner. "Eat," he said, deadpan. "She hates when you get skinny."

I forked a chunk of meat into my mouth, chewing as slowly as I dared. The taste was incredible, rich and just a little wild. I wondered if the chef was in on the secret, or if the food was as much a show for him as for us.

Kazimir waited until everyone had served themselves, then cleared his throat. "I have news. Announcements. And I want my family to hear it all at once, like we used to." His voice dropped to something softer, more dangerous. "The world has changed. Our enemies have grown bold. But we have grown stronger, too."

He looked at me. "Ryder. You know by now that the world knows that you are not only wolf. My Lucia's blood made you... more. Not since the days of our ancestors has such a thing happened. You are family, and you are prince of this house. This made you a target of the Council. I'm happy to report, you are a target no longer. The Council has been warned."

Holy shit, that sounded ominous.

I shook myself at the thought and got back to the idea of being a Kozlov "prince." I'd thought myself immune to flattery, but the word "prince" short-circuited my brain. "Yes, sir," I said, then, less formally, "Kazimir."

He grinned. "Good! Very good. You will have duties, of course. I would like you and my daughter to spend two weeks of every month here, in Philadelphia. Your other time, you serve Iron Valor. This is fair?"

I glanced at Lucia. Her eyes said, *Just go with it.*

"I can make that work," I said, surprising us both. "The hospital—my hospital—will need a new chief of staff. But I have someone in mind."

Kazimir nodded, satisfied. "See? My daughter chose well."

Maksym set down his fork. "And what about the vampires who object to a shifter in the family? Not everyone is so enlightened, Father."

Kazimir waved a hand. "They will bend the knee or lose their heads. It is the way."

Nickolay snickered into his coffee. "I will help."

Kazimir leaned forward. "Which brings me to the second bit of news. The West King, Otero, is dead. Stupid bastard thought he could cross me. I need a new king in the West. Maksym, you will go. Taras, you are his hand. Nickolay, you will remain here and serve as my hand since Lucia now has obligation to her mate. Are we in agreement?"

There was a moment of silence, the weight of history hanging in the air. Maksym inclined his head. "As you wish, Father."

Taras just grinned, as if he'd expected nothing less. Nickolay raised his glass in salute.

Bohdi looked at his father. "And I'm...?"

Kazimir cleared his throat. "Ah yes, my son who likes to play. You will learn to operate my club. This will be your job. Philadelphia is now your home."

Bohdan's face went solemn.

"This is problem for you, son?"

"Of course not, Father. I look forward to running Obsidian for you."

Kazimir turned to me again. "Now, will this be a problem for you, Ryder?"

I shook my head. "No sir. I hired a new doctor some months back. I believe he can handle the workload. I can always bring another doctor on if necessary."

Lucia laughed. "It's settled then."

She pressed her hand to mine under the table, a silent affirmation. I squeezed back. I realized in that moment I wasn't just alive. I was home.

Epilogue

Bronc

Five months ago, my world shrunk to the circumference of two infant skulls. I'd fought wars in deserts and cities, survived more than my fair share of full moons, but nothing compared to the ferocious vulnerability I felt piloting the Razor with my wife at my side and our twins—LJ and Iris—in the back. The open air warmed my skin; it carried the wild, sun-baked scent of Dairyville summer, and the constant lowing of distant cattle. The twins squawked louder than both.

"LJ, if you spit out that pacifier one more time," I said over my shoulder, "I'm trading you in for a quieter model."

Iris cackled, baby-pure and delighted, even as she clamped her own pacifier tight like a vice. Juliet, beautiful as sin and more dangerous, snorted a laugh beside me. "You say that every afternoon," she said, her voice a soft flex. "I think you secretly enjoy the chaos."

She wore a bandana on her hair to keep her curls from tangling in the wind, a retro bombshell in a faded biker tee. The twins had her eyes: dark as blackstrap molasses, fathomless and hungry for the world.

I took the long way around the compound, hands easy on the wheel. The Razor's engine thrummed low and steady, a lullaby for men with tinnitus and wolves in their souls. We started at the main gates, which the prospects had painted last fall in a blinding, military-precision red. The pack house sat straight ahead: still looking new, the Texas flag fluttering from the eaves. Where it used to look like a militia's last stand, now it could pass for a private resort.

On the porch, Wrecker rocked a glider back and forth with Parker nestled in the crook of his arm. Even at a distance, you could see how she'd tamed him; he still had the air of a pit bull behind a chain-link fence, but now his gaze softened every time it landed on her. The true king of that household, though, was the world's ugliest terrier: Rocket, snoring between them with his legs splayed and his jowls flapping in the breeze.

Wrecker raised a hand in a lazy salute. Parker lifted her coffee mug, then shook her head at Rocket's lack of decorum. I caught Juliet's eye, and she grinned like she knew the secrets of the universe.

"Remember when he said he'd never let a woman tie him down?" Juliet laughed.

"Now he lets her trim his ear hair," I replied. "True love comes for us all."

We rolled past Arsenal's new place, a clean-lined, saltbox beauty that looked like it'd been airlifted from Maine and plunked into the middle of Texas. Arsenal had built it with his own hands for Harper, who stood in the garden in a white sundress, clutching a spray of basil like it might sprout roots and drag her from this place. She still carried a dancer's posture—spine arrow-straight, feet never quite at rest. Arsenal appeared at her side in a blink, as if conjured by her heartbeat.

"They're still in the honeymoon phase," Juliet whispered.

"She makes him less insufferable."

"She makes him happy. That's all I care about."

Our little parade continued, the Razor slow enough for the twins to giggle with every bump and curve. LJ lost his pacifier again, so I braked and Juliet scooped it up, popping it back into his gummy mouth.

"Just wait until he shifts for the first time," I said. "You think he's loud now?"

"Lord help us all," Juliet said.

We passed Gunner and Brie next, two figures on horseback racing the wind. Gunner raised his hat in greeting; Brie, clad in a flowing shirt she'd probably hand-painted, let loose a yodel that echoed across the prairie. She was born for city lights, but I'd never seen her happier than on the back of a quarter horse, mud streaking her boots and paint flecked on her arms.

"Will you look at that," Juliet said. "Five months ago, Brie couldn't tell a stirrup from a saddle horn."

"Now she could teach a seminar at Texas A&M."

"Give her a year, she'll be running the place."

We took the east loop, gravel pinging off the fenders, and I let the sense of peace settle over my bones. For the first time in years, nobody was shooting at us, hunting us, or plotting to steal our children. The compound buzzed with the normal chaos of living: new construction going up near the back forty, a dozen pack members mending fence lines, the faint cry of a chainsaw from the timber yard. Even the air felt different—less like a war zone, more like home.

Juliet reached across the console, her hand warm on my forearm. "You're thinking too loud," she said.

"I was just..." I paused, searching for the right words. "I was just proud, is all. Never figured we'd have this. Not after everything."

She squeezed my arm, her thumb tracing the scar above my wrist. "You built this, Bronc. Every single one of us is here because you wouldn't let the world swallow us whole."

"Nah," I said. "I just pointed in a direction. The rest of you idiots followed."

We rumbled along the gravel drive, heading west. Big Papa sat on the porch swing with a mug of iced coffee and a grin so soft it'd make you forget he could bench press a Harley. He watched Aspen with the same pride I imagined myself wearing whenever I looked at Juliet: a man who'd seen battle, found faith, and then lost his heart to the only witch who ever made a pie crust worth dying for. Aspen knelt in the dirt, humming as she snipped lemon balm with scissors small enough for a doll.

What really did me in, though, was the prairie dog in the garden. Oscar B. Wild, who'd saved our asses more than once, was wearing an enormous straw hat and wielding a rake the size of a barbecue fork. He struggled valiantly against a cluster of dandelions, muttering to himself in an accent so posh it'd shame the Queen.

Juliet spotted him first and burst out laughing—real, from-the-gut laughter, so rare in our line of work that I wanted to bottle it. I slowed the Razor, just to savor the sound.

"Look at him!" she said, covering her mouth so she wouldn't startle the twins. "Oscar's about to start a revolution in that hat."

I waved at the porch, and Big Papa stood to return it, his voice rumbling across the lawn. "Y'all come by later—Aspen's got a lemon tart that'll change your religion."

"We will," I called. "Tell Oscar the dress code for next week's council meeting is business casual."

The prairie dog looked up at us, shading his eyes with a tiny paw. "Very droll, Mr. Baucaum. One's sun protection is not a matter for mockery."

"Noted, Oscar."

Juliet was still snickering as we puttered past. "If only you'd let me get a prairie dog, the twins would have a sidekick."

"Iris would eat him," I said. "She's got your killer instincts."

The scenery changed as we left the gardens and crossed into the estate's north quadrant. The land rose a little, rolling in soft hills toward a copse of oaks. Nestled there was the biggest house on Iron Valor land: Doc Lowrey's colonial, a stately thing with white pillars and navy-blue shutters. It had been Lucia's idea—she said the new house should feel like legacy, something permanent, not just another temporary war bunker. There was a cherry-red Tesla in the drive and a monster of a pickup next to it, Doc's dual nature summed up in two parking spaces.

Juliet sat up straighter, her interest piqued. "Think they're home?"

"Lucia will be. Doc's probably doing rounds."

"You ever think about what it's like for him now?"

"All the time." And I did. When Doc woke from Lucia's transfusion, he'd spent weeks adjusting—every sense dialed past the red line, his wolf both closer and farther than before. After Maltraz and Otero had taken him, I was afraid they'd broken him. Lucia wouldn't allow that. And he'd doubled down on the job: expanding the clinic, training more EMTs, and quietly taking responsibility for the health of every wolf and supernatural who needed it.

He'd also managed to keep Lucia's appetite for drama contained to hospital board meetings and family dinners. Considering she was the daughter of the most dangerous vampire alive, that was no small feat. All while splitting time between Texas and Philly because he was now a fucking vampire prince.

"Want to stop in?" Juliet asked.

"Let's give 'em a minute. Lucia gets testy if you wake her before noon."

We coasted past, but I caught a flicker of movement through the window. Lucia's silhouette—tall, hair a riot of black curls—stood backlit, holding a mug in one hand and waving lazily with the other. Her skin glowed in the daylight, even through glass. If the neighbors didn't know she was supernatural, they'd have pegged her as a movie star.

Juliet leaned close, lowering her voice. "I'll say it again: you owe that woman your thanks. It's because of her I made my way to you."

"She says I owe her 'a parade and a castle,'" I said. "I'm working on it."

Juliet smiled, softer now. "You like having her around."

"Yeah. She's good for Doc. Good for us, too."

I let the Razor coast, my mind cycling through everything that had changed since that impossible night. The pack had been wary of Lucia at first—outsiders were always a risk, and a vampire was worse than a risk. But she'd won them over, not with charm (she had plenty) but with blunt honesty and a work ethic that matched any wolf. She ran the hospital shift schedules, handled emergencies, and called me out personally any time my blood pressure was high enough to make her 'diagnose me by sight.'

When Doc started splitting his time between Dairyville and Philadelphia, it set the gossips in orbit. But nobody complained, not once it became clear he'd never abandon the pack for anything. He'd always return, always on schedule, always prepared. Even the kids at the nursery recognized him by the squeal Iris let out whenever she saw his glasses, which he wore now with clear lenses. His vision was perfect just like every other part of that fucker.

We took the loop back toward the main compound. I let Juliet steer one-handed while I reached back and checked the twins—LJ was knocked out, Iris drooling on a stuffed giraffe. I kissed her forehead and turned my attention to Juliet. She was humming now, the tune wordless, but I could tell she was thinking of tomorrow and the day after and all the days that would come.

"It's better than I imagined," she said, breaking her own song. "All of it. Did you ever think we'd get here?"

"Not once," I admitted. "And now I'd kill to keep it. Every last bit of it."

She slipped her hand over mine on the wheel. "We already did," she said, matter-of-fact. "Now you just get to drive the Razor."

The twins both snored at that, in perfect stereo.

We didn't go straight home this time. We circled the perimeter, past the stables, past the lake where Gunner sometimes taught the cubs to fish. Every piece of Iron Valor land held memories—some brutal, some brilliant, all stitched together by time and survival. If I closed my eyes, I could still see the night we fought off the vampires and Greenbriar, the blood and fire, the way my people rallied even when it seemed impossible.

But here's what stuck: not the violence, not the pain, but the way Juliet held my hand afterward, and the way the world kept moving forward. The way our pack learned to rebuild instead of just endure.

Juliet smiled up at me, twins in tow. "We're lucky, Bronc."

I watched the kids, the gardens, the houses, the life we'd built—crazy, fragile, stubbornly perfect.

"Yeah," I said. "We are."

Pearl's Bar & Grill glowed like a hearth on the far side of town, its neon script buzzing against the April dusk. From the outside, it looked like any other roadside diner in Texas—peeling white paint, patched roof, and a sagging sign the shape of a Lone Star—but inside, it was the heart of the pack. The only thing that'd changed since my boyhood was the addition of a row of high chairs and a "No Silverware Thrown After 6PM" rule taped to the fridge.

Tonight, every table was jammed with Iron Valor—patched jackets and baby carriers, muddy boots and high heels. Even the air tasted different, thick with fried chicken, honey, and the promise of something worth celebrating.

Menace and Savannah arrived first, both looking too good for Dairyville and knowing it. He wore a crisp shirt with the top button open, tattoos snaking up his forearms. She wore a long green dress, her dark auburn curls loose and her emerald eyes bright even after a four-hour flight from St. Louis. The room stood at attention when they walked in—once a wolf king, always a wolf king—but Menace just nodded and went straight for the coffee urn.

Savannah kissed Juliet's cheek and then mine, her perfume setting off a hundred memories. "You're still Alpha here, right, Bronc?" she teased.

"Depends on which infant you ask," I said. "Pretty sure Iris's staging a coup."

Ma, herself glided through the chaos with a tray of cornbread, followed by my little sister, Maddie, balancing three pitchers of sweet tea on one arm and a pitcher of beer on the other. Maddie was a jack of all trades, working for me at the shop and for my ma here at the diner. She was also a hot mess.

Ma set the cornbread down in front of LJ, who reached for it with both hands. "That's my boy," she said, giving his chubby fist a squeeze. "He eats like a Baucaum."

"Runs in the genes," I said, snagging a piece for myself.

Around us, the chatter rose and fell like a tide. Gunner and Brie commandeered a couple of seats at the long table, both in matching denim like they'd planned it. Arsenal and Harper arrived with a bottle of good whiskey, already locked in a mock-serious debate about whether ballet or baseball was more likely to produce an Olympic athlete. Doc and Lucia floated in last; she in a dress that probably cost more than my truck, he in a black t-shirt with "BLOOD DONORS ARE SEXY" stenciled in red across the chest. I'd bet money that Parker gave him that.

Parker and Wrecker took the seats next to us, Rocket asleep on his back beneath their feet. Parker looked different—less like a programmer who'd missed three nights' sleep, more like a woman who'd found a way to make happiness her home.

Ma made the rounds, dropping off plates and taking a headcount, never missing a beat.

"You all got drinks? Maddie, honey, top everyone off."

Maddie poured wine for Lucia, who sipped it and whispered something in Doc's ear that made him blush down to his collar.

When the noise crested, Ma banged a serving spoon on the edge of the buffet. "Listen up! If you're not eating, you're talking, and if you're not doing either, you're in the wrong bar. And I want everyone to give a hand to Bronc and Juliet—for hosting, for raising two beautiful hellions, and for keeping this pack in one piece. The rest of us just try to keep up."

The applause was a train wreck—hoots, clapping, Arsenal's wolf whistle. LJ beamed, and Juliet raised her glass, her arm around Iris.

I scanned the tables. Every face told a story: men who'd fought and bled for the pack, women who'd risked everything to find their own freedom, and children who'd grow up never doubting that they belonged.

After the first round of plates, Parker stood up, glass in hand. "Uh, I have an announcement. Well. We have an announcement." She elbowed Wrecker, who sat up straight as if waiting to be shot at.

The room stilled, every ear tuned to her.

She hesitated, then said, "I'm pregnant."

A full three seconds of dead silence. Then all hell broke loose—shouts, toasts, yips and howls from the wolves, a standing ovation from everywhere. Wrecker looked dazed, like someone had handed him a live grenade with a bow on it, but he caught Parker's hand and held it tight.

Big Papa spoke up, Aspen beaming at him. "Children are always a blessing from the Creator. May yours be healthy and happy and hopefully give you all kinds of hell!"

Menace hollered, "And if it's a girl, you can call her Menace Junior!"

Savannah snorted into her drink. "Not if they ever want her to get married."

"Here's to Rocket's first playmate," Juliet called.

Parker sat down, red-faced but grinning. Wrecker's hand was white-knuckled on her thigh.

I leaned across the table. "Congratulations. You ever need a sitter, I got a couple dozen prospects to keep her out of trouble."

"Thanks, Bronc," she said, voice thin with relief.

Ma swept by, planting a kiss on Parker's head. "You'll do fine, sugar. Just don't name it after your dog."

The rest of the night blurred into a cycle of eating, talking, and passing babies down the length of the table. The pack traded stories—good and bad, past and future, the kind that stitched themselves into your bones. Even the hard stuff got softer under the lights and laughter. I caught Doc and Lucia holding hands, Gunner teaching LJ how to toast with a sippy cup, and Arsenal sneaking bites of cake to Harper when she thought no one was watching.

Eventually, when the crowd thinned and the twins were snoring on my lap, I pushed back from the table. Menace caught my eye over the rim of his coffee. "Not bad, Alpha," he said. "Not bad at all."

"Didn't do it alone," I said, nodding at Juliet, at the pack, at Ma who was already clearing plates with Maddie. "Never could have."

He grinned, wolf-sharp and warm. "That's the trick, isn't it?"

It was. It always had been.

When we finally headed out into the dark, Juliet wrapped an arm through mine, carrying one sleeping twin while I shouldered the other.

"You happy?" she asked.

I looked at the stars above the Iron Valor sign, at the shadows of my family, and heard the echo of laughter spilling into the night.

"I wouldn't trade it for all the gold in the world," I said.

And I meant it, every word.

THANKS FOR READING

If you've made it to the end of **Doc**, thank you—truly. Reaching this point also means closing the final chapter of the *Wolves of Iron Valor MC* series, and that's something I don't take lightly. These men, their pack, and the bonds that held them together have been part of my life for a long time, and I'm deeply grateful you chose to walk this journey with me.

Doc's story was a difficult one to tell—emotional, complicated, and rooted in sacrifice. Writing Lucia alongside him allowed this world to expand in ways I've been building toward from the very beginning. If Iron Valor was about brotherhood and loyalty, this story was about what happens when those values collide with ancient power and forbidden bonds.

By now, you've met the Kozlov vampires—not as shadows, but as players. You've seen a family shaped by power, tradition, and love sharpened by centuries of survival. With Maksym stepping into his role as King of the West, Taras at his side, Nikolay assuming his place as Kozlov's hand, and Bohdi taking control of his own domain, the board has been set.

And this... is only the beginning.

The vampire stories are coming. Darker, more dangerous, and built on the same themes of loyalty, fate, and love that refuses to be controlled. If you thought the rules were strict before, you haven't seen anything yet.

Thank you for reading, for supporting an indie author, and for staying with this world through every twist and turn. I can't wait to take you into what comes next.

With gratitude,
Dex

P.S. If you ever need to debrief after this emotional rollercoaster, find me on my socials: Facebook (www.facebook.com/dexhavenauthor) Join my group page Haven for Dex Addicts (Dex Haven Readers) https://www.facebook.com/groups/havenfordexaddictsfor previews, games, and confessions I can't make anywhere else, Instagram (@authordexhaven) or Tiktok (@authordexhaven), or haunt my website (dexhavenauthor.com). You can even email me dex@dexhavenauthor.com

ALSO BY DEX

If you somehow missed the other books in the Wolves of Iron Valor MC series, you need to read them all!

Bronc- Book 1, Menace- Book 2, Wrecker- Book 3, Big Papa- Book 4, Arsenal- Book 5, and Gunner- Book 6

Be on the lookout for the Kozlov Vampire Series coming soon!